Guardians

Andrakis Book One

30th Anniversary Edition

Tony Shillitoe

Tony Shillitoe © 2024

First published in 1992 as Guardians by Pan Macmillan. Re-published in 2006 as The Waking Dragon by Altair Australia. Republished in 2024 as Guardians on Amazon.

Cover art by Kirsi Salonen
http://www.kirsisalonen.com

ISBN: 978-0-6458658-1-3

For my father, Bill Shillitoe, whose last great quest began just as this tale first took shape ...

... for Lenton Leafull, Rod Valor, Boblog, Pete Boggs, Bodicea, Shamus, Shandar and the countless questors who breathed life into the rich, imaginative world that became Andrakis ...

... and for the readers who asked for this tale again or have come to it on a new quest.

THE KINGDOM OF THANA

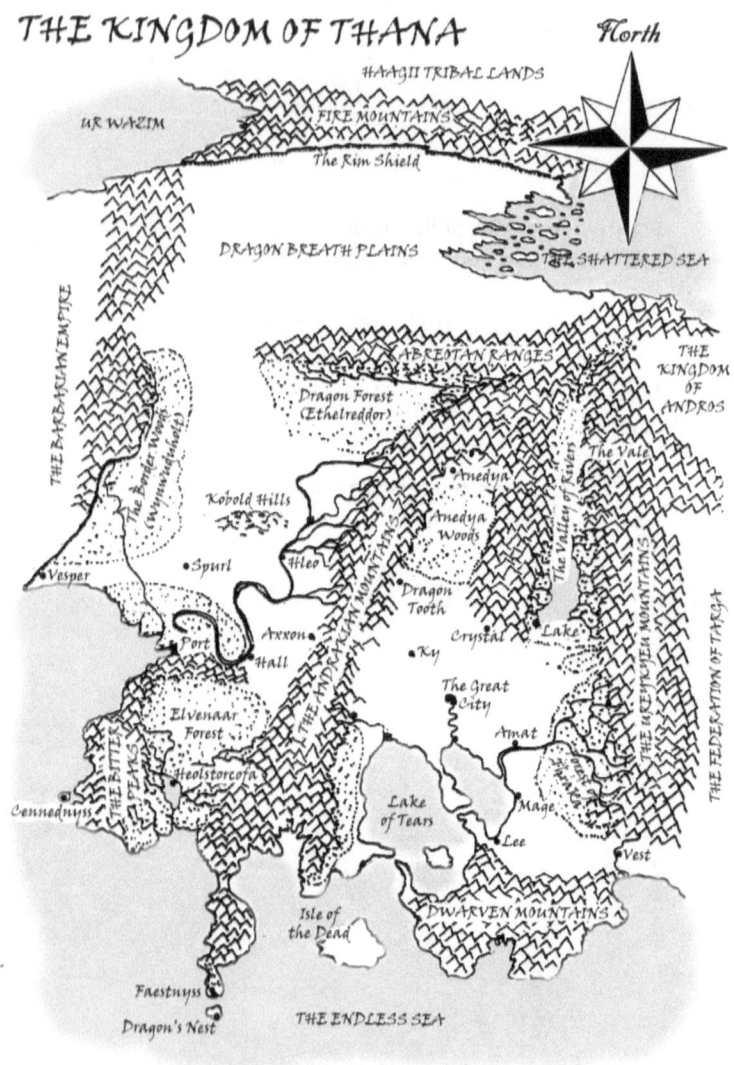

North

HAAGII TRIBAL LANDS

UR WAZIM

FIRE MOUNTAINS

The Rim Shield

DRAGON BREATH PLAINS

THE SHATTERED SEA

THE BARBARIAN EMPIRE

THE ABRENIAN RANGES

THE KINGDOM OF ANDROS

Dragon Forest (Ethelreddor)

The Vale

The Border Woods (Wyrmsdenoth)

Kobold Hills

Anedya

Anedya Woods

The Valley of Raven

Vesper

Spurl

Hleo

Dragon Tooth

Crystal Lake

THE ANDREAN MOUNTAINS

THE AKEMDELA MOUNTAINS

THE FEDERATION OF TARGA

Axxon

Port Hall

Ky

The Great City

Amat

Elvenaar Forest

Heolstorcofa

Mage

THE BITTER PEAKS

Lake of Tears

Lee

Vest

Cennednyss

Isle of the Dead

DWARVEN MOUNTAINS

Faestnyss

Dragon's Nest

THE ENDLESS SEA

RANU KA SHEHAALA

North

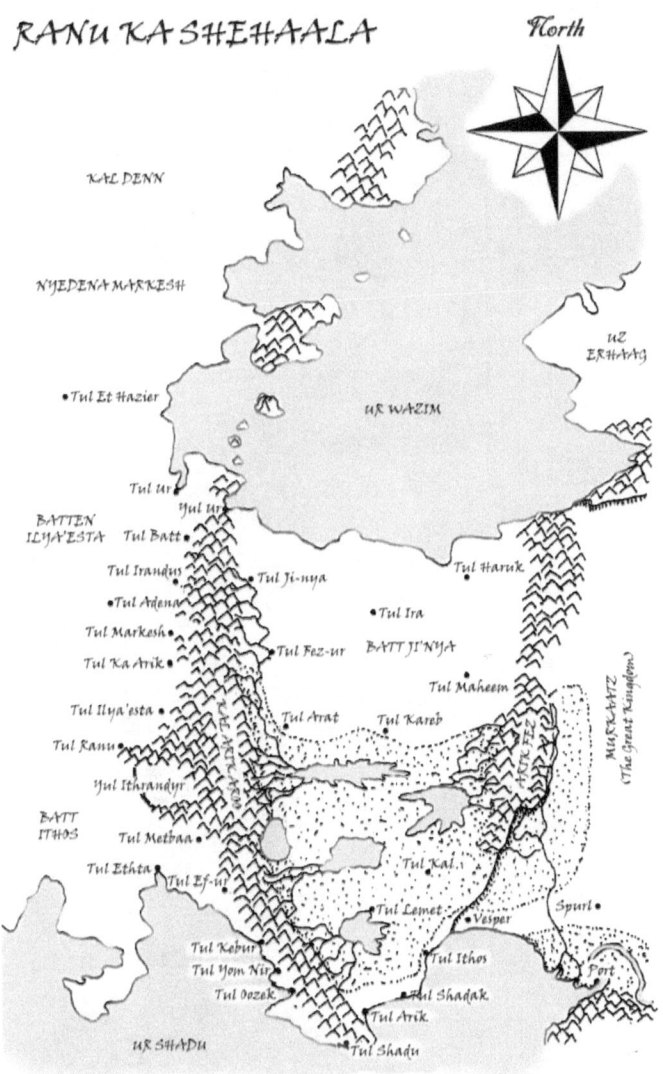

KAL DENN

NYEDENA MARKESH

UZ ERHAAG

• Tul Et Hazier

UR WAZIM

Tul Ur

BATTEN ILYA'ESTA   Yul Ur

Tul Batt •

Tul Irandus   Tul Ji-nya   Tul Haruk

• Tul Adena

Tul Markesh •   • Tul Ira

Tul Ka Arik •   • Tul Fez-ur   BATT JI'NYA

Tul Ilya'esta •   Tul Arat   Tul Maheem

Tul Ranu •   Tul Kareb

Yul Ithrandyr   MARKAHZ (The Great Kingdom)

BATT ITHOS   Tul Methaa •

Tul Ethta •   Tul Ef-ur   Tul Kal

Tul Lemet   • Vesper   Spurl •

Tul Kebur   Tul Ithos   Port

Tul Yom Nir   Tul Shadak

Tul Oozak   Tul Arik

UR SHADU   Tul Shadu

"To know where you are,
you must know where you are not.
To know who you are,
you must know who you are not.
To know why you are
is indeed a blessing."

Saying of the Ranu Ka Shehaala

"Power is formed in its own image.
Power is its own source.
Power finds that which it seeks always -
itself.
All Power is drawn unto Power.
That is an eternal law."

Prayer to Berak N'eth
from the Ithos Ashka Shadak (Vol 231)

One

He waited, listening. Satisfied he had evaded his pursuers, he slipped between the pale green saplings and emerged at the far end of the glade. A shower of pebbles clattered through the leaves. Hands on hips, he stared with insolent grey eyes at a pack of younglings, shook his long silver braids arrogantly, grinned, and asked, 'Looking for something?'

'Man-spawn!' the tallest youngling yelled. The pack started gathering stones. The same taunt, the same stupid accusation. Would they never leave him alone? He spat contemptuously and vanished between the trees before the younglings could launch their missiles.

Breaking out of the green foliage, he sprinted along the fringe of the village, racing past broad, grey elmoak trunks that soared from their gnarly roots into the dense forest canopy. In the village centre, where swaying ladder vines dangled from the entrances to living and sleeping quarters, he slowed to a jog. Giggling childlings played spell games between the great elmoak roots, and supervising adults chatted while they worked. He passed the Warming Stone and the Meeting Ground, and entered the Spell Grove, where the bending tips of giant trees formed a vaulting arched roof. Within the Grove, nine Chosen listened attentively to the Chanter, the Elder responsible for teaching Aelendyell lore to the Lore Bearers. They turned, as Terin entered, and the Chanter paused, his dark blue eyes patiently waiting for Terin to settle in his appointed place among the Chosen. 'So, we know and speak of four Ki of power,' the Chanter continued, 'but only two are bestowed upon our people - one by our heritage, one through our learning.'

Terin's interest was immediately aroused. If there are four sources of magic, and only two belong to the Aelendyell, what happened to the other two? Why did they only have access to two of the four Ki? he mused.

'We draw the First Ki from the Genesis Stone,' the Chanter explained. 'At the Time of Making, our ancestors were fashioned from the earth and forest of the First Land by Wynowyth and Laeocon, Earth Mother and Sky Father, and in their souls were sealed the Land's secrets and strengths. To these things were wedded the ancient power of the Genesis Stone which came to our people from the sky when the land was still forming. These are the essence of the First Ki, passed down through generations of the Alfyn Great Ones to the Elvenaar, and from them, in recent times, to our people, the Aelendyell. All things have, within, their own energy, their own latent magic. As descendants of the Alfyn, we have an innate link with the earth and the forests, a link that inspires the essence of pure magic in us - the First Ki - though what we can do with this source of magic is but a shadow of our Great Ancestors' powers. The First Ki is the magic of Being and Shaping.'

Only a shadow? Terin wondered. Why only a shadow? Where had the old power gone? What happened to the Genesis Stone?

'The Second Ki was formed by the great sorceresses of the Elvenaar who discovered links of power existing between Nature and the fragments of the Genesis Stone that survived the Time of the Great Dragon Burning. This is the magic of Linking and Recreating. More potent than the First Ki, it requires greater discipline and responsibility.'

'And that's the magic I want to learn,' Terin whispered. 'Powerful magic. Then they'll respect me. Then they'll leave me alone, once and for all.'

'Shh,' a Chosen Aelendyell hissed, and glared at him. Terin frowned.

'From the writings and wisdom of the Elvenaar sorceresses, the Chosen in every generation are taught the Lore of Magic. When your lessons are complete, you will carry with you, and in you, the First and Second Ki - the strength and the knowledge of every Aelendyell who has passed before you, and of those who will come after you.

4

You will carry great power, and with it even greater responsibility, for the Keepers of the Lore of Magic must be wise in thought and in deed.' The Chanter's resonating voice belied the frail, bent figure from whom it came, and Terin was fascinated by the ancient Aelendyell's clever disguise of his deep well of power under a mask of age. He gazed absently into the Chanter's dark blue eyes before he realized the Elder was staring directly at him, following the flight of his words to their mark, as if they were especially intended to target something in Terin. A message? Or a warning?

Lesson ended, Terin bolted from the grove, before anyone could talk to him. He skirted a pack of younglings huddled about a hollowed ash, moving with the stealth of a forest cat, a skill he necessarily mastered during his childling and youngling years to avoid trouble. Teasing and hatred, directed at him, made him develop abilities he might never have fostered had the Aelendyell community openly accepted him. They despised him because he was different. He was a bastard child, bred from the rape of an Aelendyell maiden, Solweonyn, who unwittingly went to the aid of a human warrior lost in the dark glens of Meerash. Taller than his peers, as tall as his human father might have been, his eyes were rounder, less almond-shaped than the eyes of a full-blooded Aelendyell. The avenging Aelendyell slew Terin's human father as he staggered from the site of his brutality, and his Aelendyell mother died from a fever contracted during his birth. Village adults and Elders fostered the orphaned Terin through his childling years. He knew little of his origins, although he recognised, early, that he was different because his peers taunted him. At first, it was because he looked a little different. Then they taunted him because of his increasing height. Finally, somehow, the older ones learned why he was different, and deeply scarred him with their barbed insults. 'Man-spawn,' they whispered. 'Half-made.' He hated them for it, hated them all. When the taunting became unbearable, he lashed out. His size and strength made fighting easy, and he quickly punished individual tormentors, but they resorted to gang attacks to counter his physical superiority, and the adults always sided with the smaller younglings.

Recognising how to avoid confrontations, he rejected his foster adults' attempts to appease him, and resorted to building a sleeping place beyond the village at the end of his youngling years, driven out by sneering contempt. He lived apart, and practised silent movement, speed, efficiency, and spells. Taunt as much as they might, his tormentors would never catch him. He could hate them with passion, loathe them, return taunt for taunt, appear and disappear in the forest at will, and always be one step ahead.

Female Aelendyell avoided him, warned by others that their status in the village would be ruined by a relationship with the half-made being, so he watched jealously as his peers partnered and crept into the forest to enjoy the pleasures of sexual exploration. Aelendyell custom forbad full sexual relationships until both partners were of age, and the pairing approved by the Elders, but there were no restrictions on sensual pleasure, at any age, so discrete liaisons were overlooked as long as the major taboo was heeded. For Terin, it was yet another form of deliberate torture devised by his tormentors to make him suffer for being a bastard. As he matured, he wanted to touch and be touched by a female, fascinated as he watched them bathe naked in the stream, but they shied away and ignored his advances, so his frustration took darker paths.

When the Elders ranked him among the Chosen to learn the Lore of Magic, his antagonists were more shocked than he was. Not only did his human body size and strength mark him as a potentially powerful Weapon Bearer, there was the matter of his impure blood. Lore Bearers were always the purest Aelendyell because they were entrusted with the duty of maintaining and passing on sacred lore. No one dared to protest his selection, because the Elders' choice was final, but he knew, from his peers' spiteful stares, that silent discontent brewed.

He relished the Elders' choice. As much as he despised the contemptuous Aelendyell society, he wanted to acquire magic because magical skill was more highly respected than a warrior's prowess. Lore Bearers rose ultimately to the highest rank of Elder, and it would give him the greatest pleasure to have authority over those who tormented and mocked him.

His selection was no accident. He meticulously learned every lesson Aelendyell childlings and younglings were expected to know. He revelled in exploring the intricacies and variations of simple spells that sprang naturally from his Aelendyell heritage. He mastered their power and experimented with embellishments, until none of his village peers could perform spells to match his flair and accuracy, or ease. He knew the Chanter couldn't overlook his potential. The Elders couldn't ignore it either. What they didn't know, when they presented him with the amber ring of the Chosen, was that his prowess stemmed from two inner needs - a deep and driving fascination for magic, and a burning desire to heap calculated revenge upon his peers.

Beyond the village margin, Terin left the narrow pathway to the Meeting Stone, and travelled a hundred paces deeper into the forest, following his own path, artfully hidden in the treefern groves. At every turn, he paused to listen, in case others were following - a habit grown from his mistrust and hatred of the younglings. He knew his Chosen peers could find his sleeping place, if they really wanted to track him, but he knew their arrogant disinterest would keep them distant. Silly younglings were the real threat, and although they lacked the finer tracking skills of their Aelendyell race he made certain he was safe. At four points along his faint path, he moved and replaced camouflaged false trail endings, and listened.

He had fashioned his sleeping place from the heart boughs of an old ash-elm, a tree smaller than the lofty elmoaks of the Aelendyell village, but thicker foliaged, and much better suited to hiding. At its base, between roots that twisted and groped at lush grass, he listened a final time. Then he conspiratorially whispered, made an upward motion with his hands before his chest, and rose gently from the ground as his spell took effect. A moment later, he disappeared into the midst of the ancient tree, ten spans above. He cupped his hands before his face in the darkness and saw their heat as his eyes adjusted to nocturnal vision, a trait common to all Aelendyell. The sparse interior took form, in the darkness and shadow, before he spoke softly, 'Leoht.' Heat quickened in the curve of his palms. An opalescent sphere shimmered into existence, lingering briefly in a ghostly half-world of faint luminescence, before expanding, in depth and brilliance, to become a floating ball of soft white light spreading its mantle across the leafy sleeping place interior.

Terin smiled, pleased with his magical talent. He nudged a rolled light green parchment back into position on a branch shelf with his fingertips, before leaning forward to draw a small dark wooden casket from behind a wall of leaves. His eyes rested on the intricate laurel leaves and vines, intertwined with figures of ancient tree giants, carved in the casket's lid, whose knotted faces were textured with character. A magical emanation tingled along the nerve webbing in his fingers, and down his spine, and he drank in the magical sensations as he lowered the casket to the floor. Squatted on his haunches, he reverently opened the lid to gaze on the object within - the sacred Aelendyell Book of Lore. If the Chanter or Elders knew he had the book - he couldn't imagine their response. But he had the Book of Lore, and every Aelendyell secret of the Second Ki.

Terin's eyes ached from poring over the ageless arcane enchantments, painstakingly written by a hundred hands, committing to memory what he could; committing to parchment what he could not remember. Sheets of scrabbled notes lay scattered about the floor. The floating light sphere waned with his exhausted energy.

When he first opened the leather-bound text, and felt the silken touch of the first page, and smelt the fragrance of time smoothed into the ancient script, he was disappointed by the volume's brevity, its lack of bulk. Instead of a mighty tome too great to comprehend at a cursory glance, the Book of Lore was lightweight and thin. But as he read, moving cautiously through the word currents, the pages seemed to expand, to grow in number as he turned each one, unfolding fluidly before his seeking eyes, exposing theorems and truths, names and relationships, strengths and weaknesses, histories, secret words and combinations, the heart of the Second Ki, until he was adrift in an ever-expanding sky of knowledge, with no guide for direction, no promise of end, no rookery for rest.

Terin closed the book. The weight of exhaustion pressed in. He slumped against a cool bough, tucked his knees beneath his chin, and let the last theories wash over his mind. On the floor, the Book of Lore was reduced in stature again to a thin text, but he knew its secret, the strong illusion binding the expansive Aelendyell knowledge within the tiny boundaries of green leather. And it held a mystery he had never imagined. The First Ki, the source of Aelendyell magic, was dependent not only on their heritage as descendants of the Alfyn Great Ones, but also on a tiny sliver of the original Genesis Stone embedded in the amber ring each of the Chosen received when they were named. And there was more. When the Chosen graduated to become Lore Bearers, they received a silver necklet with another sliver of the amber Genesis Stone embedded to enhance their magical powers. He wanted a necklet now.

Beyond the leafy walls of his hide-away, faint fingers of light traced soft golden patterns across the forest. Terin flicked back his silver locks and concentrated on the will-o'-the-wisp rays silently dancing on their leaf and bark stages, and the empty beauty soothed his tired mind. He flinched into sharp awareness. Light - morning! He scrambled to his feet, snatched up the Book of Lore, and returned it to the casket. He had tarried too long. He had to replace the casket in its niche in the Chanter's Well before the theft was discovered.

It was still dark at the forest floor, as Terin ran along the invisible paths, silently racing towards the village. He veered off the path, near the outer fringe, startled by a sound to his left, but a glance told him a nocturnal creature was scurrying home to beat the light. Relieved, he continued, cautiously traversing the village centre to the Spell Grove.

Beyond the Spell Grove, he melted into the forest to let two Night Watchers pass, and he smiled smugly as they passed, their patches of body heat shimmering beneath their jerkins and breeches. Less fortunate than he, because they hadn't been chosen to carry the Lore, they were warriors, condemned to a life of training and toil in the physical arts of fighting. A Lore Bearer carried far greater respect into old age among the Aelendyell than a Weapon Bearer. He was chosen to hold a position above them, and they hated him for it, and that pleased him.

Once the Night Watchers passed beyond vision and hearing, Terin slipped across a tiny clearing to the base of a thick elmoak, whose twisted roots gripped the earth like wooden anchors. The old tree boughs cradled the tree-home of the Chanter and guarded the Chanter's Well between its roots. He scanned for warning sounds from the lodging overhead in the last moments of darkness. High in the forest canopy, sensing the approaching sun rising, beyond the curve of the distant peaks forming the ragged spines of the Andrakian and Ureykyeu mountains, the first tentative bird calls invited others to join them in songful appreciation of impending day.

Terin momentarily listened to the birds, and then slid between the great roots to find the Cover Stone.

The Stone sat in place, guarding its secrets from everyone, but the Chanter and the Lore Bearer Elders. And Terin. He focussed on the dark circle on the ground, and deftly ran his fingers across its polished granite surface, tracing the finely chiselled rune in its face. The Cover Stone was heavy, too heavy even for a team of warriors to dislodge, and it was held in place by a spell, recreated anew by successive Chanters. The sealing spell was kept secret from those who sought to learn the lore without authority, but he watched and waited, patiently hiding for several afternoons to observe the Chanter work his magic - and then he practised the opening spell so that he, too, could draw from the Well.

He placed his palm firmly over the rune, once he finished tracing its form, and whispered, 'Un-tynan stith stan sinc-gyfa ond mund-bora.' His flattened palm became warm. When he lifted his hand from the Stone, the rune glowed white in the semi-darkness. The flat disc of granite slid silently, gracefully aside, uncovering a well, two spans wide, descending into the earth beneath the tree. He took the small casket from under his cloak, his fingers tingling with memories of potency as he caressed the carved wood. It was his to have, his to use. No one could deny him. Lying on his stomach, his heart racing anxiously, he lowered the casket into the well, found the niche in the granite wall, and slid the casket into place.

As his fingers released the forbidden object, a deep, resonating voice filled the darkness - a voice of authority, tinged with sadness. 'Why, Terin?'

There was no escape. The Chanter was too powerful to fight. The sheer shock of discovery rooted him to the lip of the Chanter's Well and stole his initiative. He was caught. He had to bear the consequence. What he hated most was knowing those who taunted him for his difference would gloat at his capture.

Two

He stood at the centre of the Meeting Stone, facing seven Aelendyell Elders who were seated in a semi-circle, on high-backed chairs, against the backdrop of the lush green forest. The Meeting Stone, a large, flat, white marble disc embedded in the thick green grass, filled the centre of a natural amphitheatre, where the Aelendyell often gathered on the grassy slopes to observe and participate in meetings, but the slopes, this morning, were empty. A guard of twelve Weapon Bearers stood along the perimeter, facing out, to keep the curious away. The Chanter, in cobalt flowing robes mirroring the colour of his eyes, his long white tresses resting on his shoulders, stared at Terin with impassive patience. The remaining Elders, robed in variegated green hues, with their high cheeked, narrow, frail profiles, and long silver-white hair, bore an uncanny resemblance to each other.

Terin defiantly returned the Chanter's gaze. They call me the bastard, he thought angrily, but they are the inbred bastards. They had caught him, and were ready to judge him, but they would not force him to be humble. He would not accept humiliation, not from anyone in the village - not even from the Chanter. He'd done what he'd had to do to sustain his spirit, in a place that hated him and he hated in return.

'You know why you are here,' the Chanter said, in a clear, low voice. Terin kept his silence, impassively smouldering. 'Curiosity is an inbred Aelendyell trait,' the Chanter continued. 'It has always been so. And you, Terin, have been more curious than most. Even when you were a youngling, we watched and saw this in you. It is one of your strengths, and a reason why you were selected among the Chosen. But what you have done this night is wed-bryce -' Terin's eyes narrowed at the Chanter's use of the old Elvenaar tongue. '- wrongful, and beyond mere forgiveness. You've taken upon

12

yourself to use, for your own purposes, that which is sacred to our people. You have presumed a right that may only be offered, on rare occasion, to the highest of the Chosen. You have broken the simple oath of trust, Terin. Why have you done this?'

Terin read no malice in the Chanter's face, and the Elder's voice carried only a gentle tinge of anger, but the direct question nevertheless demanded an answer. He broke from the Chanter's gaze and looked down. The forest seemed to be waiting for his answer, but these old fools would not humiliate him.

'As I feared,' the Chanter pronounced, with a sigh of sad resignation. The unexpected sigh drew Terin's eyes up, in time to see an Elder lean and whisper into the Chanter's left ear. The Chanter looked at Terin, and asked, 'Elder Tolenyth wants to know why you bear so much anger within?'

Terin glared at Elder Tolenyth, before returning his silent gaze to the Chanter. *As if they don't know why I hate them. I'm an outcast. Younglings taunt me. Adults ignore me. They know why I'm angry.* He looked down at his feet.

'Then you will not answer?' the Chanter asked.

The Elders sat beyond his wall of silence, awaiting a reply, but he resolved to wait them out. He studied an ant's progress across the grass, saw it briefly meet with colleagues who were curious as to the load it was carrying, before it laboured on. The Chanter's authoritative voice broke Terin's self-imposed solitude.

'Your silence speaks loud enough. Defiance. Hatred. Pride. These are evil emotions, in any Aelendyell, but especially in one who aspires to be a Lore Bearer. We had hoped your curiosity in magic would lead you from these evils, Terin of Solweonyn, but it has not been so.'

Terin winced at the mention of his dead mother's name, and his hatred flared as he looked up.

'No,' said the Chanter, slowly, seeing Terin's angry stare. 'Clearly it has not been so.' He paused, as if to drink in the verdant beauty of the vacant amphitheatre, almost as if he'd forgotten Terin, or the reason they were gathered at the

Meeting Stone. He looked either side, at his colleagues, acknowledging each, before he turned to the young half-Aelendyell standing on the milky Meeting Stone in the dappled light. 'You are dangerous and naive. You have much to unlearn before you can hope to be a Lore Bearer. You first must learn to be Aelendyell.'

Terin wanted to curse them, storm out of the clearing and retreat to his private sleeping place, ignore them, but he restrained his roiling anger. The Elders were like the younglings, taunting him into fighting them. He would not be drawn into their traps. There would be a time in the future for revenge, he reminded himself. He saw the Chanter nod to the six Elders.

'Here is our judgment!' the Chanter declared, adopting the formal tone he used for decisions. 'So let it be known. Terin of Solweonyn may no longer enter the Spell Grove, nor may he learn the lore.' He focussed on Terin. 'You will move your belongings from your hideaway, and you live among the Aelendyell families at the centre of the village. You will return to the home of Merythwyl of Lannionon, who will act as your father, and you will give Merythwyl, and his wife, Neyanna, all due respect that you would give to your true parents, were they among us. You will graciously learn Aelendyell spirit, and you will actively unlearn your spite. When you can show to us that you have done these things, then the Elders will decide the role you will be allowed to undertake as an Aelendyell adult. So are you instructed.' The Chanter met Terin's spiteful gaze with a stern expression, and said, 'Go!'

For an awkward moment, after the Chanter ordered him to leave, Terin remained motionless, unsure of how to act. The order bit deep into his pride. He turned away, numbed by the Elders' judgment, and walked up the slope and out of the amphitheatre. At the very least, he had expected to be banished from the Spell Grove. He'd even expected they would send him from the village, exile him, perhaps even put him to death for stealing the Lore Book, and practising its magic without permission. But he hadn't expected this outcome. He'd never imagined they would drag him back into the very centre of the people he despised and force him to become one of them. Of all the humiliating punishments the Elders could've chosen, this was the worst. His humiliation would be complete. Rage burned inside his breast, as he plunged along the path, and his anger surged when he reached the camouflaged entrance to his secret path. He pointed at a small shrub, and, in the ancient Elvenaar tongue, he growled, 'Byrnan!' A fierce flame erupted in the bush's heart and rapidly consumed it. He smiled grimly at the smoking ash. He was born to power. He'd made his decision.

After hiding his hoard of scrolls, and parchment scraps and notes he'd copied from the Book of Lore, in the branches and boughs hollowed out earlier in his home, he gathered his few possessions and descended to join the four Weapon Bearers waiting at the base of the tree. He let them lead him silently back to the village, content to brood on his plan and contempt for his guards. Younglings came to stare and trail after the group, as they entered the village, pointing and laughing at Terin's tall figure amid the Weapon Bearers, until two warriors chased them away.

Merythwyl and Neyanna met Terin in the village centre. Merythwyl was middle-aged, at least as near to it as Terin could guess, and wore his ash-blond hair cut short. He'd acted as Terin's guardian, before Terin abandoned the village for his own privacy. Terin considered him quiet and conservative. Although he'd been a Weapon Bearer, an injury to his thigh, when he fell from a riverbank, dodging a charging wild pig, had left him unable to fulfil his protector's role. Instead, he helped other Aelendyell repair their homes, and supervised childlings during the daylight time. Neyanna was a younger woman, with the elegant beauty of all Aelendyell women, her almond eyes shining green in her high cheeks, framed by a mantle of golden hair.

Their tree home was comfortable, if small. Leafy walls

15

separated the quarters, and Merythwyl directed Terin to a tiny alcove at the habitation's rear. As he walked through the lodging, he took in details, noting how many openings led to the forest floor between boughs, and where the occupants of his prison might be sleeping. After he'd deposited his possessions, Neyanna brought him a cup of honey wine, and asked if he wanted to share a meal, but he made no effort to talk to either Aelendyell as they tried to prompt conversation from him. Merythwyl endeavoured to reminisce on their former relationship, talking as if he was a proud father who'd been blessed with the return of a prodigal son. Terin ignored him. Neyanna was quiet, acting, as she always did, as a considerate host. Terin was amused by the pairing, given Neyanna was much younger than her husband, and attractive. He hadn't yet slept with a female, and he doubted any Aelendyell woman would offer him the opportunity because of his mixed blood, but he took in Neyanna's sensuality with a strong hunger over the rim of his drinking cup. She was wasted in Merythwyl's company.

Tiring of his insolence, his hosts talked quietly to each other, politely avoiding him in their discussions while he ate. Then, abruptly, as Terin handed Neyanna his empty bowl, Merythwyl said, 'The Elders told us why you've been sent to live with us. We know you're angry, and we understand why. It's not easy for you. There are some who are unable to show tolerance, and that's unfair on you. We know you've been sent to live with us to learn Aelendyell spirit. We accept that burden, Terin, as we accept that you are different from us in many ways. The Elders are wise, and they make their judgement for your good. While you stay with us, you are as one of our family, like a son. You may come and go as you wish.'

Terin avoided Merythwyl's face, as the Aelendyell spoke, scorning the proffered hospitality. The pretence of compassion was the worst humiliation they could force him to endure. Instead, he rose and retreated to his space in the tree home.

He listened to the motion of village life. Younglings

chattered, as they played their magical game of hideaway. He'd learned the game when he was still young enough to have friends among the childlings. The object was to cast a simple spell to make small pebbles invisible, and challenge companions to discover the hidden objects. He'd loved the game, becoming so proficient that the other childlings eventually stopped wanting to play with him, because he could make his objects impossible to find and yet he easily found their invisible objects. He listened to the laughter of young males and females fashioning pots and bowls from rich yellow clay gathered from the banks of forest streams, and he caught snippets of their courting jests between laughter. No Aelendyell girl ever flirted with him. They were afraid of him, saw him as strange because of his human features. The Aelendyell life teased him. He could hear a world to which he did not belong - a world to which he could not belong. In fact, it was a world to which he did not want to belong. He was a prisoner. He was a freak. He slumped against the wall and shut his eyes, until he finally closed out the hated world with sleep.

Daylight was fading when he woke. He sat up and discovered a bowl of fresh fruit and nuts in the doorway. Neyanna hadn't disturbed him to share the evening meal. Good, he decided. He pulled a small bag from his belongings and emptied the contents of the bowl into it. He'd be hungry later. He shifted to the darkest corner and, cross-legged, mulled over the spells he'd memorised from the Book of Lore, tracing the words of the ancient Elvenaar scripts and scrolls with the fingers of his mind, fitting them into location and time as accurately as he could remember. When he heard a light footfall, he dropped to the leaf-strewn floor and feigned sleep. After the presence withdrew, he sat up. The bowl was gone. Beyond his wall, he heard the faint murmur of Merythwyl's and Neyanna's voices.

Later, when sleep infused the village, he wrapped his possessions in a large cut of jade cloth. He crept to an opening in the tree branches, just beyond his room, listened, and when he was satisfied no one was abroad, he tucked the cloth into his green jerkin, moved his hands gently, and quietly levitated to the ground. He retraced the paths past the Spell Grove to the base of the Chanter's tree, and, as he approached, he searched for a dim glow of light within the tree's heart. The Chanter and Elders would be expecting him to steal the Book of Lore again, if they really had the insight into his nature they claimed to have, but he was prepared. Surprise in trying so quickly after being caught was his first hope for success. His second was his knowledge of the magic of the Second Ki, knowledge he was not meant to possess. He was confident the Chanter had underestimated the degree of magical power he'd already illegally acquired.

He waited for the light in the Chanter's elmoak to wane, but it burned brightly well beyond midnight, until Terin was struggling to stay awake. Worse, he observed that pairs of Watchers were regularly patrolling the base of the tree, and they moved with heightened caution, as if they were expecting to find him at the Cover Stone again. He'd underestimated the Chanter. With the Cover Stone so effectively guarded, he couldn't take the Book of Lore. Tormented by his passion to possess the book, he hunched in the undergrowth like a wounded beast, hungry for his prey but unwilling to take the risk. If he was successful in his bid, and he could steal a necklet from one if the Lore Bearers, he would have all the knowledge of the First and Second Ki. If he failed...

Twice he steeled himself to sprint to the Cover Stone, but fear and reason prevailed over ambition. Finally, frustrated and weary, he ceased his vigil, and decided to retrieve his scrolls and parchments from the secret compartments in his old hideaway. At least, in them, he had recorded a substantial portion of the Book of Lore - certainly enough to make him a potent practitioner. Then he could plot how to obtain a necklet with the sliver from the Genesis Stone to complement his amber ring.

He easily avoided the Watchers patrolling the village

perimeters and moved confidently along his secret pathway to his former tree home. There, he levitated into the tree, and fashioned a tiny sphere of light to expose the hollowed branches where he'd secreted his possessions. He was so intent on gathering the parchments that he failed to hear two Watchers scramble up the vines into his hideaway. 'It is forbidden for you to be here,' said the first Aelendyell.

'That is the will of the Elders, Terin of Solweonyn,' added the second.

Terin spun to face them, his arms full of incriminating material, and his anger and hatred welled. 'This is mine!' he snarled.

Startled by the vehement reaction, the first Aelendyell instinctively grabbed the hilt of his sword. Terin reacted. He opened his right hand, and a force like a fist hit the victim square in the chest, catapulting him backwards, over the edge of the tree platform. As he thumped onto the soft earth, his companion's jaw slackened, and his face dissolved into wide-eyed disbelief. Terin seized the moment, and hissed to the second Watcher, 'Go, before I do the same to you. You cannot stop me. I bear the Lore!' The frightened young Aelendyell backed away, scurried over the edge and down the vine rope to aid his stunned friend spread-eagled below. Terin scooped up his scrolls and notes, and bound them in a manageable bundle before he walked to the far end of his tree home and dropped lightly to the forest floor.

A stern voice startled him. 'Terin of Solweonyn.' Expecting another Watcher, Terin turned arrogantly to warn the Aelendyell not to interfere and met the dark eyes of Elder Laeocwyddyn. Behind the Elder, ten Aelendyell Weapon Bearers had their bows loaded and aimed. 'This time, Terin of Solweonyn, you've gone too far,' said the Elder firmly. Terin bolted - and hit a soft wall of resistance he couldn't push through - a spell. He was trapped. He cursed, and turned to find the Elder striding towards him. 'You cannot run from me. I am a Keeper of the Lore, and you are Aelendyell,' declared the approaching Elder.

'I'm not Aelendyell!' Terin cried passionately. 'And you

can't hold me!'

'I am. I will,' replied the Elder with calm resolution. He weaved his fingers in a deliberate pattern.

'No!' Terin screamed. 'No!' He lifted his finger and pointed with wild precision. 'Byrnan!' he yelled in panic. 'For-birnan ond fir-niman!' The old Aelendyell was astonished to hear the ancient Elvenaar incantation, as a tongue of bright yellow flame erupted within his chest. He crumpled, screaming in an agonizing inferno, and he burned fiercely, until not even a trace of ash remained to say the Elder ever existed. As the raging flames lit the bewildered and horrified faces of the Aelendyell warriors, Terin ran, and he was long gone by the time the warriors gathered their courage to pursue the renegade.

Three

The fugitive pushed north, through lush forest, twisting, backtracking along glittering streams and crossing mossy granite outcrops to lose his pursuers. Every shadow, every whisper of breeze, every animal's scamper in the forest was Aelendyell to him and sent him scrambling for cover. Capture would be death. He expected no less. He was ecg-bana - a slayer of his people - the murderer of an Elder. No Aelendyell heart would weep for him. No Aelendyell sword or arrow would speak mercy. But he didn't care. He was more than they. He was not Aelendyell. And he held the First Ki, and a great deal of the Second Ki was already part of him too. His destiny was to, one day, have it all. Then he would force the Aelendyell to kiss his feet and beg his mercy. Three times, throughout five days, the Aelendyell closed on his trail. Each time, he utilised his skill of quick and silent movement through the brush, enhancing it with magic stolen from the Book of Lore, to avoid discovery. He used every rest opportunity to weave spells, memorised from the Book of Lore, deeper into the fabric of his being. He was more than a Lore Bearer. He was free to practise magic in any form he chose.

On the sixth morning of his flight, as he walked through dew-kissed trees, he gazed up through the dark green canopy and saw snow-capped mountain peaks to his left. Mountains. As a deep forest dweller, he'd never seen mountains, although he'd heard of them in tales. He paused, fascinated by the vision, and listened for tell-tale sounds, but he heard no warnings. The forest was simply waking to a new morning. He breathed the fresh air, savouring familiar smells, and pressed on.

He reached a point where a vast, treeless region stretched ahead, larger than any clearing he'd ever encountered. Curiosity aroused by the new landscape, and satisfied his pursuers had lost his trail, he walked forward with renewed confidence. An endless blue sky hung overhead, pocked by random patches of white cloud. To his left, the forest stopped abruptly at a low dark red escarpment, which formed a natural rock step up to the base of the first peak of a mountain range stretching north and south. To his right, the forest edge curved majestically to the south, and the world broke open, across a vast, grassy sea of rolling hills that washed against the distant shores of grey, ragged mountains. The panoramic vista shocked his forest-dweller's eyes, inducing a peculiar vertigo, like the feeling he had the very first time he peered from the giant branches, atop a village elmoak, onto the ant-like Aelendyell working and playing far below - except here the world drew away from him, ever-circling outward. Dizzy, touched with fear, he shrank against the comforting bark of a tree trunk.

For a long time, he stared at the bizarre, unforested land, his senses slowly adjusting to its expanse, bracing for the moment when he would have to move from the forest's familiar security into the strange naked world. It would be sensible to stay in the forest, his home, secrete himself in hidden places, and live furtively out of sight of the Aelendyell. He could do it. He had the skill. But he knew that style of existence would be harrowing and pointless. The forest was no longer his home - it never was his home. Sooner or later, he would be discovered and forced to flee for his life, again and again. And, inevitably, the Aelendyell would hunt him down, and he would be forced to surrender and face humiliation. His future was out there. He was not Aelendyell. There was a greater motivation. He was not going to be denied access to acquiring the magical power of the elusive Third and Fourth Ki in the way that access was denied the Aelendyell. He knew, instinctively, that the remaining two Ki were somewhere in the treeless world that repulsed his Aelendyell sensibilities.

He gathered provisions from bushes and fruit trees in the forest margin and drew water from a tiny brook that struggled between lichen-covered rocks and gnarled roots.

When he discovered a beehive, he subdued the bees with a minor sleeping spell to pilfer their golden treasure. He had no idea how far he would have to travel across the treeless land, so he packed as much food as he could carry. All the while that he foraged, he listened cautiously for warnings of approaching hunters, but no one came. Food and water organised, he made his way to the tree perimeter, and resolutely strode onto the grassy plain.

He walked north for half a day, keeping the mountain range to his left. The distant escarpment gradually dissolved into low foothills huddled beneath the range, and the mountains steadily diminished into steep hills. Passes and valleys appeared frequently between the hills, until he saw a broad, flat gap leading west between two dwarf mountains. Cresting a low ridge that stretched across the plain, from the hills in the west to an extended finger of a second range of ragged-peaked mountains in the east, he saw a darkening stain that seemed to extend across the northern landscape like cloud shadow - a desolate wasteland, grey like the ashes of a dead fireplace. The vision defied his comprehension. Except at the edge, where the grass abruptly ended, as if terrified to reach into the forbidding grey dust, there was no hint of greenery in the bizarre landscape. Bleached skeletons of long-perished trees jutted acutely out of the grey dust, limbs twisted in agony, clawing at the sky. Terin recoiled, recognising the presence of lingering death in the hostile landscape, and quickly descended the rise that barred the choking grey dust from the reassuring sea of grass.

He couldn't go north. To the east, a full day's walk, was a forbidding range of rugged mountains - and travelling in that direction would involve traversing the perimeter of the grey desert. To the west, a gentler range of hills, with a clear pass through to whatever lay beyond, presented a far less threatening journey than travelling east. He'd go west.

By late afternoon, tired and sore after six days on the run, he entered the broad valley, and felt a curious sense of comfort from the presence of bushes and isolated trees, even though they were stunted in comparison to the mighty elmoaks of the Aelendyell forests. Although he had hoped to reach the heart of the pass before nightfall, he sighed with exhaustion and stopped to watch the orange sun sink to the western rim of the world, splashing the crests of the hills with soothing red and gold light. He looked for a stand of trees or a depression where he could rest and eat. The Aelendyell wouldn't dare follow him so far from the forests. The treeless world would have stopped them. He smiled, as he squatted to fossick in his food sack, and reflected on the events that so quickly brought him to this new world as he chewed a handful of berries. He had outwitted them all with his skill and his new powers, as he'd promised he would. He had humiliated the Aelendyell who, for so long, humiliated him. For now, that would suffice. They would remember him – he'd guaranteed that fact with Laeocwyddyn's death. The day he returned, to take the Book of Lore, he would enjoy reminding them just how cruelly they'd treated him, teased him, and shunned him for being only half of what they were. He would return with greater power, more knowledge than the entire council of Elders - with more authority than even the Chanter - and he'd remind them of Terin, the one they drove out because he wanted to learn magic. And he would make them tremble in his presence. 'That's my promise to the Aelendyell,' he decided aloud. Satisfied with his pledge, he stood and stretched his arms wide to relieve his muscular ache. That's when they jumped him.

A dark-skinned, bristled face filled his view. Beneath thick, knitted brows, black eyes gleamed. 'Tel alam ne bak?'

A second voice, husky, almost hoarse, spoke from behind Terin's left ear. 'Tet nya ne sarat?'

The face waited patiently, while Terin peered through the fading evening light at the worn creases that crisscrossed the skin and gathered at the corners of the man's mouth and eyes. The stranger's mouth moved. 'Tel alam ne bak?' he repeated. Faint inquisitiveness flickered in his eyes. 'Fek!' he ordered.

'Salam en yelara ned?' asked the hidden voice.

'Nye!' the stranger snapped, with a sharp shift of his head. He rose from squatting before Terin, stared down as if trying to read his captive's eyes, and walked away.

When the man, swathed in long, loose brown and cream striped robes, reached the edge of a nearby campfire, Terin eased into a half-seated position. As he settled, a hard hand locked onto his left shoulder, and a curved dagger blade flashed before his eyes, before pressing firmly against his neck. A voice hissed, 'Feyed et ne ranu ey arat! Yelara ne haru en sela!' The hand jerked Terin's shoulder roughly, as its owner released his grip and rose.

Terin watched the second captor join his companion beside the flickering campfire. Two will be hard to deal with, he assessed, as he considered escape. Two more robed figures emerged from the darkness to stand at the fire. Four made the odds much more difficult. He shrugged, and watched his captors for clues as to their intentions. From time to time, as they talked, they glanced in his direction. Their alien language, the coarse tongue of a barbaric culture, lacked soft Aelendyell resonances. So how had they caught him unaware? He was far too cautious to be easily surprised. He wondered if the Aelendyell Elders had contracted mercenaries to catch him if he left the forest. The notion was absurd. As far as he knew, the Aelendyell community kept aloof from the world beyond the forest, dealing with humans, only as a last resort, in times of great need. The Elders would never hire human mercenaries when their dignity was at stake. So the strangers must have come upon him by accident. But he couldn't remain a captive. What if they considered taking him to the forest for profit, or ransom, when they recognised his Aelendyell heritage? He wriggled his wrists and ankles and cursed when he discovered they were bound tight. Without the free use of his hands, or fingers, he couldn't conjure a useful Aelendyell spell, because he hadn't yet memorized the Second Ki spells that didn't require hand movements. Securely tied, unable to work his magic, his only option was to sit and observe. And wait.

Three strangers wore dust-ridden, cream robes, fixed with black sashes at the waist, and loosely tied into pantaloons. Brown capes draped over their shoulders, and gleaming scimitars were thrust through the sashes. All four were bearded. The one who tried to speak to him wore striped robes. Their gestures, and frequent glances in his direction, told him their discussion centred on what to do with him.

He also discerned vague silhouettes of large animals, resting at the edge of the firelight, periodically snorting and grunting. He'd never seen anything larger than a deer in the forest. He had heard descriptions of horses that humans favoured for travel, but the animals in the darkness were more unusual than he imagined horses to be, and larger.

The discussion became animated and erupted into argument. Two debaters drew swords and confronted each other. He couldn't understand their spoken words, but the tone was obvious. His fate rested in the outcome. The other two intervened, the weapons were lowered, but more sharp words were exchanged. Abruptly, two men strode into the darkness. A third came towards him, carrying a water sack. He kneeled in the semi-light, before Terin, and asked, 'Dena?' He lifted the sack, uncorked it, and held it towards Terin's lips. 'Adena. Ne denyet.' Throat and tongue dry from travelling, Terin gladly accepted the offer, and the cool liquid eased his parched aching. The sack was withdrawn and placed on the ground. 'Tel alam ne bak?' the water bearer repeated. Terin shook his head to show confusion. The man stared at him and Terin read strong intelligence in the man's dark eyes. He made a pointing gesture at his chest, and said, 'Rahmud.' He repeated his action and word twice and pointed at Terin. 'Ne? Alam?'

Realising the intent, Terin hesitated before answering the questioning finger. 'E - Ellandryll. I am Ellandryll,' he lied.

Rahmud repeated the name. 'Ellandryll. Ne et Ellandryll. Aa.' As if satisfied, he picked up the water sack, and returned to the fire's warm circle. Terin watched him retreat and wondered what Rahmud and his companions would do with a renegade who killed an Aelendyell Lore Bearer. Whatever their plans, he had to have one of his own. Somehow. He wriggled his wrists.

Despite his bonds, he slept, but when he woke the morning sunlight lacked warmth, and the bitter cold of the night earth gripped his ribs with chilling fingers. He was cramped from lack of movement. There was activity in the small camp. The four men were gathering the cloth and poles they erected for shelter and loading their bags onto the backs of the beasts. Now that he could see them in the light, they were the colour of the grey dust he saw on the dead plain the previous day, large bodied, with elongated necks, and a prominent distortion on their backs. Loaded, six of the seven beasts were prodded to their feet, and he marvelled that such skinny legs could support the towering bulk. The creatures looked spindly, ungainly, and illogical.

Rahmud approached, carrying a small bowl of steaming broth. He knelt before Terin and dipped his fingers into the warm liquid, scooping out a portion, and lifting it to Terin's mouth. 'Hakeemya ne,' he offered.

'What is it?' Terin asked suspiciously. He stared into Rahmud's eyes, searching for a clue to the man's emotions. The eyes were serious, nothing more.

'Ne hakeem. Hakeem,' the man insisted.

Terin acquiesced. Food was food, and it was warm after the chilly night. It tasted good, but the flavour was unlike anything he'd ever eaten. Rahmud spooned the last fragments with his fingers.

When Terin was finished, Rahmud hoisted him onto his shoulder, carted him roughly to the remaining kneeling animal, threw him onto the creature's back and lashed him securely to prevent him from falling. The animal's faecal stench was repulsive and Terin gagged. He heard the four men bickering and arguing as they completed cleaning their campsite. Terin's beast was prodded to its feet, and the sudden upward lurch was ferocious. His wrists were already chafed and sore because he tried to work his bonds free during the night, but he succeeded only in increasing his discomfort. If he'd been able to work his hands free, he could easily dispose of these strangers. To be tied like a beast to a beast was humiliating. At least, though, they hadn't merely decided to kill him. If only he could get his hands free...

Face down on the curved hump of a beast that dipped and heaved as it walked, he saw very little of the countryside through which they passed that morning, but he knew they'd travelled well beyond the long valley and had descended a low outcrop of foothills onto grassy plains. They moved at the men's walking pace. He expected them to rest when the strength of the sun on his back and the shadows of the beasts on the ground told him it was midday, but they pressed on, rarely speaking, as if they were intent on reaching an important destination.

Mid-afternoon, the slight breeze carried the rhythm of rapidly approaching hooves. There were shouts and cries, and, for a moment, Terin considered the misfortune he would suffer if the arrivals were foes of his captors. It quickly became apparent, however, the riders were kindred people, even though their greetings and exchanges were unintelligible. His beast was goaded into kneeling, and feet appeared at the periphery of his vision. A hand jerked up his head, and he found himself under the harsh scrutiny of a dozen faces, along with Rahmud's. More argument erupted, when they released his hair, and it continued for several heated moments. He heard a sharp ring of metal, shouts, and high-pitched cries. Fighting.

The melee was brief. Triumphant shouts and laughter rose. Boots reappeared before his eyes, and, again, rough hands pulled his hair to lift his head. He was forced to look into a grinning, bearded face - a face he didn't recognise. He glimpsed a bloodied scimitar blade as his head was dropped against the stinking haunch of his pack animal. Yells and movement erupted in a wall of sound, and his animal scrambled to its feet. Other animals drew alongside, smaller beasts on which men sat, and his animal was goaded forward. As his beast lunged into a canter, he spotted a blood-spattered body on the ground, arm outstretched, hand grasping a scimitar, eyes staring vacantly skyward. Rahmud.

Four

Men and children pressed in, talking eagerly as they vied for a clearer view of the captive. At the back of the crowd, black raiment from head to foot contrasting markedly with the creams and fawns of the robes of those hemming him in, women watched in unanimated silence. His three guards vainly tried to beat back the crowd by throwing random, vicious kicks and punches, but curiosity had the better of the people's sense of self-preservation.

When he arrived in darkness the previous night, Terin was thrown into a pit, and he remained there until morning, bound tight, unable to move, awaiting his captors' will. He wallowed in his own piss and shit, mortified anyone could be treated so vilely. Death at the hand of the Aelendyell would be better than this. The strangers who captured him in the mountain pass weren't imprisoned with him, so he suspected only Rahmud died in the brief fight. He assumed Rahmud was slain because he'd been too kind, while the others were ready to kill Terin. He felt he understood the ruthless justice that prevailed in this culture. They admired strength and despised weakness. And Rahmud had been guilty of being kind to a captive - of being weak.

His tongue and throat were aflame. He had not been given water since Rahmud's final offering. Now they had dragged him out of the pit into public view, an oddity on display in their world. The treatment reminded him how his peers teased and provoked him in the Aelendyell village, and his rage rose. If he could release his hands, he would show them strength worthy of their respect.

Just as he was convinced the crowd would press too tightly and suffocate him with their noise, a hush fell, and the mob dropped to their knees, burying their heads between their arms to hide their faces. Even his three guards fell into the absolute position of subservience, and he was taken aback. Someone held unquestionable power over these people. He would love to wield such power. He turned to the source.

Two men stood directly behind him, having emerged from a domed mud brick building. One wore pure white robes, with a mail over-jerkin, wisps of gold thread interlaced between the rings. Of medium height, thickset, his bearing was upright. He had the same olive complexion as the men who'd captured Terin, but his neatly trimmed beard and moustache differentiated him from the rest. At his waist, was a broad leather belt studded with opaque gems, and gleaming scimitars adorned either side. He had a red wrapped cloth on his head, pinned at the front with a bright blue jewel. The jewel matched his eyes, eyes full of commanding presence.

Menace emanated from the second figure. Swathed head to foot in deep red robes, his dark burning eyes peered from the depths of his apparel, but Terin's eyes fixed on a silver amulet hanging from a leather thong around the man's neck. It was worked into a figurine, and, heightened by the absence of food or water for over a day, Terin's innate Aelendyell senses tingled in the presence of a source of magic present in the amulet.

Both men surveyed the gathering, and Terin almost succumbed to a compulsion to prostrate himself before them as well, but he fought the urge, and stared unflinching back, determined to assert his courage. The man in white took a step forward, raised both hands, and spread-eagled his arms to address the kneeling assembly. 'Anyat ne haruk ey ranu. Fekala ne sel arat shebu shehaala ferad. Sek feran yaseem!'

The people responded as one, without lifting their heads, 'Yaseem ferad!' They rose, and dispersed to their homes, avoiding eye contact with the speaker. Only Terin's three guards remained face down in the dust.

'Ned nyaru!' ordered the man in white.

'Yaseem ferad!' the three guards responded. They scrambled to their feet, and firmly ushered Terin towards the domed building's entrance in the wake of their leaders. Inside, the guards again dropped to the floor. The man in white motioned his hand to summarily dismiss them. They rose, bowed, and backed from the room.

Terin briefly met the gaze of the two leaders, before he turned to survey the interior. To show his will was the stronger, he would ignore their presence. The space was lit by a circle of torches, suspended on dark metal rods that jutted from the smoke-stained white adobe ceiling. The ceiling, supported by a single central stone column, curved to the earthen floor. There were two carved wooden chairs with padded seats, and a low railing crossed the width of the building, separating the chairs from where Terin stood. Directly opposite the entrance was a closed wooden door. A low, broad hearth sat between his hosts and himself.

'Selne et ne?'

Terin's attention moved smoothly to focus on the speaker - the man in white.

'Selne et ne?'

He understood the questioning tone, but he deliberated on his answer.

'Fek!' commanded the man in white.

Terin shrugged. 'Your language is not my language. I cannot answer what I cannot understand,' he replied in Aelendyell. The man dressed in red leaned across and whispered in the first man's ear, and the man in white's eyes widened. The one in red withdrew, via the far door, and the room fell into silence, as if a great yawning chasm of distance had opened between the two figures. Terin studied the man, awaiting his next question, but he seemed content to be expecting Terin to speak.

When the wooden door swung open again, the man in red reappeared, bearing a statue. Terin recognised its similarity to the amulet about the man's neck. The red robed man gently placed his burden on the floor, prostrated himself before it, rose to his knees, placed his arms across his chest, palms pressed against opposite shoulders, leaned forward, and reverently kissed the statue. He leaned back, his knees still on the ground, until his shoulders touched the floor, and opened his arms wide, staring with closed eyes at the ceiling. He remained in his utterly vulnerable pose, chanting silent words, while his companion in white remained impassive, except that he crossed his chest with his arms.

The ritual fascinated Terin, especially because his spirit tingled with magical awareness. The source was the red robed figure. Slowly, the statue glowed a honey colour. Terin's excitement grew. Magic! It's here, in this place. The one in red is the Chanter of these people - a Lore Bearer. It must be so. But the fact the stranger was calling magic from a hand-fashioned object made Terin's mind race through the possibilities of what he was witnessing. No Aelendyell Elder had ever drawn power from a statue.

When the glow subsided, the man in red sat up and stared straight at Terin, his eyes smouldering with same amber glow that had shone in the statue. 'Fek. Speak. Alam. Your name. Leiksha Harud et Maheem orders you to speak.'

The man spoke Aelendyell, albeit poorly, and the mixture of familiar and alien words caught Terin off guard, because he responded involuntarily to the deep commanding voice. 'I am Terin.'

Both men regarded him, but the one in red approached. His eyes were filled with amber light, and Terin was overwhelmed by the presence of strong magic. 'Why are you come unto the land of the Ranu Ka Shehaala?'

'I am a wanderer. I come in search of the Ki,' Terin quickly explained. It is partly true, he thought. Why should this one, even with such power, doubt me? If only he could work his hands free and use his own magic.

The interview was brief. They dismissed him, without explanation, and let him be dragged back to the pit, wondering how the man in red had learned to speak and understand his Aelendyell tongue. The ivory statue he'd kissed was a source of magic. Terin wanted to get to that source. Perhaps, he wondered, trying to make sense of it, perhaps these strangers know one of the Ki denied to the Aelendyell.

The late afternoon sun was slanting into the pit, and creeping up its eastern wall, before anyone came to break the boredom of his confinement. A guard lifted the grill from the top of the pit, and effortlessly dropped to the floor. He wore an impassive, grubby, heavily bearded face, and when he opened his mouth, he displayed a broken set of yellowed teeth with gaps where at least three had been knocked out. He carried a length of rope that he tied about Terin's waist. Then he climbed the rope out of the pit, pulling Terin up after him. Waiting at the top were four more guards in dusty cream robes, scimitars thrust through their red waist sashes. They watched him with disinterest. Black robed women huddled nearby, like crows.

Scattered on a cloth blanket, on the sparse grass at the edge of the village thoroughfare, was food - clay bowls of fruits and raw reddish strips of matter. A pitcher stood at the centre. Terin's hunger leapt inside his stomach with ravenous talons, and he stumbled towards the offering. A guard stepped in his way and produced a dagger. Terin's reaction was reflexive. He ducked, and lunged at the guard, sinking his shoulder into the man's stomach, knocking him aside, but his attack was in vain. The guard's companions quickly subdued him, holding him prone on his back. The victim of his attack leaned over him, turning the dagger wickedly before his face. Dying like this is stupid, he thought, as the man turned the knife blade towards his chest. The man inserted his blade in Terin's jerkin sleeve and slit the cloth from wrist to shoulder. He repeated the process on the other sleeve, and on both leggings. Terin's restrainers lifted him to his feet, and pulled the clothing away, leaving him naked. Nudity held no shame in Aelendyell culture. Clothing was worn for protection, warmth, and adornment - Terin's Aelendyell upbringing had taught him this - but he felt vulnerable, as if the act of being forcibly stripped before a fully clothed pack of alien women stripped away his pride and power in full sight of their eyes. He wanted to hide. They even left his wrists tied, and his ankles partly hobbled. If only they would untie his hands -

The guards lifted him backwards and immersed him in a warm water tub, leaving him wondering what bizarre punishment was planned. Then the whole purpose of their actions dawned as the gaggle of women descended. A bath - they intended to clean him. Publicly. His humiliation was complete. Female hands washed over his body, methodically, thoroughly, regardless of his squirming protests, and throughout the ordeal the women remained totally silent, their faces hidden, personalities visible only through their dark eyes. When the women were finished, the guards lifted him from the tub, and the women dried him with coarse towels. An ochre yellow bundle was brought forward and unfolded before him. Loose sleeves identified its role, and he cursed when he saw the sleeves were laced to allow them to be fitted without the need for untying his hands. His anger subsided, as two women gently tied the sleeves along his arms, and it subsided further when they led him to eat.

He did not recognize the fruits. Their bright yellow, green, and orange skins were dimpled and harsh, and their taste was bitter. The nuts were also unfamiliar. Some were large and tasty, while others were like seeds - tiny, black, and unappetising. But hunger prevailed, and he ate what the attending women offered to his lips. The pitcher contained a white liquid he did not, at first, recognise, until he recalled Aelendyell mothers gave milk from their breasts to their younglings, and so he presumed he was being offered the same liquid drawn from the breasts of the village women. The curious custom amused him, but he eagerly drank the milk they poured into his mouth to sooth his parched lips and throat. The red strips he refused. Something was wrong with that food. It bore an uncanny resemblance to flesh, and his Aelendyell mind couldn't entirely grasp the concept of eating meat, since no Aelendyell hunted or killed or ate wild creatures. Each time the women offered the meat, he shook his head, and ignored their insistent prodding, determined not to eat what he did not trust.

He had a strong feeling of being watched throughout the meal, and he finally spied the observer, the man in white, across the thoroughfare. Only when the crow-women finished their task, cleaned away the bowls, and left, did the man in white approach. Terin's five guards stretched out on the ground in full supplication, but the man in white ignored them as he stopped directly before Terin and squatted on the blanket. Terin's eyes were drawn to the faint glow of the talisman about the man's neck. 'Hakeemya.' the man began. He cleared his throat and seemed to concentrate harder, while his right hand enveloped the talisman. 'Food. You - have - eaten well?' he asked, unsteadily, as if speaking while simultaneously thinking different words. Terin nodded. Fresh clothing and a bath, together with a satisfied stomach, had combined to ease his anger. 'Good,' the man said simply. He studied Terin's face. 'Rekama, he introduced me to you. I am Leiksha Harud et Maheem. This,' he gestured with a broad sweep of his arm, 'is my Tul, my village, my ranu, my people as you might say. I am lord here, as those of the Barbarian Kingdom to the east would call me. I am life and death here. It is necessary that you, a stranger, should know this.' Maheem held out his left hand with the palm cupped to symbolize his power. 'Your fate now lies here.' Terin knew the man did not boast. He spoke with too much calm assurance. It was fact - nothing more, nothing less. 'Why you have come to Ranu Ka Shehaala is of no importance to me,' Maheem continued. 'It is no longer your destiny perhaps either. Where you now go I have already decided. Yaseem sel feran. It will be done. May you be at peace with the destiny I have chosen for you.' Terin wasn't invited to reply. Maheem rose, dismissed himself without a word to the guards who were still face down on the earth, and walked into the heart of the village, leaving Terin to ponder the man's solid belief in his own power.

Five

The horseback journey lasted fifteen days. Maheem chose his twelve best men to take Terin on the journey, and the man of magic in the red robes, Rekama, led the party. They rode northwest, across rolling plains with sweeping oceans of grass and wild oats, each day drawing further from Terin's Aelendyell birthplace, opening a world he never imagined existed. Strapped to the bare back of his horse, the lands of the Ranu Ka Shehaala moved like a vast kaleidoscope. To the south, he glimpsed a broad edge of jade green, a forest stretching the width of the plains, far larger than his Aelendyell home, and he was consciously denying a pain that spread through the fibre of his soul whenever he saw the distant, alien, yet compelling verge. His Aelendyell spirit burned within, and he cursed its rebellious nature. To the north, and closer each day, was a glittering vista, an enormous body of water spreading across the horizon, like the southern forest, a barrier to the world. West, another wall rose, a long spine of mountainous peaks thrusting at the sky, and they trapped the grass plains by linking with the water at the point towards which the travellers were headed.

The party rode across the plains at a steady pace, from dawn to dusk, for seven of the fifteen days. Terin tired of their stony silence and assumed they couldn't understand his Aelendyell tongue any more than he could understand theirs, but he also sensed they were under strict orders not to converse with him. He remembered Rahmud's fate and wondered if these men would suffer the same harsh justice if they broke their orders.

If the escort silence was irritating, Rekama's presence was stifling. He rode at the head, his body stiff with arrogance. Terin knew Rekama wore his talisman, so Rekama almost certainly understood what Terin was asking, or saying, on every occasion, but he refused to acknowledge Terin. He kept a wary, aloof eye on his captive, and the care with which he ensured Terin's hands were secured told Terin that Rekama guessed at his potential if he were loosed.

They were never alone once they left the Tul of Maheem. Bands of riders swept in across the plains with amazing speed on stocky little horses, and rode parallel to their group, stopping when they stopped, moving on when they moved. At night, the campfires of the escorting groups could be seen flickering a short distance from their own fire. Terin noted that neither group tried to make contact, even when the intervening distance narrowed to a point where he could see the riders' features. He also observed that the riders who shadowed them the full distance on the first day, and overnight, didn't continue the following dawn. For half that morning, they travelled unaccompanied, until another party of horsemen raced towards them from the south and took up the same escort pattern. They shadowed Terin's party for two and a half days, before they wheeled back to the southeast, just as a fresh company of riders appeared from out of the west.

Rekama was their right of passage. Terin noticed the manner with which the riders took special note of Rekama's presence at the head of the party. It appeared everyone respected Lore Keepers, regardless of their place of origin. But he kept Rahmud's fate in mind, a man who obviously rode in haste, with his humped beasts, across the lands of another Tul without permission. Rekama was their protection on this journey, not the sharp scimitars hanging from the guard's sashes.

Terin had time to observe Rekama's powers. He created the campsite cooking fires with a simple ritual and soft words. When Terin's horse developed a limp on the sixth day, Rekama stopped the group, dismounted, and, after ascertaining the cause as an inflammation of the hoof from a sharp thorn, he gently ran his hands around the infected area and healed it - completely. Each time he carried out a simple act of magic, he held the talisman firmly in his palm.

Terin had to have that talisman. He was convinced it was a vital link to one of the missing Ki, magic the Aelendyell Lore Book didn't contain. He lay awake, long after his captors were sleeping, staring at the wheeling stars, plotting how he could release his hands and escape, until he drifted into dreams, no closer to his goal.

At the end of the seventh day, Rekama's party reached the north-western corner of the plains, where the mountain peaks sank into the earth before reaching the sea, leaving a wide passage open to the west. The remains of a decayed and ancient stone wall, still standing over twenty arm spans high in places, ran from the foot of the mountains to the seashore. A central gap, once a great gateway, led into a small town nestled in the crumbling ruins of larger buildings that had formed a large city. As they approached the gateway, the last escorting band of horsemen curved away to the south.

Terin gazed at the sea's dark blue expanse and wondered at the existence of so much water in one place. He watched the ebb of its surface and heard the susurration of waves on sand. No river had beauty like this. Then he realized why he was seeking the Four Ki. The Aelendyell held two sources of power and were like rivers running with force; the power of movement and change, but that power was limited by constraints. And it only fed into a vaster power, the Four Ki - the ocean of power. Combined, the four Ki became a strong and constant ocean, with enormous dimensions he could only guess at. That was his aim - to possess that power - to be the ocean encompassing the world with his strength, commanding respect. When he returned to take the Book of Lore from the Aelendyell, they would not stop him, because he would be an ocean of power that would drown their feeble rivers.

He became aware of Rekama's silent stare - the stare of someone understanding something for the first time, and it made Terin uneasy. He broke eye contact, believing Rekama knew precisely what he was thinking.

No one questioned their passage through the town, although Terin noticed how eagerly people moved aside to let them pass. Occasionally, he heard calls of 'Irand shadu arat shehaal!' and Rekama bowed his head in response. The street entered a small market square, bustling with late afternoon bartering, as men argued and bought, and sold everything from fruit, and strips of raw meat, to turbans and horses. The place was a chaotic jumble of goods, animals and people, and the hubbub caught Terin unawares. Again, as their party rode through the crowded place, men moved aside, and faces were averted from Rekama, but they stared at Terin with hard, inquisitive eyes, recognizing an alien face in their midst.

In the street beyond the market, a group of solidly built men in brown robes greeted Rekama with low bows, and avoided his eyes, as they said, in unison, 'Irand shadu arat shehaal.' One came forward, his bushy beard obscuring his features, except his sparkling dark eyes, and he bowed again, pointing with a generous sweep of his right arm to a barn, and a small building. 'Hakeemya asham esta en Ithosen, feshpa ey feshan esta ne sela ferapa. Haruk ey, haruk ne.' He bowed again, as he finished.

Rekama paused to think, and replied, without looking at the man 'Irand shadu arat shehaal.' He turned his horse towards the barn.

They rested overnight. Rekama was given quarters inside their host's house, while Terin and his guards remained with the horses in the barn. Hay provided comfort, and they were served simple but nourishing meals by dark-robed, faceless women, who moved like silent shadows, and who sat patiently in the dark corners while the men ate. Terin marvelled at the iron discipline to maintain silence, for days on end, the men and women of this land had. Given their natural dispensation for chatter, no Aelendyell could do it, he decided, and no Aelendyell male would dare expect his female companion to wait upon his every whim, unless she chose to serve him. These people had highly refined concepts of authority affecting everyone, and each knew his or her place in the society. It was a wondrous world.

In the morning, Terin was led to his horse, but as he stepped out of the barn he saw a company of thirty horsemen drawn up. Their horses were taller than the beasts he'd been transported on, and they were dappled grey. Their riders wore purple robes, cloaks and turbans, fastened with red gems, and Terin glimpsed swords beneath the robes. At the centre of the line, a man in red robes sat astride a black horse, and Terin immediately took him to be Rekama, but at that moment Rekama emerged from the front door of the house with his host in train. The troop crossed their chests, and bowed to Rekama, and it was then that Terin became aware that everyone around him was prostrate on the street before the new man in red. He smiled at the absurd complexity of the ritualistic greeting and watched to see how the two men in red would welcome one another. The stranger was the first to speak. 'Irand shadu arat shehaal, Ithos Rekama,' he said, with a mild bow of his head.

'Irand shadu arat shehaal, Wazeem,' Rekama responded.

The stranger studied Terin. 'Ferad a en ka selne fek ne?' he asked, turning to Rekama.

'Aa.'

The stranger nodded. 'Sek feran yaseem!' he ordered.

'Yaseem ferad!' the gathered groups responded, and they rose to continue their various duties. Rekama's men were soon mounted and positioned in the centre of the troop of new riders, with Terin at their centre. Rekama and Wazeem moved to the head of the company, and the riders wound out of the town, into open land.

The remainder of the journey took eight days. After riding west, around the spur of the mountain range, on a paved road, for part of the first day, they turned south, and followed the edge of the mountains. There were still stretches of wide, rolling grass plains to the west, much like those they'd crossed to reach the gateway town, but the vista was broken by outcrops of trees, and low ranges. Each day, they rode over stone arch bridges across narrow pebbled stream beds, and as they travelled further south, Terin saw more and more creatures wandering in groups about the countryside, tended by men and boys. Some creatures had horns and were smaller than the smallest horses. Others were almost hornless, and their grey fur was thick and matted. The creatures seemed content to graze, and their keepers equally content to sit and monitor them from the shade of broad bough trees. They passed travellers atop wooden vehicles, pulled by horses, and the vehicles carried large pottery urns. Each day, they rode through four or five villages, but no one ventured near them, and when they camped it was always outside a village. Food, water, and other gifts mysteriously awaited their arrival at the chosen campsites, but Terin never saw the providers and that puzzled him. Towards the end of the sixth and seventh days, the company passed through two woods, with low trees and broad grass-covered spaces between, and Terin felt a pang to be loose among even such sparse vegetation - anything to break the constant cone of silence in which he was forced to travel. He was alone, sustained only by the burning frustration of his arrogance, and a hope that he was being led to a place where the Third or Fourth Ki would be revealed.

On the fifteenth day since they'd embarked from Maheem's Tul, they were forced to cut west by a spur in the mountain range, but by midday they were heading south again. A short time later, their road swept into a broad highway, on a flat plain pushing east, toward the ranges. The volume of people multiplied and filled the highway in both directions. Terin had never seen so many people - people bearing goods on their backs, or on the backs of their horses, or other beasts of burden, people following wooden vehicles drawn by the beasts. The highway was a moving river of people, and the troop flowed into its current, turning east, towards the heart of the mountains.

When Terin saw the wall, he was filled with awe. It rose

one hundred spans out of the plain, with smooth majesty, and swept in a gentle arc, from a point in the northern arm of the mountain spur to the southern extremity, where it abutted a smaller spur. As they drew closer, he saw the wall was formed from massive blocks of hardened sandstone, so cleverly interlaced that only practised eyes could discern the joint lines. Where the broad highway ended, two huge open iron gates, daubed in purple and gold, let the torrent of travellers enter and leave at will. If the destiny Maheem decided for him lay beyond the wall of the Ranu Ka Shehaala, then Terin was prepared to face it after such a vision.

Six

Yul Ithrandyr - Holy City of Light. Terin gazed from a turret window, carved into a white cliff face, over an ocean of flat white rooftops that spread to the very walls of the city. Rising like fingers, white towers thrust at the sky, splashed with black banners, proclaiming to all who set eyes upon them the rank of Ithosen - Holy One - of those residing within. He had been locked in his tower for four days, since arriving in the city. His hands remained bound, and his wrists were chafed raw. Silent crow women dressed him, fed him, washed him, and bathed his wrists to prevent infection from the sores. He longed to free his hands, no longer to practise magic against his captors but just to feel movement in his arms and ease his aching muscles. White birds, wheeling in wavering formations above the towers, made him long to be free, to be his own master, to explore this magnificent, this powerful, city.

He accepted that his captors had no connection with the Aelendyell. Neither did they seem intent on harming him, despite his bonds. He felt as much a curiosity for them as they were to him, but he wanted to know why they were keeping him isolated and bound. And what had happened to his few possessions, the scrolls and parchments taken when Rahmud's men captured him? Only one other face appeared in the four days: the furrowed and whiskered countenance of a bulky man who guarded his prison door, but, like the women, he refused to acknowledge Terin's questions, or speak to him. The worst prison was neither the physical room, nor the bonds, but the wall of silence enclosing him. It locked him in as it locked him out.

His cell was austerely furnished. A wooden plank served for his bed and a coarse hide as a blanket. A bucket with a wooden seat, a hole in the centre, was placed in his room each morning, although he initially had no idea of its purpose until the women silently indicated it was to take his bodily wastes. He thought the custom quaint, but useful in his confined space. A small table and stool completed the setting. The walls were smooth and white, the floor grey stone, and the ceiling was domed, with a crystal sphere suspended at its centre. The sphere drew his attention the moment he entered, and it frequently attracted him because he sensed an aura of magic about it. He tried reaching it by putting the stool on the table, but the sphere was too high, and his tied wrists hampered his efforts. He tried to invoke a levitation spell, but without free hands he failed.

His eyes wandered from his room to the birds again, and then to the city. He never imagined so many people lived in the world, let alone could be gathered in one city. He pondered the complexities of living in crowded, unnatural conditions, and he was keen to see the High Elder or Chanter who held the power to oversee a place so vast. He recalled Rekama's parting advice when he delivered him to the tower, the only words he spoke to Terin throughout the journey. 'Leiksha Ithrandyr Shehaal now controls your destiny. What he will decide for you, only he knows. I am merely his servant, and I have done as he bade. Be grateful Maheem placed your fate in his hands, stranger from the east. While your eyes can still see the Great City, Yul Ithrandyr, beg mercy of Leiksha Ithrandyr Shehaal. He is the Light, the Darkness, the Power.' Rekama's awkward Aelendyell words ran through Terin's mind every morning and evening, becoming a litany, until he longed to meet this Shehaal, the one who commanded so much from so many.

His door opened. Six black robed women, bearing a wash basin and a freshly pressed light grey robe, were bundled in by a troop of six guards in light chain mail corselets and purple cloth. The women fussed with extra zeal over his cleanliness and appearance and wove his long silver locks into a thick braid. He was sprinkled with sweet-smelling fragrances, reminding him of blooms in his distant forest. He was amused by their close attention, familiar now with their intentions, especially as he was merely a prisoner and not a guest. This time, however, when the women withdrew, the guards motioned he should accompany them.

They led him down the broad steps he'd ascended when he arrived. The walls were stark, uninviting white, and he reflected on his mixed emotions when Rekama brought him to the place. Overawed by the city's expanse, its bustling humanity, his reaction was magnified when he approached the palace - a structure carved from the heart-rock of the cliff forming the city's eastern wall beneath the vaulting mountain range. Its architectural scope and magnitude confounded his limited Aelendyell experiences, and its grandeur dwarfed the mundane simplicity of his forest home.

Halfway down the steps, the guards halted on a landing before a metal door in the inner wall. One opened the door, and Terin was ushered through. He walked into opulence: a chamber lined with beaten gold overlaid on the walls and ceiling, and a floor fashioned from pure white, seamless marble. Lengths of silk hung from the domed ceiling - purples, creams, scarlet and black - and animal hide cushions were scattered about the floor in comfortable piles. Floating a hand span below the ceiling, a glowing sphere bathed the room with light.

He was led across the plush room to a pair of obsidian doors with gold handles. They opened at the head of a flight of marble stairs that swept down to floor level, halfway along a huge hall - the Kal E'haruk Ka Irandu - the Great Central Hall of Light. The sheer size and airy brightness stunned him. Two thousand people could comfortably assemble here, he thought. Everything - columns, walls, stairs, seating - was carved from white marble, and in the ceiling, thirty spans above, translucent segments let diffuse daylight mix with magical light emanating from myriad floating spheres. The only aberration lay to the left, near the head of the hall on both sides. Twenty figures sat on marble benches, each in red robes, each wearing a silver talisman. As the guards prodded him down to floor level, and urged him along the hall, he looked left and right at the audience, wondering if he was already known. He thought he saw Wazeem, who escorted Rekama from the northern city by the ocean, but it was difficult to identify anyone behind the heavy robes.

Movement at the head of the hall attracted him, as the robed men slid from their benches to kneel face down. Steps rose to a proscenium, and a white marble throne, padded with purple and scarlet cushions. A figure in white stepped into view, flanked by two huge warriors in purple armour, and followed by three men dressed respectively in red, purple, and black robes. The group moved to the head of the steps and stopped, and the hall echoed to a chant from the prostrate guards and red magicians behind Terin. 'Ithos Leiksha Irandu Shadu arat ilya'esta. Shehalak arat nes shehaal!' Nine times the chant was repeated, voices resounding from walls and ceiling, filling the hall with a sound equivalent to a crowd many times larger.

When the final syllables rose into the lighted spaces, the figure in white lifted both hands, as if encompassing the small assembly, and gently replied, 'Irand shadu arat shehaal.'

The listeners responded in unison, 'Irand shadu arat shehaal,' before they lifted their heads and knelt upright.

Terin knew the man in white, unadorned with rich robes or jewellery, had to be Leiksha Ithrandyr Shehaal. His presence carried the power of majesty. Rekama had warned him his life lay in the hands of this man. Now he would learn his destiny according to the leader of the Ranu Ka Shehaala.

Shehaal gracefully descended the steps. He had piercing green eyes, large and rounded like an owl's, framed by thick, trimmed eyebrows. The rest of his face was shrouded, but a wisp of black hair peeped from beneath his turban. Shehaal circled, studying Terin, before he stopped directly in front of him, staring into his eyes for a long moment, reading. He took Terin's bonded wrists in his hands and studied them. He looked once more into Terin's grey eyes and turned away. He remounted the steps, and, at the top, he faced the small assembly. 'Ned kana jinna!' he ordered. A guard ran to Terin and drew his scimitar.

So, this is to be my destiny, thought Terin. Not without a fight.

As he tensed to roll, to make his death more than a simple stroke, someone yelled, 'Leiksha nye! Ki bak nek! Ki bak nek!'

The guard paused, looking from Shehaal to the red robed intervener. Terin recognised Wazeem, but Shehaal dismissed the protest, and signalled to the guard. Before Terin could move, distracted by Wazeem's cry, the scimitar slid forward. His wrists were freed! The guard dropped on his face, quickly cried, 'Yaseem ferad Ithos Leiksha!' before he scampered to his position at the foot of the stairs with his companions.

Terin flexed his arms. Could he conjure spells? They were stiff and sore at shoulder and elbow, but his wrists and hands were free for the first time in twenty days. He stretched out to enjoy his freedom in the great hall of Shehaal, thinking quickly through a host of First and Second Ki spells he could invoke to escape, oblivious to those watching.

'My most Holy Lord of Light and Peace would like to know why you chose to leave the land of your people to enter the realm of the Ranu Ka Shehaala?' The perfectly intoned Aelendyell spoken by the man in the black robe descending the steps caught Terin off guard. He couldn't detect magic assisting the speaker. He wasn't clutching the silver pendant hanging from his neck chain as Rekama did to communicate. Besides, his fluent expression was far too natural. 'My most Holy Lord is impatient.'

Terin cleared his throat. 'I come to learn. I want to learn the Third Ki.'

The black robed interpreter relayed Terin's words, but they brought no response from Shehaal. Nevertheless, the interpreter continued, as if cued. 'My most Holy Lord hears your voice, and knows it to be Aelendyell, and there are signs in your features that mark Aelendyell breeding. But you have the stature and bearing of a man. Which are you?'

The blunt question added to Terin's discomfort, and he

flushed at the reference to his mixed parentage, but he was committed to his position and responded bluntly with a lie to blur the true reasons behind his arrival. 'My mother was Aelendyell, so I was told, though I never knew her. My father was - is human - a magician. He taught me a little of his ways, but then he sent me on a quest for knowledge. I came to your land because I'd heard rumours there is a powerful source of magic here, and I would like to learn as much as I can.' Terin hoped a complimentary story would enhance his chance of a favour from Shehaal. He watched the white figure for a response, a positive gesture, as the interpreter passed on his story, but Shehaal remained impassive.

'My most Holy Lord wishes to know what you can offer to his people in exchange for this knowledge you claim to seek?'

These questions are designed to harass me, Terin decided, but I won't be discouraged. 'I can teach his people what few things I know in the skills of magic. I have nothing else to offer, except for my service to your most Holy Lord.'

The interpreter relayed his response, waited for a sign of silent approval, and turned once more to Terin. 'My most Holy Lord accepts your offer of service. You will be apprenticed. Leiksha Ithrandyr Shehaal is your new master, and he has spoken.' The interpreter lifted his face towards the others gathered in the Kal E'haruk. 'Irand shadu arat shehaal.'

'Irand shadu arat shehaal!' the assembly responded. Shehaal and his retinue, minus the interpreter, turned and disappeared behind the marble throne.

This man, thought Terin with puzzled relief, who possesses so much power, has readily accepted me. Why? So lost was he in his thoughts, again, that he was unaware of the interpreter until the latter touched his shoulder. He glanced down, and realized, for the first time, just how much shorter and slighter than he the interpreter was, especially as he was no longer standing on the steps. The man's eyes were very different, and yet very familiar - deep green, and almond-shaped - Aelendyell eyes. 'You are to accompany

49

me,' the interpreter said.

He led Terin along the gleaming floor to the far end of the hall. As they passed the red robed magicians, Terin noticed how they bowed their heads in deference to the man he followed, and the guards remained prostrate on the floor until they passed. Double doors opened into a large courtyard filled with hanging plants, ferns, and palm trees, and there were three bubbling water fountains, each carved in the shape of the silver talisman worn by the red-robed magicians. Enlarged, the figure was clearly feminine, but the features remained blurred, indistinguishable. 'Who is that?' Terin asked.

'Fareeka, Akid Akis ka Shehaal,' replied the interpreter. 'She is the Strength and Shape of Life. She is the Mother of the first and of all Ranu Ka Shehaala.'

'Why are her features blurred?'

'Why not?'

Terin's dissatisfaction with the answer went unobserved. Beyond the courtyard's iron gates, was a space of open ground where Terin surmised groups gathered before being summoned into the Kal E'haruk. As they crossed the space, he paused to look up. Sheer, smooth walls soared towards the cliff top from which they were carved, marked haphazardly by windows of blue and green crystal. The sight thrilled him. 'It is magnificent,' said the black robed interpreter, returning to stand beside him. Terin nodded his appreciation. 'There are a thousand rooms inside the Palace of Peace and Light - the Palace Irandu Shadu. And those are only the known ones that the Holy Lord allows to be seen by others. It is said there are a thousand more that mortal eyes never set eyes upon.' Terin listened, enthralled, all the while gazing up at the white surface. 'Come,' ordered the interpreter. 'You must follow closely from this point.'

They passed through a large gateway, under the scrutiny of ten guards who bowed as the interpreter approached. Outside the gates, a crowd threw themselves face down on the ground at the appearance of Terin's guide, and remained there, until Terin and the interpreter moved on. There were old men, children in tattered robes, and crippled beggars, some with terrible sores and deformities. One small child looked up at Terin with pitifully hungry eyes, and Terin had to look away, filled with a sense of guilt he didn't understand. He hadn't expected to see misery in the heart of a city so wondrous.

The interpreter led him through a maze of streets, and everywhere people moved aside, and bowed to the earth. They arrived in a circular space, from which many streets ran, at the centre of which a white tower rose to the blue sky. There were no doors, no visible entrances. The interpreter placed his hand inside his black robe, withdrew a pyramidal amber crystal, and placed it on the ground against the tower wall. 'Follow my exact movement, and do not hesitate. We enter here,' the interpreter instructed. He crossed his chest with his arms, shut his eyes, and walked at the wall. Terin watched him dissolve through it, so without hesitation he followed, and was inside the tower when he opened his eyes. The interpreter was kneeling, completing a whispered command in the language of the Ranu Ka Shehaala, and the pyramid crystal appeared beside the interpreter's right knee.

Like the cell in which he'd been confined, the furnishing was simple: a red mat at the centre, a small wooden chest near the wall, a plank bed, and a cupboard, supporting six pottery vessels. The ceiling was five arm spans above, and in its centre was an arm span diameter hole. 'This is your first space for study,' explained the instructor. 'My Holy Lord Shehaal has instructed me to be your mentor and guide, since we share a common background.' He loosened his shawl and the cowl of his robe and drew them back. Terin was startled. Before him was a full blood Aelendyell, with locks of flowing silver-grey hair like his own. He'd been wrong. These captors were agents of the Aelendyell. He'd been duped into believing he'd escaped. He stepped back involuntarily, defensively, preparing to weave a spell. The interpreter noticed his reaction, and with a stern look remarked, 'My Holy Lord said that you hide more than you cared to reveal in the Kal E'haruk, and now I see it's true.' He shook his head. 'You needn't fear me. I'm no more Aelendyell than you are. I am Ranu Ka Shehaala, one of the People of Life.' Terin did not relax, but the interpreter turned, exposing his back as if he completely trusted Terin, and continued his explanation. 'My Aelendyell world has been long forgotten in this place, and only its external shadow remains to remind me what I left it behind of my own choosing.' The interpreter faced Terin again, his face serious. 'Your reasons for leaving it are not my concern, and mine are not yours. We are here. Now. That, and only that, is your concern.' The interpreter picked up his pyramid and walked to the centre of the room. He formed brief, soundless words, and rose from the floor to pass through the hole in the ceiling.

Terin crossed to the mat and peered up. Another room lay above, but there were no further holes visible in its ceiling. He incanted his own levitation spell, and followed, and heard the surprise in the interpreter's voice as he stepped onto solid floor. 'Wazeem wasn't exaggerating when he warned the Holy Lord that you already possess some power. Interesting. But if my memory serves me, you are too young to have access to the Aelendyell Lore Book or its secrets. Who taught you this simple magic?'

'I taught myself,' Terin replied, quelling his desire to boast. 'It's not the most difficult magic I've learned.'

'Indeed,' was the interpreter's disinterested reply.

Terin wondered why the interpreter showed a lack of interest in his skills. Surely he could sense Terin knew more. If only he could impress him somehow. 'I've learned other spells. I can show you.'

'Yes. In good time. 'The interpreter's tone reflected no desire to accept Terin's offer. 'But for now you have lessons to learn, if you want to serve Leiksha Ithrandyr Shehaal as you promised, and especially if you wish to learn the Third Ki. I have more important things to do, including preparing your future instructions, so I leave you to your lessons.' The interpreter began to whisper.

'Wait,' asked Terin, on impulse. 'Where do I sleep? What do I eat? What do I call you?'

The interpreter paused. 'You are here. You already have access to all you will need.'

'But what do I study? Where are the scrolls and books? What happened to my scrolls? Who has them?'

'What you must learn is here already.'

The response frustrated Terin. 'At least tell me your name.'

The interpreter smiled enigmatically. 'That is one of your lessons.' He whispered a final word, and ascended through the ceiling, twenty hand spans above, passing through solid stone. Terin was alone.

Time was meaningless. The light was permanent, and he couldn't trace its source. Had only a short time passed? Or days? He slept twice. He was thirsty. He was hungry. No one came, not even the black robed interpreter. There were no lessons. Perhaps there was never meant to be any. Perhaps he'd fallen prey to a complex imprisonment and cruel form of execution.

He searched both floor levels. The ground floor pottery vessels were empty, although he detected the odour of fresh food in two pots that made his mouth water. The wooden chest was empty, except for a piece of parchment and a quill. No ink though. The cupboard revealed a rolled fur for bedding, and when he unrolled the fur a silver amulet dropped to the floor. He retrieved the object and inspected its blurred feminine form. The hands were clasped in prayer. Fareeka: but no inscriptions, no distinguishing marks, no clues to its use. Dissatisfied, he tucked the amulet inside his white robe, and ascended to the second level.

On this level was only a locked chest against the wall. Terin tried picking the lock, without success. Defeated, he searched the walls and floor again. They had come in. The interpreter levitated through the ceiling. There were ways out – all he had to do was find a way. Levitating to the second ceiling earned him a sore head and greater frustration. Searching the walls proved fruitless. He was all too completely trapped.

He awoke from his second sleep with renewed enthusiasm. He had some knowledge of the Second Ki - if he could recall the text of the Book of Lore. He squatted on the red mat, at ground floor level, and focussed on searching his memory. He folded back the richly textured cover, the pages, at first straining to read the text in his mind, and then relaxing, letting the source wash over him, as it had when he first read the Lore. He visualized text detail, the keys to understanding, spells, the tomes of wisdom gathered through a thousand years of Aelendyell and Elvenaar research. He slipped into sharper focus, and the brilliant clarity of the text hurt his inner mind's eye, making him flinch, and lose concentration.

On his fourth attempt, Terin braced for the shift into bright focus, and fully opened his conscious mind to allow the stored volume of magic in his sub-conscious to flow between. There came a surge, a wave of subliminal thought that rose and crashed through, spilling bright flashes of light and understanding like a ceaseless tide into the recesses of his mind. The flood of knowledge peaked, and ebbed, waves diminishing, until the last trickles of light faded and were gone. He collapsed, exhausted by his effort in his weakened state, but he gloated over his success. The spells, the magic, were his. No more would his hands control his spell making. The secrets of the Second Ki, the workings he pored over in the confines of his tree home, were locked from him no longer. He rolled over, and descended into a deep, extended sleep.

The chest on the second floor was easy to open. He placed his hands on the lock, recited the unlocking spell, and threw open the chest with gusto. Within was a small leather-bound book with peculiar writing, and a larger compendium of pictures of exotically dressed men and women, each carrying a gold or silver weapon or item, each either mounted on a fabulous beast, or standing above miniature representations of the world. As he stared, each picture flashed before his eyes without his hands moving the pages, and the compendium merged into a single page. He was fascinated by the unusual magic as each figure appeared and disappeared. Some frowned, some laughed. Some stared with appealing expressions. But one face flashed with increasing frequency and sharper clarity, commanding eyes burning, and each time the face flicked by, Terin was conscious of a prickling surge of power creeping through his veins. The face demanded his attention, called on him to choose. He acceded to the compulsion. He wanted to see that face above all others.

The flicking ceased. Terin shook his head to restore his senses, but when he looked at his hands the compendium had disappeared, leaving a single vellum sheet. He gazed at the page: the portrait of the dark-eyed face, the ruggedly handsome visage framing the eyes. Yet, oddly, he couldn't remember the features when he turned from the page. The only lingering image was the dark eyes with immense authority and intelligence emanating from their depths. Who is this? he wondered.

He turned his attention to the small book. Placing his hand on the text, he uttered the Aelendyell magical command to decipher language, 'Ge witan writ.' His mind shifted focus and the words on the first page metamorphosed into meaning. He held a prayer book. Each page was adorned with an illuminated picture within the silver outline of Fareeka, the symbol Terin associated with Ranu Ka Shehaala magic. As he carefully read the prayers, he recognised their function - spell texts. There were ten pages of prayer spells, each addressed to an un-named deity, while the remaining pages were vacant, blank, as if awaiting inscriptions of their own. He considered his discovery. Were these the lessons the interpreter mentioned? He flipped through the small spell book, until he found prayers referring to provision of food and water. These he needed. He read a spell aloud, skipping the blank where a deity ought to be named, and waited. Nothing. Without the missing name, the spells wouldn't work. A name. He needed a name.

Intuitively, he picked up the vellum page with the dark-eyed portrait and stared at the face. Are you the source of power? he wondered. The dark eyes stared back. There was a subtle shifting across the face, a change in the page's grained texture, and a voice rose from the lips.

'Who seeks to serve the will of Berak N'eth?'

The manifestation startled Terin. It had a resonating timbre, and he was mystified how he could understand what was an alien tongue. 'I am Terin.'

'What do you presume to gain from serving me?'

Terin's mind raced. He'd stumbled on a source of power. 'Access to the Third Ki. I want to learn the magic of the Ranu Ka Shehaala,' he replied with growing confidence. He'd asked directly. He expected nothing less than a direct answer.

'Oho!' The face beamed with pleasure, and a deep rumble of laughter followed. 'You seek power. We have something in common.' A pause, and the voice asked, 'Do you know who I am?'

'No.'

'I, Berak N'eth, am power. I am the Lord of Power. No storm surges but I will it. No volcano erupts unless I bid it. Great kings rise and fall as I see fit. I gave the force to create the energies of the Thirteen Worlds and caused the suns to burst into first light at the Beginning of all things. Beneath all magics, I am the Source. Know this, for it is I whom you offer to serve. Serve me well, serve me honestly, serve me as and when I bid you to serve, without question, and you will have the very power you seek. If you will strike that bargain, and willingly serve Berak N'eth, hold this icon to your amulet, and know that I am with you and you with me.' The voice ceased. The shifting image on the vellum solidified.

Excited, nervous, Terin withdrew the silver figurine from his white robe and touched it to the surface of the picture. A brief brilliant blue flash exploded at the point of contact, and the vellum page vanished. The amulet tingled sharply with magical static. Terin smiled. When he studied the amulet, he discovered a sliver of amber crystal embedded in the metal. He scratched at the amber. It was impervious and immovable. He placed his amber ring beside the sliver in the amulet, saw the similarity, and knew he had access to the Third Ki.

He ate a meal provided by the spell book when he inserted Berak N'eth's name, after he discovered the food had materialized in a pottery jar on the first level. He drank his fill of fresh water. Refreshed, he set to memorising the spells in the prayer book. Two particularly caught his attention, and he took thorough care to learn them, before applying them.

'Hello, Karrilyon,' Terin said proudly, as he completed his levitation through the stone floor into the third level of the tower.

Karrilyon turned, nodded, as if expecting Terin's arrival, and said, 'Good. You've completed the first lesson.'

Seven

'You cast an imposing figure!' Karrilyon declared, as he settled the red cape over Terin's shoulders. 'You have the bearing of a true Ithosen.' Terin smiled at the mention of the Ranu Ka Shehaala word for a Holy One. He liked the sound of the word, in a language that, barely two years earlier, was alien to him. Neither he, nor Karrilyon, used Aelendyell any more for conversation, and Terin saved it only for working spells of the First and Second Ki. Karrilyon stepped back to admire his protégé. 'Indeed. You will stand out at Kal Metbaa. The Most Holy Lord of Light and Peace Himself will see you, and that will be a true blessing.' Terin's smile widened to a grin, which Karrilyon interpreted as a sign of appreciation of his compliments, but Terin grinned because he had moved one step further on his quest for power.

As Karrilyon gathered minor items from a silver chest on the table, Terin moved to a circular tower window that faced east and stared towards the looming white cliff face that formed part of the Palace Irandu Shadu. Grey clouds closed most of the sky, but patches of brilliant blue refused to withdraw. Directly below the tower, the flat roofs of the city spread in every direction. Two years ago, he was brought into the land of the Ranu Ka Shehaala and condemned, by his own wish, to the isolation of the tower, under Karrilyon's guidance. For two years, he'd worked hard, studied hard, practised and prayed relentlessly, and mastered each of the twelve tests represented by the twelve floors within the tower. He'd found a spiritual guide - his deity - Berak N'eth. He'd learned the holy arts of creating and purifying water. He had learned minor healing spells. He'd mastered rites of passage, adopted a new language, and a new culture - learned laws. And he'd achieved much, much more. He had synthesized spells from Aelendyell Lore with artefacts of Ranu Ka Shehaala magic and created unique spell variants.

He felt power coursing through his soul that he dared not reveal. And he'd begun to learn the intricacies of mind magic - skills of judging and influencing the thoughts of others, though the knowledge of the Ranu Ka Shehaala in that art seemed limited. Today, for the first time in two whole years, he would walk in the world of people again. He wondered how the Elders of the Aelendyell council would react if they could see him, dressed in the red Ithosen robes, the master of a magic they believed was forever denied to them. Ithosen magic had to be magic from one of the missing Third or Fourth Ki the Chanter referred to in the Spell Grove. Aelendyell Lore Bearers could not purify waters, or cast healing spells, and Terin knew of no magic in the Aelendyell village that could be attributed to a benefactor like Berak N'eth. If he returned to the forests of his taunted childhood now, they would learn to respect him, because he was more powerful than they ever could be.

'Come!' Karrilyon called, interrupting Terin's thoughts. 'It is time we went to Kal Metbaa.' He descended through the solid floor of the tower chamber. Terin cast his spell and followed.

He had noticed and dismissed the phenomenon from the tower window, but it was directly evident when they emerged from the tower that the streets were quiet. 'Where are the people?' he asked.

Karrilyon turned to his taller companion. 'It is the Day of Kal Metbaa. Only Novitiates and their Masters may walk the streets between sunrise and sunset during Kal Metbaa. It is Holy Law, and must be obeyed, on pain of death.'

Terin considered Karrilyon's explanation and tried to recall where he missed this event in the Holy Laws during his studies, but he could not, and realized, to his concern, that his learning during the two years was not as thorough as he'd thought.

Two more Ithosen joined them, bowing deferentially to Karrilyon. Terin was no longer surprised by the gesture of respect from other Ithosen. During his studies, he learned Karrilyon was an Advisor, a key figure in the administration of the Holy Lord of Peace and Light, Leiksha Ithrandyr Shehaal. Terin, however, never considered bowing to Karrilyon, and Karrilyon never indicated he should. Terin had no intention of bowing to anyone.

The Palace Guards were remarkably absent, and the gates were open into the assembly space. When Terin entered with Karrilyon, he observed a group of red robed figures patiently waiting outside the courtyard that led into the Palace. All bowed respectfully as Karrilyon passed between them to the doors. Terin followed, but Karrilyon turned, raised his hand, and said firmly, 'No. You are not permitted to enter until you are called.' He smiled when he saw the disdain in Terin's expression. 'Your Aelendyell pride is the burning energy of your learning. So it was with me, although I did not have the eagerness you have for power. Therefore, I teach you one final lesson on Kal Metbaa Day. Do not let pride hinder reason. Do not let your search for power blind you to yourself. You will understand what is meant by that, I know, for it is your destiny to learn.' He turned to open the door, but he paused briefly before turning back to face Terin with a peculiar expression of bewilderment. 'I know not why I know this, but you must enter last on this day. You will do - you will - you will find a greater destiny today. There is a change coming, a terrible change.' He stared through Terin, and confusion flickered in his eyes as his speech faltered, and his tone shifted. Hypnotically, he said, 'It is your destiny to be a part of this terrible change, but not mine. I - will - not - see - it.' He blinked and vanished through the doors.

Self-consciously aware others may have overheard Karrilyon's eerie speech, Terin looked around, but no one appeared to have listened. Not Karrilyon, but someone else spoke through him. Clutching his amulet, Terin moved away from the others to a corner of the broad courtyard, where he recited a brief prayer to Berak N'eth. He waited, but the prayer was unanswered. He repeated the words, focussing into the silver figurine in his hand, but there was no response. Not since his first contact, two years earlier, had he spoken directly with the deity. He sometimes doubted the contact was anything more than a hunger-induced hallucination, but he knew more than his innate curiosity and desire to master magic had enabled him to learn and create with a vigour and rapidity of success that Karrilyon told him outshone any apprentice before Terin. Had he not mastered the twelve levels in less than a third of the time of other apprentices? Novitiates completed at least six years of study and training before being brought to Kal Metbaa. He'd taken a mere two. Berak N'eth was real and hadn't deserted him, his deity worked in silence, and with purpose, but he needed an explanation for Karrilyon's speech. Or was it a warning?

Terin looked over his shoulder to discover the waiting Novitiates were gone and the courtyard empty. He released his grip on his amulet and hurried to the doors. He swung them open and hurried through the courtyard of fountains and plants to the double doors leading into the Great Central Hall of Light. As he ran, he puzzled over the absence of guards, before remembering Karrilyon's explanation about the Holy Law of Kal Metbaa. No one was allowed outside, but Novitiates and their Masters: on pain of death. People in this city obeyed power.

He glimpsed movement to his right, in the green ferns, as he reached the doors. A figure in dun-coloured clothing slid from view. A rope dangled from a window, a white rope blending carefully with the white rock of the Palace wall, and he spotted the feet of another dun-coloured figure scrambling silently through the window. Something was terribly wrong. The hairs on the nape of his neck rose. Intruders? Sensing a presence, stalking him through the courtyard undergrowth, with the keen Aelendyell skills he had all but forgotten since his capture in the mountains, he focussed his mind in the direction of the source of threat. Someone intended to kill him - a man - someone who thought in the language of the Ranu Ka Shehaala - someone raising a dagger. Terin spoke, his right hand rapidly tracing the air, as a figure stood and threw a long-bladed dagger at his chest. The dagger spun through the air, hit an invisible barrier in front of Terin's hand, and clattered harmlessly on the cobblestones at his feet. His assailant hesitated, surprise quickly turning into terror, before he spun on his heel to run, and he made three steps before Terin cut him down with a small missile of magical energy that punched through the man's back and out of his chest.

He had precious little time. He wrenched open the doors. Light from overhead skylights splashed through the hall, and shone squarely on the backs of the prostrate Novitiates and their Masters on the marble floor. Red robed Ithosen sat in groups on seats, left and right, near the great dais at the head of the hall. Seated upon his throne, in the pure white simplicity Terin remembered, was Leiksha Ithrandyr Shehaal. Beside him, kneeling with heads down, were his Advisors, Karrilyon's black robe clearly visible against the white floor. No one looked up, despite his noisy entrance, so he yelled, 'Look to the ceiling!' and sprinted into the hall, ignoring indignant protests from the Ithosen rising at his intrusion on Kal Metbaa. He couldn't see what he was searching for against the glaring light of the windows and magical floating spheres. Someone whispered sharply, 'Kneel!' and he heard Karrilyon call, 'Terin. Obey the Law. Kneel before -' but the sentence remained incomplete. A collective gasp rose. Karrilyon clutched a shaft of wood protruding from his chest. Terin judged the angle and turned his gaze towards a section of the ceiling. He'd looked in the wrong place! A bowman clung to a ledge, below a skylight, nocking another shaft. No time to plan. Terin raised his hand, spread his fingers, and focussed his energy. The bowman jerked upright, lost his balance and footing, and plunged to his death on the marble floor, thirty spans below.

The Novitiates and closest Ithosen milled around the spread-eagled assassin, and several Ithosen moved up the steps towards the Holy Lord of Peace and Light, but Terin continued to search the ceiling. Then he saw it - an arrow speeding in a shallow arc towards its target, the white figure on the throne. A thought – one Aelendyell word, 'Byrnan!'

The arrow exploded in a fierce ball of bright green flame, crashed into Shehaal's chest, flared, and died, leaving a patch of charred cloth. Leiksha Ithrandyr Shehaal flinched and sat upright, staring down in wonder at the inconsequential damage to his robe. Terin moved his fingers rapidly through the air, pointed at an arrow on the marble floor that had tumbled from the quiver of the first bowman, and sent it flying to impale the figure clinging to the ceiling. The second assassin fell, scattering Novitiates who leapt aside to avoid being struck by his body. Terin checked there were no further threats, lowered his hands, and sighed with relief.

Eight

'Each object contains its own energy. It doesn't matter that you cannot see the energy. In objects, like this goblet I hold, the energy is at rest. But, at my bidding, with the guidance of my personal Deity, the energy within can be called upon, and then the object released to do as I please.' Terin held the copper goblet at arm's length, resting in the palm of his hand, and made a brief incantation. The goblet quivered, rose, and floated above his open hand, and the students gasped. He broke the spell. 'You have seen. The lesson ends. Return to your Masters, and your studies.' The green robed youths bowed their faces to the floor from their kneeling positions, and chorused 'Yaseem ferad,' before they withdrew from the marbled room.

He waited, until their whispering feet faded along the corridor, before moving to the courtyard window to gaze on the bright green plants clustered around the glittering crystal blue pools below. A red robed Ithosen crossed the courtyard and disappeared into an archway. Terin fingered a thin filigree chain about his neck and stopped at the diamond arrow jewel pendant. Four years had passed since his Kal Metbaa - four years since he cradled the head of the dying Karrilyon, whom no power could save from the assassin's poisoned arrow. The Ranu Ka Shehaala spent a week mourning the loss of the Holy Lord's Principal Advisor, and, at the week's end, his mortal remains were publicly burned, to free his soul to fly into the realm of his personal God. Then Terin was summoned before Lord Shehaal. At the full assembly of Ithosen, Shehaal praised him, honoured him, and presented him with the diamond arrow as a token of gratitude, calling him 'Aroo Shehaal' – 'the shield of Shehaal' – and welcoming him into their midst as true Ranu Ka Shehaala. Shehaal placed the red cloak of Ithosen about Terin's shoulders, an honour reserved for those whom the

Most Holy Lord held in highest esteem, before ordering him to teach each new year's selection of apprentices all he knew of Aelendyell magic, and how it might be married to the power of the Ithosen. Shehaal made him the Ranu equivalent of an Aelendyell Chanter, and Terin barely hid his satisfaction at the gift of authority bestowed on him. Shehaal also ordered him to remain within the Palace Irandu Shadu to study and experiment. No Ithosen had ever been accorded such status, and Terin knew many, like Wazeem, were intensely jealous of his favoured position. All the better, he thought. Power is far more satisfying when it's held over others. He made a point of always politely smiling whenever an Ithosen passed him in the Great Central Hall. His destiny passed, as Rekama prophesied, into the hands of Leiksha Ithrandyr Shehaal, or, more precisely, became welded with Shehaal's fate.

Four years passed quickly. Terin immersed himself obsessively in every book of Ranu Ka Shehaala and Ithosen Lore he discovered in the Palace archives. Shehaal, like his predecessors, insisted all practices of magic be thoroughly and accurately recorded so that he could know which Ithosen were attached to what deities, and the strength and commitment of their powers. The demand for attention to detail spurred Terin to memorize everything in every spare moment he wasn't required to be teaching apprentices. What surprised him was his uncanny ability to learn rapidly, though he couldn't understand what had changed in himself. Pages rolled through his mind, like the first time he opened the Aelendyell Book of Lore, but he also saw fleeting glimpses of Berak N'eth's eyes staring from hidden pages in the thickest archive tomes. He had a gift for learning, and he revelled in it every day.

He loathed teaching. His ego gorged upon his self-importance when his first class bowed before him and listened unquestioningly to his every word. He recalled his Aelendyell Chanter, and the awe with which he had beheld the old teacher and saw the same emotion in the faces and eyes of his students. But the novelty quickly faded. Within six months, he was scheming ways to annul his contract with Shehaal, though he knew that course of action was neither remotely possible, nor wise to contemplate. Instead, he became resigned to the daily teaching chore with thinly veiled arrogance, accepting it was small discomfort when weighed against the time he could freely spend swimming through the pools of Ithosen lore. The Third Ki was at his disposal, and he had time to master it.

His desire to return to the Aelendyell forests, to heap revenge on those who teased and denied and despised him, cooled as he worked and studied, but the embers did not die. Sometimes, in the darker period of morning, he would lift his eyes from a page and stare at an abstract point in the middle distance, letting his mind wander over the possibilities returning to his village might create. How would the Chanter react? Could he force them to kneel before him like his apprentices? Whatever their reactions, he held the greater power. One day, when the time was right, he would return to teach them the true essence of power, show them he was much more than they ever could aspire to be, make them realize, forever, that he was not the bastard child of misfortune.

Aware of a presence, he turned from the sun-splashed window to see a prostrate guard in the doorway and wondered how long the guard would remain in that position if he chose to ignore him. Very likely forever. Those without power, in the presence of those with it, had no other choice. It was a universal law. He grinned, shook his silver locks, and commanded, 'Fek!'

The guard spoke, as ordered, but he didn't dare lift his eyes. 'Ithosen. My Most Holy Lord of Light and Peace requests that you attend his presence immediately.'

Terin deliberately held the guard to the floor with his silence, until he answered, 'His Will be done.'

He followed the guard along the broad lengths of polished marble floors, and up the familiar white steps. They passed the Library, the Great Banquet Hall, and the iron doors to the Great Central Hall, before stopping at a delicately carved oak door Terin realized he'd never entered.

The room differed from any he had seen in the Palace. Instead of stone-hewn walls, there were richly coloured wooden panels, regularly interspersed with heavy beams, and tapestries hung on the walls, depicting forested lands, full of exotic wild creatures. A light orb floated above a mahogany desk, illuminating all corners of the room. Shehaal was present, along with Ahket El Nabar, in his customary purple robes, and Parnash Seraphen, Karrilyon's successor, in the Advisor's black robes. Four Holy Guards, silver scimitars glittering at their sides, purple headgear complementing their armour, stood to the side. He sensed formality weighing on the room's atmosphere, as if the people present were waiting for him to begin. But begin what? Or perhaps this was another formal ceremony of reward for his work. He flicked through the pages of his mind, searching his enormous knowledge of Ranu Ka Shehaala Lore, but no understanding of a purpose for this clandestine meeting presented itself. He was at a loss. And still they relentlessly stared. Parnash was even daring to use a Mind spell to probe his thoughts. 'Most Holy Lord, why have you called me here?' he asked, to prevent Parnash's intrusion, and break the silence.

No one spoke, but Parnash answered psychically. Where is your respect? You stand before Power. You stand before Leiksha Ithrandyr Shehaal. Kneel before your Holy Lord.

Terin reacted angrily, responding to Parnash with a thought projection he immediately regretted because it wasn't carefully constructed. I kneel before no one!

A wave of indignation erupted from Parnash. You must respect Power!

I respect myself. I will be Power, Parnash! His wilful reply brought surprising acquiescence. He anticipated righteous indignation from Parnash for his heretical statement. Instead, Ahket drew a collection of parchments from beneath his robe, spread them upon the desktop, and asked,

67

'Are these your writings?'

Terin knew they were copies of his research into synthesizing Aelendyell and Ithosen magic, but they didn't explain his true work or his greater successes with the Ki during his four years within the Palace Irandu Shadu. Nor did they detail important discoveries he'd stumbled upon in Karrilyon's tower. 'They are copies of my research.'

'Yes,' Ahket acknowledged, without further explanation.

Parnash spoke next. 'Leiksha Ithrandyr Shehaal has blessed your works. He has seen a growth in the proficiency of new students under their Masters because of your influence. It would seem that, within six years, you have gathered more knowledge about the Ranu Ka Shehaala, and created greater knowledge, than that contributed by the entire Assembly of Ithosen. You serve Berak N'eth with ardent fervour.'

He had never revealed his deity to anyone, because his research warned him the Ithosen considered Berak N'eth dangerous, but Shehaal obviously knew who Terin served. 'Yes. I know.' Leiksha Ithrandyr Shehaal's deep green crystal eyes were peering through him. 'Nothing is hidden from me. You, of all, with your research and work, should know that. Yet, foolishly, you try to hide things from me. You build your power to serve only your own ends, not the needs of the Ranu Ka Shehaala, and you share only that which you believe is safe to share. There is an ancient Ranu saying, some even call a prophecy. Perhaps you've already read it. It says 'Beware the one who comes seeking power, for from you he will take all he can, and in its name unleash darkness among you, and he will rise to rule over you in the time to come.' The Gods talk. Great Shehaala talks to me. Fareeka talks to the Ithosen. They know the ways of Berak N'eth, and I have been warned. Now I warn you.' Shehaal caught his breath and continued. 'He who seeks power walks a twofold path. There is a choice of journeys. One direction leads towards power that grows and shares beauty and wisdom. One direction leads to a terrible power, raw, selfish power that destroys all it touches. You seek power. You seek it for yourself. You walk a deadly path. And when power comes, what will you do, Seeker of Power? What will you do?' Again, the Holy Lord of Light and Peace paused to let Terin ponder the gravity of his questions, the implications of his answers. 'Your presence here, within Irandu Shadu, within Yul Ithrandyr, is a two-edged sword that threatens to slay that which it is meant to protect. Here, we have peace in our work. We work for enlightenment. We seek harmony through power. You threaten that harmony. You have much to teach us, with your experiments in the arts of magic, and we will gladly learn what you have to teach. But you, too, have much to learn, and I am to blame for not seeing that sooner. You lack the most important quality of a seeker of power: humility. Your pride is like a slow-burning fuse, threatening to ignite and bring down ruin. I cannot endure that risk within the Great City of Light. I must make changes, and you will obey them.'

Shehaal's words resonated in Terin. The Holy Lord's eyes flashed, and Terin felt compelled to kneel. He faltered, as the others around Shehaal dropped to their faces, and although he relented and kneeled, he steadfastly refused to lower his face to the floor. That he would never do. Never.

Shehaal fixed him with a knowing stare. 'You will leave Yul Ithrandyr and journey to Tul Et Hazier, in the Sands of Fire. There, you will establish a new order of Ithosen to follow your teachings under the blessing of Berak N'eth. You will build a black tower of stone, and each year a new student will be sent to you, to learn what you have learnt. And you will send reports of your research to Yul Ithrandyr for the archives, as all Ithosen must do. And you will hide nothing from me, or the Ranu Ka Shehaala. By your duty, you are bound. And there is one thing more,' Shehaal added, breaking into Terin's confused thoughts. 'From this moment in time, Terin is a forgotten name of a forgotten past. You are reminded that the Ranu Ka Shehaala embraced you when you came uninvited into our lands, and it is right that you bear a name befitting your people and your rank. When you rise from this place, you are A Ahmud Ki, Seeker of

69

Power, born unto a new destiny shaped by the Great Shehaala Himself. Whatever was is no more. Sek feran yaseem!'

Nine

Jezarba liked his task less every year. For twenty-two years, he had served a Most Holy Lord of Light and Peace, father, and now son, as their Collector of Wisdom, the Murzat Ka Shet. He travelled the land of the Ranu Ka Shehaala, visiting the Ithosen towers and the Tuls, to collect research and writings, and return them to Yul Ithrandyr for perusal by Shehaal and his Advisors. He was received with open arms and feasting in some places, and dark looks and disdain in others. The Ithosen, he concluded early in his career, were a moody lot. But the one he now had to visit was his least favoured of all, and not only because his black tower lay in the heart of the Sands of Fire. Jezarba shifted his buttocks. Mules, no matter how well padded, were uncomfortable beasts, but he already missed his mule as he gingerly edged himself onto the rough spine of a camel.

'Do not break the poor beast's back, o little large one,' warned a dark bearded soldier, and he turned to his companions, grinning at Jezarba's discomfort.

'Your insolence will reap its reward, you offspring of camel dung!' Jezarba retorted, angered by the jibe. The soldiers of his personal guard had scant respect for him, frequently using him as the butt of their jokes. His threats fell on deaf ears, because his soldiers knew his threats were hollow. Jezarba had little real authority, and no courage. He was, after all, a glorified messenger, one of low status in the ranks of the Ranu Ka Shehaala. He adjusted his corpulent mass on his mount, wiped his dripping forehead, wet from the heat reflecting from the red desert sands and his exertions, and squinted at the dune ridges rolling forbiddingly away to the northwest.

A Ahmud Ki stood on the parapet, silently watching two

black robed women tending the garden shrubs. His eyes followed the lush green pattern of foliage until they met the harsh red edge of desert burning in the mid-morning sun. The contrast in heat and colour between the two worlds always pleased him, though three years had passed since he completed a greening project to satiate an inner Aelendyell longing for the forests of his former life. He inwardly smiled at his successful venture - an artificial oasis created out of dead sands. He looked at his fingertips and congratulated himself for blending three sources of magic to conjure his black tower and its environ from fierce desert – all in nine short years. He shifted his attention to the approaching camel train and recognised Jezarba's fat silhouette. For all his shortcomings, the Murzat Ka Shet was always on time.

A Ahmud Ki walked to the centre of the tower, said the words for descending, and passed through the black marble to the floor below. As his feet touched the cool surface, he commanded an orb to shine. Light spilled across his workbenches, his desk, and shelves stacked with vellum parchments, and vials, and caskets - a collection of portables acquired or created during the nine years of exile. Nine brief years - fifteen years since he'd left the Aelendyell forests. Consumed with passion to master the three Ki, he made the years race as he delved into Ithosen Lore, transcribed from his memory what he could recall from the Aelendyell Book of Lore, and wrote down the spells he could generate internally as a natural consequence of his Aelendyell parentage. Experiment followed experiment. He felt Berak N'eth's guidance charging him with curious energy, driving him to alter and change, blend and mould each source of power into a single unity that he could call upon at will. He recorded his successes, and his failures, according to the command of Shehaal, and despatched his research, annually, with the obese Murzat Ka Shet who came panting across the sands, to the distant city of Yul Ithrandyr. He served the few writs he received from Shehaal's Advisors with respectful indifference, ruthlessly trained each student he was sent, and remained isolated and aloof from other

Ithosen who populated the city and Tuls. Here, in a place of his making, he was a law unto himself - the Seeker of Power - and every day he grew stronger, opened new secrets, mastered new arts, according to the blessings of his silent deity, Berak N'eth.

'Help me off this clumsy beast, you laughing fools!' Jezarba bleated, as he lurched precariously across the back of his camel. The animal bucked and sent him sprawling into the red sands, amid raucous laughter. In a desperate attempt to regain dignity, Jezarba hefted himself upright, and glared at his guards. 'You'll pay this time, all of you, for this - this - insolence!' he screeched. 'Leiksha Ithrandyr Shehaal Himself will hear of this, and his anger will be unending! How - how dare you humiliate the Murzat Ka Shet? You will be made to burn in the deserts for an eternity! Your guts will be fed to vultures while you lay bleeding and alive under the hot sun. I swear I will see this done, may Fareeka be my witness!' Jezarba marched up and down before his guards, as he delivered his vitriol, while they stood perfectly still, in mock fear, of the small fat clown whom they were forced to serve. Then, as he turned to face the gardens and the black tower, they grinned like naughty vagabond children behind an adult chosen for ridicule.

Four women escorted Jezarba through the grounds of the tower. The fertile oasis' climate, relatively cool despite the blazing mid-morning sun of the Sands of Fire, always unnerved Shehaal's messenger, unlike any other Ithosen's residence. He knew very little of magic, even after his twenty-two years of carrying communications and research back and forth, but in this place he always felt the threatening presence of power, and it made his nerves tingle and his flesh creep. He understood why the Great Holy Lord of the Ranu Ka Shehaala had sent this Ithosen so far from the Holy City of Light and Peace, and why Shehaal was most intent on receiving the annual reports and research of this one more than any other. Jezarba was always pleased to be leaving the tower and heading across the hot sands. The desert seemed less hostile, less potentially lethal, than the Ithosen within the black tower.

A Ahmud Ki listened to the approaching messenger's thoughts, and grinned. This strange little fat man, who Shehaal was content to entrust with powerful secrets, was always a source of amusement, and, although Jezarba did not know it, he was always a source of information. In his second year of exile, his black tower constructed, A Ahmud Ki enhanced the Ithosen ability to read other minds. He practised and prayed, and blended a portion of Aelendyell and Elvenaar Lore into the Ithosen skill, to make it possible for him to unravel even prior experiences from people's memories. Not only could he listen into a person's current thoughts, he could uncover former thoughts. There were limitations. It was impossible to maintain a conversation and concentrate simultaneously on the audience's thoughts. He also wondered how secretive the spell would be if applied on another user of magic, because he had no difficulty sensing attempts to use mind spells on him. Limited by Jezarba's own perceptions, A Ahmud Ki nevertheless used the messenger's visits to glean news and changes in the world beyond the Sands of Fire, and once or twice he was able to stumble across ideas other Ithosen shared with Jezarba.

A Ahmud Ki levitated to a receiving room on the ground floor, passing through the bedrooms of the ten serving women he kept in the tower to fulfil his various needs. As he descended, he checked that the six women indoors were busy, writing and mending, and preparing for his experiments, according to his instructions. He did not want male servants. The Ranu Ka Shehaala women lived to silently obey their men, and A Ahmud Ki wanted only selfless obedience for his study, and for his pleasures. Men would serve with constrained obedience because they obeyed the code all Ranu Ka Shehaala observed, but obedient men still had to be reminded of their place. Not so the women. They served unquestioningly. They did not exist.

When Jezarba was led, wheezing and puffing, into the receiving room, the women bowed their faces to the floor, dissolving their physical being in A Ahmud Ki's presence. A Ahmud Ki smiled, not to greet Jezarba, but with the satisfaction of an omnipotent lord. He clapped his hands, and the women retreated to the gardens. A Ahmud Ki turned to Jezarba, and said, 'Irand shadu arat shehaal.'

Jezarba bowed his head. 'Irand shadu arat shehaal, Ithosen. My Most Holy Lord Shehaal sends you his greeting and hopes that you have been in good health and have had a productive year in your studies.'

'Shehaal can be assured all my studies are productive, this year even more so than the last.'

Jezarba heard, in A Ahmud Ki's voice, the confidence of equality of standing, and it made him uneasy. No Ithosen, anywhere in the land, spoke with so much irreverence for Shehaal.

'You think I should have much greater respect for Shehaal, don't you Jezarba?' Jezarba's startled expression made A Ahmud Ki smile. 'True. I know everything you think, and you know I know. He is the One Holy Lord of Light and Peace - the most powerful man in the land of the Ranu Ka Shehaala. I should serve him without question.' He laughed lightly. 'And I should be grateful that he chose to send me into isolation, into exile amid this infernal sandpit, so that I might learn humility. But after all, Jezarba, he's just a man, no more or less than you are.' He let Jezarba dwell upon his heretical statement.

Jezarba fidgeted with his fingers.

'Well, Jezarba, today you will learn just how grateful I really am for Shehaal's blessing, because I have something very special to show you, something I'm sure you won't hesitate to carry back to your Holy Lord Shehaal. Are you ready?'

Jezarba squirmed anxiously. He had felt unusually exposed when this Ithosen greeted him, but now he felt in positive danger, threatened by the magician's tone.

'Uncomfortable?' A Ahmud Ki inquired, with mock concern. 'You should be. I – not your precious Shehaal – I am the most powerful man in the land. I hold three Ki - not a mere paltry one like your squabbling, struggling Ithosen, who stay locked in their quaint white towers, or serve in the Tuls, and pay lip service in their self-effacing manner to the Great Shehaal, who would be long since dead if I hadn't saved him from the assassin's arrow.'

Jezarba was perspiring, no longer from the heat, because the desert heat didn't seem able to penetrate the walls of A Ahmud Ki's tower, but from fear overflowing in his gut. He avoided the Ithosen's eyes, frightened he would see more than he wanted to see in them, as he considered possible excuses he could safely offer to leave.

'Now you're afraid,' said A Ahmud Ki, grinning, his deep grey eyes glowing. 'But I won't hurt you. You're a guest in my tower, and you will have important news to carry back to Shehaal. Come. You must pay attention to what you are about to see.'

Before he could refuse, Jezarba felt his body lighten, as the Ithosen rapidly weaved his hands, and he swiftly rose to, and through, the ceiling. He flinched, but he felt nothing as he passed through the air. When the motion ceased, he felt as if he was standing on stone. He heaved a deep sigh, relieved to be in one piece, but he was in darkness, and he suffered another surge of panic.

'Relax. You have nothing to fear.'

The disembodied voice was calm, reassuring, and Jezarba reconsidered his opinion of the Ithosen, as though he felt he could trust the man.

'Leoht!' A Ahmud Ki commanded.

Jezarba saw a deep blue rectangular glow forming, and the vision was enticing despite his heightened nervous disposition. The light deepened in hue.

'Watch carefully, Murzat Ka Shet, for what you are seeing no other has ever seen in this land. Watch carefully, for what you are witnessing is all you will take from A Ahmud Ki to

76

Shehaal this year.'

Jezarba wanted to ask questions, wanted to leave, but morbid fear held him rigid and silent. He heard the Ithosen's footfall and saw the dark outline of the tall half-Aelendyell against the blue haze. He was unsure, but he imagined he could see shapes, and a figure, within the haze, as if he was looking through coloured glass into another room. He also knew that wasn't possible. They were near the outer wall of the tower, weren't they? He wasn't sure, anymore, of anything.

'Murzat Ka Shet, I've opened a door to another place. Three hundred years ago, a holy man, Kerat N'i Qadir, tried a similar experiment with magic, and it killed him. The Great Holy Lord of Light and Peace of that particular time forbade any further tampering with such magic. Qadir's studies were locked away in the vaults of Palace Irandu Shadu. But I found them. I have unlocked what Qadir could not. I can see where the door leads.'

A Ahmud Ki pointed at the shimmering blue, and when Jezarba squinted he saw a woman, with long tresses spilling over her shoulders, beckoning, forming words with her lips. She was in an austere room, the colour indistinguishable because of the blue haze.

'That is where I go now. There lies the Fourth Ki, of that I'm certain, and when I master it no one will match my power. And I will return to the Aelendyell and be master over them, and one day even you will see me again, and bow to me as your new Leiksha, for I will inherit all lands, including the land of the Ranu Ka Shehaala.' He quietly laughed.

Jezarba saw a bright red glow emanating from the Ithosen's eyes. He dropped to his knees, in obeisance and terror.

A Ahmud Ki uttered a forced whisper. 'Sek feran yaseem!' Then he stepped into the shimmering rectangle and vanished. The haze dissolved.

In the same instant came a sharp crackle of static, and a rushing wind smashed Jezarba's fat body against the stone floor. He clawed at the marble with his fingers, as mounting pressure pushed down on his back, squeezing breath from his lungs, crushing him. The darkness rushed in.

The sun was hot. Its harsh touch scalded his face. When he opened his eyes it almost blinded him. He rolled onto his stomach. Sand. He eased into a sitting position, shielded his eyes with his hand, and looked around. Others were doing the same. Soldiers – women - everyone seemed as dazed as he felt. He rubbed his eyes and peered at the desert. There was no black tower, no green gardens. A Ahmud Ki might never have existed. Jezarba staggered to his feet. As he did so, a tiny gleam of reflected light caught his eye in the burning sands. He bent and picked up a black crystal. It was cold, uniquely cold, as if the sun's heat had no impact, and it caused Jezarba to break into a cold sweat.

"Each traveller in life must choose a path to follow, but the path's fruits and labours are unknown until it has been walked from beginning to end."

from The Teachings of The Way - various Elders

Ten

Andra turned westward to gaze along his narrow home valley. The golden dawn half-light was already brightening the slopes, but, directly below him, the huts and larger buildings of the village were wrapped in purple and grey hues. White curlicues of chimney smoke spiralled into the air. An open doorway spilled a yellow patch of firelight onto the cold ground. In the southeast section, where Vale cattle often strayed, invisible dogs barked, and Andra knew his friend, Erik, was busily beginning his daily duties for Cattle Master Neldrin. The long, rolling and thickly wooded spurs of The Vale stretched west, until they melted, beyond the mists, into the Valley of Rivers, so named because a multitude of streams and rivers tumbled down from the eastern Ureykyeu Mountains, and the Andrakian mountains to the west, through myriad vales and convolutions, to empty their souls into the heart of Rainbow Lake at the valley's southern end. He ran his hands through his long and thick black locks, and his brown eyes narrowed as he studied the weathered railings and brush shelters of the pig stalls. Task Master Flintok wasn't up yet. That didn't surprise him. The grey-haired Master often came late to the stalls. He told Andra one penalty of age was that sleep came early and left late. Besides, he warned the youth, it was Andra, not the Pig Master, who the Council of Law was testing. An advantage of age, he said, was wisdom.

The early morning pungent pig stench – mud, stale milk and urine, sodden straw and grain – irritated Andra and he'd been obliged to tolerate it for three moon cycles. Every morning, as raucous roosters roused their human keepers before sunrise, he threw aside his warm sleeping hides, dipped his face in the bitterly cold trough inside his family hut, gathered his weapons, and quickly dressed. After filling his food sack with nuts, meat, and chunks of mada-fruit, he ran the length of the village, through the mist, and scrambled up the dew-laden eastern slope to the pig stalls before the Sun Caller's horn echoed across The Vale. For generations, the Sun Caller's ancient ivory horn signalled the breaking of the first rays of light over the peaks of the Ureykyeu Mountains, and youths undergoing initiation and training into the Guardian ranks had to be at their assigned duties before the notes of the Sun Caller's horn ended. Failure meant the offender's time to serve at the place of duty was extended by two moon cycles. The lesson was simple. Guardians were neither lazy nor unreliable.

Andra reminded himself that he was lucky to be assigned to the pigs. Master Flintok took a kindly attitude to youths under his care. Cattle Master Neldrin, a man in his middle years, thickset and stern, always strictly dealt with youths attached to his service, according to The Way of The Vale. He never failed to be at the cattle pens before Sun Call, and most youths serving him had their duty extended for lateness. Erik started his duty one moon cycle before Andra, and he was already destined to finish it one cycle later.

The sounding of the deep horn from the northern heights broke his reverie, and he turned east, to catch the first rays gilding the snow-capped, craggy peaks of the Ureykyeu. He collected a wooden staff that was leaning against the railings of the stalls, and unhitched the gate, lugged the rough gate open, dragging it against the previous evening's sludge, and plodded into the yard. Queenie, the old boss sow, heavy jowls besotted with caked straw and mud, watched him enter, snorted, and lurched drunkenly to her hoofs. A litter of piglets scattered in squealing confusion as their warmth moved. Queenie needed no direction from the youth. She squelched heavily across the yard and out the gate, haphazardly pursued by her insecure horde. Andra prodded the rest of the herd into action, and amid protesting grunts and snorts and squeals he shuffled the pigs onto a run, leading down the hill to the creek marshes.

Every morning, he let the pigs out to root for sweet potatoes and mada-fruit, and every evening, at Sun Fall, he gathered the herd and drove it to the safety of the pens. Between Sun Call and midday, he cleaned the stalls, raked the sodden earth smooth, cut and prepared fresh, dry bedding for the pigs, and tended animals needing care. At night, before leaving, he made swill for the pigs' supper from buckets of milk brought by Erik. Flintok monitored his efforts every day, and every five days the old man reported on his progress to the Council of Law.

The mist had cleared from The Vale, and Andra was finishing his morning chores, raking the mud, when he spotted a bent figure walking up the narrow, winding path from the village. Flintok was later than usual. As the grey-haired elder approached, he called, wheezily, 'Hai! Young man! You have been at your work early.' His smile creased his leathery face into multitudinous wrinkles.

Andra straightened from his raking. 'Greetings, Master Flintok. I was as early as I must be. But I could have been late, this morning, and you wouldn't have known.'

The old man hobbled closer, chuckling. 'Ay. A wise observation for a young mouse, but young mice seldom see the mouse hawk that takes them unprepared. Be wary of the hawk, lad.' The old man turned to spit, before continuing. 'This morning, this old hawk slept. The mouse prospered. See that it is always so.' He placed a weathered hand on Andra's shoulder. 'How was my Queen?'

'Morose, Master.'

'Ay. She grows grumpier with age. But she is a lady, and one to be mindful of. She has delivered many generations. She has a right to her moods.'

The old man's fondness for the sow intrigued Andra. The Pig Master knew each pig by sight, named them all, and they responded to his call like old friends and loving children. Andra, before he began his service, found the old man's rapport with his beasts repugnant, but he quickly learned to respect Flintok's uncanny and caring skills with the pigs. Flintok frequently spoke of each pig's personality, and he fretted over every beast that fell ill or strayed. 'Come lad,' he said, taking the rake from Andra, and motioning towards a scythe hanging inside the shelter. 'You have grass to cut. Go to it, and then make your way to your lessons. I will visit the family at the marsh and talk to old Queenie. We have stories to share.'

Andra appreciated the change in task. The fresh scent of the grassed clearing on the eastern side of the hill was a pleasant change from the sty. As he bent to cut the first tuft, he paused to watch Flintok descend the slope, to the marsh. The old man's needs were simple. His life was peaceful and ordered. He was the spirit of The Way and all good things in The Vale. He would endure.

The rush of air from the wooden blade ruffled Andra's hair. He sidestepped from his crouched position, span and faced his opponent - Alain, the blacksmith's son - broad of shoulder - almost a hand span taller. The youths circled, searching for a weakness in the opponent's guard. Andra lunged - missed! A stinging blow from Alain's sword sent him sprawling.

'Enough!' The Guardian Master stepped between the combatants.

Andra scrambled to his feet, trying to ignore the pain from the welt across his back, and the smile that fleetingly crossed Erik's face. He gazed into the eyes of the Guardian Master – cold, hard, steel blue eyes.

'Your timing is poor. Do you think speed, alone, will win?' Andra didn't answer. The Guardian Master didn't ask questions, he made statements. The pupil's task was to listen and learn. All three youths listened. 'And you, Alain. Does a good warrior always win through sheer size and holding his ground?' He paused to let them consider his challenges. 'You have much to learn yet. You fight like brawlers in city taverns, and soldiers in the King's Armies. You fight to win or lose. You fight to die. That is not The Way of The Vale. That is not The Way of a Guardian.' The Guardian Master turned from the youths and strode towards the northern ridge.

Andra studied the Guardian Master with admiration. Short, stocky in build, dressed in leather-plated tunic and green leggings, a broadsword strapped to his left side, and a faint limp in the right leg, his appearance masked the subtle form of a consummate warrior. He held high authority and respect in the village, along with those who sat on the Council of Law, because he was responsible for training the youths who would become the protectors of The Vale. He wore his long dark hair in a braided ponytail, as was the custom and badge of all men who served as Guardians. The Guardian Master was not village-born but an outsider. He had chosen to settle among them, several years earlier. A man who had seen and travelled more of the world than anyone in The Vale, his past was shrouded in mist, like the Valley of Rivers in early morning.

'What is he doing?' Erik whispered.

'Perhaps he's testing our patience,' Alain suggested.

'I think we've failed,' ventured Erik. 'How's your back?'

Andra forced a grin. 'It smarts.'

'I didn't mean to hit so hard,' Alain apologized. 'No offence intended.'

'None taken,' Andra replied.

Erik kicked a clump of short grass out of the earth.

'Look.'

Heeding Alain's warning, Andra and Erik saw the Guardian Master was walking briskly towards them. He held his sword in his left hand, and as he reached the group he swung the point of his weapon sharply into the earth, released the handle, and stepped back, folding his arms. 'You must learn faster. You've played at warriors long enough. Prove to me you can be Guardians.' His voice, like his eyes, was cold, and filled the youths with nervous tension. 'Which of you would be the new Guardian Master?' The challenge astonished them. Andra stared at Erik, who lifted an eyebrow. 'Come. I offer you great honour. One of you, pick up the sword, wound or kill me, and the title is yours. Who will it be?'

'No one would dare do that,' Alain said. 'There is the

Law.'

'Do not be concerned with the Law of The Vale,' the Guardian Master answered. 'You have witnesses. I told the Council I would make this offer. Come. Who has the courage to be Guardian Master?'

His tone made it clear the challenge was genuine, but Andra couldn't fathom the Master's purpose. Erik remained rooted to the earth. Alain went to speak again, but held back. Awkward silence crowded in.

When the Guardian Master spoke again, his voice was impatient, insistent. 'Come. I am waiting. Where is the challenger? Who has the courage?' The youth did not move. 'So,' the Guardian Master said, spitting out the word. 'It is all true.' He shook his head and glared at the three youths. 'There are those in the village who say that none of you have the character of a Guardian, that you are cowards and boys, fit only to tend cows, and sheep, and pigs, that you don't have the strength of heart to take a sword against an unarmed old man!' He sneered contemptuously. 'You are the offspring of weak men who cry themselves to sleep at night.'

The insults stung Andra more than Alain's weapon, but Erik lunged and lifted the sword. 'Take back the insult to my father!' he yelled angrily. The ungainly weight of the Guardian Master's weapon made the blond-haired youth lose balance, but he steadied, and snarled, 'Take it back!'

The Guardian Master's tone became cutting. 'Erik. Spawn of a fisherman. Chaser of calves. Milksop. You dare pretend to be the man of this pathetic trio? What can you hope -' He ceased in mid-sentence, as Erik thrust the sword at the taunting figure. The Guardian Master neatly sidestepped and tripped the gangly youth. 'To fight with a sword, you'd best stand up.' The barb pricked Erik into furious action. He scrambled to his feet, swinging wildly, but each sweep cut air as the Guardian Master deftly dodged the attacks. Erik swung the sword high and brought it down. The Guardian Master was motionless, as if waiting for the blade to cleave his unguarded head, but in a blur his iron hands gripped

Erik's wrists, the pair collapsed in a backward roll, one of the Master's feet swung into the youth's midriff, and Erik spun crazily through the air, landing in a bone-crunching heap several paces down the slope.

The Guardian Master bounced to his feet, gathered his sword, dusted it, and returned the blade to its scabbard. To Andra and Alain, who were staring at their companion's motionless body, he said calmly, 'Erik will be bruised and sore, not only his body, but also his pride. Take him to his father's home and tend to him. Teach him what you learned. The lesson is at an end.' With that, the Guardian Master turned on his heel, and headed down the slope for the large wooden hall, near the village centre, where the Guardians shared residence, leaving the two friends staring at his retreating figure.

Eleven

'He was in complete control.'

Andra considered Alain's assertion before lowering his gaze to Erik, who was lying on straw bedding.

'I was a fool,' Erik muttered, lifting his head. 'I've humiliated myself.'

'Don't take it so badly,' said Andra. 'What you did, we all should have done – if we'd been quick enough.'

'Or brave enough,' Alain said, shaking his head.

'My head still hurts,' groaned Erik. 'All I remember is the world spinning. And then a stop.'

'He deliberately tried to make us angry,' said Alain, more to himself than his companions. 'He wanted us to be angry. He wanted to show us how an angry man can lose control of a fight. Erik lost his temper - he lost the fight.'

'True,' Andra agreed. 'But there's more to it. Erik went mad for most of the time, didn't you?' Erik nodded painfully. 'But I saw you take control just before he threw you - when you held the sword high.'

'Yes. I tried to calm myself. Swinging the sword wasn't achieving much, but when he stood still I thought I saw an advantage. I thought it was my chance.'

'That's exactly what he wanted you to think,' said Alain, as he stood at the foot of Erik's bedding.

'No. There's more,' Andra argued. He crossed the earthen floor to a small window. Long shadows were spreading across The Vale, and a soft breeze caressed his face. 'He used your own body and mind against you.'

Erik rose to a sitting position. 'He did what?'

'Yes, explain,' Alain prompted.

'I don't fully understand it yet, but he wanted you to attack his vulnerable position,' Andra slowly, thoughtfully replied. 'He wanted you to believe he was defenceless – only he wasn't, because he took the force of your downswing, and the weight of your body, and used them to defeat you.'

'Like a bird uses the wind to keep aloft.'

The intrusion of a deeper voice startled them. Erik's father, Adrik the Fisherman, stood in the doorway, lithe and sinewy, tanned like cured leather. 'I see my son and his young friends have begun learning the First Principle of The Way.' He entered, and put his fishing baskets by the rough-hewn table, before he unhooked his afternoon's catch from his belt, two rainbow trout, and swung them onto the table as a simple statement of his day's work. 'A good catch. I left the rest at the storehouse. All will eat well tonight who wish to eat fish.' He approached Erik's bed, and stood beside Alain, peering down on his son. 'Does your pride hurt?' he asked.

Erik looked up into the shadows of his father's worn face. 'A little. The greater hurt is in my head.'

Adrik laughed. 'Ha! Then all is well. You take your lesson with a Guardian's grace. Pity your father did not do so.' The youths looked at the fisherman for further explanation, but their querying expressions only caused Adrik to chuckle again. 'So?' he asked. 'Surprised a fisherman understands The Way of Guardians?' He grinned. 'Well, you must learn that not all who are chosen, or who ask, to begin that path, follow it to its end. At your age, like so many men of this valley, I, too, had dreams of honour. I chose to follow the Guardian Master of that time. But his path was too hard. I was too impatient. When I was tested, I failed. I did not want to learn the lessons. I left the Guardian's path and searched for a much easier one to follow. Now, I laugh whenever I remember that I chose to become a fisherman - I, who has so little patience,' and he laughed quietly.

'Do you regret failing?' Alain asked.

Adrik straightened his shoulders, but a firm, friendly smile spread across his lips. 'I regret nothing. You see, Alain, son of Irwin, I, like your father who works metal for the village, did not fail in The Way of The Vale. We chose other paths. And, on the path I chose, I learned all the lessons the Fish Master taught. Fishermen are Guardians too. We learn the same lessons, but apply them to different tasks. We all bring life to, and protect life within, The Vale - Guardian or Fisherman, Cattle Master or Blacksmith. All are the same. I have nothing to regret.' The resonating note of the Sun Caller's horn filled the room and stopped Adrik. Andra noticed the creeping shadows outside, and instinctively began to excuse himself. 'Yes. Go,' Adrik urged. 'To your tasks, as indeed you must.' He leaned over Erik. 'Come, son. No hurt can stop you either. If you are to be a Guardian, you must never fail your duties.'

Erik gingerly rose to his feet, swaying slightly, and followed his friends to the door. He turned to farewell his father, but Adrik's back was turned, because he was staring through the window at the blue haze settling across the deeper parts of The Vale.

The last sunrays lanced across the sky, piercing the encroaching evening clouds in a final, vain attempt to keep light in the world, and the sun was no more than a deep red colouration on the distant Andrakian peaks when Andra plunged into the marsh. Moisture welled between his toes. The pigs weren't difficult to locate, because they grazed on the grassy verge of the marshes, or lolled about in overgrown spots where the old sow and larger pigs used their weight and girth to flatten and shape the reeds into beds. Andra called, and prodded the herd into action, and he soon had them labouring up the slope towards their stalls. Queenie and her litter sauntered along at the rear. The old sow wasn't going to be hurried. Flintok waited at the gate. 'Come, children,' he crooned to the pigs. 'The night is near, and you must rest from the day's labour. Come, my Queen. Your most royal chamber awaits.' The old Master's familiar voice hastened the animals' pace, and Andra noticed that even the sow quickened her gait as she neared the crest.

When the final pig entered the pen, Andra searched the village path for the reassuring sight of Erik, and saw him, lugging two heavy wooden milk pails up to the pigsty. Erik's daily carrying labour was a bane and a blessing. Despite the strain of the task, he was physically filling out, and he appeared to be finding the daily chore easier with the passage of time. He made good progress on the final part of the slope, but as he reached Andra, sweating under the yoke of his load, Andra felt a hand grip his shoulder. He turned to Flintok, who said, with a wavering note of concern, 'I have counted. Two pigs are not in their beds. Senna and Artera are missing.'

The import of Flintok's message went deep. Andra hadn't checked the herd thoroughly before driving them home. If animals were missing, there'd be a penalty. Not even a Master as lenient as Flintok could allow carelessness to pass unpunished. Indeed, Flintok's love for his beasts meant Andra had failed in a duty close to the old man's heart. He had to make reparation. 'It's my fault, Master. I'll fetch them,' he said, turning to collect the wooden staff. 'When I return, I'll feed them their gruel and milk.'

Flintok nodded. 'I will feed these,' he replied. 'You must find Senna and Artera. They will have wandered into the northern part of the marsh where it is easier to root out the sweet shoots. Go. Chastise them for their forgetfulness.'

And chide myself for my own forgetfulness, thought Andra.

'I'll come with you,' Erik offered.

'But your duties?' asked Andra.

'I'm finished for today. Master Neldrin has released me. Delivering the milk was my final task. Besides, it's growing dark, so you'll need good help to find the pigs in the marsh.'

Andra smiled at his friend's confidence. He would certainly appreciate Erik's company, rather than trudge through the marshes in the closing darkness alone. 'Let's go,' he agreed, grinning, and the pair strode down the hill to the north of the pig run.

The evening purples and blues were darkening when Andra and Erik hurried into the broadest quadrant of marsh.

Twisted trees spread their spidery roots, threatening to entangle the unwary foot, and giant clumps of grass formed soft islands in the shallow stretches of water that seeped from an invisible source beneath the marsh. Patches of algae and ooze sucked at their feet, and mud under the water clutched at their ankles. 'It's already too dark,' Andra muttered. 'Even pigs won't be easy to see now.'

'There's still time. They'll come to your calling,' Erik prompted. 'Our movement may already have frightened them home. Cattle seek shelter if they are unsure of noises.'

Andra trudged deeper into the marsh, with Erik in train, pushing a path through thicker reed masses, but neither found signs of the missing animals. Night pressed in. Speckled starlight peeped between the dark tree canopies. Andra halted. 'This is pointless,' he said despondently. 'I've lost them. I've failed in my duty. You know what that means!'

'Don't be so lost yet. I bet they're already back at the pens,' Erik said, to bolster his friend's flagging hopes. 'Besides, Master Flintok is not unkind. He might forgive the oversight and not report it to the Council.'

'Unlikely,' Andra murmured. 'No one could find the pigs in this. Let's go back.'

They retraced their steps through the murk, working from clump to clump, treading warily with bare feet in cold patches of water, but, without a guiding light, except for the weak glow of the distant stars and a quarter moon, they had difficulty identifying anything that could lead them back to the makeshift path by which they'd entered. Andra felt the chill creeping into his bones. He tried to ignore the discomfort and near silence by losing himself in thoughts about Flintok's likely punishment for his failure, but he gradually became aware of the more immediate predicament that Erik and he faced, and he wondered if his friend shared his concern.

'Look!' Andra stumbled through knee-deep slime to stand at Erik's shoulder. A small fire shone in the dark marshes. 'Who could it be?' Erik whispered. 'We didn't pass through or near an area large enough to make camp.'

'Who'd camp in the marshes anyway?' asked Andra.

'We'd best check. Perhaps it's someone who could help us find our way out of this sodden place.'

Drawn by the light, they approached warily, and Andra's curiosity took him to the very edge of the firelight. The earth beneath his feet stopped oozing water, so he was at the edge of the marsh - but where exactly? The clearing was empty. The small fire burned, feeding on a crude pile of sticks, and a pair of forked limbs were arranged to serve as simple spit supports. Broken logs lay near the fire. The enticing tang of cooked meat lingered. He was about to creep closer, but Erik's sharp whisper halted him. 'What are you doing?'

'I'm going to have a look.'

'This is someone's camp, Andra. They can't be far away.'

'I won't disturb anything. I'll be careful. Besides, there's something by the logs I must see.'

'What if they return?' Erik insisted. 'We don't know who's staying here. I've a bad feeling about this place.'

'So do I. That's why I must look. Wait here.' Andra moved towards the nearest log, several paces into the clearing. The small, dark shapes by the log grew clearer as he neared, until he recognized what they were. The larger chunks were two pigs' heads, severed at the neck. The smaller pieces were trotters and bones. Nausea cramped his stomach, as shock, panic, and anger welled in his chest. He stood and took in a full view of the clearing. Shadows from the fire danced crazily on the trunks and limbs of surrounding trees, mocking his emotions. His fists clenched tight.

'Andra!' Someone hissed his name. 'Andra!' The second hiss dragged him from his raging thoughts. Erik was gesticulating, and calling, 'Hurry! Something's coming!' He took another look at the grizzly remains of Flintok's animals, before he dashed into the trees to join Erik. They slipped further into the undergrowth and took watch.

In the dark, beyond the clearing and to their right, a creature moved clumsily through the trees, its progress betrayed by a cracking of dry twigs and grunts, but into the flickering firelight stumbled not one but three men, carrying armfuls of firewood. They their way to the fire and dropped their bundles. All were broad, and stooped at the shoulders, with long, shaggy and dirty hair. They wore rough sheepskin coats, and buckles and strips of leather armour were visible under the coats. Sword blades glinted in the firelight. 'Soldiers?' whispered Erik.

Andra shook his head. 'No. I don't think so.' He watched them shuffle before sitting on the logs. One kicked a handful of sticks onto the fading flames. A second picked up a chewed bone from their earlier meal and tossed it in his hand like a dagger. Their muffled voices drifted through the still air as a series of grunts and guttural utterings. 'They don't speak our tongue,' he observed. 'Have you heard this speech before?'

'No,' Erik replied. 'They're strangers to The Vale. They may even be strangers to Thana. Father said all men in Thana spoke a common language.' Startled by rustling leaves to his immediate left, Erik span and saw metal glinting in the flickering firelight. 'Run, Andra!' he cried. He tugged at his friend's tunic and bolted into the marsh.

Andra froze, his eyes riveted to the apparition, his heart filled with cold terror. The stranger was like the three in the clearing - broad, stocky, not overly tall. He wore the trappings of a foot soldier - leather armour, rough boots, a short sword in a flimsy scabbard. Both hands, large and covered with tufts of hair, were firmly wrapped about the shaft of a metal-tipped wooden spear levelled at Andra's chest. But his face was neither human nor animal. Long, dark, dank, unkempt hair hanging about leathery skin, large dark eyes staring from deep sockets above heavy jowls, nostrils flaring fiercely in the flattened nose, he was taking in the smell of Andra's fear. He grunted a challenge, menacing Andra with his spear. Glancing at the clearing, Andra saw the others prowling towards the point where he crouched, and he caught snatches of the sounds of Erik's fading escape. He was trapped and alone.

He leaped sideways, into the rushes. Something sharp grazed his thigh. Guttural shouts exploded. Scrambling

94

blindly to his feet, he plunged into the marsh, running for his life. He ran hard, until his chest was hurting, and he was gasping for air. Something snared his foot in the black water, and he pitched forward, arms outstretched in a desperate effort to protect himself, but pain cut his cheek as he struck the water. He winced and rolled aside, and lay motionless in a shallow mud pool, letting the chill moisture cool his fatigued body. He waited, listening, his heart pounding. Only the brief whisper of the breeze through the tree canopy disturbed the night. The sounds of pursuit had ceased.

He relaxed and assessed his situation. Cuts and scrapes to his feet and legs and hands and arms were stinging. His cheek throbbed, and he winced when he touched the wound. He had no idea where he was. He'd bolted into the marsh with no sense of direction - driven by the fear of death. He'd lost Erik, his companion, swallowed by the marsh and the night. He'd lost Flintok's pigs. He was lost. He fought rising panic, until he relaxed again, and exhaustion flooded over him.

Twelve

Whiskers tickled his ear. He opened his eyes to dull daylight, and the dog's pink, wet tongue. It lifted its head, barked, and shook its tawny coat, before sticking its muzzle directly into Andra's face again. He pushed the snout aside and sat up, and the dog barked again. Voices reached his ears. Shouts. Men stumbled through the marshes towards him, scattering the early waist-high mist, and the dog bounded away to greet the approaching people. Andra recognized the Guardian Master, two Guardians, his father and Erik. His father, Malcolm, lifted him from the moist turf. 'Are you hurt?'

'No, Father.'

'The boy is cut. Here. And here.' Someone touched his legging at the thigh, and Andra winced with pain. 'And here is a wound. Not deep.' Fingers brushed his left cheek. 'There's a deep cut here.'

'Where's Erik?' he asked.

'I'm here.'

'Are you hurt?'

'No. Just tired,' replied his friend.

'How did you find your way out?'

'I don't know. Luck. I came out of the marsh at the western end near the cattle run.'

'Carry him carefully,' a voice instructed. Arms gently swept him into a prone position.

'I can walk,' Andra protested.

The Guardian Master's face appeared. 'Bravely spoken, but not true, my young friend. Rest. You have much to do soon enough.'

A hand gripped his left arm. He turned his head to catch sight of his father looking gravely at him. 'You look as though I'm about to die, Father. I'm not. I have too much work to make up for Master Flintok.' His father nodded, and a thin smile crossed his lips. The trees overhead lurched into a bobbing motion, and the gently rocking world sent him back to sleep.

They were closing on him. Leather buckles rattled. Dark swirling hair. Spears. Hundreds. He lifted his hand in a futile attempt to fend off the missiles. They cut, jabbed, stung. A spear lanced his cheek. A pig's head loomed in his face. Sickening grin. Death rictus. Leering. Trees. Everywhere trees. Shouting. Faces of leather - sneering. Hands reaching – groping, tearing, stabbing. Andra kicked, scratched, hit out savagely, screamed.

'Easy, lad. Easy. Calm down. Come on, lad, take hold. Break the dream.' Andra opened his eyes and stared into his father's bearded visage. Firm hands held him. 'They still chase you in your dreams?'

'Yes.' Andra felt weakened, exhausted. Sweat beaded on his brow and soaked through his clothes.

'At least you are awake. The fever is leaving your body.' Malcolm stood back from the hewn bunk. Tall and slim, almost gaunt, he was a carpenter, and the furniture in the two-roomed hut came from the skill of his hands. 'Hungry?'

Andra became acutely aware he was very hungry, and thirsty. 'I am, Father. I feel as though I could eat a full day's meal.'

'Little wonder,' Malcolm said. 'You've been in the fever beyond five Sun Calls since we found you in the marshes. You've eaten nothing and drank very little. I'll bring you broth, and mada-fruit to give you strength.'

Andra edged up to a semi-sitting position in the bunk, after Malcolm withdrew. Five days: he couldn't remember anything of them, except fragments of dreams and fears. He had never been ill in his childhood. How strange it felt to lose time.

His thoughts were interrupted by his father's returning

footsteps. 'Here. Sip this. And eat these to regain strength.' Malcolm offered a warm bowl of broth. Andra took it in both hands and cupped it to his lips. The liquid tasted strong and good, and soothing. He looked at the two mada-fruit Malcolm had placed on the bed's edge. The tiny, green-skinned fruit looked like wrinkled, unripe lemons. Within, they had a tasteless red centre that made mada-fruit relatively unpalatable, but locked in the fruit's bitter rind was restorative nourishment. Malcolm bent forward and swabbed thick yellow cream on Andra's cheek. It stung at the touch and Andra yelped.

'Keep still. The wound is deeper than we thought. It will take time to heal. Jenna has made a special poultice to aid the process. Even so, you will bear a scar.' Malcolm dabbed at the cheek again.

'Where's mother?' Andra asked.

'She attends Council. They've been meeting these past five days. Hold still.'

'Why so long?'

Malcolm squatted beside the bed and tilted his head as he explained. 'It would seem your discovery five nights ago is of great import to several who sit on the Council of Law. They've spoken to Erik and gathered all they can from his story. The intruders are not from Thana. Anedra will not say, but I know that she and the others on the Council are concerned by Erik's report, and they are keen to speak to you.'

Andra's head was racing. 'I can't tell them anymore than Erik. They were strangers. They weren't men like us. They —' he started, but his father cut across his words.

'Then the Guardian Master is right, and we must prepare for their coming.'

The bitter edge to his father's tone surprised Andra. 'What is the Guardian Master right about?'

'That is not for me to say,' Malcolm replied. 'You will learn soon enough, I have no doubt. But enough talk. Eat. You must rest. Tomorrow, you go with Anedra before the Council. You will need your strength.' The carpenter rose and placed his left hand on his son's head. 'Enjoy your peace while you can. Soon you will be a Guardian.'

He followed her at a respectful distance, as they walked the worn path towards the Hall of Council. She walked precisely, proudly, her green gown and flowing robes hiding her feminine form, but the locks of jet-black hair swirling sensually around her shoulders in the breeze highlighted Anedra's uncommon beauty. In their two-roomed hut, she was his mother, a source of comfort and caring. Here, she was authority. The bright morning light added crispness to her bearing, and Andra felt compelled to dutifully follow, as any inhabitant of The Vale called before the Council would.

Anedra revealed nothing to him. She woke him with a meal of nuts and milk, and fruit, and asked him to dress. When he asked if he was to go before the Council she simply said yes, but the finality in her reply warned him not to ask further, so he dressed in silence. His father watched them leave together, also maintaining the silence to ensure the occasion's formality was strictly observed.

Andra studied the Hall as they approached. He'd passed it many times, but he had never entered. The huge oaken door hung on a massive frame, which seemed to hold the whole wooden structure together. Ancient tree trunks, implanted in the firm earth at intervals, formed the Hall's skeleton, and the structure could comfortably shelter two hundred people. The peaked roof was sealed with slabs of pitched bark. The Hall was the centre of decision-making - the very heart of the people – and generations of dwellers in The Vale had sent their representatives to sit in the Council of Law. All laws emanated from the building. As long as the Hall of Council stands, thought Andra, The Vale will endure, Flintok will endure, he will endure. It symbolizes our existence and oneness.

Anedra halted before the weather-worn door, placed her hands on the smooth wood, and said, 'I am Anedra, daughter of Landor of The Vale, wife of Malcolm, mother of Andra, keeper of Council Law. I enter this sacred place with the peace of The Vale in my heart, and the need of the people in my thoughts.' In response to her words, the door slowly opened. Anedra turned to her son and said, 'In here, you speak only with an open heart. Truth is valued above all things. Herein, you serve only The Vale. You obey the ancient laws.' She bade him to follow silently.

The simplicity of the interior surprised Andra because he expected to find the walls carved with ancient legends and furnished with long tables of finely crafted wood. Instead, the rustic exterior walls, with their axe-hewn trunks, rudely intruded, and exposed beams ran the width and length of the peaked slab roof. A hole in the roof's centre served as the chimney for an open hearth in the earthen floor. Large logs were arranged around the hearth, flattened to serve as bench seats. Yellow light flickered from torches that were hung at angles to prevent them burning the walls.

Six people sat or stood at the circle. He recognised four. The Guardian Master stood with his back to the hearth, the silver circlet at the base of his ponytail catching the glow from the orange coals. An older woman, hair greyed with age, sat near him, and Andra knew she was Mistress Orlin, the village Metal Master. Another old woman, whom Andra did not know, sat beside her. Master Tomas, the Bird Master, stood opposite, and his portly frame partially hid someone from Andra's view. At the head of the circle, a tall, solid man Andra knew well - Master Renfrey, Master of The Vale, Head of the Council of Law – gazed at him from under his bushy eyebrows.

Anedra indicated Andra was to wait by the entrance. She walked towards the inner circle of Councillors, acknowledging each member, and bowed her head as she confronted Master Renfrey. After a brief exchange, Anedra turned to Andra, and said, 'Andra, son of Malcolm and Anedra, the Council of Law invites you to enter the Inner Circle so the Councillors might welcome you and speak their thoughts with you. If you accept, approach with peace in your heart and truth in your voice, for you enter a sacred place of The Vale.' Momentarily startled by his mother's formality, he hesitated before moving silently towards the Circle. The Councillors stood to face him, and Anedra invited him to sit on a log with his back to the entrance. The Guardian Master sat to his left. To his right sat an ancient being, bent with rheumatism and age, long straggly wisps of grey hair dropping from a balding pate. Andra was fascinated by the decayed appearance of the old one, an individual he could not remember ever seeing in The Vale.

Master Renfrey's voice drew his attention across the glowing hearth. 'Welcome to the Council of Law, Andra of The Vale. We trust you are better?' Andra nodded politely, but self-consciously touched his cheek. Master Renfrey continued. 'Good. Very good. You know why we have chosen to summon you to Council?' Again, Andra nodded. 'I cannot impress upon you how important it is for you to answer our questions, and to speak honestly. A matter of great concern has arisen, and only you hold the key to unravelling our immediate destiny in this matter. Keep your mind alert and clear. Answer accurately all that is asked. Keep no secrets. Do you understand, Andra?' The Master of The Vale raised his eyebrows, seeking an answer. Andra nodded. Perspiration formed on his palms.

Mistress Orlin spoke, her voice throaty and strong. 'Well, lad, tell us how you came to be in the marshes after Sun Fall.'

Andra glanced at the group of faces awaiting his reply, and lowered his head. Shame swelled in his throat, causing his voice to tremble. 'Master Flintok told me I had overlooked two pigs, Senna and Artera, when I brought them out of the marsh from feeding for the day.' He swallowed. 'I - I knew I had - failed my duty - so I offered to fetch the two pigs before it became too dark.'

'Did you expect to find them?' Master Tomas asked, raising a quizzical eyebrow.

'Yes. They don't usually stray far. I was curious they weren't with the rest, but then I thought my carelessness had made me miss them in the roundup.'

'Were you careless?'

Andra looked up into the dark eyes of the Guardian Master. 'I - I don't know.' He dropped his head again.

'Did you go alone?'

Master Renfrey's question surprised him because he knew they had already spoken to Erik. 'No. Erik joined me.'

'And where did you search for the animals?'

Andra paused to remember, and carefully explained in detail where he and Erik had searched for the pigs. As he finished, Mistress Orlin asked, 'Why did you not return to Master Flintok when the sunlight had dissolved?'

'I was concerned for the pigs. I had failed my duty, but I knew Master Flintok would be very disappointed if I returned without them.'

'Be that as it may,' interrupted the Guardian Master, 'but one who serves a Master knows that it is not appropriate to risk the dark, especially in a place like the marshes. Had Master Flintok not taught you this?'

Andra nodded slowly, submissively. The Councillors waited, as the lesson ran home to the youth, until the silence was broken by a brittle, cracked voice. Andra turned to meet slitted eyes inside the wrinkled head beside him. 'Describe them to us.' Andra heard a murmur of voices, but he was unable to break contact with the elder's eyes. 'Describe them, boy.'

His mind flicked through images in the marshes. He focussed on a campsite. A fire. Roasted meat. Pig's heads. Hunched figures in the firelight. Leather. Swords. Dark shapes in the bushes. Trembling, he slowly described what Erik and he had seen. Cold fear spread in the pit of his abdomen. His knuckles whitened. He tightened his grip on the edge of the log seat. He wanted to cry out, run, but the determined squinting eyes held him in place as he stammered his images of the intruders - ran again in wild panic - stumbled - fell - sliced open his cheek - fainted. He was unaware of finishing. First, the whole Council seemed frozen. He sensed the Guardian Master beside him. Master Renfrey was bent forward, his head buried in his hands. His mother was staring, her eyes wide with terror, her face rigid and pale. Pressure relaxed in his head. Focus returned. He looked at the old being beside him, but the elder ignored his presence. The Councillors re-gathered their composure, all except the Guardian Master, who was pacing back and forth, his left hand locked on the hilt of his sheathed sword. Something was terribly wrong, and Andra knew he'd precipitated it. Something he said had unsettled the gathering, yet when he stopped to recall his words he could remember nothing.

'Mistress Anedra,' said Master Renfrey calmly, 'direct the boy to his home for the day. Tomorrow he must return to his Task Master at Sun Call to continue his duties. I will personally speak to Master Flintok about what is to be done for this time.' Anedra rose and came around the circle to her son. She gently touched his shoulder and led him to the door.

Thirteen

Master Flintok did not punish him for the butchered pigs. In fact, no one mentioned them, or his meeting with the intruders in the marsh. Erik shared the secret, but neither youth had opportunity to speak of the incident because the intensity of their training consumed everything. In the mornings, they worked through independent tasks for their Task Masters, and in the afternoons the Guardian Master rigorously trained all three in The Way of The Vale. By evening, Andra collapsed on his bed, exhausted. The meeting with the Council was forgotten. The spear wound on his thigh healed. The scar set on his cheek. Warm summer days ran into early autumn.

But Andra sensed a different mood in The Vale. Though Master Flintok never mentioned any discussion with the Master of The Vale, Andra noticed subtle changes in his daily routine. Master Flintok arrived before him at the pig enclosure and grumbled less about his rheumatism and age. He carried his staff everywhere. He directed Andra to herd the pigs down to the marsh each morning, and to remain with them until Flintok relieved him. Most mornings, the old man went with Andra to the marsh, and wandered along its verge, searching the open patches of earth. The pigs were kept from entering the thicker sections, and Andra was ordered to bring them home before Sun Fall, which meant he had to run, without delay, to the sty the moment the Guardian Master dismissed him from afternoon training.

The Guardian Master remained stern with his three apprentices, but Andra sensed greater urgency in their instruction. They were allowed less time to reflect on the skills, and the Guardian Master dealt abruptly with anyone who forgot what had been taught, or was slow to acquire a new skill. 'What is the paradox of a Vale Guardian?' Dark eyes fixed on Andra.

'That he must learn to fight in the belief and hope that he never will.'

'As it is,' said the Guardian Master. He spun and swung an open hand at Andra's head. Too slow to block the blow, Andra willingly rolled with its force, cartwheeled, and bounced to his feet. 'The lesson?' barked the Guardian Master.

'A powerful force is weakened when it is not resisted.'

'Such is The Way.'

The Guardian Master's hand flashed to the hilt of his sword, and he drew it from its scabbard with deadly intent. 'Now you die!' he scowled, and lunged.

Andra neatly stepped aside, smiled, turned both hands palm upward, and extended his arms. The Guardian Master spat and stabbed at his chest. Andra jumped back and smiled again. 'Put away your weapon,' he said mildly.' I mean you no harm. Pass friend. We have no quarrel. I —' The sword ripped through the air in a wide arc, but he rolled to his left, and returned to his feet, still smiling.

'Curse you!' the Guardian Master snarled. 'Fight!'

'It's not The Way,' Andra amiably answered.

The Guardian Master stared menacingly for a moment longer, then shrugged his shoulders and sheathed his sword. 'As it is,' he said. 'But not every traveller through The Vale will as willingly put up his sword at your request.' There was an icy edge to his words. 'You must learn The Way of The Staff.'

From that afternoon, all three were ordered to carry a staff, and they went home from successive trainings with a multitude of scrapes and bruises. The Guardian Master seemed intent on breaking every bone in their bodies, as he went about his task of teaching them all that he knew in The Way of The Staff. Fighting with wooden swords, even the lessons in The Way of Hands, were neither as demanding, nor as viciously taught, as those of The Staff. And throughout it, Andra remained acutely aware of the Guardian master's determination that they should learn quickly.

Other changes were also evident in the village. Guardians

normally went on patrols alone, but now they went to watch points in pairs, and they were well armed, even when not on duty. Women and children stayed close to the village, while older boys, under the watchful eyes of two Guardians, were set the task of collecting nuts, berries, edible roots, and mada-fruit. People did not venture beyond their homes after Sun Fall. Andra questioned his mother only once on the changes. 'It is a time for caution,' she told him. Her grey eyes flashed, reflecting the candlelight, before she returned to fashioning a tunic from rough brown material. The matter was closed.

The veil of silence that drifted over the adults after the arrival of the intruders in the marsh badgered Andra every night, as he lay in bed, but he was comforted knowing that, within a matter of days, his three-moon cycle ordeal with Master Flintok would end, and he could stand with pride with the other Guardians. The smell of pigs wouldn't greet him in the mornings. He would miss Master Flintok's company, and his passion for his animals, but lately the old man's distant manners had estranged Master from pupil. Trainings with the Guardian Master would continue. 'A Guardian never stops learning,' was one of many maxims the youths were taught. Andra wondered if the pain of learning, like the pain that scarred his cheek, lessened with time.

A boy loped up the hill and Andra guessed him to be about fourteen summers as he tried to identify him. His voice carried urgency, like the keening of a hawk. The Guardian Master dropped his defensive stance and turned from Alain. 'Master! Master! Come!' the boy gasped, as he staggered to a halt.

'Why are you interrupting training?'

'Master Renfrey - he wants you to return to the village, Master. Something bad has happened.'

Andra saw fear in the boy's eyes as he delivered his message, but the Guardian Master was impassive. 'What happened, lad?'

'Strangers - they took Master Neldrin's cattle. Gavin was killed! Please Master, you must come!' the boy pleaded.

Andra's gut tightened. Gavin was a Guardian, three years his senior. He glanced at his friends. They were staring with shocked ashen faces. 'You have no time for emotion,' the Guardian Master growled. 'Grab your staff and follow! There will be much to do.' He briskly led the group down the hill.

As they entered the village, people were milling at the entrance to the Council Hall. Master Renfrey stood in the doorway, blocking access. Neldrin, the Cattle Master, was arguing heatedly with him. The crowd moved aside for the Guardian Master, but Master Neldrin grabbed his arm as he reached the step. 'You! You're Guardian Master,' he said angrily. 'What are you going to do about my cattle? Get your weapons and kill these marauders!'

The Guardian Master removed Neldrin's hand with a deft shrug and fixed him with a cold glare. 'That, Master Neldrin, is not The Way,' he said, with finality. He followed Master Renfrey into the Hall, closing the door behind them.

Andra turned to Erik and Alain and found them engrossed in animated conversation with Alain's father, Blacksmith Irwin. The crowd dispersed. Men drifted away, in twos and threes, whispering. Mothers directed children to the safety of their homes, but several older children loitered a short distance from the Hall, awaiting further developments. Master Irwin stopped his explanation, as Andra joined his companions. 'That is how it is. But enough. I must attend to the forge. It may be that I will have many tasks ahead if today's events follow a certain path. Go with care.' He placed his hands briefly on his son's broad shoulders before he headed towards his smithy.

'What have you learned?' Andra asked.

'A great deal,' replied Erik.

'More than we expected,' added Alain.

'Alain's father heard a lot about events, and beyond this day too.'

'But what happened to Master Neldrin?' Andra asked.

Erik took a breath and explained. 'We put the cattle out

to pasture this morning, after Sun Call. I saw nothing unusual, but Master Neldrin complained that the beasts were uneasy. After I was released to come to training, Master Neldrin tended the cattle alone, and it was then the strangers came. Six of them. They ambushed Master Neldrin, and drove him off with spears, so he ran to find the Guardians on the South Spur, Gavin and Derwent, but when they returned the cattle were scattered. Some had run off, and some had been slaughtered, but four beasts were missing altogether. Gavin and Derwent found their tracks and followed them into the foothills. They came on the strangers butchering the carcasses of the four beasts they'd stolen, and Gavin was killed before the strangers ran into the marshes. Derwent carried his body back to the village.'

'Does Derwent, or Master Neldrin, know who the strangers were?' asked Andra.

Erik shook his head. 'No. But, from the descriptions, it sounds like they are the same ones we encountered.'

'What are they be doing in The Vale?' Andra asked.

'Not only in The Vale,' Alain interrupted. 'My father says he's heard many worrying tales about events in the realm of Thana, beyond The Vale. He says there's war brewing. Passing travellers, who rested their horses, or had them re-shoed by Father, spoke of dark troubles spreading throughout the land. Bands of ill-intentioned creatures have been raiding villages and farms, stealing and killing livestock - killing people. They say we're lucky not to have been seriously affected this close to the northern lands. One who passed through, only four days ago, said the Great King is mobilizing a huge army to deal with the intruders.'

'The war could spread here?' Andra asked.

'My father doesn't think so. But he says we must prepare as if war is coming. The strangers will come again. That's what all the adults believe.'

'We'll be ready,' said Erik, grasping his staff. 'We three will all soon be Guardians. We will protect The Vale.'

'Andra and I will be ready to teach you when you join us in the Guardian Hall, Erik,' chuckled Alain, reminding Erik that the latter still had at least another moon cycle to complete his services for Master Neldrin. 'At least you can thank the strangers for reducing your workload.'

Erik smiled, and swiftly cuffed Alain behind the ear. A scuffle erupted, and Andra joined in on the pretence of attempting to separate his friends. All three were quickly embroiled in conflict, whirling their staffs, dodging and weaving in mock combat.

'What manner of behaviour is this!' boomed a deep voice. Andra turned to acknowledge the speaker, only to receive a sharp blow across his shins from Erik's staff that sent him sprawling in the dust at the feet of Master Renfrey. 'Stop! At once!' Renfrey commanded. 'You! Andra, son of Malcolm, stand up!' He waited for Andra to scramble to his feet. 'You dare be frivolous when you are meant to be waiting patiently for your Master to call or dismiss you? Perhaps Council will need to reconsider the Guardian Master's request after this public display of foolishness.' All three blushed with shame. 'Dust yourselves,' ordered the Master of The Vale, 'and follow me.'

Andra and Erik had been in the Hall before. Alain had not, and he stared in awe. All the members of Council were present, but none sat at their places. Beyond the Inner Circle, the Guardian Master stood, his solid frame broken by brief flashes of reddish light reflecting from buckles on his armour. Behind him, on a raised board, lay Gavin's bloodied corpse. 'Stand at the foot of the Circle,' Master Renfrey instructed. Andra, Alain and Erik moved to the designated point, facing the Guardian Master. As they did, the Councillors sank to their knees, facing the youths. Master Renfrey joined the Circle. The Guardian Master spoke.

'Know, all of you, that I, Artega, Guardian Master of The Vale am Chief Protector of all who enter or live within The Vale. I am the Teacher of The Way, and of the many ways within The One Way. It is I who carry the wishes of the Council of Law into the training of those who desire to be Guardians and protectors of The Vale. Know that this is my sacred duty, as carried out by those who have served as

Guardian Master before me.'

'As it is, so it will be,' chorused the kneeling watchers.

'As it is,' responded the Guardian Master. 'I stand within this sacred space to offer truth, with the need of the people in my thoughts. Who will listen?'

Master Renfrey rose to face him. 'We know you, Artega, and welcome your words. What would you speak to Council?'

'I bring today, before the Inner Circle of Council, three young men - Alain son of Irwin, Andra son of Malcolm, Erik son of Adrik. These have been my pupils. They have studied The Way of The Vale. They have served their assigned duties with their Task Masters. I present all three as rightful candidates to become full Guardians of The Vale.' He stared directly at the youths. 'They are ready.'

Artega's speech caught all three youths completely unprepared. Andra was acutely conscious of his companions' gaping mouths as he stared, wide-eyed, at his mother kneeling before him. Her eyes reflected her pride. 'We of the Inner Circle hear your request, Artega. Does any Councillor object?' asked Master Renfrey. The atmosphere of the Hall was tense, as if awaiting a denial, but none came. 'Your request is accepted,' the Master of The Vale confirmed. 'Proceed with the Induction.'

The Guardian Master moved across the Inner Circle and directed the youths to turn towards the entrance and kneel. He drew a length of braid from inside his tunic and began to tie Alain's hair into the traditional ponytail that distinguished the Guardians of the village. As he did so, he recited a litany. 'You are here because you have chosen your path. You are here because you have shown your desire. You are here because you are a Guardian. Your path is not easy. Your path demands patience. Your path requires strength. Your path is to serve. Your path is The Way.' The voice floated behind Erik, and then Andra felt hands tug at his hair. 'You will act for truth. You will act for the peace of The Vale. You will act according to your training. You are a Guardian, protector of all in The Vale that has been, is, and will be. You are now one

110

with the sacred traditions. You can now sing the stories of those who have gone before you, and in time to come, may there be songs sung in honour of you. You are a Guardian.' Andra heard the Guardian Master move away.

Master Renfrey broke in. 'Turn to face the Council.' The youths rose and turned. The Councillors were standing. 'Before us we see three new Guardians. We do not know you. Come into the circle. Name yourself. Be welcomed.' The Master of The Vale extended his hands towards Alain, who hesitated, before stepping into the Inner Circle.

'I am Alain, son of Irwin, Guardian of The Vale.'

'We know you and welcome you Alain, son of Irwin,' responded Master Renfrey. 'Keep truth, peace, and love of the people always in you. Join us, and be seated.' In turn, Andra and Erik were formally welcomed and took their places in the Circle. Andra looked at his mother. Anedra was smiling but her eyes held an indefinable sadness.

Fourteen

'I still can't believe this. Yesterday I was a boy to be ordered about by Master Neldrin. Today, I'm a Guardian. I am a man!' Erik shouted, and laughed.

'Ha!' grunted Alain, grinning cheekily. 'I see no change from the boy I beat with my staff.' He slapped Erik heartily on the shoulder and swung onto his bunk. 'No more sleeping on straw or the floor for me!'

'No more pigs!' shouted Andra. 'No more evil-smelling, vile, fat, grunting pigs!'

'I still can't believe it,' Erik repeated.

'It all happened so quickly,' said Andra. 'Why so quickly?'

'Are you complaining?' Alain asked, leaning out from his bunk.

'I thought there'd be something more.'

'Like what?' asked Erik. 'A celebration? Mystical cutting of our wrists?'

'No,' Andra faltered, and added, 'Well, yes.'

Erik and Alain laughed. 'Does it matter?' Alain asked, as he caught his breath. 'We're Guardians, with or without a big ceremony.'

The double entrance doors to the Hall swung open, and daylight glowed brightly behind the dark figures striding in. The last one closed the doors. The Guardian Hall was a single room. As in the Council Hall, angled, exposed beams supported a wooden shingle roof. Half the interior, closest to the entrance, was given over to an eating and meeting space, where a long, sturdy table sat in the left portion, and a cooking hearth, and a patch of bare earth filled the remainder. Andra, Erik, and Alain were on bunks in the sleeping half of the Hall. The wooden double bunks were arranged in two rows, enough to accommodate twenty sleepers. The hewn timber walls were decorated with spears, shields, and assorted weaponry, and forlorn tapestries clung to the walls, reviving dusty memories of greater times. The voices of the new arrivals filled the Hall. All six were involved in an animated argument that attracted the interest of the three friends. 'Well, I say we're foolish to go on ignoring what we've seen. Their tracks can be found in almost every remote corner of The Vale.'

'I found fresh marks at the western watering hole,' offered an auburn-haired speaker.

'Then they are becoming more purposeful,' chimed in a third speaker.

'Soon they'll be stealing more than pigs and cattle and fowl.'

'But he'll remind us of our duty according to The Way. Ours is not to wantonly kill intruders.'

'Oh Liam, you're such a fool!' chided the first speaker, a burly, dark-haired man. 'Did they stop to ask if they could kill Gavin? No! They slaughtered him, like they'll slaughter us if we sit back and do nothing.'

'We owe them for the death of Gavin. We must avenge our brother!' added someone.

'Vengeance is not The Way, Bryon. Have you so easily forgotten your teachings?' The others turned to the blonde-haired man who'd asked the question.

'What good were Gavin's teachings to him at the end?' snapped his adversary. 'The Way did not protect him!'

'But The Way protected Derwent. He drove off as many of the intruders as there are of us here,' cut in Liam.

They stopped, aware of the three youths, and the two groups regarded each other. The dark-haired man broke the silence. 'Well. Seems there are three more Guardians. And whom do we have the pleasure of welcoming?'

Alain stepped forward. 'I am Alain, son of -'

'Yes, we know who your father is,' interrupted the older man, 'and I certainly know you, son of Anedra,' he said, fixing his steady gaze on Andra. 'And you must be Erik,' he added, shifting his gaze. 'We're indeed honoured.' He motioned for the youths to join them at the long table. 'I am Bryon,' he said. 'My companions are Karl, with the hair of flame, Liam,

113

Renwith, Mark. And Stephen, here, who always reminds us that we are servants of The Way.' The blonde Guardian smiled at the mention of his name.

'The Guardian Master has brought you here earlier than we expected,' said Liam. 'You must feel honoured.'

'I'm confused,' said Andra. 'I still had time to serve with Master Flintok. Now, I'm a Guardian.'

'Don't be surprised,' grunted Renwith. 'You're needed. There aren't many of us, and there are too many strangers in The Vale. You will not enjoy the time that you have chosen to become a Guardian.'

'You may well wish you could go back to tending pigs,' Bryon added.

'Don't let their foolish talk dishearten you,' said Stephen. 'You chose your paths, and you are Guardians. As it is.'

'How many of you, I mean us, are there in The Vale?' Andra asked. 'There are only twenty beds.'

'There were ten, until this morning,' replied Mark. 'Now, twelve.'

'Why so few?' I always thought there were more.'

'The Vale is not a big place,' explained Liam. 'I'm youngest, and I'm already two full summers older than any of you. After you three, there's no boy closer than four summers to reaching Guardian age. The village has too few people. We're lucky to have so many Guardians now.'

The doors opened again, and four girls entered, accompanied by an older woman, carrying pottery containers and jugs. A meal was hastily laid on the table under the woman's watchful eyes. Bryon and Karl slipped into quick banter with the girls, who smiled and blushed as they worked. Then, as quickly as they arrived, the girls and their chaperone left. 'Come,' said Bryon with a sweeping invitation of his arm. 'Shall we eat?'

When the meal was finished, the six older Guardians rose and moved to their bunks. They withdrew swords from under their mattresses and went to the walls to select shields and armour. Andra observed that the precision of their actions suggested they were motivated by an identical but silent message. They gathered on the bare earth, before the hearth. Bryon interrupted. 'We forget. Our new companions don't understand. You, Erik, come with me. Liam, see to Alain. Stephen, Andra.' The young Guardians joined their indicated tutors.

Stephen led Andra to the back wall, and as he followed Andra studied the young man. Stephen moved confidently. Lightly built, but wiry, strength flowed through his body. He had the traditional ponytail, in his blonde locks, neatly fixed with silver wire. He motioned towards a long box. 'Select a weapon.' Andra peered in at a dozen swords, packed in animal fat to prevent rust. He hesitated. 'Go on. One is for you. We follow The Way of The Staff, because a sword is a poor weapon, but these are for tomorrow's ceremony.'

'Ceremony?' asked Andra. 'What ceremony?'

'For Gavin. Tomorrow, we carry his body into the mountains, to free his spirit, so that he may follow his new path beyond this life. It is The Way. As Guardians of The Vale, we honour our brother by accompanying his last mortal remains to their resting place. We dress as the ancient Guardians dressed, wearing armour and bearing swords.' Stephen's voice was solemn, but there was no sorrow in the young man's eyes or face. Andra chose his sword. In turn, Stephen led Andra to select a shield and armour. They rejoined the others at the hearth, and set to burnishing metal, and greasing leather, until they shone in the flickering firelight.

So diligent was Andra at his task, he failed to notice the light fade outside the Hall, and he didn't hear the Sun Fall horn echo across The Vale. Nor was he aware that the Guardian Master and the remaining three Guardians had entered the Hall. The blades began to gleam with reddish hues from the flames, as darkness sank into the eaves, and steadily one, two, and then several voices enjoined in a Time Old song of mourning for a lost companion.

'Mountains hang their shaggy heads
Purple mists about them creep
Grey faced clouds above them gather

115

Sorrows rumble in valleys deep
Their tears tumble.
Shining shields and swords a-glitter
Uplift we old companions
On shoulders stooped with heavy death
March we into the canyons
Of the mountains.'

The verses poured from the Guardians' hearts while they toiled, and the haunting melody drew unanticipated sorrow from within Andra.

'He watches now from craggy rims
Spirit freed beyond The Vale
And we must keep our duty daily
Keep The Way and never fail
Until we join him.'

After the final strain melted into the dark corners, for a time, each man stared silently into the flames of the dying hearth, lost on a pilgrimage through the forests of his thoughts. Then, wordless, each rose, carefully put aside his weapon and armour, and went to his bunk.

The procession climbed the steep, winding path from The Vale, along the rocky Ureykyeu cliffs, where only two could walk abreast. Behind Renwith came Alain and Andra, and six Guardians bearing Gavin's burial stretcher. Villagers accompanied Gavin's mother behind the pallbearers. Erik and Bryon brought up the rear. Ahead, and out of sight, Mark and the Guardian Master led the party, scouting for danger. To Andra's left, the earth dropped abruptly into a rocky valley. He felt the tension. For the first time, he was aware of the mortality that stalked life in The Vale. Gavin's bloodied body on the Council Hall slab was incongruous amid the life surrounding it. The deaths of village elders, and Master Aubrey's little girl drowning in the wintry flow of the river, three summers past, had been fleeting incidents with no emotional attachment for him. He'd never walked the path into the mountains. Now, each step drew him irresistibly closer to the resting site of everyone who died in The Vale. They carried Gavin, who had been a young and healthy Guardian, and it filled him with a strong sense of loss. Yet, he still felt as if he was observing the experience rather than acting as a participant, and his emotional state was confusing.

'These are fresh!' Mark shouted, as he turned the bend on the mountain path, and bent to study the ground.

'I don't like the feel of this,' Renwith muttered, and he nervously fingered his sword as he peered up the slope. 'The strangers are likely to desecrate a sanctuary. Stay alert!' The procession continued, but the Guardians were searching every crevasse and possible point where an attack could be launched. The path narrowed and squeezed through a cleft in the rock face. Further up, it curved back on itself, and passed between two towering pinnacles. 'The Twin Guardians of the Dead,' Renwith announced, as they walked between, but Andra only half-heard his comment, being lost in his own thoughts about death and uncertainty about the security of where they were.

Beyond the Twin Guardians, the path ended at a flat, open space, cradled in a natural bowl, as large as the interior of the Council Hall. The cliffs were honeycombed with caves in the cliff face, but Andra's attention flicked to the centre, where Mark and the Guardian Master crouched, back-to-back, staffs ready. A dozen stocky figures surrounded them. A stranger shouted, they charged, and the Guardians vanished in a flurry of arms, legs and swords. Andra didn't hesitate. He drew his ceremonial sword and ran into the melee, followed by Renwith, Alain, and others. Wild clattering and cries filled the air, but, as quickly as it began, the fight ended. The intruders scrambled up the cliffs and fled into the mountains. Andra and Alain started to pursue them, but the Guardian Master intervened. 'No!' he ordered sternly. 'You have a duty to finish here. We must attend to the dead.' When he saw the swords in their hands, he scolded them. 'Put these up. A staff is the weapon of a Guardian. Remember that. These are ceremonial toys.'

The bearers, who joined the skirmish, returned to collect Gavin's body, and they carried it into the centre of the flat area. 'Just my luck to miss the action!' Bryon scowled, as he joined his Guardian companions.

'There wasn't much action, hungry Bryon of Robert,' jibed Renwith. 'We let them go for you.'

The death rites were simple. Andra joined the circle around Gavin's fully armoured corpse and the Guardian Master repeated the words he recited at the Guardian's induction. Master Renfrey briefly spoke about Gavin's duty to The Vale, before he led the gathering from the area, leaving Gavin's mother, the Guardian Master, and Derwent to inter Gavin's corpse within one of a multitude of small caves that pocked the cliff.

While they waited beyond the Twin Guardians, the funeral assembly sang a dirge, and as it echoed mournfully, down through the rock valleys to the lush green meadows and woods of The Vale, the final poignant reality of death reached Andra's heart. Tears welled, and he shamefully wiped them away. A hand rested on his shoulder. 'Never be ashamed to show sorrow, Andra.' The voice belonged to Stephen.

'Children cry,' Andra mumbled, embarrassed another Guardian had seen his tears.

'All cry who have feeling and compassion for their companions and those whom they love. You will see no dry eyes about you, Andra, not here, not now.' At Stephen's prompting, Andra looked, and saw Stephen was right. The singers sang through tears.

The Guardian Master was the last to return from the sanctuary. The Guardians were patiently waiting, but the others had left, returned to The Vale, to go about their duties. 'I have decided,' he announced. The finality in his voice was plain to Andra. 'The strangers are too great a threat to our safety. They've even plundered the bodies of our dead. They do not respect, or know, The Way, and it is something I know they will never willingly learn or accept.' He looked at his charges. 'I speak as Guardian Master. Hear and obey my words.' Andra sensed there would be no questioning of the coming instructions. 'I am going into the mountains to find the strangers. With me will go Bryon, Renwith, Mark, Derwent, Karl and Farel.' A stirring passed through the group. 'Liam will lead in The Vale in my absence. With Alain, he will watch the Eastern Ridge. Stephen and Andra will guard the Southern Spur and the Outward Road. I leave Kevin and Erik the care of the village, and watching of the Northern Spur. Guard The Vale well.' The Guardian Master shifted his stance to stare over the precipice towards The Vale. 'I do not have the blessing of the Council of Law in this decision. They won't countenance any notion of hunting down the intruders. But they don't understand these strangers as I understand them. Before I came here, to live and serve, I met this kind in the wider world. They are evil, wrong, beyond the experience of any living person in The Vale, save perhaps the venerable Master Geat. The Vale means nothing to them. Life has no value to them, except to kill.' The Guardian Master's voice saddened. 'If I don't follow this path, against the wishes of Council, The Vale will disappear beneath the cruelty and malice of the strangers. I have been Guardian Master here for too long to let that happen.' He turned to the group, and the familiar tone returned. 'We leave at once. Tonight, once Sun Fall has sounded, Liam will go to Master Renfrey and inform him. We will be gone for several days, perhaps a week. We will need to use all our training and live off the fruits and waters of the land. But we are Guardians.'

His final statement brought the Guardians to rigid attention. 'The die is cast,' Bryon muttered.

'As it is,' responded the Guardian Master.

Fifteen

Grey autumn clouds drifted across the sky, leaving dull light to filter onto the rolling plain, but every now and then a shaft of yellow sunlight traced the hillocks and copses. The brooding mountains, their craggy peaks threatening to tear open the bellies of the travelling clouds, kept silent guard at the eastern end, but their sombre presence only enhanced the green hues in The Vale. From his vantage, atop a rugged red granite outcrop on the southern spur, Andra surveyed his home, and drank in the cool morning air. The fresh breezes carried a hint of rain, and he glanced at the racing clouds. Soon winter will settle on us, he thought, and we'll sit inside, wrapped in skins, by roaring hearths. Then who will watch The Vale?

'Yes,' said Stephen. 'Winter is coming.'

'How did you know what I was thinking?'

'Your eyes. The clouds,' his companion explained. 'Soon we will be watching from here, crouched against the rocks, trying to hide from the freezing winds and sleet.'

'You mean Guardians keep watch in rough weather?'

'As long as there is a chance someone may come into The Vale, that is The Way.'

Andra hunched into a squatting position and reflected on his six days as a Guardian. His chosen path had already lost its glamour. Sitting on a pinnacle of rock for days, waiting for people to enter The Vale, lacked appeal. The only consolation was the Guardian Master's absence, hence no continuation of the rigorous training – that, and the beauty of The Vale. Liam's message from the Guardian Master to Master Renfrey was greeted by a brief outburst of anger, but there had been no further response from the Council of Law. The remaining Guardians were allowed to go about their duties, without question or comment, and village life continued as if nothing was changed. This, Stephen explained to Andra, was simply The Way. The Council could only wait patiently for the Guardian Master's return. Anedra did not ask Andra about the Guardian Master's decision when he visited his home, and Andra felt no obligation to offer an explanation on the Guardian Master's part. He was, after all, a Guardian now.

He turned his attention to the narrow track that wound down the slope below his watch point. The Outward Road squeezed between the points of the northern and southern spurs of the hills ringing The Vale and dropped rapidly into the thick forest that flowed into the region of the Valley of Rivers, and the wider world; the Land of Thana, the Great King. He could only guess what lay beyond the forest. His parents never travelled beyond The Vale. There was nothing to draw the people out of their tiny world because it provided them with everything they needed. They had peace and contentment, and disturbances, like those by the recent intruders, were rare. Even that minor problem would end once the Guardian Master and his band dealt with them. The Outward Road led only to the unknown, and the troubles of other people. Andra remembered the talk of the war that was brewing in the Great Kingdom of Thana. War meant warriors locked in battle, but Andra couldn't imagine the scale or purpose of a war, or a battle, no matter how hard he tried. To deliberately seek battle with a foe, without first seeking friendship, was unthinkable. It was not The Way.

He spotted dark specks on the crest of the hill on the Outward Road, so he tugged Stephen's arm and pointed. The specks grew as they topped the crest, and black shapes separated and melted together as they passed between the spurs and entered The Vale. 'Riders,' whispered Stephen. 'Can you see how many?'

'No,' Andra replied. 'Not yet.' He examined the close group of horsemen moving directly below, fascinated by the horses. Horses were rare in The Vale. Only the Guardian Master and Master Renfrey owned riding horses. The Guardian Master rode his horse, every day, to reach watch points in The Vale. Master Renfrey used his horse to travel on the Outward Road to villages in the Valley of Rivers. Alain's father tended to both animals. Andra loved them, and often wished more horses lived in The Vale, but Anedra told him there was no real need. The Vale provided all they needed. 'Eight,' he announced.

'Good. Now, go quickly,' Stephen urged. 'Take word to the Council. There are strangers entering The Vale. They wear much armour. Go!'

At Stephen's insistence, Andra scrambled down from the rocky ridge and sprinted onto an earthen path. From every watch point in The Vale, the Guardians of old had beaten narrow, hidden pathways, along which they could run while remaining unseen by anyone travelling the Outward Road. Long ago, the Council of Law planned that the approach to the village would follow a winding course, deliberately designed to delay travellers. The running paths, however, were as straight as the topography of The Vale allowed, giving Guardian runners ample time to warn the village before the travellers arrived. The air was mild. The earth under his feet was soft, and the sharp wind in his face heightened his senses as he slipped into a comfortable pace. The horsemen were moving slowly, so he'd have the news to the Council in good time. He ducked overhanging branches from low trees and weaved between thicker bushes. Low hillocks hindered his view of the Outward Road, but he knew that a short distance further on he could pause in a copse to check the riders' progress. His breathing adopted the rhythm of his feet, and he relaxed. Running felt good. He remembered the Guardian Master's earliest trainings. 'Be ready to run. A Guardian can protect by running. Running warriors can win where it appears they are retreating. Learn to run. There is a time for it. Such is The Way.' Andra recited the lessons in rhythm as he ran. Twice he stopped to check the riders. The first occasion, they were still winding along the Outward Road, a mass of shadows under a dull, sunless sky. The second time, they'd made even less progress than he anticipated, because they hadn't yet crested one of the higher hills in The Vale. He pressed on, making the village in easy time, and went straight to Master Renfrey's hut.

By the time the riders reached the village, the Council was fully assembled, and most inhabitants had gathered to greet them. Master Renfrey was noticeably troubled by Andra's news, although he said nothing to the young Guardian, and went about the business of gathering the Councillors from their homes and their duties. Andra waited at the Hall, where Liam, Kevin and Erik joined him. Stephen and Alain remained on watch in the hills. The riders walked their horses up the incline to the head of the village, riding two abreast, in regimental lines. They wore fine, jet-black plate armour, head to foot, and it appeared keenly polished, even under the dust of travel. The muscular horses, bred for speed and strength, were as black as the riders, and black pieces of chain and plate armour were fitted to the horses' heads, necks and chests as added protection. The only distinguishing feature on the black shields, hanging from their saddles, was a rampant creature, half-lion and half-eagle, etched in emerald. The riders' faces were hidden behind ebony visors, and their hands within black, studded leather gloves.

The troop halted several paces from the Council, but one rider continued forward, until his horse's nose almost pushed into Master Renfrey's face. He spoke with a cold, authoritative voice. 'Who claims to be head of this village?'

Master Renfrey glanced at the Council members. Each nodded, so he turned to the rider, and said, 'I am Master Renfrey. I am Master of The Vale, Head of the Council of Law. To whom do I speak?'

'I am Devi Senok, first in line of the Great King's Personal Guard. I am Haardrishii.'

Andra heard self-importance and finality in the rider's statement. Everything about the man's manner reflected confident, aggressive arrogance that angered and unsettled him. 'What is your purpose in coming into The Vale?' asked Master Renfrey.

Devi Senok tilted forward in his saddle and deftly unfastened a saddlebag buckle. From it, he withdrew a rolled parchment, which he held up. 'This is an order from the Great King that all subjects, in all villages of the Kingdom of Thana, must obey.' He unrolled the parchment.

Erik whispered to Andra, 'Liam says the Guardian Master should be here. These King's men will only bring trouble.' Andra glanced beyond the mounted figure of Devi Senok towards the other riders. They sat rigid in their saddles, apparently oblivious to the people watching them. 'Liam says it's best if two of us were -'

'Sh!' Andra interrupted, as Devi Senok read from the parchment.

'I, Thana, Royal Majesty of the Lands of Thana, Great King and Eternal Liege, hereby decree that the cities, towns and villages of Thana shall send to the Great City all young warriors to serve in the Royal Armies, to crush the rebellious uprisings, and repel the iniquitous invasion of the subjects of Uz-Erhaag from our northern borders. I command the Great King's Personal Guard to travel the land, and escort all eligible men, and those worthy of the honour, to serve as a warrior of Thana to the Great City. The Personal Guard have the Great King's Right to free provender in all places, and power to discipline any who do not comply with the Great King's decree. Thus have I, Great King Thana, Eternal Liege, ordered. Let it be obeyed.' Devi Senok stopped. The villagers whispered. Andra stared at Erik and the other Guardians, his heart pounding fearfully. The King's decree included each of them.

'Your news stuns us, Devi Senok,' Master Renfrey replied. 'What you - I mean what the Great King asks of us is no small request. Our Council must meet. We must consider what has been requested.'

Devi Senok nodded. 'We stay until morning. My men have travelled for a long time, and will enjoy an opportunity to rest, eat, and refresh their horses. I will join you and your Councillors to see that your discussion and decisions are informed.' He dismounted with surprising ease, given his armour, and he handed his reins to Alisa, Master Flintok's granddaughter. 'See that he is fed, watered, and brushed well,' Senok ordered. He took a silver piece from a money pouch on his belt and gave it to Alisa. 'His name is Sharpwind.' The girl's eyes sparkled, and she reached up to stroke the black horse's nose. Senok made an inaudible comment to Renfrey, who nodded, and ordered the villagers to go about their duties. As the crowd dispersed, Senok joined the Councillors, and the group headed for the Hall of Council.

In the Guardian Hall, the young men fervently discussed the situation. 'The Guardian Master must be told,' Liam insisted. 'These soldiers come from the King to strip The Vale of Guardians at a time when we are most needed here. The intruders threaten to take all we have, especially if the Guardian Master and the others aren't successful in the mountains.'

'We owe no allegiance to a distant man who calls himself a Great King,' Kevin agreed. 'But what are we to do? What will Council decide?'

'The Council will obey the King's law,' said Liam, with disgust. 'It has always been so. Without the Guardian Master's influence, it will be even more so. The Way is to be part of the Whole, if the Whole so demands. Remember?' He paced across the meeting area in the Guardian Hall towards Erik and Andra, who were standing by the doors. 'What are our visitors doing?'

'Nothing,' said Erik.

'They've sat on their horses at the end of the village without moving or speaking since they arrived,' Andra added.

'Not even to each other?' asked Kevin.

'No.'

'They are disciplined,' said Liam. 'Too much so. They are dangerous.' He clapped the two young Guardians on the shoulders and gestured that they should move to the meeting area. 'The Council will agree to send at least some of us. That is certain. I'm bound by the Guardian Master to remain here. But I have a plan.' Liam leaned forward conspiratorially. 'Kevin, I want you to find the Guardian Master and bring him back to the village. You must seek him in the mountains, and you must not fail. These two, and I, will go with the soldiers in the morning, if the Council directs us to do so. We'll try to slow their progress beyond the Spurs on the Outward Road, until the Guardian Master can reach us, if that is his wish. Stephen and Alain will be told to stay at their watch points to escape this fate. They will protect The Vale.' He looked each companion deliberately in the eye. 'It is a dangerous plan. Will you accept it?' All three nodded. Andra felt the pit of his stomach tighten. 'As it is,' said Liam.

The Haardrishii warriors remained motionless and silent throughout the afternoon, until the Sun Fall horn echoed across The Vale. Senok emerged from the Hall of Council and casually joined his followers. Master Renfrey emerged and came towards the Guardian Hall. Liam met him at the entrance. 'What is the Council's decision?' he asked.

'I will tell you, and the others, later. Gather your things, and bring them to the Hall. Tonight, you will sleep there. The Haardrishii will sleep in your quarters.' He didn't wait for a reply, but left.

Liam turned to his companions. 'It's as I guessed. Come, gather your gear. Leave nothing valuable to tempt these King's men,' he added contemptuously.

The gloom of the Council Hall matched Andra's mood. As he and his companions sat in the Inner Circle, the oak door opened, admitting Stephen and Alain. 'Who's on watch?' Liam asked of Master Renfrey.

'No one,' Master Renfrey replied. 'Council has matters of urgency to discuss with all of you. The Vale must care for itself tonight.'

'The Guardian Master would not allow this!' Liam angrily challenged.

126

'The Guardian Master would not approve of a Guardian rebuking the Master of The Vale within the Hall of Council of Law either,' croaked a withered voice. Everyone turned to the oldest man of the village, Master Geat. 'Sit, young man,' he quietly told Liam. 'Time is too short to waste in argument.' Andra saw Liam hesitate, but he acquiesced and sat.

'I will explain as much as I can, but briefly,' said Master Renfrey. 'You may ask questions, if I do not answer your thoughts in my speech.' He moved to the centre, beside the dead ash and coals in the fire pit. The last grey daylight angled through a gap in the roof to lay a mantle on his shoulders and created a soft halo about the edges of his hair. The effect gave the Master of The Vale's normally solid figure an ethereal quality, but his face was obscured by shadow. 'The world you know is The Vale,' he began. 'It is our world. Your ancestors were born here. Most of them walked their worldly paths here, and their remains lay in the Caves of the Dead. The Vale is ancient. Our Way and our Laws are ancient. We live in a constant world. But, beyond The Vale, lies a larger world, a world of Great Kings - the world of Thana. That world is a place of constant change. Great Kings come and go. Their laws change. Before Great King Thana came to the throne, King Naxos ruled his lands. Before him, Queen Lycanae reigned, and the sons and grandsons of Aian Abreotan the Dragonslayer. Before King Abreotan, Mareg the Dragonlord annexed the lands, and before his evil rule, the lands were simply called The Land. Always, throughout these changes, The Vale has existed, and for much of recent time The Vale has been left alone, left apart from the broader world, left in peace.' He took a breath. 'Yet we also remain part of that world, sworn to serve those who rule it. That is The Way of The Vale. All who serve on the Council of Law swore allegiance to Great King Thana when we took our places. Such is The Way.

Many generations have passed since any of our people were called to serve the rulers beyond The Vale. The last time, they were volunteers who chose to aid young King

127

Naxos defend the eastern borders of his Kingdom. In volunteering, they also protected The Vale, because we live in the eastern part, and the threat affected us as much as it affected the Kingdom. Now a great war threatens to erupt from the north. Devi Senok told us the forces of the Dark Ones are rising in the lands of Uz Erhaag, as they did long ago. Throughout Thana, small bands of Haagii, the strangers we have already seen here, are raiding travellers and merchant wagons, and pillaging villages, stealing and wantonly killing. They are spreading like a sickening disease, and their numbers multiply daily. The Great King is massing his armies to take the war to the Haagii, and drive the pestilence from the Kingdom before it becomes too widespread. He and his Royal Advisors believe that is the right path to follow. It is the path they've chosen. And that's why the Haardrishii are here.

We must send what help we can to the Great King. The Council has spoken with Devi Senok. We told him we need protection in The Vale because the strangers have already touched us. Devi Senok granted that we might keep two Guardians to watch and protect us.' Andra saw Liam move, as if to speak, but Master Renfrey glared at him, so he bit his lip irritably. The other Guardians shifted uneasily. 'Do not underestimate the Council, Liam,' said Master Renfrey. 'We know two Guardians could not keep The Vale safe from harm. So, we've ensured that more will stay.' Master Renfrey squatted and beckoned the Guardians to come closer. 'Listen to my words, and then forget you ever heard them spoken. We profaned these sacred walls of truth-speaking with lies today, but it is time for decisions of necessity. Devi Senok has seen only six Guardians. We told him we have only six young men of age and training to serve as Guardians. He knows nothing of the others in the mountains. So, four of you will go, two will stay. That is the decision. Council has agreed this is what will be. This way, we honour the request of the Great King, and keep The Vale safe from further threats from Haagii wanderers.'

The last daylight struggled into the Hall, as the Master of

The Vale concluded, faltered, failed, and darkness pressed in. Andra could only distinguish a bulky shadow standing in the centre of the circle. The Master's words echoed in his thoughts. Four must go. Two stay. A great war. Lands beyond The Vale. Haagii. The group sat, rooted to their log benches, locked in individual thoughts.

'Who will go?' Liam asked.

A moment passed, before Master Renfrey answered. 'We could not decide. Council could not name them. You must decide. You each must consider the path you are following now, and the path you will be following this time tomorrow. Four will be following a path beyond The Vale. Tonight, in the Hall of Council, you must decide.'

A further pause followed. 'I will light the torches,' Mistress Orlin quietly offered. 'There will be food brought soon. Master Tomas, can you see to that?'

A shuffling, a stumble, and Andra sensed a figure making for the oaken door. A scraping of flint came from the side wall, and the first torch flickered into life. Mistress Orlin cast an imposing shadow. Andra turned to his mother, and found Anedra gazing at him, from across the circle, studying him, trying to read his thoughts, as he was trying to read hers. He stared into her face, recognising the beauty of the woman who'd borne him in her arms, laughing and smiling, but he seemed to be watching her from a distance, and she was gazing through him, past him. Then she softly smiled.

'We will share food. Your fathers and mothers will join us,' said Master Renfrey as the last torch was lit. 'When we have feasted, we will leave you to your decisions.' As he finished, Master Tomas returned, leading several women and younger girls who carried platters and bowls of food, and jugs of water and milk for the feasting. The families of the Guardians entered and joined the hearth circle. Master Renfrey lit the fire and stoked the coals, and soon the Hall was filled with sounds of talking, laughter, and eating.

Andra ate, and shared his thoughts with his parents, Malcolm and Anedra, and he drank in the pictures of activity. The Vale was alive – filled with joy and love and caring – but, when he saw the Master of The Vale in the dancing light, the man looked visibly aged. His broad shoulders and tall frame were bowed under an invisible weight, and he stood apart from everyone, unsmiling. And when Andra re-joined conversation with his family, he remained acutely sensitive of his mother's gaze, looking at him as if she was searching for an answer – asking him why.

It was settled. Liam, Stephen, Alain and Andra would go with the Haardrishii. Erik would keep watch on the village. In the morning, they would explain Kevin's absence by saying he'd left early to set watch over the Northern Spur. Kevin gathered leftover food from the eating, collected his staff, whispered luck to his friends, and slipped out of the Hall and into the night. They waited nervously, as he crept out of the village and into the eastern hills, but no one stirred, so they returned to their makeshift beds around the glowing hearth and drifted into fitful sleep for their last night in The Vale.

The moon made vain attempts to peep between the ragged clouds, and a cold, biting breeze cut into The Vale from the south. The huts of the tiny village huddled like cattle on the meadows, waiting for approaching winter winds and rains to lash them. Outside the Guardian Hall, masked in shadow, a dark figure lingered. A solitary moonbeam touched an arm, and black metal glinted, as the figure silently stared at the eastern ridge above Master Flintok's pigpen.

Sixteen

The Outward Road sloped steeply into the Valley of Rivers forest, where the tree canopy stretched westward to the rugged faces of the Andrakian Mountains like a sea of green into which the party of travellers were sinking. Andra had watched the face of the forests for several days from the Southern Spur, but now his companions and he were walking into a land none had entered. Beneath the canopy, the Outward Road disappeared between large tree trunks into a twilight aura, and Andra felt apprehension, because he was leaving behind a world of security and meaning to plunge into a world full of uncertainties, a world where he no longer had importance as an individual. The guarded nature of the eight Haardrishii astride their smooth black horses, silently pacing the four young Guardians, only filled him with less confidence as The Vale dissolved in their wake.

When they gathered outside the Hall of Council at Sun Call, the dying echoes of the Sun Caller's horn struck a chord in Andra's heart, its melancholy sound reminding him of his sorrow at leaving The Vale. Malcolm and Anedra embraced him. For the first time that he could remember, his mother's cheeks were wet with tears as she urged him to take care during his service in the Kingdom. But his father surprised him most of all, because Malcolm brought a gift, wrapped in oiled cloth; an old sword, and a belt and scabbard. 'Here,' he said. 'Wear it well. Your grandfather was Cedwyn, Master Swordmaker, and he wrought this blade in a place beyond The Vale, long ago. It has never seen battle, and it is of little use here, but where you choose to go, my son, such a weapon will have its use.' As Andra accepted the gift, Malcolm retained his grip on it, and in a commanding tone said, 'I charge you, as my son, to keep the sword with you, always. Lend it to no man. Use it only when you must. And remember the teachings of The Way before you resort to this weapon. Am I understood?' Andra nodded assent. He strapped the sword securely to his back, but he couldn't suppress his wonder at the gift, or the sword's existence in his family.

Kevin's absence wasn't queried when Liam gave his explanation. Devi Senok and Master Renfrey exchanged formal farewells, before the party of eight riders and four walkers left. Children walked, skipped, and ran beside the group for a short distance beyond the village, but they stopped once they crested the first hillock on the Outward Road, and watched with wide, inquiring eyes, as the four young village men trailed in the wake of the dark riders.

The dark forest greedily swallowed them, and, barely a few paces in, Andra felt it was almost necessary to light a torch. He turned to his companions to comment, but only Liam nodded understanding, and he remained tight lipped. As his eyes adjusted to the dappled light, Andra noticed changes. The Outward Road continued its gentle downward slope, but it was increasingly covered with debris. Dry rivulets and runnels, filled with small, smooth pebbles, and larger creeks, cluttered with flat stones and dead wood, tracked the ground contours, crisscrossing the forest floor and the Outward Road. The trees appeared to have an ancient agreement to evenly space their trunks, and, the deeper into the forest they travelled, the wider the spaces became. The trunks were solid, smooth, and rose as straight as arrow shafts to the height of four people, before branching into intertwining boughs and leaves. Thick berry bushes clustered where the sunlight filtered through to the ground, and lichen, bracken and moss festooned rocks. The forest floor was littered with a rich carpet of dead vegetable matter.

Time lost perspective. Rare patches of sunlight afforded glimpses of the sun's direction and angle, but Andra felt as though he had been walking for days. The group's silent progress annoyed him. Eventually, it mystified him. The Haardrishii were closed within the metal bounds of their armour, and Liam, Stephen and Alain were content to keep to themselves. Only the steady clip-clop of horse's hooves, and infrequent chatter of unseen birds, high in the trees, broke the silence.

The Outward Road reached a fork. One road led south, dipping and twisting lower among the trees. The second wound north. A short distance from the fork, Devi Senok reined in and motioned with his right hand. The Haardrishii turned their horses from the road, and moved quietly into the trees, and began to dismount. Senok wheeled his horse and casually approached the Guardians. 'We wait here for the others to come,' Senok explained. 'Go and rest, and eat, in the trees.'

'Who and what others?' Liam asked.

'The rest of my company.' The conversation was over. Senok turned his horse smartly, touched its flank with his heel, and cantered to the fork. He stopped, and waited in full view of the open roads.

'That one's evil,' Alain muttered, staring at the Haardrishii leader.

'Not evil,' replied Liam. 'Cold. No blood of life runs through his veins. He has no feelings. They have been trained out of him.'

Andra continued to stare at the silhouette of horse and rider fused to a spot in the fork. Liam's observation of lifelessness was too true. Stephen broke into his thoughts, saying, 'Come, Andra. We have a chance to sit and eat. Let's not waste our time with these blackbirds.' Andra nodded and followed his friends into a space between the trees.

Once they'd shared a meal, Liam called them together. He judged the proximity of the nearest Haardrishii, and, satisfied his lowered voice would not be heard, he outlined his plan. 'We must encourage our hosts to travel slowly. It's fortunate that they've already decided to wait here. I hadn't expected such luck. But we must use it to our advantage and stall them. Kevin will bring the Guardian Master and the others, and we will leave these vassals of the King to tend to other matters. Our sworn duty is to The Vale. The Kingdom has many others to protect it. Without us, The Vale will have no one.'

Andra obediently listened, but as Liam continued, he became aware of growing concern spreading across Stephen's countenance, and when Liam paused Stephen spoke out. 'Liam, the Guardian Master placed you in charge for his absence. You have made the serious decision whether we should go with the King's men. You made an honourable decision, according to The Way. We hid the existence of the others so they could remain as Guardians. In turn, we are here. But your plan to return us to The Vale is not sound. It will bring disaster. These black warriors will only be replaced by many others who will come to take whatever they want from The Vale in the name of the Great King.'

The accusation stung Liam. He retorted with, 'You would rather go with these soldiers and leave The Vale unprotected, would you?'

'No,' Stephen firmly replied. 'I will go with them to ensure The Vale is protected.'

They faced each other, for several uncomfortable moments, until Liam broke the impasse. 'So be it,' he said. 'The Guardian Master will come. Let him decide who has learned the better lesson.' Liam's response was respectable, but Andra recognized that the icy underlying emotion in his words highlighted a wide rift between the two Guardians, and the rift disappointed him. He wanted them to clasp hands, forgive each other, and be friends, but he didn't know how to draw them together. He looked to Alain, who was staring in bewilderment at him.

'On your feet!' Senok called from his horse. The Guardians gathered their sacks and goods, and trudged to the Outward Road, where the Haardrishii were assembled in two columns and waiting. At the fork, Andra saw a second troop of Haardrishii, greater in number than the Guardians' escort.

'Where have they come from?' whispered Alain.

'Senok was waiting for them,' Liam explained. 'And it appears we're not the only ones to volunteer for service in the King's army.' At the rear of the new column were two large wooden wagons, drawn by oxen, with cages, and in the cages sat a collection of shabbily dressed men and women. 'They were obviously reluctant to come,' Liam observed. Devi Senok saluted the Haardrishii horseman at the head of the new troop with a clenched right hand and fell in beside him. The company moved forward, and the four Guardians and their escort pulled in behind the lumbering wagons.

Hampered by dry creek beds, and stony runnels cutting across the rocky, winding southern road, they made slow progress. The oxen moved with dogged determination, and the wagons clattered and heaved from side to side over each obstacle, with frequent oaths bursting from the occupants who were thrown about by the rough travel. The undergrowth thickened as they travelled. Squirrels, and tawny-coated rabbits, paused to watch the passing procession of silent horsemen and noisy cages before skittering into cover. Elk appeared in the later afternoon, the larger animals well into the forest for the time of year, which Andra knew signalled the approach of a cold, hard winter in the foothills and mountains. There would be snow in The Vale.

The column halted, before evening, at a point on the road where the overhead canopy thinned appreciably to form a clearing. Two creeks encircled either side of the clearing, and lush green grass and clumps of blackberry bushes flourished at its centre. The road wound around the western end, but the Haardrishii crossed the shallow creek, into the clearing, to set camp. Senok sent the four Guardians and two Haardrishii into the forest to gather firewood. The task was onerous, since the only wood at ground level, close to camp, was large trunks and boughs, and they struggled with heavy burdens. When they returned, four Haardrishii, in full armour, set to chopping the logs as the light waned.

'Don't they ever take their blasted armour off?' bellowed a captive from the wagons. Curious as to the source, the Guardians approached. The Haardrishii ignored them, and the guard at the wagons stepped aside. The voice's owner greeted them. 'So. We're permitted to meet.' The man's physical bulk, even crouched in the cage, was intimidating. His shoulders were broad, his arms knotted with muscle. Andra was certain the man would stand at least a full head taller than he, or any of his companions. He wore crude leather leggings and a loose jerkin laced over his massive chest, and his face was hidden beneath a thick, matted rust coloured beard, the same shade as his shaggy hair. Three more men, and five women, smaller in stature, but comparable in dress and muscular conditioning, were crammed into the cage behind him. Andra counted eight more men squatted in the second cage. 'I take it you also joined the Great King's Armies. Freely, I might suggest, by your condition,' the red giant quipped.

'We are physically free. But not in spirit,' Liam replied. 'And we may not yet be joining the King's army.'

The man in the cage tipped back his head and laughed heartily. 'Oho! An interesting answer!' he exclaimed, and his companions laughed with him. 'And why are you so certain you have a choice?'

Liam stared at the man. 'That,' he said slowly, 'I cannot say.'

The red-haired giant chuckled. 'So be it. Keep your secrets as you please.'

'Who are you?' Stephen asked.

'I am Claarn the Red,' the big man responded, 'Keeper of Tressel Deep. And these are my travelling companions on this wondrous journey to the place of kings - Korgan, Marella, Aian of the River, Nessa, Talan, Mercur, Larsa, Pearl.' As Claarn the Red introduced each prisoner, they nodded, grinning at their leader's royal tone. 'Well met, hearty fellows, on this free and open road!' Claarn concluded with an attempted sweep of his broad arm, but he only succeeded in barking his knuckles on the rough wooden cage, bringing a roar of laughter from his companions. He feigned brief anger before composing himself, to ask, 'To whom do we speak?'

Liam introduced the Guardians, but he said nothing of The Vale in his response. Claarn didn't appear to acknowledge Liam's omission. He seemed content with their names. 'How did you end up in these cages?' asked Stephen.

Claarn laughed again. 'Simple,' he said. 'We defied the Great King's men. These black vultures rode into the Deep several days back, and their captain spoke with Lord Radnell. The Lord sent for us and told us the soldiers of the Great King had come to take volunteers for the Great King's Armies. He didn't want us to go, unless we wanted to. Well, Lord Radnell has always been good to us.' Nods and murmurs of approval came from the other prisoners. 'No one wanted to leave the Deep, so Lord Radnell told the captain that there were no volunteers, and the Great King would have to look elsewhere. Well, ten of the vultures came back the next day to take whomever they wanted. We stood our ground at the head of the Deep and sent them packing. Lord Radnell had ordered us not to kill any of them, so we didn't. We took the armour off those we caught, and sent them skulking back, naked, to their captain. They're men enough, when that fancy black metal is stripped away.'

'And not as big a man as you Claarn, you big python,' chortled the woman named Marella. General laughter followed her ribald quip.

'And you should know best of all,' retorted Claarn, to another burst of laughter, and Marella hit him playfully on the head. 'So we celebrated,' he continued. 'We drank and laughed and sang into the night. But we hadn't figured on their returning with thrice that number. We battled long and hard for two days. We slew none of their men, for Lord Radnell had ordered it so, but seven of our people were killed. They drove us back into the very gates of Lord Radnell's stone keep, and there we gave them a lusty fight, one of the best. For all their pompous armour, these black vultures are good warriors, and worthy opponents in battle. I would have enjoyed fighting them to the death. But, in the end, Lord Radnell asked us to put aside our weapons, and we did. Seventeen of us were taken and caged by the vultures. We are in the Great King's Armies. But it was a good fight!' he grinned. 'A good fight, win or lose, is a good fight,' he added, and looked to the four Guardians for approval of his warrior's philosophy. Andra smiled, fascinated by the giant's casual nature, even in defeat, but he felt Alain tugging at his arm, and turned. Three Haardrishii were walking swiftly towards them. 'Aha! We've spoken too long,' said Claarn loudly. 'Take heed, my new friends. Be cautious with our black hosts.' The leading Haardrishii indicated for the Guardians to move away from the wagons, towards where Senok stood in the company of the horseman who led the second company. All four followed the silent instruction. 'Good! Good! Be obedient! Serve your new masters well!' Claarn taunted at their backs. 'You are the Great King's soldiers now, just like us!'

'It is The Way,' Andra heard Stephen say quietly.

'For now,' Liam responded, in a half-whisper.

Dusky gloom spread through the trees. The air was cold. Hordes of insects swirled above patches of broken earth and stagnant pools in the streambeds. Crickets rasped a rhythmic cacophony to celebrate the enclosing night. Locked away beneath the forest trees, an alien presence closed about the campsite. Three low fires crackled near the camp's centre, and a single, dark, motionless figure sat at each. The glow from the furthermost fire barely reached the first prison wagon, where Claarn and his friends huddled, sleeping.

Senok was brief with his words, earlier in the evening. He introduced the Guardians to the second Haardrishii leader, Devi Neylor. Andra understood the word Devi implied rank, but neither Haardrishii wore distinguishing features to signify their position. As far as he'd seen, the only distinction between the Devis and the soldiers was the formers' right to speak and give orders. Then Senok took a risk before he dismissed the Guardians. He informed them they were to take their turn in the watch that night. When he walked to the horses with Neylor, the Guardians conversed excitedly.

'If we are going to escape,' said Alain, 'this has to be the one opportunity.'

'You're a fool!' snapped Liam. 'He's trying to trap us into doing exactly that. Give him an excuse, and he'll slap us into the carts with Claarn's lot.'

'So why put us in charge of a section of the watch?' asked Andra.

'Simple,' said Liam. 'To tire us and rest his men. He suspects us.'

'I do not think that is true,' Stephen argued. 'I think he is testing us.'

Liam shook his head, but Andra understood the implication of Stephen's comment. 'You mean he wants to test our loyalty?'

'Yes. As the Guardian Master would test us. I do not believe he wants us to fail, either, or he would not have offered the responsibility so curtly or indifferently.'

'Surely you don't expect us to obey his order?' Liam asked.

'I do,' replied Stephen. 'That is The Way.'

Andra took second watch. Alain finished his turn and went to eat. Liam and Stephen were sleeping. He huddled into the roots of a giant oak and stared north, along the winding road, as the last vestiges of light disintegrated. The sounds of the waking night echoed through the forest. Invisible birds trilled shrilly. Crickets increased their song intensity. Flutterings, scratchings, scrapings kept Andra alert, as he peered into the night, forcing his eyes to discern impressions of light or movement. The watch, he realized, relied on senses other than sight. Twice he was certain he heard the shuffling of larger creatures along or across the road, but the sounds were brief, and ceased as soon as he began to focus on them. When Liam came to relieve him, he was exhausted, and he gladly scrambled back to the camp to collapse into deep sleep.

Guttural cries. Muffled screams. Chaos. Metal clashed. Confusion. In the red fire glow, figures appeared - black armour - leather - weapons glinting - disappeared. Shouting from the wagons. Andra struggled to his feet. A bulky figure loomed out of the darkness and knocked him over. More shouts. He looked up. A black figure moved by him. A groan. A body fell against the earth. More shapes leapt across the open space at the fires. One fell into a hearth, sending sparks flying in a red and gold shower into the night. The fleeing figures hit a solid wall of darkness at the edge of the clearing. Screams. Bodies fell. Others reeled back into the circle of fires, staggered, crumpled like sacks. The darkness at the edge closed in. Haardrishii. As he gathered his wits, Andra heard faint shouting in the woods. Silence. 'Are you alright Andra?' Alain's voice.

'Yes.'

Stephen stepped out of the darkness. 'Come. Let us see what happened.'

Seventeen

Claarn tossed aside the plate of gruel that Andra handed through the bars, and bellowed furiously, 'I am a warrior! No warrior is left out of a fight!' He smashed his fists against the bars. Grunts of dissension rose from his caged companions. 'How many of the Dark Ones were there?'

'Liam said the Haardrishii caught fourteen,' he replied.

'Only fourteen? Dead?'

'Yes. All of them.'

Disappointment clouded Claarn's face. 'How many of the black soldiers are hurt?'

'None.'

'Pity!' Claarn spat. 'It would do them good to bleed. Perhaps they'd see we are needed outside of these cages. We would fight well together.'

Andra excused himself, after he finished doling out food and water to the captives, and crossed the clearing, past the heaped corpses of dead Haagii. He glanced at the pile and shuddered as he recalled his flight through the marshes of The Vale. Last night, death brushed by a second time, fortuitously diverted by a Haardrishii sword. In one of many lessons, the Guardian Master told them that, in the Outer World, beyond The Vale, there were foolish men and women who entrusted their lives to good fortune. They called it luck. That was not The Way. Guardians were taught to rely on skill and knowledge of The Way for protection. Luck had nothing to do with life in The Vale. Yet Andra knew he'd already had a share of luck. He lifted his hand to his cheek and touched his scar, remembering his night of terror. He looked again at the bodies of the Haagii and wondered whether his own should have been lying there in the pile after last night.

'Andra!' Liam called. 'Come! Prepare yourself. The Haardrishii are ready to leave.' Andra nodded, and considered how much Liam had changed since the Guardian

Master journeyed into the mountains. He was fresh and young, but leadership made him more like the Guardian Master - abrupt, cautious – and youth had disappeared from his face.

Dull light filtered through the trees, as the company crossed the pebble-strewn creek bed. The wagons rattled and shook, and curses burst from the caged passengers. Andra smelt moisture; a close, cool, sweet smell, mixed with the trees' fragrant juices, and the rotting compost on the forest floor. The rains were coming. From what he could see, the forest would become a maze of watercourses, rushing down from the mountains into the lake in the south, and travel would be arduous and dangerous. If the rains were constant and heavy, the roads would be impassable.

Throughout the day, the Haardrishii Devis set a brisk traveling pace. Andra and Alain were ordered to pass food and water to Claarn and his followers on the move, while two Haardrishii teamsters prodded and cajoled the oxen. It seemed the Haardrishii well understood the necessity to be out of the Valley of Rivers before the rains came. The road followed a tortuous route south, avoiding deeper sluiceways and channels, and dense thickets, winding in and back like a demented, rough-scaled serpent set loose in unfamiliar territory. The main Haardrishii body rode in two lines, but six horsemen were dispersed at various points off the road to shadow the column as outriders, keeping watch for the Haagii.

By late afternoon, Andra's calves and lower back ached. He was conditioned to long periods of running and walking, but he also recognised weariness. The rugged, uneven forest floor was testing his fitness gained from flat valleys and sloping hills, so he tried to forget his discomfort in idle chatter with Alain, and occasional trips to the wagons with water skins.

Claarn greeted him with burly humour, and the others in the wagons took interest in him. They exchanged names. Marella and Talan shared their version of their capture at Tressel Deep. Andra told them how he came to be accompanying the Haardrishii. The prisoners spoke roughly, even with a little contempt, about the Haardrishii, but they respected the prowess of their captors, respected the skill and commitment and loyalty of hardened warriors. Their difference in nature and philosophy, from people Andra knew in The Vale, filled him with increasing curiosity. He knew he was asking too many questions, but he asked regardless, first about Tressel Deep and their homes, and then about Lord Radnell, and lastly about themselves.

'Why are you a warrior?' he asked Marella, as he passed her a cup of water. He tried not to stare at the young woman in the cart, but he couldn't resist. All the women were attractive – dark skinned, with long hair – except Larsa, whose skin was a shade lighter, and her hair deep red. All had the physical conditioning of trained warriors - strong, lithe bodies, honed to athletic perfection. Andra had never seen women, or girls, like them in The Vale. In fact, it occurred to him, as he watched the women while he was walking, that he'd never taken much interest in the women, or girls, of The Vale. The village women were older, and the wives of other men, and the girls were at least three full summers younger than him.

'Why are you a warrior?' Marella retorted, with a flick of her tangled hair. She gazed at him confidently from deep green eyes.

'I mean,' said Andra, feeling foolish, 'I mean why does the Deep have women as warriors, as well as men?' He phrased his question awkwardly and knew it. He stared through a loose tie in Marella's leather jerkin at an exposed portion of her breasts, and when he looked up he looked straight into her eyes. Caught. He stumbled, regained his footing beside the wagon, and turned to watch where he was walking.

A knowing smile touched Marella's lips as she answered his question. 'Not all women in Tressel Deep are warriors. Are there any in your village?'

'No,' he replied. 'Only men learn The Way of a Guardian.'

'Then your village has many men?'

'No. The Guardian Master said we don't have enough

men to become Guardians. So did Liam.'

'So it was in Tressel Deep,' interjected Talan, 'for a long time. And much danger came to the Keep, because Lord Radnell's grandfather had too few trained men to defend the whole of Tressel Deep. Even boys were used, but they were too weak, too inexperienced, and too few.'

'Lord Radnell's grandmother,' Marella continued, 'was a person full of fire. She rallied the women of the Keep, and together they held back Lord Radnell's enemy from the southern wall, while the men fought in the main gates. The enemy fell back. The Deep was released. And so it was that old Lady Radnell forced her husband to accept that women should be trained as soldiers in the same fashion as his men. It was the only way Lord Radnell could field a large enough force to protect the Deep from intruders. Like you, I choose to be a warrior because it is the strongest way I know I have to protect my people.'

Andra didn't look up, but he listened closely. He'd never thought of women as Guardians in The Vale. His mother served on Council, but she was different from the other women because she had a commanding presence, and a keen intelligence. He couldn't picture her wielding a staff, or sword, against enemy warriors.

'Have you a woman in your home?' Marella asked.

'Yes. My mother,' he innocently replied. The wagon erupted in a burst of raucous laughter that stopped him in his tracks. What had he said wrong? He stared at the men and women, laughing at him with wild-eyed amusement, as they rocked and swayed in their cages.

The figure stood in the middle of the road. Silent. Dark. Unmoving. The column of riders stopped. 'Who is it?' Andra whispered to Alain. The latter shook his head.

'He's come!' Liam announced.

'Who?' asked Andra.

'The Guardian Master.'

'Alone,' added Stephen. The Guardians passed the lines

of Haardrishii to the head of the company.

The Guardian Master stood balanced, legs apart, staff in his left hand, one end firmly rooted in the road. Dusk was descending on the forest, but a single ray of sunlight angled behind the Guardian Master, adding a dimension of luminescent power to his imposing appearance. He spoke in a cool, controlled, deliberate manner. 'Senok, I would speak with you. Alone.'

Andra looked up at Devi Senok, who was making complex gestures with his hand to Devi Neylor. When Neylor nodded in understanding, Senok dismounted.

'Come!' said Liam. 'We'll join the Master,' and he started to move forward.

'Stay where you are!' Senok curtly commanded.

Andra, Alain, and Stephen obeyed. Liam looked at them with silent appeal, but when he saw that they were unwilling to disobey Senok he shrugged with reluctant resignation and stepped back beside them.

The Haardrishii strolled towards the waiting Guardian Master, moving smoothly, unencumbered by his snugly fitting black armour, until the two men faced each other. If they were talking, there was no indication. Andra saw no gestures, no movement. Then, as if by mutual assent, the men stepped back. Senok removed his black helmet. The Guardian Master removed his pack. For another moment, they faced each other, rigid, patient. In a blur of action, sword and staff collided overhead. The ringing clash of metal reached the watchers.

Liam grabbed his staff, urged his companions to follow, and started towards the fight, but a black Haardrishii horse cut off his path. Infuriated, he swung his staff at the rider, but Devi Neylor deftly leaned away from the flashing weapon's path. Liam swung again. This time Neylor let the staff find a mark - his left hand. He grabbed the end and held it rigid. Liam was amazed by the horseman's extraordinary strength. 'Put it down,' Neylor ordered firmly. 'This is not your fight.' Liam tried in vain to wrench his staff free of the Haardrishii's grip. 'Put it down,' Neylor repeated. Liam glared, but he relented. Neylor released the staff and backed his steed away.

Liam turned to his companions. 'Why didn't you help?'

'As Neylor said,' replied Stephen, 'it is not our fight. The Guardian Master has chosen this confrontation for reasons only he knows. We must watch. It is The Way.'

'I'm tired of The Way,' Liam muttered despondently.

The fight intensified. The combatants swung, parried, thrust, and turned away their opponent's weapon with precision. Neither held advantage. As Andra watched the conflict in awe, he felt as though he was watching a dance - a ritual. The warriors appeared perfectly versed in each other's movements, knowing, before it came, what the next action would be. The weapons arced through the air, and clashed, ringing with energy, as the two men danced in the darkening roadway.

'And who commands you now, in the Great City?' asked the Guardian Master, between mouthfuls of tender baked rabbit.

'Surdrok. The Surly One,' replied Senok. 'He replaced Dominic.'

'It was time,' the Guardian Master noted, with a nod. 'Dominic is old enough to sit on the Great Council of Elders. But I see he taught you well.'

'Yes,' said Senok simply, and continued eating.

'So. What is this Surdrok like?'

Senok looked up from the crackling fire, and Andra spotted a hint of bitterness in the Haardrishii's eyes. 'Surdrok is harsh and cruel. There is mad dog in his breeding. Dominic was a strong disciplinarian, but this one is ruthless without feeling. He knows nothing of the Old Way or the Silent Order.'

'How was he chosen?'

Senok shook his head as he put down the bones of his meal. 'He wasn't chosen. The Great King ignored the Old Way. The Great Council of Elders was not consulted. The

Silent Order was not invited to choose. He did not come from the ranks of the Silent Order, as Dominic, or the others have done. He is an outsider. He has the stature of a Shaddite - solid, not tall - and ugliness, not unlike the Haagii. The Great King commissioned him. But many say the Great King's new Advisor appointed him, in return for an old favour.' Senok stared into the fire. 'You should not have left, Artega. You would have been Dominic's successor, had you remained.'

The use of the Guardian Master's name, and the Haardrishii's tone, along with a sigh of disappointment, caught the attention of the four young Guardians. The Guardian Master's unspoken past lay before them. He had been Haardrishii before coming to The Vale. 'I could not stay,' Artega quietly replied. 'You know that. I felt the direction of The Way, and it led me here. Here I must stay,'

'But your talent is wasted here, Artega,' Senok insisted. 'You could have trained many Haardrishii in the skills of sword and staff. Return with us. There's still time. Your skills are needed by the Order. And there is a great peril rising in the north.'

Artega shook his head. 'No. No, my young friend, I stay here, in The Vale. My skills are not wasted. I've trained many warriors in The Way. You have four here, and they will serve the Great King well. But I will stay and teach others. And when the time comes to meet the northern threat, let Great King Thana know the Valley of Rivers is secure, and at peace.'

'As you wish,' Senok replied. He leaned forward to stir the glowing coals.

Alain tugged Andra's jerkin. Andra looked at Alain, who nodded towards Liam. Their companion was walking away. 'Excuse us, Guardian Master,' said Stephen, as he rose, and the younger Guardians followed. They caught Liam at the edge of the campsite, staring blankly into the wall of darkness of the forest. They stood beside him, Stephen imitating his gaze, and Andra and Alain studied his partially visible face. Stephen broke the tableau. 'What thoughts run through your mind, Liam?' Liam's eyes remained fixed on the darkness. 'A Guardian does not hide his secrets from a fellow

Guardian. That is not The Way,' said Stephen, attempting to coax him to talk.

Liam whirled on his companion, rage searing his face. 'Damn you, Stephen!' he spat. 'Damn you and The Way! Are you deaf? Blind? Don't you understand what just happened? Can't you see?'

Andra recoiled from Liam's anger, but Stephen remained facing him. 'What should I see?' he passively asked.

Liam threw up his hands in frustrated disbelief. 'You don't see it, do you? No, of course not! You couldn't,' he said, and exhaled heavily.

'Tell us. Perhaps we can help,' Stephen offered.

'Help?' asked Liam. 'How can you help?' A desperate laugh escaped his lips. 'You can't help, you fools! You're as helpless as I am. And why? Because he sold you. Him!' He pointed directly at the campfire, but when they all turned they saw a figure less than an arm's length from the tip of Liam's accusing finger: Artega, Guardian Master. Liam's finger wavered, and fell, and he dropped his head. A horse whinnied from the far side of camp. Faint voices drifted in the air from the prisoner wagons.

'You are correct Liam. I have failed you,' said Artega sadly.

Liam lifted his head. 'I - I was angry Guardian Master. Forgive me,' he said, in a steady voice.

'You were not angry, Liam. You were much more. You should not ask my forgiveness. I ask it of you. I let you all be deliberately taken from The Vale, to become part of the Great King's Armies. I chose to let you go, but I did not ask if you wished to leave. In that, I have failed.'

Alain stumbled to intervene. 'But Master, you have come for us now.'

'No, Alain,' Artega quietly replied. 'I have not come to take you back.'

Understanding spread to all four Guardians in the darkness. 'Then why did you come?' asked Andra.

'To see an old friend,' Artega explained. 'And to see that you are treated as warriors, especially when you reach the

Great City.' He let his revelation sink in, before he continued. 'But now, Liam must be heard. You must choose your own paths from here.' He turned away, quietly returned to the fire in the tiny clearing.

All four Guardians watched the Guardian Master's back until he sat beside Senok. Stephen spoke first. 'Come. Night passes. Let us sleep before we are asked to take watch. We have a long way to travel.'

'My choice is already made,' said Alain to Andra. 'I'm keen to see the Great City. My father's spoken of it many times, and I've listened to the speeches of the travellers who've entered The Vale, so I'm not turning back.'

Andra laughed, and slapped Alain on the shoulder. 'So be it then. We must go to the Great City.'

Stephen inclined his head towards the place where Liam had been standing, and asked, 'Coming Liam?' But the young man had already melted into the darkness.

Eighteen

The forest dissolved in rain. Jewelled drops crashed through the leaf canopy, and a fine mist blanketed the air and tree trunks. The earth turned fluid and treacherous beneath their feet. Runnels became swollen creeks of mud, cutting back and forth across the forest floor, forcing the party to retrace their progress along the rapidly melting path. Andra drew the neck of his rough leather hide tighter about his chin, but the downpour trickled inside his tunic, and his leggings were thoroughly soaked from constant wading through knee-deep washes and turbulent streams. He measured each unsure step, glancing up every so often to see where Stephen's stooped back was leading him through the watery world. Ahead, and behind, Haardrishii riders picked paths between trees, rocks, and muddy swirls. Their black armour glistened, as if freshly forged and polished, but each rider bent to the rain's mastery, and their steeds stumbled forward in blind obedience to prods and nudges. The oxen wagons and their human burden formed a pitiful vision. The beasts dumbly struggled through obstacles, their hides matted, their hocks caked with mud and blood from falls, and great clouds of steam rose from their gaping mouths. In the wagons, beneath oilskins, Claarn and his people huddled for warmth, their boisterous, mocking voices silent. Rain dominated. Water roared in their ears.

Senok shifted in his saddle and squinted into the rain. He was frustrated. The rains had come too early. He had miscalculated their journey through the Valley of Rivers, and they were caught unnecessarily in a dangerous, alien environment. Surdrok would be angry. Haardrishii did not make mistakes - Devi Haardrishii especially so. For now, he had to lead the group to higher ground before the volumes of water, collecting in the ravines and vales of the mountains, burst their temporary confines and flooded the

Valley of Rivers. It was too late to turn back, to the town of Forge, and Mist was another two full days' travel south. So he had to find a natural haven.

Andra plodded through the rain with his companions. Liam had not returned. When Artega farewelled them, Liam was absent, and he hadn't reappeared in the two days since they passed through Forge. Stephen believed he returned to The Vale. His pride suffered a serious blow from the last lesson of the Guardian Master, and he would feel obliged to prove his worth as a Guardian, the path he chose as a youth. Stephen's reasoning was compelling, but Andra wanted to argue, although he couldn't fathom why. Liam's anger was directed at the Guardian Master and The Vale. Going back was only one of several possible choices for Liam. In fact, Andra expected to see him walking with them the following morning, and he was concerned when the young man failed to appear as the day drew on. 'Liam is strong,' Alain said. 'You worry too much, Andra.' And gradually Andra accepted that Stephen had to be right. Liam didn't appear. Then the rains came and dulled his thoughts.

The stream was shallow, but crossing it would be challenging because of the fierce current. Senok hand-signed an order to a horseman, who urged his horse into the stream. Muddied water swirled around the horse's legs, but the animal was strong, and drew confidence from its rider. On the far bank, the rider halted to signal that he was fine before he moved into the woods. Moments later, he emerged to signal that he'd found higher ground. Senok urged his horse into the boiling broth, and the others followed.

The crossing was relatively easy for the riders, but Andra and his companions struggled to keep their footing on the uneven pebbly bottom. Alain twisted, and plunged into the seething water, pulled out of Stephen's reach, but a Haardrishii rider wrenched him out, and lifted him onto the back of his black stallion. Before Andra or Stephen could marvel at the act, two more riders wheeled and worked their horses back to offer mounts to them.

For Claarn's people, hunched inside the wagons, the crossing was cruel. The oxen strained and bellowed, as four Haardrishii drove them into the stream, and the wagons rocked and lurched violently as their wooden wheels fought over submerged traps. The waters swirled into the cages, drenching the prisoners' feet and legs, and sweeping away loose bundles of belongings and supplies. A thunderous roar of water drowned all sound, but Andra knew the oaths and curses Claarn would be directing at the Haardrishii as the oxen lumbered out of the stream.

The high ground they had to climb rose abruptly, for fifty paces, and was slippery with patches of mud, wet grass, and thousands of rivulets. At the top, they could see a grove. Andra assessed that, if floods did sweep in from the Ureykyeu and Andrakian mountains, the hill would remain above water. The stream was creeping over its banks, into the trees, getting wilder by the moment.

Four Haardrishii coaxed their horses up the incline, the animals' hooves digging into the soft earth, slipping, digging again, slithering back, faltering, digging in again, gaining precious distance. Each horseman had a length of rope entwined about the pommel of the saddle and played it out as his mount gamely struggled against the treacherous surface. Andra willed the riders up the hill, then shouted, exhorting them to beat the elements. The horses strained, lunged, slipped, and struggled towards the trees. And then a rider fell. He toppled sideways, arms spread-eagled, and slid to the bottom. The broken haft of a wooden spear jutted from the dead warrior's neck. At the top, dark figures swarmed around the remaining three horsemen. Spears arced towards the troop at the bottom.

Chaos broke loose. A Haagii band burst through the streaming rain from the forest, charged through the stream, and crashed into the Haardrishii ranks. Warriors grappled and fell, rolling and writhing while they desperately tried to regain their feet to stay alive in the rain and mud. Stephen disappeared into the fight, and Alain followed.

Andra looked up to discover that the three Haardrishii horsemen had vanished in the turmoil. As he clambered past the wagons, intent on joining the fray, a huge arm grabbed his belt and pulled him against the wooden bars. 'Open it!' Claarn shouted, above the din. 'It's our only chance! Open it!' Andra stared into the red giant's fierce eyes and saw the fire raging within. 'Open it!' Claarn snarled.

'I don't have the keys!' Andra yelled.

'Then get them! And quick!' Claarn bellowed, and he released the youth.

Andra knew Senok had keys to the cages, as did Neylor, but finding individual Haardrishii on a battlefield was virtually impossible, because they wore identical black armour, regardless of rank. The only hope he held was that one of them was at the edge of the skirmish, directing the troop.

Luck was with him. He spied Neylor near the crumbling banks of the expanding stream that was fast becoming a swollen river. Two attackers lay motionless at his feet. Keys dangled from his belt. Skirting the brawling melee, Andra made for him, but when he indicated the keys Neylor shook his head. Andra made a second plea. Neylor shook his head. What could he do? He assessed the battle and was sure the Haardrishii were not in control. Senok was nowhere to be seen. Claarn's desperate order echoed in his mind. He lunged at the Haardrishii, but Neylor anticipated his move and stepped back - and fell, and the rushing waters swallowed him. Andra plunged into the muddy torrent and groped beneath the surface for the Devi's armour, hooked onto his belt, and with supreme effort dragged the spluttering and coughing Devi to the bank. As he hauled Neylor out of the water, he wrenched the keys from the Haardrishii's belt and scrambled back to the wagons.

He fumbled with the heavy iron locks, before turning the key and swinging open the gate. Claarn tore the keys from Andra's grip and tossed them to Talan, but he slapped the young Guardian on the shoulder, and yelled, 'We are in your debt, but for the moment we have other business!' He gathered his people and led them into the turmoil. Andra unhitched his staff and followed.

The earth churned to liquid underfoot, as bodies clashed and slithered with abandon in the morass. The Haagii mercenaries refused to yield before the skill and strength of the Haardrishii, but the battle was turning in the Haardrishii's favour. Andra glimpsed Senok rallying and orchestrating his men at the centre of the tumult, but his attention switched to a hulking Haagii warrior lumbering at him through the mud and rain, a pitted broad sword held menacingly in his right hand. The Haagii thrust at Andra, Andra sidestepped, and the Haagii lost his balance, falling on his face. Andra brought the tip of his staff smartly down on his attacker's neck, exerted too much force, and collapsed on the prostrate Haagii. His face buried into the Haagii's half-cured shaggy hide jerkin and the stench was unbearable. Someone wrenched at his arm, and he looked up to find Alain, with a mud-smeared face and a gaping cut across his cheek, motioning urgently for him to get up. He rose, and followed Alain up the slope, scrambling frantically, clinging to every meagre tuft of grass or secure rock with all the strength they could muster. Around him, Andra saw Haardrishii warriors climbing too, some on horses, some leading their animals, some without. The mad ascent pumped adrenalin through his veins and made him giddy, even as the drumming rain dulled his senses, until a subtle shift in the background sound stopped him. He peered into the rain at the others. They also had stopped, and they were staring down the hill.

The Haagii horde milled at the base, organising to pursue the Haardrishii. The keener ones were struggling up the first section of the slope. Ominous thunder rumbled across the Valley, and the earth vibrated beneath everyone's feet. The Haagii stopped. As the shaking spread, and grew in intensity, drowning the drum of the rain and rush of the wild river, Alain pointed to the west. The thunder reached a crescendo, and the Haagii scattered like ants before a strong gust of wind. The ring of trees at the base of the hill buckled, and a

154

boiling wall of water smashed through. The Haagii, the carts, corpses, and oxen were swept into a seething flood that rushed across the valley floor towards Rainbow Lake, the mistress to whom the flood bore its ragged toys and twisted gifts.

For a long time, the Haardrishii and Guardians sat in the rain, astonished by the devastation, watching the spinning and eddying waters. Then, as if a silent agreement passed between the Haardrishii, they rose to continue the climb. Andra and Alain exchanged glances, and followed the Haardrishii, weary beyond the limit of feeling.

They were last to reach the grove at the summit, and they were surprised to see the Haardrishii assembled in battle formation - until they saw the reason. At the grove's entrance, sheltered from the rain, Claarn, a sword in hand, blocked the way with his companions. For the first time, Andra saw the man's full stature, and even wet and bedraggled the Giant of Tressel Deep was imposing. Senok and Neylor faced Claarn, warily eyeing him, until Claarn lowered his sword, and laughed. He strode through the rain, gripped Senok's arm, elbow to wrist, and hugged him warmly. 'So,' he said, cheerily. 'I welcome a warrior and a brother. Come in from the rain. We have dead to mourn, songs to make.' With that, he led the company past the Haagii corpses, into the centre of the grove where the bodies of three Haardrishii

"A trap, set too surely, may fail by killing that which it only meant to catch."

from the Aelendyell Book of Lore

Nineteen

'I speak fourteen dialects and nine languages. I learned the Aelendyell tongue as a child. My mother took me on a journey through the western lands, and we stayed for a long time in the Forest of Thraka. We met and were feasted by Aelendyell. A Chanter named Baenowyth taught me the language.' Seralinna's eyes danced with memories, before she shook her long auburn tresses and smiled at A Ahmud Ki. 'But you are very different from anyone I've ever met. Your eyes, your language – they're Aelendyell – but you're too tall to be Aelendyell. And your name. It's adopted, isn't it?'

'I have Aelendyell blood, but I despise it,' A Ahmud Ki stated flatly. 'As for my name, I am A Ahmud Ki.' He wondered if she could read his mind and find fragments of Terin, the hunted Aelendyell outcast. If she could, she was subtle and clever, because he felt no mind search energy. He refrained from probing her thoughts in case she could detect his spying and know his spells. Whatever her intentions, he would let her make the first move. Then he would know more of her power, and her potential to threaten him. 'Where am I?'

Seralinna smiled again, with warmth that he could only perceive as friendliness. 'You are in the Travel Chamber of my Keep.'

'Do you know how far from Yul Ithrandyr your Keep is?' he asked.

'You come from Yul Ithrandyr?'

Her tone revealed she did not know the Holy City, so he knew he'd travelled a considerable distance through the magical door. 'No. I come from Tul Et Hazier, in the Sands of Fire,' he answered, awaiting her reaction.

'What land is this place in? And where is it?'

Her interest was oddly infectious and genuine, and A Ahmud Ki began to relax in the presence of a woman whose

159

beauty surpassed all the Ranu women he'd kept as servants in his black tower. 'It is the land of the Ranu Ka Shehaala. As for where it is, I can only guess from what you've told me that it's to the west.' He noticed her puzzled expression, and he was tempted to invade her thoughts, but he restrained his impulse, and asked 'What is it?'

'I don't understand,' she said, tilting her head gently to the right, an action that A Ahmud Ki immediately thought was unique and attractive. 'To the west lies the Kingdom of Thana, and the Aelendyell forests. Beyond that, there is only a barren land populated by a race of barbarians. No one bothers to go there because the land is harsh and the people primitive.'

'Have you been there?' he asked.

'No.'

'Then how can you be so sure the people are primitive?'

'My mother taught me that barbarians treat their women like slaves, and they have no magic except a limited form of religious polytheism - witchcraft. They live in small villages scattered across their lands, and fight and kill each other for no more reason than the sheer pleasure of it.'

'When did your mother last see the land of the Ranu Ka Shehaala?' he asked quietly.

Seralinna looked away. 'My mother has never been there. No one goes there. The barbarians have nothing to offer us. Where have you really come from?' she asked.

'I told you,' A Ahmud Ki replied, alert and wary of her sudden, direct question.

'And I've told you that what you say isn't possible,' she asserted. 'No portal has ever had the power to open across the distances you claim to have travelled. So from whose Keep have you come?'

A Ahmud Ki hesitated. If he reiterated his answer, he knew she wouldn't believe him, but her observation about the portal's power intrigued him. Wherever Seralinna's Keep was, her attitude made it clear that she and her people had access to considerable magical power, almost certainly the Fourth Ki, and they believed other forms of magic to be inferior. Yet he'd already obviously superseded their powers of portal projection and travel, which meant he possessed secrets they did not, so it was in his interests not to reveal any more to Seralinna. Besides, he'd travelled to a destination from which he wasn't even certain he could return, so he had to learn as much as he could to solve his own dilemma. 'I'm not from anyone's Keep. I've been experimenting with the magic door, the portal, and it accidentally brought me here,' he explained.

'Your mother or sister needs to teach you more control,' she chided, and grinned. 'Do you know how to return?'

The question hadn't occurred to him. When he studied, built, and activated the magic door in his tower, he only searched for a point of entry. His door led one way. He hadn't planned on returning. But neither had he anticipated travelling so great a distance. He was unsure as to where he was – apparently, according to Seralinna, east of the Aelendyell forests. 'No,' he replied. 'No, I don't know how to go back. I thought I only needed to step back through the door.' He looked at the mirror, suspended between two ebony poles, in the centre of Seralinna's room.

She tilted her head and laughed. 'You do have a great deal to learn. There are hundreds of places to go. You must know the energy level, direction, point of focus, colour, height, even a password of entry for some.' She stopped laughing and stared at him. 'You have the presence of a sorcerer, but you speak as if you are an apprentice.' She raised her eyebrows in a wry smile.

He grinned good-naturedly. What she doesn't know, he thought to himself, won't interfere with me.

Seralinna led him down three flights of wooden stairs to an eating room. He considered the stone construction of the Keep's inner walls. Crudely hand-built, lacking the smooth finish of the buildings he'd inhabited in Yul Ithrandyr, nowhere could he feel a presence of magic holding the construction together, and he wryly wondered who were the barbarians when it came to building with stone.

'I will bring food and drink. We'll talk further, before I

work out how to send you home,' Seralinna told him, as she moved elegantly towards an adjacent door.

He watched her go. Slim, lithe, her blue gown washed about her body with tantalising ease, and her hair hung in waves down the middle of her back, bouncing softly with her steps. He sighed when she closed the door. What game is she playing, he wondered? She had been shocked to see him in the centre of her Travel Chamber, as she called it, when he first stepped through from Ranu Ka Shehaala, but she acquiesced - almost too quickly - appearing to drop her defences in favour of curiosity. She studied him as she questioned him, but he sensed increasing softness in her voice and in her eyes, as if she was accepting his presence. She easily slipped into his native Aelendyell tongue when she noticed his features, though her accent was foreign. It had been fifteen years since he'd spoken Aelendyell consistently with anyone, except Karrilyon. Is it a complicated ploy to catch me off guard? he wondered.

The Keep's furniture and floor and ceiling were wooden and rudimentary, and the old building was in a state of decay. As he rose to go to a window to look out, Seralinna returned, carrying a gold tray of pottery goblets and food, which she placed on the table. 'Please eat and drink what you wish. I don't own a great deal, but you are welcome. I'll leave you for a short time, but, if you want anything, whisper my name.' She smiled when she saw A Ahmud Ki's quizzical expression, and explained with a cheeky wink, 'The stones will tell me.' She turned and headed up the stairs.

He listened to her footfall on the wooden steps and ascertained that she was returning to the Travel Chamber. The food was inviting. He grabbed a handful of red berries from a wooden bowl and ate them, and drank the white liquid in a goblet. Like milk, it was sweet and filling. When he finished, and Seralinna still hadn't returned, he moved to a window to survey the landscape. The outside world was bright and green, full of hillocks and hills, sturdy oaks and fig trees, under an azure sky. Flocks of birds wheeled across the sky and a glittering creek tumbled along a broad, rocky bed through a shallow green valley. He estimated he was ten arm spans above ground level. There were no more visible buildings, but mounds covered with luxurious grass, at the base of the Keep, suggested the presence of long-overgrown ruins, and clusters of hewn stone broke through the green mantle in patches to confirm his thought. The Keep was the surviving structure of a larger building, or collection of buildings. But he was drawn, again, to the raw beauty of the surrounding country, and the intensity of the green force pulsing through the natural life hurt his eyes. The ghost of Terin felt an inexplicable longing for his long-forsaken forests.

He didn't hear Seralinna descend the stairs or approach from behind, so her voice startled him. 'We have a journey to undertake,' she said gravely. 'I've tried to find where you belong, but no one's heard of you, by name or by description. There's more to your arrival than I can fathom, or you're willing to tell.'

Lady Tarnyss peered forward from the height of the upper step, and a frown creased her brow. 'An interesting story, one with more to it than you choose to reveal, young man, but you are advised not to lie to anyone here. Not publicly.'

A Ahmud Ki read the sincerity of her threat in her dark eyes. He gripped the symbol of Fareeka hanging from his neck chain, his fingers caressing the tiny amber jewels embedded in her eyes, and applied the Translation spell he learned during his Ithosen training to comprehend and speak in Tarnyss' foreign tongue. 'All I've told you is true,' he wearily reiterated. 'I built a door, a portal as you call it, and it led to Seralinna's Keep. I research magic, and experiment with new ways to combine different pieces of knowledge. That's how I created the door.'

Tarnyss straightened her posture and glanced to her left at her fellow Councillors. The eight women and two men nodded, without shifting their gaze from A Ahmud Ki. 'Very well,' she said quietly. 'Let's assume that you actually did build a portal more powerful than any built by wizards or sorceresses before you. How many of your barbarian people know your secret?'

A Ahmud Ki couldn't suppress a smile. 'The Ranu Ka Shehaala are not barbarians,' he corrected. 'And no one else has my knowledge of the door.' He wondered what Jezarba had told Shehaal, and how Shehaal reacted to the messenger's news. He almost wished he had been there.

'That, at least, is comforting,' said Tarnyss. 'But surely someone might stumble upon your portal in your absence?'

'I don't think that will happen, Lady Tarnyss,' Seralinna politely interrupted.

'Why not?'

'He didn't know how to return, and I couldn't find an alien source for transference through my mirror when I tried to determine from where he'd journeyed. I think his portal was singular in direction, and highly unstable. It's most likely already closed.' She smiled at A Ahmud Ki, who felt a warm tingle through his body as she caught his eyes, like the thrill of magic, but when he returned his attention to Tarnyss he noticed that she had also observed the silent communication.

'Yes,' she breathed, dissatisfied by what she'd witnessed. 'Another complication.' She walked slowly to her left, and abruptly wheeled to face A Ahmud Ki. 'If you are who you appear to be, then your coming is a matter of great concern for the Supreme Council of Targa. Wizards are rare in our world, very rare, and –' She glanced in the direction of the two elderly male Councillors, with their long white beards and shocks of white hair stringing out from balding pates '- young wizards are unknown.' Catching the folds of her flowing emerald dress, she swept down two steps to stand level with A Ahmud Ki, and stared directly into his grey eyes. 'There is one way to prove if you are a charlatan. The Test.' The Councillors muttered approval, but A Ahmud Ki heard Seralinna gasp. 'Of course,' Tarnyss continued, 'you don't have to take The Test, if you are willing to admit this is all an elaborate hoax, or a prank of the Lord Keeper's warriors.'

Her undisguised cynicism goaded his arrogance. Calming his voice with the discipline Karrilyon had taught him, he asked, 'What is The Test?'

He detected the faintest trace of surprise in Tarnyss' reaction, but she laughed dismissively and gave a cryptic answer. 'That is The Test. But there's no need to explain it to you. You merely have to decide whether you think you are ready for The Test or not. Answer?'

A Ahmud Ki was aware of Seralinna's concern, and wondered what The Test involved, but when he cast an eye over the Councillors, all awaiting his decision, he realized they thought he was nothing more than a warrior conducting a silly joke. What relationship exists between the warriors and magicians of this place if the Councillors are so ready to believe the warriors would play a practical joke to embarrass the Council? he wondered. And are all women the main source of magical power and men merely warriors? This place had so many puzzles. He looked straight into Tarnyss' dark eyes and moon-white face, framed by thickly curled black hair, and said, 'I'll take The Test.'

Seralinna led him to the door. When she opened it, he looked into a circular space, thirty arm spans in diameter, lit artificially. She touched his arm. 'This isn't a joke gone horribly wrong, is it?'

He smiled. 'This is no joke. I don't even know who this Lord of the Keeps is, Seralinna. I've never been to your land. I told you the truth.' He went to enter the arena, but her grip on his arm tightened, and the serious expression on her fine-featured beauty disturbed him. 'What is it?' he asked.

Her eyes glistened, like deep pools, urging him to leap into their depths, but her lips trembled as she said, in a half-whisper, 'If you really do have magic in you, then you will survive The Test because - because only magic can get you out of it.' She released his arm and retreated along the corridor. He watched her retreat, until she rounded a far corner leading to the stairs, fascinated by her uncompromised show of concern. Love was alien to his experience. He felt pangs of lust often enough, and the Ranu women served that need wonderfully, but Seralinna's unsolicited affection was fresh, scintillating, and he felt increasingly attracted to her. If it is a cruel emotional trick to unmask me, it is almost working, he decided. He composed his thoughts, drew a deep breath, and stepped into the circular room.

A smooth dark rock wall, possibly granite, he surmised, ran the circumference of the room, and rose at least four arm spans. Overhead was a milky-white dome, the source of light, and A Ahmud Ki imagined himself within one of Shehaal's spheres, floating in the Palace Irandu Shadu. The floor was rough earth, trampled and hacked by hundreds of feet and hooves. There was only one visible wooden door in the opposite wall. 'You lay claim to belong to the Order of Wizardry by submitting to The Test of the Supreme Council of Targa,' Tarnyss' voice boomed from an indefinable point overhead. 'If you can escape from The Test arena, after overcoming its obstacles, then your right to be accorded the title of Wizard shall be recognized and granted by the Council. Should you fail – that is another matter entirely. May you be guided by your powers and prove to be a great wizard. Let The Test begin!'

Getting out of here will be easy, A Ahmud Ki mused. Simple levitation: a novice's trick in the white towers. So what are the difficulties? A whir and clank of chain disrupted his thoughts, and the opposite door creaked. As it opened, he was aware of a gleam at his feet, and looked down to see a red-handled sword and a shield on the earthen floor. Part of The Test, he thought. No use to me. I am a sorcerer, not a warrior. Across the arena, three humanoid creatures, with hunched shoulders, excessively long arms, and protruding lower canines, loped towards him, wielding brutal axes. He calmly measured the distance, extended his arms, and cast a spell. It was a simple spell, one designed to temporarily incapacitate an opponent, and a prequel to his performance, but its limitation was the area it covered. Two creatures stumbled and fell into the dirt. The third, outside the area of effect, hefted its axe, and hurled it with deadly accuracy, but A Ahmud Ki waved his fingers, and the axe hit an invisible barrier in front of his face, before harmlessly dropping to the ground. The creature stared at him, puzzled. A Ahmud Ki pointed his finger at the heart of the confused being and uttered 'Byrnan.' Flame erupted in the creature's chest. It squealed in surprise, and then roared with pain as it collapsed. Simple, thought A Ahmud Ki. So much for The Test. They would now know that he was a wizard, but he deliberately used the simplest of spells to mask his full ability. He glanced at the sword and shield again, and inwardly grinned at the simple-minded trap they laid to see if he would resort to warrior instincts and take up the weaponry. They thought him a charlatan and they were wrong.

He turned to the door through which he'd entered. The door was gone. In its place stood a warrior, in shining plate armour. A visor hid his face, but A Ahmud Ki sensed the presence of a warrior of outstanding prowess. Not that he was concerned. No warrior could match a practitioner of the First, Second, and Third Ki.

The warrior drew a broad sword from a golden scabbard and advanced, and A Ahmud Ki allowed him to take several paces, before pointing at the warrior's left leg. He would cut this opponent down, methodically, to emphasize his ability. He uttered the spell word. A ball of flame exploded against the warrior's leg armour and disappeared in a flash of blue light. The warrior continued unaffected. A Ahmud Ki retreated, across the arena, astonished by the failure of his spell. He directed a wind gust at his target, testing the warrior's reaction, and, to his horror, saw that spell also had no effect. Fear pulsed through his being as he dodged to his left, the warrior's sword barely missing his ear, and he put several paces between his pursuer and himself to gather his thoughts.

Magic isn't affecting this warrior. Why? The warrior closed the gap, so A Ahmud Ki resorted to an Aelendyell spell of invisibility, using it to retreat to another sector of the arena, leaving the warrior to search for him while he reconsidered the circumstance. Hiding surely isn't the answer to this part of The Test? Why isn't magic affecting the warrior? He watched his hunter, and another pang of fear clawed at his gut when he realized the warrior was approaching purposely, as if he could see his quarry. A Ahmud Ki rolled to the right, the sword clanging against the granite wall and drawing sparks. He scrambled to his feet and sprinted to the opposite side of the arena.

Perhaps the Test isn't destructive, he reasoned, as he straightened against the wall. They are testing my response to danger. I've made a mistake attacking this warrior. There are other ways. He cast a suggestion of friendship at the warrior, but the warrior closed in menacingly. A Ahmud Ki shifted yet again. Surely they aren't expecting me to grab the sword and shield and fight hand-to-hand? No. It is a test of my magic. It must be. I need to use something more powerful, more impressive. He shuffled sideways, to delay his opponent's attack, and concentrated directly on the approaching warrior's mind – and was startled to find it empty of thought. Impossible! he decided, but in the instant he caught the essence of a thought and honed in – and followed the thread to a second mind: Tarnyss! She was controlling the warrior. He broke contact to avoid a vicious lunge of the sword, and scampered away, wrestling with his challenge. Tarnyss. The warrior. Why? How? No magical effect. Is she protecting him? Unless – He stood upright and grinned. Of course, he thought, and strode cockily towards his opponent, mouthing the words of an Aelendyell unmaking spell from the Second Ki. The warrior lifted his sword in a swift arc and screamed a blood-chilling war cry, but A Ahmud Ki laughed and shook his head as the sword swept down. His long grey locks, and head and body, shimmered with dispelled arcane energy as the illusory sword passed swiftly through him. The warrior stepped back, shimmered as A Ahmud Ki had, faded, and vanished. On the ground, where the warrior had stood, an amber crystal sparkled. A Ahmud Ki smiled and bent to retrieve it. Clever, he thought, as his fingers touched the gem. Very clever. Tarnyss tried to defeat him with an illusion, with nothing. The gem was a vehicle for generating the warrior's image. Now he would leave.

As he straightened, he saw oil spreading through the dirt towards him, leading a wall of flame that threatened to engulf the arena. Another illusion? he wondered. The flaming oil washed over the humanoid bodies and consumed them. No illusion in that, he decided, and motioned with his hands to elevate. Flames spread under him as he ascended to the ceiling, and he felt heat rising – real heat. Hate to fail The Test, he thought. With a final phrase, he passed through the mass of the dome, to be greeted with applause from the Supreme Council of Targa.

Twenty

'How many of these visitations must I endure?' A Ahmud Ki asked irritably, as he turned his back on Seralinna and her shimmering portal.

'There are forty-seven members of the Order. You've met thirty-two so far,' she explained patiently. 'You really can't blame them. They're all curious to welcome a new wizard to the Order, and you are especially important because you're - well, unusual.' A Ahmud Ki glanced at her. 'I meant because of your age, and where you've apparently come from,' she added with a smile.

'I'm tired of their stares and smiles and pleasantries,' he scowled, and turned away. At first, he bathed in the glory of passing The Test and proving his power before the High Council. He especially enjoyed the effect of his success on Tarnyss, who reluctantly applauded him. He touched and read her mind in The Test and that visibly shocked her, as if mind touch was a skill these people did not possess. He was pleased when the Council instructed Seralinna to return to her Keep, with him, to prepare for the Order's formal reception, and when the first members entered through the portal, one by one, and greeted him, and welcomed and praised him for his success, he relished the honour and accord. He had sought the same recognition of his power from the Ranu Ka Shehaala Ithosen, but they snubbed him, and the Great Shehaal sent him into exile rather than acknowledge his power. Only women and underlings were left to bow to him, and they bowed to anyone in a red cloak. So, he revelled in the compliments and questions of the sorceresses, and the occasional elderly wizard, but the novelty was becoming tedious. The smiles were the same – polite, but indifferent. He answered the same boring questions. He was growing tired of questions about his Aelendyell heritage, and the disbelief concerning his coming from the Ranu Ka Shehaala, or the barbarians as these people persisted in calling them. Names blended.

A hum rose in the portal mirror. Another visitor. But A Ahmud Ki saw something different in the woman who appeared. She bore a striking resemblance to Lady Tarnyss. 'A Ahmud Ki,' said Seralinna, 'I am pleased to present Lady Corinna, sister of Lady Tarnyss of the High Council.'

Corinna bowed her head slightly, almost in mock politeness, and glared at Seralinna. 'If you don't mind, girl, I wish to speak to our new wizard. Alone. Kindly leave us.' Seralinna looked from her to A Ahmud Ki, curtsied to Corinna, and silently left. Corinna held her posture erect, as she approached A Ahmud Ki. 'I haven't come to fawn upon you, like most of the hypocrites in the Order will have done today. I never approve of men being allowed to practise magic, and I approve even less of one so young. I only wish that what my sister has already told me were not true, though my eyes tell me that it is. Be that as it may.' Her eyes seemed determined to physically penetrate A Ahmud Ki's thoughts, and he felt compelled to turn away from her, but he refused and held her gaze defiantly. In the end, she broke her gaze, and shifted to his left, before continuing. 'My questioning will be brief, young man. What are your politics?'

Having never heard the word 'politics', A Ahmud Ki carefully inquired, 'What specialist magic is that?'

Corinna's eyes narrowed. 'Are you mocking me?'

'No.'

'Have you never decided which point of view to uphold?'

'I admit I don't understand your question,' he replied, wondering what plot or trick the sorceress was preparing.

'I would have thought barbarians, at the very least, would have had political squabbles. Plots? Intrigues? Alliances?' A Ahmud Ki's blank expression irritated Corinna. 'Are you telling me that you took no sides in politics in your homeland?'

'I heard the Ithosen talk and whisper at meetings, but I had no interest in their petty matters, and no one ever explained those matters to me,' he calmly replied.

'How irresponsible!' she declared. 'Who ruled your strange land?'

'Leiksha Ithrandyr Shehaal.'

'One woman?'

'One man,' he corrected.

His correction brought an icy stare from the sorceress. 'A man? Alone? How primitive! These people are barbarians indeed! Surely you must have known his opponents?'

'No one opposes the Holy Lord of Peace and Light. Everyone serves him. He is Protector and Lord of the Ranu Ka Shehaala. All obey his word.'

Corinna shook her head in disgust and disbelief. 'Surely women opposed him?'

A Ahmud Ki grinned. 'Women are not even allowed to speak to men in the land of the Ranu Ka Shehaala.' He enjoyed observing the effect of his comment on Corinna.

'Don't be impudent, young man, or I will remind you of your place here. My sister said you are filled with male arrogance, which is obvious, but don't trifle with me. I don't like you, and I would enjoy chastising your boyish ignorance.'

Her barbed comment stung his pride and he wanted to react, but he controlled his desire, and said, 'Perhaps you will have that opportunity one day, Lady Corinna.'

She glared viciously and spoke acidly. 'I have one final question, wizard. It concerns The Test, and my sister. She said you discovered the illusion by reading her mind. Is that true?' A Ahmud Ki held back his answer. 'Is that true?' she demanded.

He savoured the note of urgency in her voice, because he knew for certain that he possessed a Ki these people did not. 'Of course it is.'

Corinna turned on her heel, her dark grey robes wheeling lightly about her, and returned to the portal. As she was about to step through, she halted, and turned to him. 'Don't come to learn my arts. I will not teach you. But I will leave you with a double warning, young man.' She spat the last word with contempt. 'Whether you choose to ignore it or not, every decision you take is political, and all others will see it that way, especially in Targa. Learn your politics, or perish. As for your pride, one day it will be your downfall, I assure you. Curb your arrogance.' With that, she disappeared into the portal's blue haze.

Seralinna's face appeared in the doorway. 'Has she gone?'

'She has,' A Ahmud Ki replied.

Seralinna entered. 'I ought to have warned you about her, and others in the Order. They quite dislike all new sorceresses or wizards. They see them as threats to their own positions in the Order.' A Ahmud Ki looked for further explanation. 'Lady Corinna probably mentioned politics?' He nodded. 'She's obsessed by them,' she said. 'Are you?'

'I didn't even know what she was talking about,' he replied.

Seralinna looked at him quizzically. 'For a wizard, wherever you come from, you're awfully naive.' A Ahmud Ki's eyes narrowed, which only caused her to laugh. 'Oh, I'm sorry if I offended you,' she apologized. 'I didn't mean to. It's just so unusual to meet someone in Targa who isn't concerned about her or his position in the Order of Power. Most of them spend all their time devising new ways to improve their standing over the others. They bicker and argue, and they all despise the Councillors, even though every single one would love to be on the Council. It's so petty.'

'So, politics is a struggle for power?' he asked, becoming interested.

'Oh, it's not so simple,' she replied. 'It's about making friends and gathering support from people who would just as likely do anything to ruin your position, if they could. You have to learn how to cheat and lie, without offending too many people. You must make yourself seem more impressive than you really are. You see, you have to be assessed and voted into a new position in the Order, and, if you can cajole and convince enough supporters, you'll eventually be voted onto the Council, which controls the destinies of every sorceress and wizard in Targa. Every year, a new President of the High Council is elected, although the position always goes to the most powerful person in the Federation. Lady Tarnyss has been President for the last nine years. That irks her sister, Lady Corinna, but the success of her sister also makes Corinna a highly respected person in the Order. It's very silly. And your sudden appearance has ruffled a few feathers, because, like everyone else, you'll be added to the Order of Power, according to the Council's assessment of your merit, and your knowledge of magical lore.'

'But why were they so eager to applaud me after The Test, and to visit me, if my presence offends them?'

'Passing The Test is a worthy achievement,' she answered. 'You've earned their respect. As for visiting you, they're merely being polite, while they ascertain the extent of your powers. Some will see you as a threat to their position in the Order - others will assess you as less than a threat. And others come merely to be known to you in the hope that, later, when you're admitted to the Order, they can foster political friendships with you in their favour.'

A Ahmud Ki turned from her and stroked his chin. 'So why do you accept me in your Keep?' When she didn't reply, he faced her, and caught the glow in her cheeks, colour that added radiance to her beauty and hinted that she was hiding more than political manoeuvring. Although he was tempted to probe her thoughts to find the answer, he resisted, and diverted the conversation to other matters. 'When will my assessment be made?' he asked. The sooner the better, he thought.

'When you've taken ownership of one of the old Keeps. Then you will be assessed.'

'A Keep?' He gazed into the crystal depth of her eyes and her beauty teased him. 'No, not a Keep, Seralinna,' he said, no longer veiling his arrogance, 'not for me. I will create a tower of the Ranu Ka Shehaala, a tower befitting true magical research. A Ahmud Ki will not live in an old Keep.' Seralinna drew back, afraid, but he smiled, and then he laughed, knowing that his quest for control of the Four Ki had led him to the right place again.

The black tower rose fully thirty arm spans, unblemished by joins or cracks, free of visible windows or doors. An exotic garden of tree ferns, palms, and a multitude of brightly flowering plants clustered around the base, watered by fountains from three springs. Set against the natural greens of Targa's hillocks and tree clumps, the tower and its garden were more impressive than in the centre of the Sands of Fire. No Targan sorceress or wizard could create such a perfect building, thought Seralinna, as she winged towards the tower, and its existence thrilled and filled her with dread. She alighted on the ground, morphed from her robin guise into human form, and waited for A Ahmud Ki to emerge from his tower. She didn't have long to wait. Her host appeared through the ebony wall, where no door existed, and came forward with extended arms to greet her. He had exchanged the red Ithosen robes for deep blue robes, and a silver cloak to match the tint of his Aelendyell locks, and his finely chiselled features charmed her. 'I'm pleased you've come,' he said, as he took her by the arms. 'As you welcomed me into your home, when I stumbled through your portal, so now I welcome your beauty to my home.' He made a sweeping gesture towards the tower. 'What do you think?'

'I - I've never seen such craftsmanship. The finest buildings, even in the heart of the city, don't compare. Who built it? I mean, how did you build it?'

'A little barbarian magic,' he said, grinning, 'blessed by my Deity.'

Seralinna was puzzled by his reference to a deity, but he led her to the wall before she could ask him to explain. One step from the wall, he opened his palm to reveal a pyramidal amber crystal. 'My key,' he informed her.

'Can't you conjure a spell to go through?' she queried, as she watched him place the crystal on the ground, at the base of the wall.

'Of course - that's basic Aelendyell magic. But no one can simply pass through Ithosen walls. Try it.'

She looked at him and saw the mischief written in his face. 'No. I believe you,' she replied.

'Ithosen are very jealous of their magical research and devotions. If the towers could be entered with spells, anyone with magical knowledge could break in uninvited. That's why the Ithosen developed buildings of magic rather than stone. Access to each tower is by individual crystals, and the crystals are only activated by individual voices.' As he finished explaining, he bent and uttered two silent words to the crystal. He took Seralinna's hand and led her through the solid wall.

A floating sphere lit the circular room. A single, square table graced the centre, complemented by six chairs. A low chest, curved to the arc of the wall, filled a space, and on the chest were bowls of food, and a pitcher of wine. Seralinna noticed there weren't any stairs to the next level, and the ceiling was solid. 'Please excuse the furnishings. I've never needed much more than this. Would you like a drink, or something to eat?' he offered.

She shook her head. 'You've learned quickly about the nature of political influence,' she said. He smiled knowingly, so she shifted tack. 'Why did you invite me here?'

He drew closer. 'You see how quickly I learn, Seralinna? I need to learn. That's why I stepped through the portal to come here. I want to learn your magic. I want you to teach me.'

His confession made her to step away, and anger flashed through her eyes. 'You want to use me, you mean!'

He was hurt by her jibe. 'No. I don't want to use you, as you put it. Believe me, Seralinna, all I want to do is learn. And I can teach you what I know if you want. No tricks.'

'No tricks,' she responded, 'but lots of political gain. When is your assessment?'

She didn't trust him. He knew it. Yet he wanted her trust. He never wanted anyone's trust before, but he wanted hers - really wanted it. 'That's unimportant,' he tried to explain.

'What I want-'

'When is your assessment?' she repeated.

There was no point in lying to her. 'Three days.'

She nodded, as if understanding a fact that eluded him. 'And what do you want from me?'

'I want you to show me how to construct one of your portals.' She smiled as if relieved, and he reddened at her reaction. 'What's so funny?' he asked hurtfully.

She took his hands in her own. 'Nothing, really. I thought you were going to ask for something of far-reaching importance to enhance your political standing. And all you want is help with a simple portal. All this wonderful Ithosen magic,' she indicated the surrounding tower, 'and yet your people cannot create portals.'

He felt discomfort at having a weakness exposed, especially by Seralinna, but his indignation remained within, held by her captivating smile and shining eyes. He said, quietly, 'I have much to learn from you.'

'And I will teach you,' she answered.

He was amazed at the speed and ease with which the people of Targa could create a portal. Seralinna finished the task late in the afternoon, using ebony rods that A Ahmud Ki fashioned from Ithosen spell weaving in the place of the manufactured rods Targans normally used for a magic mirror frame. He watched with interest, and memorised each chant and ingredient, storing the information with the skill and accuracy mastered under Karrilyon's tutelage. He also made modifications and improvements according to his research when he created his portal in the Sands of Fire, but he kept the improvements to himself, to apply when Seralinna wasn't present. To begin with, he needed a portal to allow him the freedom to travel that the sorceresses and wizards of this land took for granted. He pestered Seralinna with questions, and she patiently answered, teaching him about her culture and herself. 'No one really questions it. It's been that way for many generations. Mothers pass their magical knowledge to their daughters, who, in turn, pass their skills to their daughters. Men have always been warriors, a few exceptions being old men who somehow seem to attain magical talent with age. Women are naturally adept with their minds, men with their hands.'

'So, all sorceresses know the magic of your people?'

'No, of course not. There's too much to know for one person to remember. Each member of the Order specializes in her field.'

'What's your speciality?'

Seralinna smiled. 'Shape-changing - mainly into small creatures and birds. Especially birds. My great Granmama loved forest creatures, so she chose to learn their ways. She perfected the art of shape-change spells, and her knowledge and skill were passed from my mother to me.'

'Is that all you can do?' he asked, disappointed to learn her magic was limited.

'Oh, I know the Central Arts of Magic we all have to learn, like passage spells, or multiplication, or portal construction, and others.' His interest brightened at the mention of more spells, some new to him. 'But my Pledge to the Order is study into shape-changing.'

'So, you're the only member who can shape-change?'

'No. I'm the only one in my specialist field. Danyella studies shape-changing into larger creatures. Mariska alters her shape to water creatures. Lady Winter can shape-change into reptiles, although her Pledge is in the field of weather conjuration.'

'And what's Lady Tarnyss' speciality?'

'She's pledged to illusion. But like so many who play the game of politics, she dabbles in other fields. We all know she's become adept at spells of energy. She shows them off to impress others. There are also rumours that she delves into the Secret Dark Arts of the Dragonlords.'

A Ahmud Ki heard a shudder passing through Seralinna as she uttered the last words. Tarnyss' powers apparently disturbed her, but he wanted to know who or what were Dragonlords?

After describing Tarnyss' skills, Seralinna worked in silence on the last vestiges of the portal. Finally, she stepped back, and took his right hand in her left, with a sparkle in her eyes that reflected the blue haze flickering on the vertical black rods. 'Finished!' She released his hand and raised both of hers. 'Now to activate your portal.' She shook back her auburn hair and snapped out a command. 'Haeraeni!' Blue light sizzled from pole to pole, crackled with electrical static, and settled into a smooth blue incandescent light.

Twenty One

The portal shimmered, and A Ahmud Ki emerged in the Great Hall of the Targa Council. He strode down the wooden steps to the long narrow expanse of floor. The Council was fully assembled. Tarnyss, at the centre in a high-backed chair reserved for the President, was watching him closely, so, with impish delight, he projected a simple 'Hello' into her consciousness and smiled inwardly when he registered her shocked and angry response, though he resisted looking directly at her face. The Council was arranged in two tiers at the head of the Hall. Members of the Order sat along the left wall in three tiered rows, with those of highest rank in the Order of Power seated closest to the Council. He searched for Lady Corinna's face and found her in the front row first seat. Sisterly influence is a powerful political tool, he decided. He also noticed eight seats were empty. Seralinna told him there were currently forty-seven members, but he counted thirty-nine. He recalled only thirty-three visiting him in Seralinna's Keep, Corinna being the last. Something was amiss, though Seralinna hadn't indicated there was a major dissension in the Order. He reminded himself to ask her more about the situation after his assessment. After all, it was his assessment, and he was confident he would receive high ranking among these people. He possessed three Ki. Who, among the Targans, could boast as much?

As in his first visit with Seralinna, he compared the tall angular wooden interior of this Hall with the bright airy marble construction of the Great Central Hall of the Palace Irandu Shadu and found the former wanting in majesty. For all their magic, he reminded himself, these people of Targa cannot build with beauty. Projections, points, edges and beams intruded on lines of sight, reminding him of the forest architecture of his Aelendyell birthplace. He could not bring himself to extend more than formal respect to a people who lived in ragged stone keeps that were remnants of ruined castles.

He approached the bar, separating the Council from the floor space, and Tarnyss stood, lifting a golden sceptre high above her head. 'I, Tarnyss of Lessa,' she began, 'President of the Supreme Council of Targa, call upon the Order to give attention to the one who stands before us.' She stared directly at him. 'Who comes to be assessed?'

A Ahmud Ki cleared his throat. 'I am A Ahmud Ki, former Ithosen of the Ranu Ka Shehaala, former Advisor to Leiksha Ithrandyr Shehaal, and Holder of the Three Ki. My name means 'The Seeker of Power', and I come before you to be assessed.' He appreciated the formal tone of his voice as it echoed through the Hall, and he wondered how impressed the assembled sorceresses and wizards were with his titles. He glimpsed Seralinna's face in the third row, halfway along the Order, but he couldn't determine her mood. A stifled gasp escaped from an unidentified person in the Order.

'What special skill can you offer to the Supreme Council so that your position in the Order can be assessed?' Tarnyss asked, with her usual abruptness.

He knew she expected him to say mind spells, or something similarly singular, but he had an altogether different agenda. 'I specialize in learning,' he announced. 'I specialize in everything. Already I understand and can use magic from the Aelendyell and the Ithosen. I possess three Ki. My task, in your land, is to learn the Fourth Ki, the magic of Targa.' Tarnyss' eyes widened, as he expected, but the reaction from the assembled gallery was unexpected. Sharp whispers and animated discussion broke out between members of the Order. He caught snatches of words and phrases and heard 'The Prophecy!' and 'It's true!' Seralinna stared at him, and her face had visibly whitened.

Lady Tarnyss asserted her authority. 'Come to order! An assessment is in process, and you will have the sense to observe appropriate decorum. Come to order at once!' When silence was finally restored, she addressed the members of the Order with perfunctory vigour. 'That is enough! Witches' tales, and the rampant moaning of insane village warlocks, have no place in the Great Hall. That talk will not be tolerated. It's utter nonsense!'

A Ahmud Ki, however, wanted to know what he'd said to prompt the disturbance. What prophecy are they whispering about? Who are these witches and warlocks? He had to know. Something has clearly upset Seralinna as well - but what?

Tarnyss broke in on his thoughts. 'If your claim is true, then your position in the Order of Power is, fittingly, the highest rank, and not even the Supreme Council can oppose your right. But no one has ever mastered more than two specialities, although some have tried, or dabbled in more, so how are we to believe that your wild claim is true?'

'Simple,' he replied. Tarnyss had taken the bait. 'Give me the authority to visit with members of the Order, and Councillors if you like, for extended periods, with the express purpose of learning their individual specialities. Then order me to return to the Hall, in a year, to demonstrate what I've learnt, and if I haven't mastered more than five specialities my words are mere boasting and you've lost nothing. However, if I'm successful, your Council will naturally award me an important position in the Order of Power.' Whispers and argument broke out, all over the Hall. Tarnyss looked to her fellow Councillors for support, only to see them embroiled in intense discussion, so she joined them, and A Ahmud Ki watched the heated exchanges with amusement. He knew the majority of the Councillors rejected his challenge, but it was clear that Tarnyss was arguing for acceptance. He concentrated on her thoughts, gently reaching out with a mind spell in the hope of perceiving her plans without her aware of his spying, but as he touched her consciousness she spun from her argument and glared at him, her eyes glittering with indignant anger. He withdrew immediately, smiling.

Tarnyss regained her composure and ordered the assembly into silence. She stared at A Ahmud Ki as she spoke. 'The Supreme Council has deliberated on your proposal. We accept your proposal.' He noted several Councillors shaking their heads in disapproval, and a further outburst of whispers, and hisses, erupted. Tarnyss raised her voice over the dissension. 'The Council directs members of the Order to welcome you to their Keeps, if you choose to visit them, and we ask members to teach you all you can learn. However, in twelve months, you must return to the assembly and demonstrate that you have learned five new speciality skills, at which point your position in the Order will be decided. If you fail, you will forfeit your freedom to the Supreme Council, and offer to freely teach your skills to any member of the Order who seeks to learn them. Are you agreed?'

A Ahmud Ki bowed low, with mock humility, and replied, 'I accept your terms completely.'

'Why did you do it?'

A Ahmud Ki casually ran the brush through his hair as Seralinna repeated her question. 'Why not?' he replied.

She wrenched the brush from his hand and forced him to pay her attention. 'You really don't understand, do you? You've promised the Supreme Council that you'll learn five specialities in a year. Five! It's taken me a lifetime to learn just one. And yet you claim you'll learn five!'

'I learn fast, Seralinna. I learned how to construct one of your portals.'

'Portals are child's play,' she snorted. 'Every sorceress in Targa can make one, some much quicker than I. A portal isn't remotely like a speciality. You have to live a special skill, make it part of you. You must learn all its beauties and its vagaries, its pleasures and traps. You can't just learn these things from a lore book.'

A Ahmud Ki assumed a stern expression, although within he was smiling at Seralinna's passion for her art and her concern for him. 'That's why I chose to learn from you, first. Already you're teaching me an important lesson. I must make the special skill part of me. Good. I believe magical power without passion or belief is weak magic. Teach me, Seralinna. Teach me so I will learn.'

She held his gaze, locked with him in silent argument, before she broke the frieze with a shake of her head. 'What else can I do?' she sighed. 'Yes, A Ahmud Ki, I'll teach you everything I know. But,' she added quietly, 'I also know my efforts will be futile in the long run.'

He raised his eyebrows. 'Why do you say that?'

'Did you hear them? Did you feel the mood in the assembly? They despise you. They fear you, A Ahmud Ki.' She looked at him with hurt in her eyes.

'I thought it was just womanly jealousy,' he flippantly replied, 'a feature of the political in-fighting you said takes place in the Order. But I did mean to ask you about a prophecy. What is that all about?'

Seralinna moved across the room to a marble bench in A Ahmud Ki's study, and he sensed her reluctance to answer. 'It's nothing really,' she said. 'Most of us know it's an old witches' fable, spread by the common folk, a good story for sharing around night fires. No one could really believe it. But your arrival is making even level heads wonder.' She broke off, and stared at him curiously, and took a very deep breath before she continued. 'You see, there is an old prophecy, one of many hundreds, that one day a stranger will come, who will possess greater power than all the Councillors combined, and that stranger will bring down the Supreme Council and all of its followers. The stranger will be a man, a young man unlike any wizard before him, and he will change the world, and bring it to great evil and darkness.' She paused to assess him again, before she started to walk the circumference of the circular room. 'The witches promulgate a great many prophecies, and most refer to the downfall of the Order of Power because that is what they hope for in their limited worlds. They never come true. Why should this one?' She stopped directly before him. 'I certainly don't believe it,' she concluded.

'But others do.'

His statement trapped her. 'Yes. Others do,' she

admitted. 'And that's another reason why you won't succeed, even if you could learn five specialities. No member of the Order will offer to teach you. They protect their skills as much as possible from each other, as it is. Now their fear of a wretchedly silly prophecy will doubly ensure they will refuse your requests.'

'But Lady Tarnyss -'

'Was being politically shrewd and polite,' Seralinna cut in. 'She gave an instruction to the Order that she knows full well will be disobeyed completely. It's an old game, and you'll be its victim this time. Some of them will even take you into their Keeps and pretend to teach you, but they'll neglect details, important details, so, when you're put to the test at assessment in a year's time, you'll be found deficient. Lady Tarnyss has no intention of giving you a fair chance at success. As a pawn to the Supreme Council, you'll merely enhance her prestige as President.'

Her revelation shook him to the core of his being. While he'd been planning his strategy to learn the Fourth Ki, Tarnyss and her Council were skilfully outmanoeuvring him. Corinna said that his pride would be his downfall. Now he understood her meaning more clearly than she probably thought he would. They weren't going to teach him their magic. They intended to starve him of it, lead him on in a false belief that he was gaining power, and destroy him when he most expected success. He grinned, as he sifted through his thoughts, and then chuckled aloud. This, he thought, could be more fun than ever, a challenge worthy of me, one I will relish, if I play my part of the game with rare cunning. On impulse, he hugged Seralinna, lifted her off the floor, and kissed her cheek. She gasped a foreign word and became a white dove, fluttering out of his grasp, but her startled transformation did not dampen his joy. As she settled on the bench, he cried, 'With you as my teacher, I will master much more than a mere five specialities, Seralinna! I understand the nature of these political games you so dislike, and frankly, I enjoy them!' A puzzled dove peered at him from the bench top.

Twenty Two

'Ironim ornyth!' A Ahmud Ki stretched his arms wide.

'Focus in! You must believe! You must want to be the creature!' Seralinna yelled, as she drifted in a circle overhead.

'I believe! I believe!' he rasped, through gritted teeth.

'Try again!' she encouraged. She dipped her falcon wings and mounted a warm upward current. She loved thermal flying.

A Ahmud Ki concentrated inwards, worked back over the spell theory, checked the feathers were tucked into his belt, and repeated the words. 'Ironim ornyth!' Nothing happened. 'Damn! I want to be a bird! I want to be a bird!' he muttered, and his frustration intensified as he recanted the order and ingredients of the spell. I will be a bird – anything - even like that stupid swallow over there. He watched the bird roll and dart between the mounds at the foot of Seralinna's Keep. Even that! 'Ironim! Ironim ornyth!' The air was punched from his chest, and the earth rushed to meet his face. Overwhelmed by vertigo, he pitched forward, face-first, his beak digging into the soil. Beak? Yes! A beak! I've done it!

Seralinna shouted congratulations. 'You've done it! You've done it!'

'Of course I've done it,' he mumbled, and struggled to his feet, disoriented and awkward so close to the ground, trying to balance with a tail. He flicked dirt off his beak, stretched out his left wing tentatively, and toppled over. A rush of wing beats settled beside him.

'Are you alright?' Seralinna asked, chuckling.

A Ahmud Ki righted his swallow body after a short struggle, and declared, 'Of course I'm alright. The spell unsettled me a little, that's all. Let's fly!'

'Wait -!' she warned, but he launched forward, only to topple helplessly, wing over wing, down the side of the mound that had become a steep hillside for a swallow. She glided down to join him at the bottom. 'Are you hurt?' she asked.

He stood, with all the dignity a swallow could muster, puffed out his chest, and snapped, 'No! This is so cursed clumsy! I can't even fly. I made a mistake in the spell conjuration.'

'No, you didn't,' she laughed. 'You'll fly. But remember, you've only created the shape of a swallow. Have you ever flown before?'

He shook his head. 'Levitation's the limit. I was studying how to make objects fly, or at least move through the air, in the Great Palace Irandu Shadu, but I wasn't able to complete the study.'

'Then you'll have to learn the way all small birds do,' she said. 'You must become one with your new shape, learn its balance and its intricacies. You must get a feeling for air movement, how it flows over and through your feathers, how it can be made to lift you. You must learn the speed you need to flap your wings to get lift, and when to bend your wings back or forward to climb or stall. Then, and only then, will you have any idea how to fly.'

'But that will take too long!' protested the swallow. 'Why didn't you teach me bird-shaping first?'

'Because bird-shaping is the hardest of the shape-changing spells I can teach you, and flight is the most difficult skill to master. That's why I taught you the others first, and you've mastered them in three weeks. No one has ever learned so quickly!' Her eyes sparkled with excitement. 'But now you'll need time to learn flight from your mother bird.' When he looked puzzled, she laughed, and said, 'Me of course!' and, with that, she leapt into the air, leaving him floundering in the grass.

He flew for the first time five days later, after exhausting sessions of adjusting to the balance and weight of the body he adopted in the spell. He wobbled into the air from a Keep window, six arm spans up, while Seralinna was grinding flour on the ground floor, and he glided a full circle around the Keep. The flight thrilled him. He dipped towards the lower floor window where she was working, to show her what he'd learned, misjudged the width of the window, and flew smack into the wall of the Keep. She heard a thud against the stone, after which her walls whispered that a bird had hit them, and a man lay motionless on the ground outside her window. She rushed out to find A Ahmud Ki unconscious and bleeding. He took a full week to recover. She scolded him for his recklessness, and threatened to teach him nothing more because he was lucky to be alive, but he felt only a growing love for her, and the more she fussed and bullied him about the incident the more he teased her, and he smiled at her chiding. If he'd ever wanted the company of a woman, this young sorceress with her mane of auburn hair was that woman.

Seralinna sensed the change in his approach and secretly liked what she felt and saw, but she maintained her mock anger in case he misunderstood her real feelings. She loved him, wanted him, but deep inside a moth burred its wings whenever she watched him practise a new magical feat, as if warning her that the old prophetic words were closer to being true than she wanted to accept.

He surprised her, one afternoon, when he said he no longer wanted to practise magic. She wondered if the accident caused him to lose interest, but she knew that would never be the case for him. Yet he arrived in her portal later each morning, and left her Keep well before sunset, explaining that he needed more time for sleep. During the ensuing days, he insisted on walking with her across the bright green rolling hills and beside eager bubbling creeks cutting to the east, and standing beneath the shady boughs of the few trees in the valleys to take in the vista. He asked about her childhood, about her learning, about her land, and listened intently to everything she said. He spent long moments staring at her, which she found initially disturbing, and eventually flattering. His oddest requests were for her to repeat comments, asides and unimportant statements she hadn't realized she'd made, and he would strain to listen, as if they were the most significant words she had uttered. His interest in shape changing had disappeared. She hadn't seen him practising the intricate and taxing spells she'd taught to him, and feared he'd discovered the risks involved in altering to bird shape too demanding. She also found herself falling all too far in love with the stranger of whom she knew too little.

'You said forests were destroyed to build the city and ships?' he repeated, interrupting her thoughts.

'Uhuh. That's why there are no forests in Targa, no homes for woodland-dwelling creatures. All that remains is what your eyes show you, small clumps and isolated single trees. Even the mountain ridge forests have fallen to the axes.'

'But how do your people build new ships or new towns?'

Seralinna stopped to rest under a giant spreading fig and sat on a twisted root. 'The ships range across the oceans, and our foresters forage in other lands where forests are plentiful.'

'So now your men cut down the forests of other people.'

'I suppose so. What does it matter?'

He walked on several steps. Within, a fragment of his Aelendyell spirit protested the wanton destruction of trees, the deaths of kindred souls, but a coal of hate also burned, and grim satisfaction filled his heart at the description of the destruction. 'It doesn't matter,' he agreed and stopped to look at her. 'I must see these ships you mention. I know a place where there are large tracts of forest that would build thousands of ships for Targa. I'll take you there one day.'

Hearing the hard edge in his voice, she knew something was wrong. 'You've asked all the questions, during the last few days, and I've answered as best as I can. Now I want to ask you something.' She caught her breath. 'Why aren't you learning your skills? Have you forgotten the Council and Tarnyss?' He threw back his head and laughed – a response that astonished her, and, for a moment she was too numb to speak, until she blurted, 'What's so damned funny about that?' She blushed at her own passionate outburst when he levelled his cool grey eyes at her, and she looked away.

'Seralinna.' His soft voice drew her gaze back to where he'd been standing, but he was gone. Hovering, wings beating faster than her eyes could see, was a bright yellow, red, and green hummingbird. The hummingbird changed colour and shape to become a magpie that flew effortlessly from under the fig's boughs into the blue sky. As the bird gained height, it changed into a majestic eagle, circling on wind eddies, before hanging motionless, momentarily, on an updraft. She stepped from under the tree to watch the eagle rise higher. A sharp keening cut the air, the eagle stooped, and plummeted towards the earth with fearful speed, levelling to disappear behind a hillock fifty paces from where she stood. A moment later, A Ahmud Ki crested the hillock, carrying the fresh carcass of a plump quail in his hands, smiling broadly. She understood why his manner had changed.

The mild bright days swiftly cooled, and a crisp, white layer of sparkling snow blanketed the Targan hills. Seralinna kept her Keep shutters closed against the chill, and practised warming spells that A Ahmud Ki taught her before he left on his first visitation to a member of the Order. Seralinna advised him to go to Katrin. Her Keep was to the north, nestled in the foothills of Westridge Range. Like Seralinna, she had no interest in the politics of the Order of Power. Her speciality was controlling spells, but Seralinna warned that she was reluctant to share her skill with anyone she distrusted, and so Seralinna offered to go on A Ahmud Ki's behalf to ask for Katrin's help. He declined her offer, saying he preferred to convince her alone, but he'd been gone for more than four weeks, and Seralinna hadn't heard from either A Ahmud Ki or Katrin to indicate how he was faring. She considered visiting Katrin's Keep, but she resisted her curiosity, knowing that too close an interest might be misconstrued as jealous prying - which set her to wondering if Katrin had too eagerly favoured her handsome visitor, or whether A Ahmud Ki was using his charm on Katrin as he'd done on her.

She descended the cold wooden steps from her sleeping chamber and entered the Travel chamber, with its familiar blue haze, shivering from the touch of the room's icy air. Three paces took her to a low shelf, and she collected a small lump of igneous rock, silky smooth from years of polishing. She cupped it in her hands, as A Ahmud Ki had taught her, and uttered the Ranu Ka Shehaala words, 'Ne esta ka markesh jinn nyaru.' Her palms were lit by a warm, orange glow, as she carried the stone to the centre of the room to place it on a low table. Warmth gradually spread through the room.

'Impressive.'

The intruder's statement startled her. Turning quickly, she saw a silhouette in the further shadows of the room. 'Who are you?' she challenged.

Lady Tarnyss stepped into the dull circle of light. 'I apologize. I thought you would have recognized my voice. You must attend Council more often, Seralinna.'

Seralinna relaxed a little, but the President of the Supreme Council of Targa's uninvited presence made her uncertain and cautious. Out of respect for authority, she curtsied, saying, 'I accept the great honour your Ladyship bestows upon me with this visit. I did not expect you, so I am unprepared, but please share what provender I have.' She indicated for Tarnyss to follow her out of the room, but Tarnyss waved aside her offer.

'I don't have time for your formal speech or pleasant trivialities. I came to ask you a couple of questions, and that is all. I'll be brief. I expect your responses to be equally so. Am I understood?' Seralinna nodded. 'Good,' added Tarnyss. She moved towards the warming stone and its orange glow. 'Where did you learn this?'

'A Ahmud Ki showed me.'

'And what else has he shown you?'

Seralinna heard the malicious tone in the question and wondered what degree of honesty she ought to give in her answers. Tarnyss was playing one of her political games. 'Not a great deal - some simple purification spells, like Renatha uses, but different because of the language. He hasn't had time to teach me a great deal.'

'No doubt,' Tarnyss quipped. 'Has he tried his mind spells on you?'

She watched Seralinna's face for a guarded reaction, but the question drew genuine surprise from the young sorceress. 'Not at all. I wasn't even aware that he knew mind spells. I thought he'd gone to Ka –' She stifled her speech and cursed herself for her carelessness.

'He's gone to Katrin's? When?' Tarnyss demanded.

She didn't know, thought Seralinna. 'Several weeks ago. He left after he'd stayed here for a time.'

'Before you went to Katrin's, you mean?' Tarnyss said, as she walked towards the portal.

She didn't see Seralinna's surprise. 'I haven't been to Katrin's for some time,' she replied.

Tarnyss' measured tone carried a cold warning edge that cut into Seralinna's confusion. 'Don't lie to me, girl. I know you've been at Katrin's Keep for three weeks or more. You've been seen there, and Katrin came to ask me if I minded her teaching you some of her skills.' Her dark eyes became glistening slits of suspicion. 'What game are you playing? I thought you were too good to frolic in politics?'

Seralinna's confusion worsened. 'I don't know what you're trying to prove. With all respect, Lady Tarnyss, I've not been near Katrin's Keep, and I doubt Katrin would –' She broke off again, struggling to control her inner turmoil.

Lady Tarnyss smiled. 'You doubt that Katrin would come to me for advice? Once, perhaps, but people change, Seralinna. People change. Katrin has. So too, it seems, have you, though I can't see you'd learn much in the time you spent with Katrin. We all start small, though. Who knows, perhaps one day you'll rise to sit on Council? I very much doubt it, though. You're far too naïve, Seralinna, even now.'

Lady Tarnyss returned to the warming stone and passed a hand over it. The glow subsided and the stone returned to a cold, hard object. 'A simple trick - useful, but not terribly rare.' She sat on the edge of the table. 'Which reminds me - where is your brash male friend? Oh, that's right, off to visit Katrin. That's a pity really, because Katrin is terribly superstitious, especially where prophecies are concerned. She won't be very co-operative.'

Tarnyss' calculated jibe angered Seralinna. She had to endure the taunts, there was no alternative for her, but her hands shook with rage, so she clasped them to steady herself. 'Is that all you wanted to know?' she asked, with cool deliberation.

'No, not quite. Be patient, young lady. Don't let irritations upset your manners. I have two more questions. First, why did you visit Vanyessa this week?'

The question perplexed Seralinna further. She hadn't been beyond her own Keep for over a fortnight, and that excursion was to the village for provisions, because the hawker failed to stop by her Keep before the first snowfall. Something was dreadfully amiss with Lady Tarnyss' information, or else her political game was exceedingly complex. She withheld her answer with a question of her own. 'Who told you that I was at Vanyessa's Keep?'

'So, you admit being there!'

'I never said that. I merely asked where you get your inaccurate information from.'

The smile faded from Tarnyss' lips. 'If you intend to play word games with me, girl, I assure you that you will be the loser. I have my sources, and they are good ones. You were seen there.'

'If you say so,' was Seralinna's non-committal response. 'What was your other question?'

Tarnyss was discernibly annoyed with Seralinna's diffidence. She moved to the portal and stared at the blue sheet of light. 'We know your friend has his own portal. You helped him to construct it. Can you visit him whenever you wish?'

'Why do you ask that?'

'Just answer the question!'

Tarnyss' order was full of threat and anger, and Seralinna knew it was wiser to answer this question honestly. 'I haven't been in his tower since he left to study with Katrin. In fact, I haven't been in his tower for at least six or seven weeks. There's no need to go there.'

'But you could go?'

'I suppose so - if I wanted.'

Without further consideration, Lady Tarnyss stretched out her arms and incanted the spell to open the portal into A Ahmud Ki's tower. Seralinna instinctively stood behind her, surprised by the President's impulsive move. The portal shimmered, and focussed on a crimson curved inner wall, and Lady Tarnyss stepped in - and simultaneously stepped out again into Seralinna's room. Anger surged. 'No!' She slapped her arms against her sides and stamped her feet with rage. 'Urgh! Curse him!' The scene so frightened Seralinna that she retreated graciously from the room, as Tarnyss worked out her tantrum. There was a blue flash, and when Seralinna peered into her Travel Chamber the President of the Supreme Council was gone.

Twenty Three

She watched the snow owl skim across the undulating ground, heading for her Keep, using its wings to dip and rise and turn with consummate ease. Birds were by far her favoured creatures, and she felt deep satisfaction that her mother taught her exceedingly well in her art. She was surprised when the owl flew through her open window, landed on the floor, shook moisture from its feathers, and became a tall half-Aelendyell wizard with piercing grey eyes. A Ahmud Ki smiled. He loved how Seralinna's auburn hair fell about her shoulders, and the cool winter air brought a fresh touch of red to her lips and cheeks, enhancing her natural beauty. Her sparkling eyes made him want to laugh with sheer joy. He'd missed her and was glad to be back in her Keep. 'You've learned very well,' she said, in greeting.

'I was taught well,' he replied, and laughed. 'I've returned from Vanyessa's Keep.'

Seralinna studied him carefully, as she said, 'Yes, I know. I thought you may have been there.'

'How did you know?'

'Lady Tarnyss visited me, two days ago.'

A Ahmud Ki nodded. 'I might have expected that. What else did she tell you?'

'Strange things,' she replied. 'I think she has some plan afoot, but I really can't fathom her purpose. She claimed I was at Katrin's, and Vanyessa's. Why would she do that?'

A Ahmud Ki's smile altered to a cheeky grin, and he looked out the window at the snow-draped landscape. 'Perhaps she was informed you were there.'

'But who would tell her that? I wasn't there.'

'Katrin would for a start,' he replied, as he strode across the room. 'You were wrong about Katrin's political neutrality, Seralinna. She sits firmly in Tarnyss' palm. She warned me about the perils of being associated with the evil wizard who claims to come from the land of barbarians. She was reluctant to teach me any skills before consulting with Tarnyss.'

His explanation was puzzling. He had to be confused. Why would Katrin warn him about himself? 'Did she teach you?' she asked.

A Ahmud Ki chuckled with delight. 'More than she even knows.'

'But how am I involved in all this?'

A Ahmud Ki grinned. 'Katrin taught you all her skills, not me.'

'I don't understand.'

'I know,' he said, touching her shoulder. 'Watch.' He moved from the wooden table, and reached inside the fold of his robe, to hold something hidden against his chest. He extended his left hand and wove an intricate pattern around his head and body, intoning the spell. 'Met Shehaal Kis! Ka Seralinna akis n'tel jinn nyaru! Sek feran yaseem!' A red glow of energy enveloped his body, and his shape blurred and altered dimension. When the glow dissipated, Seralinna was staring at her own image. The hair bristled on the neck. Her image smiled and shook back its auburn hair. 'Well? What do you think?'

The transformation shocked her. She felt numb, empty. What could she think? A Ahmud Ki saw her reaction and cancelled the spell, assuming his own form, but when he moved gently towards her, she cried, 'No! Don't! Don't come any closer!'

He stopped, but he extended his hands. 'I'm sorry,' he apologized softly. 'I didn't mean to upset you.'

She bit her lip and turned away, and he heard choking sobs in her voice. 'Wh-why did y-you do th-at?'

'I had to, Seralinna. It was the simplest way. You understand that. Tarnyss would never let Katrin teach me. She's filled her head with nonsense about the prophecy. And Vanyessa's too. So, I made them teach you, and Tarnyss is none the wiser that it was really me, not you, they taught.'

When Seralinna turned, her eyes gleamed with tears and

anger. 'And that explains why Tarnyss came here to mock me. Me! Not you! You had no right to do that! You didn't even ask if I minded!'

A Ahmud Ki dropped his hands. 'If you knew what I was doing -' His voice trailed away.

'I know,' she said. 'If I knew, I might have told someone, like Lady Tarnyss. Is that all the trust you have in me?' she asked, anger crackling in her voice.

'It's not trust I'm considering,' he replied. 'It's your safety.'

'What danger am I in?' she snapped. 'Who would dare threaten me in my own Keep?'

'You befriended me,' he calmly explained. 'That makes you an opponent to Tarnyss and the Council. You said so yourself, before you chose to teach me your speciality.'

'You make it sound like Tarnyss' politics. I'm opposing no one! I simply wanted to help you.'

'Every decision, every action, is political, Seralinna. Lady Corinna taught me that law on her first visit here.'

She glared at him. 'I'm not interested in playing political games!'

'You are already playing.'

She looked bewildered, before she ran up the stairs, leaving him in the room, staring after her.

He locked himself in his tower Spell Room for three days, working long sessions to modify and improve the spells Katrin taught him. They were simple spells, like the Ithosen mind spells, and he learned them with ease because the field was familiar, though the language and the focus were different. He made no attempt to visit Seralinna's Keep. Her response to his impersonation of her caused him deep regret, and he didn't know how long it would be before she might forgive him. He would wait. She would visit when she was ready. He knew she'd come when she forgot her anger.

In the Portal Room, he stared at the red energy lighting the curved wall. Its colour differed from the blue haze of the

197

Targan portals because he modified it according to his studies in Ranu Ka Shehaala, making his portal more powerful and easier to control. Targan portals were two-way affairs, allowing anyone with a portal to tune into them, and come and go at will. He could make his operate one-way, locking access to it from anyone, except those whose voice imprints he commanded it to recognize. Only two people could use his portal - himself, and Seralinna. He wished she would step through.

He ascended through the ceiling to the Devotional Room. The space was entirely black, and unfurnished. Spinning at the centre, suspended from the ceiling by its own volition, irradiating a soft amber glow, was a talisman of Berak N'eth, the God of Power. A Ahmud Ki kneeled beneath it, face to the floor. He knelt to nothing but Power itself. The amber light intensified, permeated his being, and filled him with renewed energy, new desire to learn. This land of Targa was the source of the Fourth Ki, and already part of it was in his grasp. He would become all-powerful – a wizard beyond anything the Aelendyell, or Ithosen or Members of the Order could imagine. His God willed it. He, A Ahmud Ki, willed it. He meditated beneath the spinning icon, practising chants and hand motions associated with his newly acquired skills. Lady Tarnyss and the Council were blocking his path to learn from Members of the Order. There had to be a way to circumvent them. His guise as Seralinna worked on Katrin, but Seralinna's angry reaction prevented him from using that ploy any further. If the emotional objection had come from another person, he wouldn't have cared, but Seralinna was different. He cared for her. No doubt Lady Tarnyss would have advised Vanyessa, though he'd already given up learning from her speciality – fire spells – because he'd mastered fire skills from Aelendyell Lore. Yet he had to learn three more specialities, and that meant finding three more members of the Order whom Tarnyss couldn't influence.

He leapt to his feet, cast a spell, and descended to the Portal Room. He portalled into Seralinna's Keep and listened for her voice or movement. Her Keep was silent, cold. He descended the stairs to the ground floor, searching for Seralinna as he went. Finally, he placed both hands on the wall and concentrated. 'Where is your Mistress?'

A whispering, resonating voice replied. 'Gone. Gone away. She is gone.'

He removed his hands and ran them through his silver locks. Where would she have gone? He had questions to ask, a plan to explain. He'd thought of the obvious answer to beat Tarnyss at her own game. He wanted Seralinna to know, even if she didn't approve. Now she wouldn't know and couldn't help him. He could wait for her to return, but that might cost days in time. The answers to his questions – perhaps – perhaps Katrin. No. Vanyessa. Yes, Vanyessa! She'd have the answers – if he beat Tarnyss to her. He morphed into Seralinna's shape and ran upstairs to the Travel Room.

The instant he stepped through the portal, they were on him, their weight pushing him to the floor, a hammer-like blow smashing the breath from his chest. He coughed, gasped for air, as strong arms lifted and pinioned him against the rough stone wall. 'Who in the three hells are you?' a deep male voice boomed. A Ahmud Ki could only see a bulky form towering over him. 'I asked you a question, dog food! Who are you?' repeated the voice.

'I am A Ahmud Ki.'

'Never heard of you. For what purpose do you arrive through Milady's portal uninvited?'

'I want to speak to her.' A Ahmud Ki slowly made out his aggressor's features. The man was fully bearded, his hair cut close to the scalp. He had a broad, flat nose.

'Are you from Council?'

'No.'

The warrior glanced over his shoulder. 'Wilfred! Come look at this, you old bag of horse fodder!' Feet shuffled, and a wizened face peered around the warrior's side at A Ahmud Ki. 'Have you seen this one at Council, or in any assemblies of the Order?'

The wizened face pushed closer and A Ahmud Ki could see the fuzz of white hair barely covering a bald pate. The face was a mass of wrinkles. 'No. Not this one. Not at all, friend Boeris. I've never seen this face at assemblies. He must be new, he must be. Hee, hee, hee,' giggled the old man hoarsely. 'Ooh, won't they be upset! Another wizard. And a young one too. Hee, hee, hee.'

'Shut up, you babbling old idiot,' growled the impatient warrior.

The old man turned on Boeris, straining in vain to straighten his hunched shoulders and stooped back. 'You mind your manners, young sonny,' he wheezed.

'Get back to your doddling cleaning,' the warrior ordered. He took hold of the old man's shoulders and effortlessly pushed him behind his back.

'Cheeky young reprobate!' the old voice croaked, but as Boeris wheeled, A Ahmud Ki heard footsteps shuffle to safety.

'Old fool!' the warrior spat. The pair restraining A Ahmud Ki laughed. Boeris leaned forward and grabbed A Ahmud Ki's cheeks in one hand. 'Now for you, my friend.' He inspected A Ahmud Ki's features. 'Your face isn't familiar at all, is it? Strange face. You don't look like one of our kind. The eyes are different. But old Wilfred can't be right about you not belonging to the Order of Power. You dress like them, all tarted up to look impressive.' Boeris fingered A Ahmud Ki's robes. 'A wizard, is it? What's your speciality?' he asked derisively.

A Ahmud Ki focussed on patience, to quell his mounting anger. 'I haven't come here to discuss my power with a lowly servant,' he coldly replied.

Boeris straightened, and raised a huge, menacing hand. 'We don't have much time for the Order of Power, or whatever you belong to! One more smart answer from your pretty mouth and I'll turn your face into pigs' gruel! Understand?'

A Ahmud Ki smiled too confidently. 'I understand

perfectly.'

Boeris glared, lifted his hand higher on the backswing. 'That will do Boeris!' a woman's voice warned. Boeris held his hand high, his eyes fixed on A Ahmud Ki.

A Ahmud Ki's smile widened in response to the voice. 'Go on Boeris, complete the job. Pigs' gruel. Remember? Like you,' he quietly taunted, and watched rage smoulder in the man's face.

'Boeris!' the woman ordered firmly. Boeris' hand fell to his side, and he turned to the approaching figure. A Ahmud Ki laughed quietly, and watched Boeris' back flinch. The woman came into view, surrounded by a soft halo of light. Her brown hair neatly tied into a bun, exposing her slender neck, she wore a grey smock, with a light grey cloak draped over her shoulders. The light accentuated her face in the otherwise dull room. Neither beautiful, nor young, her face held a dignified charm, and a sparkle of intelligence played in the corners of her brown eyes. A coronet, laced with diamonds, sat lightly in her hair, and she held a green staff in her right hand. She studied A Ahmud Ki, as if searching for minute hidden detail, before directing her attention to the two men holding him. 'Release him. He will do no harm here.'

The warriors relaxed their hold, and A Ahmud Ki shook his arms to restore circulation. 'Thank you,' he said, grinning at the warriors, and he bowed to the sorceress.

'I'm sorry,' she said. 'I gave Boeris strict instructions that none of Lady Tarnyss' prying Council should be allowed to enter my Keep, without my permission. He's a little too enthusiastic, at times.' Boeris looked at her with the expression of a whipped dog as she held her hand towards A Ahmud Ki. 'I'm Jasmin.'

He took the proffered hand. 'I am A Ahmud Ki.'

'Yes,' she said. 'I know. You're the one the Members of the Order claim is here to fulfil an ancient prophecy. I know why you've come.'

They stood on the tower, looking across the castle battlements and craggy rocks towards the snow-capped peaks far to the west. The morning sun at their backs cast gold across the distant snow. 'The land of Targa ends there, at those mountains, as it also ends here, in the steep foothills of these mountains. Beyond the western peaks lies the Kingdom of Thana. Beyond the mountains here lies another Kingdom, Andros. I've never been to either, and I have no desire to,' said Jasmin matter-of-factly. 'My home is here.'

As the sunrise extended its golden fingers westward, A Ahmud Ki glanced at Boeris, who was a polite five paces away. Everywhere Jasmin and A Ahmud Ki went, he went, like a persistent shadow, or a jealous lover. Whenever Jasmin looked at Boeris, he glowed with pride, but he scowled at A Ahmud Ki, especially when the latter smiled graciously at him. A Ahmud Ki asked Jasmin why Boeris had to follow them, and she replied, 'It's his duty,' with no further explanation.

Jasmin happily taught him her specialities, because she held no love for Tarnyss or the Council, or the Order of Power, and she was fascinated by the half-Aelendyell. She was a master of two specialities, not one, and that discovery made A Ahmud Ki secretly ecstatic, more so when he learned from her that one – store magic spells - wasn't accorded her by the Council. A surprise for him meant a certain surprise for Tarnyss. Jasmin's legitimate speciality was locking spells. Both were new areas of study for A Ahmud Ki, so he applied himself to everything she taught with added zeal. In return, he taught her simpler Aelendyell spells, and he began to instruct her in shape-change spells, giving her access to a third speciality, though she would take many, many months to acquire the knowledge and skills that he took for granted after only weeks. She was enthralled by his capacity to learn quickly, and marvelled at his abilities to modify spells, speed the process of creation, and enhance the magnitude and duration of them. She asked questions, and he taught her the Ithosen techniques for learning, but he knew he couldn't help her acquire his talent; a talent that was innate to his being, and became so the night he opened the Aelendyell Lore Book. By accident, or by design, he inherited an Elvenaar talent, which ought to have perished with the passing of that great race of magical beings. It was why he was A Ahmud Ki.

Winter passed. The white landscape dissolved, the hinterland snows melted into fast-flowing creeks, and hues of green emerged as far as the eye could see. Birdlife and wildlife multiplied, and the small creatures reminded A Ahmud Ki of Seralinna. He'd finished all he needed to learn from the gracious Jasmin, and he was tired of old Wilfred's prying questions, and Boeris' icy stare. He stayed longer than he intended, but he had learned much more than he anticipated, so the time spent was justified, but it was time to leave.

On the morning he was preparing to take his leave, his door echoed to the heavy knock of a warrior's glove. When he opened it, a sword point flashed to his throat. Boeris grinned at its extremity. 'I know who you are,' he scowled. 'The village witches warned us. It's time we listened to them.' He gestured to two warriors accompanying him. 'Bind him. And bind his arms especially well.' A Ahmud Ki flinched, and felt the sword point press menacingly against his flesh. 'I wouldn't,' snarled Boeris. 'Wizard you might be, but I'll make you whistle through the side of your neck before you complete one word of your fiendish spells.' A Ahmud Ki relaxed, letting the warriors tie his hands behind his back. Boeris stepped aside and indicated the tower stairs with a gesture of his sword. 'Take him up. I'd like this wizard to see the beautiful land he threatens to destroy.' A Ahmud Ki ascended the stairs in silence, with Boeris following. The group stepped into bright daylight, and A Ahmud Ki breathed in the sweet freshness of the crisp morning air. 'Enjoy it,' growled Boeris. 'It will be your last.' The warriors manhandled A Ahmud Ki to the edge of the tower, and hoisted him onto the low parapet. He looked down to the razor teeth of the ragged rocks; dark, ugly, and hungry for blood.

He smiled inwardly as he turned to Boeris. 'Since you're about to kill me, you could oblige my last request.'

Boeris spat on the stone with contempt. 'You get no favours. But ask anyway.'

'Why are you killing me? And does Lady Jasmin approve?'

Boeris' face reddened. 'You know the reasons. I dearly would love to have cut out your liver the first morning you blundered into this castle and laid eyes upon our lady. If you had once touched her, in any way, I would have cut you apart, you sewer rat! But that's not why you're here. The good lady doesn't know. She's away, searching the hills for dew and herbs, and other things your kind favours. When she returns, you'll be long gone, and she'll be none the wiser.'

'So?' repeated A Ahmud Ki. 'What's the reason?'

Boeris thrust his face forward. 'You are evil. Filth! You're the coming of the prophecy. Don't think I don't know. I know! I've watched you. You're not like the rest of them. You learn too much, too quickly. You're only interested in what you can get. That's dangerous in any man, or woman. But in you, it's worse - and much, much more. It's wrong! The ancient prophets warned us. Drive out the One who comes seeking all power for He will unleash Evil on the World and destroy Good. If you live, we all die. I'm making sure you don't live. For everyone.'

A Ahmud Ki focussed on Boeris' mind, something he should have done many times before, but he'd underestimated the man. The real answer was there, in his mind; Lady Tarnyss. Boeris was her paid servant. His duty was to keep an eye on Jasmin to make sure she plotted no tricks against the Council or its President. It made perfect sense. 'So how much does Tarnyss know?'

His question visibly affected Boeris. The warrior cursed under his breath before turning to his companions. 'There'll be no prophecy fulfilled in our time! Throw the pig swill over!' Both men heaved, and A Ahmud Ki tumbled over the edge. Part way down, there was a sharp flash of light, and a peregrine falcon cartwheeled out of the falling knotted rope, gathered speed, and climbed steeply. The empty rope thudded against the rocks. The bird stooped at the three astonished men crouching on the tower, and as it sped down the hillsides to the south a voice whispered in the rush of its wings, 'You're a dead man, Boeris.'

Twenty Four

Lady Tarnyss glared at the peregrine falcon on the window ledge. The bird ruffled its feathers and cocked its head inquisitively. 'Why you have any interest in such trifling creatures I'll never know,' she said disdainfully.

'They don't harm people,' Seralinna replied. She moved to the window ledge, to stroke the bird's head. It waited for her touch. 'And they know whom to trust,' she added.

'Fools trust other fools,' Tarnyss retorted, 'which is why I come to visit you again. Has your wizard returned?'

Seralinna kept stroking the falcon. 'No. Not yet.'

'And if he had, I doubt very much that you would tell me, would you?' said Tarnyss with a mocking smile.

'Don't tar me with your dishonest brush.'

Lady Tarnyss raised her eyebrows. 'I see your manners haven't improved. Little matter. I take it you've at least heard from your A Ahmud Ki?'

Seralinna shook her head. 'No.'

'Come now, girl. You hardly expect me to believe that. He's surely communicated something to you in all this time.'

'He left while I was absent, Lady Tarnyss, and I've neither heard from nor seen him since.' Seralinna stopped stroking the bird and returned to the centre of the room. 'For all I know,' she added quietly, 'he returned to his home.'

'You and I both know he hasn't done that. The tower still stands,' said Lady Tarnyss. She reached inside the fold of her cloak, and withdrew a small amber ball, which she held in the palm of her left hand. She passed her right hand over it in a deliberate pattern, uttering a short magical phrase and the ball expanded, changing colour to a milky hue. She placed it on Seralinna's table. 'Do you know what this is, girl?'

'A ball of communication?' Seralinna offered.

Tarnyss nodded. 'Correct. That's how I know where your

friend has been. My informants each have one so they can tell me what is happening, and where people are. Your wizard has been stirring up trouble among the rebels.'

Seralinna was puzzled. 'Who are the rebels?' she asked.

'How little you understand,' scoffed Tarnyss. 'The ones who fail to attend assemblies of the Order and High Council. They refuse to be part of the Order. They oppose my Presidency. They are the rebels, especially, now that they've aided him.'

'If you know so much about what he's been doing, why bother asking me?' Seralinna asked, irritated with Tarnyss' arrogance.

Tarnyss flashed angry eyes. 'I knew he was going to Jasmin's castle on the northern hinterland. He asked Vanyessa who the rebels were, who didn't support me, or the current High Council. He chose to visit Jasmin first. Vanyessa told me. My informant in Jasmin's castle kept a close eye on him while he was there, and I know Jasmin defied me by teaching him. Then, he apparently flew away.' Lady Tarnyss paused to throw a quick glance at the window. The falcon was gone. She drew a breath, before continuing. 'Next, I learned he arrived at that idiot fool Marcus' Keep, and he convinced Marcus to dismiss all his people for a time. My informant there tried to persuade Marcus not to listen, but the idiot turned him into a spider, and gave him to a servant to carry away until the spell wore off. What concerns me most is that, the following day, all the rebels disappeared from their Keeps, even Jasmin, and I'm certain they assembled at Marcus' Keep.' A faint smile crossed Seralinna's lips. 'What is so amusing?' snapped Lady Tarnyss.

Seralinna composed herself. 'Pardon my forwardness, Lady Tarnyss,' she politely began, 'but I can't help feeling, even given my naiveté, that you so politely point out in these matters, you've been beaten at your own political game.'

Lady Tarnyss smashed her fist down against the table, and the communication ball, jumped, rolled over the edge, and shattered on the slate floor. 'How little you know!' Her voice sparkled with anger. 'Even with their help, he cannot withstand me, or the High Council!'

'You talk as though he wanted your position of President. He's merely completing your challenge.'

'And doesn't he want it?' Tarnyss asked. 'Do you think that such a challenge, especially if he overcomes it, will be all a man like him would want?' she screeched. 'He wants more! Much more! And if he succeeds, when no sorceress or wizard has succeeded before, who can oppose him? No one! No one!' Her voice reached a note of hysteria, which made Seralinna step back, frightened by the lady's passion. Tarnyss' eyes were wide, staring at Seralinna, fixing her fear in the mind of the younger woman. She shivered, sighed deeply, and turned away to walk to the window. Silence filled the room, leaving both women lost in their thoughts.

A footfall on the stairs broke Seralinna's reverie. She saw A Ahmud Ki descending and motioned for him to withdraw, but he continued down, and entered. 'I've just returned,' he announced, and feigned surprise at Lady Tarnyss' presence. 'I beg your pardon. I didn't know you had a guest.'

Tarnyss turned with a sweet, insincere smile that matched his words. 'Even your timing is too perfect,' she said. He faintly bowed his head and reached for Seralinna's hand. Lady Tarnyss' voice cut across his movement. 'You will have plenty of time for that later. I wish to speak with him. Alone. Leave us, Seralinna.'

Seralinna tried to release A Ahmud Ki's hand, but he merely tightened his grip. 'I'm certain anything you have to say to me, Lady Tarnyss, can be shared in Seralinna's company.'

Tarnyss glared at Seralinna, then at A Ahmud Ki. 'Very well, have it as you wish.' She moved from the window and approached them. 'I take it that your time away has been fruitful?'

A Ahmud Ki smiled. 'Surely you, of all people, Lady Tarnyss, know that.' He glanced at the broken crystal pieces on the floor.

'You have no right to meddle as you have done,' she said tartly.

'You set the rules for the contest,' he dispassionately replied, and met her sharp glare with a broader grin. She scowled and returned to the window. As she did so, he bent forward, gathered the pieces of crystal from the floor, and set them on the table. When she turned back, A Ahmud Ki was holding a perfectly formed, milky ball in his hands. 'I believe this was broken.'

Lady Tarnyss visibly shuddered. 'How did you -' she blurted, but regained her composure to ask, 'Chana taught you mending spells, didn't she?'

'A little of her art,' A Ahmud Ki replied, placing the ball on the table. 'The Ithosen are far more adept at those skills than your people. She helped me modify finer, technical aspects of the spells.'

Lady Tarnyss was alert. 'What else did those rebellious fools teach you?'

'More than enough to meet the challenge of the High Council, Lady Tarnyss: I am ready to be tested.'

'Don't be so brash about what you may have learned, young man. You have a full month before you must take the test again, and a great deal can happen in that time.' Tarnyss straightened her robes and crossed to pick up the ball. She cupped it in her hands and carefully inspected it. She spoke a word, and it shrank to its original tiny dimension and amber coloration. She replaced it inside her robes, shrugged her shoulders, and resignation crossed her features. 'Perhaps I have been wrong to interfere with what seems to be inevitable,' she said, in a tired voice. Seralinna and A Ahmud Ki looked at each other, and Tarnyss hastily addressed their unspoken disbelief. 'For all you may think of me, Seralinna, I can accept when there is no alternative. I give credit where it is due. I appear to have been wrong. If you really have mastered five specialities -'

'Seven, Lady Tarnyss,' A Ahmud Ki cut in.

'Seven?' He smiled at her fleeting astonishment. She recovered her composure. 'Seven, then,' she said. 'If you have done this, then I will lose nothing in teaching you an eighth.' Seralinna gasped, and tightened her grip on A

Ahmud Ki's hand, but he remained unmoved. Within, however, he wondered at the sorceress' reasoning, trying to guess at her political gain from such an offer. Lady Tarnyss repeated it when he failed to respond. 'I offer to teach you one of my specialities,' she said.

'At what price?' he asked.

Lady Tarnyss smiled. 'Corinna said you would learn the game. Yes, a price. Naturally. The price is that I will be allowed to observe how you learn so quickly, and I expect to be taught something in return.'

A Ahmud Ki paused, before answering. He'd set his own trap to be given free rein to learn Targan magic, and triumphed, despite Tarnyss' concerted efforts to deny him. He held the balance. But her conditional offer had to have hidden advantages for her. She didn't strike him as one who would easily relinquish political control over her opponent, particularly if he was a potential threat to her status in the Order, which he obviously was with his magic and association with the rebel factions. He revelled in her last challenge. Now his growing political curiosity was aroused by her renewed duplicity. 'I accept your offer,' he finally replied, 'though I tell you, openly, that I suspect you have more in mind than you reveal at present.' Lady Tarnyss adopted a hurt expression, at which A Ahmud Ki smiled. 'But I, too, have a condition,' he added.

'What is it?' she asked cautiously.

'Seralinna accompanies me.'

Tarnyss tried to remain calm, but her reaction belied her true feelings, and he knew she didn't want Seralinna anywhere near him. 'I don't think that's very wise,' she advised. A Ahmud Ki shrugged to demonstrate indifference to her offer. 'But it will be arranged,' she conceded.

'Good. When do I come?'

'Now,' she said. 'You need nothing. Everything will be catered for in Targa.'

A Ahmud Ki shook his head. 'No. We'll come at sundown. I have matters to attend to first.'

Lady Tarnyss smiled and glanced at Seralinna. 'As you

wish. I've already overstayed my time here. I'll be ready for your arrival this evening.'

Seralinna led the sorceress upstairs to the Travel Room and its familiar blue haze. Moments later, she descended, to find A Ahmud Ki bending over her table. Two opaque creamy spheres sat on the table beneath his hands. 'Communication balls? How?' she asked.

He held one out. 'This one is yours.'

'Thank you. But how?' she repeated.

'Simple. I kept two fragments of the shattered crystal from Tarnyss' ball.'

'But mending spells only work if the whole is present.'

'True,' he acknowledged, 'but I didn't use something as simplistic as a mending spell. I created these with forming spells. You only need a part of the object to recreate the whole. Several parts mean that it's perfectly possible to create duplicates of the original whole. I learnt from Marcus that communication crystal is rare, very rare, and when I saw Tarnyss' shattered here I couldn't resist the opportunity. Now we have one each, and Tarnyss still has hers. Wherever we are, we can use these. But first I need to teach you an Aelendyell spell so you can keep the ball hidden on you. You must concentrate. You'll need this spell when we visit Lady Tarnyss, of that I'm all too certain.'

A Ahmud Ki concentrated, and pushed through the portal with a spell, searching beyond the blue haze. He touched six minds - five servants, or soldiers, with no apparent intent of harm. The sixth, Tarnyss, recoiled at his touch, bristling with indignation. 'It's safe,' he said, relaxing from the effort. 'There's no plot to catch us unaware, at least not yet.' He stepped through the portal. Seralinna followed. They entered the Great Hall and its familiar wooden architecture.

'Was that really necessary?' asked Lady Tarnyss.

A Ahmud Ki's demonstration of power rankled her. 'The last time I casually stepped through a portal, I was jumped, coincidentally, by one of your political servants. Learning involves avoiding the same mistake next time.'

'Very philosophical. You are under no threat from me.' She indicated her five unarmed male servants. 'If you would follow, I'll show you to your quarters. Stewards will attend your needs.'

She led them through a door, at the far end of the empty Hall, into a corridor with doors in either wall, evenly spaced. They passed through another door, into a courtyard covered with white gravel, through which coloured stones had been worked to form the outline of a great white steed with wings. The picture attracted A Ahmud Ki because he saw the resemblance to the horses the Ranu Ka Shehaala rode across their sweeping plains, but he'd never seen a horse with wings. He stopped Lady Tarnyss, to ask, 'What is that?'

She said, offhandedly, 'A Pegasus,' and went to continue across the courtyard, but A Ahmud Ki, enthralled by the vision, asked her another question.

'Do these creatures live in your land?'

Tarnyss halted, annoyed. 'No,' she said. 'There may have been Pegasii once, long ago, but, like the Elvenaar, and the Giants, and the Dragonlords, they've gone. They're legends, nothing more, although sailors, who've journeyed to distant islands, occasionally claim they've seen them.' She looked up at the purpling evening sky, before turning her eyes on A Ahmud Ki again. 'I doubt it, though,' she concluded, and continued across the courtyard.

The walls of the next building were hung with myriad tapestries, mainly depicting warriors in pitched battle against a background of mighty forests and raging rivers. Here and there, strange shapes blotted the pictures, like lizards flying. Some spouted sheets of flame, wreaking havoc among troops of warriors. On several tapestries, a fair-haired warrior, in golden plate armour, stood defiantly, legs astride the turmoil of battle, a great two-handed sword of flame firmly grasped in his hands. Heads of the giant lizards, black and bloodied, lay severed at his feet. A Ahmud Ki was keen to ask Tarnyss about the tapestries, but she hurried on, and led them up a winding staircase to a landing. To the left and right were doors. 'You'll sleep here. I'll come for you in the morning.'

'Where exactly are we?' A Ahmud Ki asked.

'In the Hall of Study,' Lady Tarnyss explained. 'Seralinna knows this building well. All who learn a speciality come here to research, from time to time. Rest. Tomorrow I shall begin your instruction.' Lady Tarnyss excused herself and descended the stairs.

Attendants opened the doors. 'Your choice,' offered A Ahmud Ki with a grin.

Seralinna stepped into the right doorway. 'I'll bathe first, if you don't mind, but I'll join you, to eat, in a short while.'

'Should I come in and bless the waters you bathe in?' he asked. She replied by closing her door.

A Ahmud Ki found basic and austere wooden furnishing in his room. A bed, a desk with ink, parchment, and writing implements, and a small clothing chest lined one wall. A bathing tub, water jug, and shelves spread along a second. Evening's last light spilled from a high arched window, where he went to gaze over the city of Targa. A dark conglomeration of low buildings spread to the dark waters of the bay, in places lit by flickering torches. Shapes on the water he presumed were the ships he'd heard of, but encroaching darkness reduced them to silhouettes. Directly below his window, a street ran left and right, and he heard the steady clip-clop of horses' hooves as the twin lanterns of a vehicle moved by. The night revealed little of Targa, but he could tell it had none of Yul Ithrandyr's grandeur.

A knock signalled the arrival of attendants fetching food and drink. He let them enter, carrying two wooden trays with bowls of sweetmeats, and salads, and a carafe of amber fluid. They placed the trays on the desk, and one pulled the curtain across the window while the other lit a lantern on the wall. As they made to leave, A Ahmud Ki called one back. 'Before you go, I want to ask some questions.'

The man smiled beneath his bristly beard. 'I'll answers what I may, sir.'

'The tapestries on the walls downstairs – what are they?'

'I take it you means what be they about, sir?' He scratched his beard. 'I thought all folks knew about the Dragon Wars. Them tapestries is like a record of what happened when it all happened.'

'I'm from a different land,' A Ahmud Ki explained. 'I've never heard of the Dragon Wars.' Memories of Aelendyell Lore flickered through his mind, and he recalled stories of the flight of the Elvenaar before the Dark Ones; the terror and the battles.

'Ah well, begging your pardon, sir, but I did suspect something like that, on account of the shape of your face and eyes, and the colour of your hair too. But as to your question, all I knows is that back a whiles there was a series of great wars, where some evil body, and a horde of them dragons, took to messing up the lands and killing folk, until King Abreotan cut them to pieces with his magic sword. That's him what you seen with the flaming great sword, and all them dragon heads lying at his feet.'

'The dragons were the flying lizards?'

'That they were. But I hear tell that there aren't none of them about no more. Except that some of them sailors, what's got touchy imaginations after a bit too long at sea, says there's dragons still, in other places.'

A Ahmud Ki dismissed the attendant. Seralinna would be arriving soon. He wanted the time alone with her, not just to be in her company but to ask her more questions about her land, questions he hadn't even considered before. Dragons were obviously powerful creatures, and he recalled descriptions of similar creatures in the Aelendyell Book of Lore; except there they were much more fearsome, more potent than the tapestries depicted them.

A gentle tapping broke his thought. When he opened the door, he stared in awe of Seralinna's beauty, her hair in curls of red and gold to her shoulders, and her green eyes sparkling above the warm red softness of her lips. She wore a green cloak for warmth, but he glimpsed a light green sheer cloth beneath it, and he was seized by an intense desire to sweep her into his arms and hold her. She smiled with the same charm as the first day he'd met her in her Keep, and her smile shifted his thoughts far from questions of ancient battles and extinct dragons. Tonight, he thought, he would drink in her essence, and taste her love, as he'd longed to do since he first saw her. He bowed, and Seralinna entered, closing the door behind her.

Twenty Five

Lady Tarnyss ascended a short flight of stairs to greet them. 'I trust you both slept well last night?'

A Ahmud Ki smiled at Seralinna, who blushed in response. 'Yes, thank you,' he replied.

'Good,' said Tarnyss. 'You'll need all your energy and concentration during the next week to begin your study.'

'And what do you propose to teach me?' asked A Ahmud Ki.

Lady Tarnyss said, 'Energy spells.' Her gravity emphasised the importance she gave to her speciality. Seralinna touched A Ahmud Ki's arm, and he saw the questions and mistrust in her eyes.

'I'm honoured,' he quietly said, and bowed his head.

'No doubt,' remarked Tarnyss. 'And no doubt you would like a demonstration of what energy spells can do. Seralinna, lead him to the Observation Chamber.'

She left, leaving A Ahmud Ki to follow Seralinna through a wooden door, beyond the small platform on which Lady Tarnyss had been standing.

'What do you think she's playing at?' he asked, as they reached the door.

'I wish I knew,' said Seralinna. 'She's never offered to teach her energy spells to anyone. She's refused anyone who has dared ask her for instruction.'

'What about her daughter?'

'She has no daughter. She never had a child, and never will. She hates men. She will never sleep with one. That's why I'm so frightened by all this. It's not in character for her to teach you, a man, anything.'

He entered the room, and immediately recognised it as the one to which he ascended at the completion of The Test. Large, roughly circular, it was filled with a floor of magical energy, like a floor of light on which one could walk, and through which one could view the arena below. He looked down, and saw Tarnyss in the centre of the arena, staring at a far door. Seralinna joined him. 'Have you seen her spells?' he asked.

'Once. She created a tower of light to impress the assembly, as a statement of her new skills. But I have no idea what she can conjure, because she's never taken any test — not like this one.'

The far door swung open. In lumbered a massive, four-legged beast, covered with thick leathery brown hide, reinforced with hard metal squares, each square sporting a hideously sharp spike. Two horns sprouted from the monster's broad, lowered head, and a shorter horn stood at the end of its snout. It halted, tossed its head, and flared its deep nostrils, taking in the scents of its alien surroundings. It fixed its beady black eyes on Tarnyss, who remained unmoved, snorted a challenge, and kicked up a piece of the earthen floor as it charged. A Ahmud Ki was impressed by the beast's speed because it was upon Lady Tarnyss, the horns goring into her. But the beast passed straight through, and when it wheeled to face her again she was unharmed by its attack. The creature appeared confused, but it lowered its head and charged again. As it closed the distance, Tarnyss made a simple pattern in the air with her fingers and stepped nimbly aside from the path of the raging creature. She pointed at it as it thundered by, and a spot of light appeared in the centre of its spine. When it reached the farther side of the arena, the beast exploded in a ferocious ball of flame, and disintegrated, leaving a blackened, scorched shadow on the ground. A Ahmud Ki recognised a much more potent form of the Aelendyell spell he could already cast, and instantly he wanted to learn how to create Tarnyss' intense energy.

Two doors, invisible until they opened, released identical creatures. Like the first, they lowered their horns, and charged. This time, Tarnyss levitated out of the creatures' paths, and they narrowly avoided collision. They halted and backed off, eyeing each other with deepest suspicion. From her elevated vantage point, Tarnyss directed a finger at each beast in turn. An ear-splitting crackle of energy rent the air with each pointing, and thin, ragged lines of lightning neatly felled the creatures, like paper in wind. Tarnyss returned to the ground, dusted her robe, and disappeared. 'Sufficient demonstration?' she asked, as she reappeared beside A Ahmud Ki in the Observation Chamber.

He turned with a smile. 'When do I start?'

The books of the Targan Council's Library were cumbersome, leather-bound, fragile things, not at all like the neat volumes stored in the Holy Library of the Palace Irandu Shadu. Worse, the entries in the Targan Spell Books were written in a variety of hands, some almost unreadable, and not a few were in languages unfamiliar to A Ahmud Ki. As he searched the titles Lady Tarnyss selected for him to read, he relied, in the initial stage, on Seralinna to translate pieces he didn't understand, until she taught him enough so that he could research independently. His burning energy to master anything that might open doors to greater power spurred him forward, making him labour through volume after volume at a rate that amazed Seralinna, and Lady Tarnyss when she came each afternoon of the first fortnight to observe his progress. He settled into a regime reflecting the discipline of his Ithosen training. He was up before sunrise, meditating, running words and actions of new spells through his mind, improving and perfecting them through dogged repetition, and as the sun peered above the rim of the ocean he left his chamber and went to the library to read until midday, when he ate and bathed. He meditated a further period in the afternoon, before descending to the arena to practise the spells he'd studied and memorised through the morning session. He then returned to the library, pre-read the next day's area of research, and went to the evening meal as the sun set. At the meal, he answered questions Seralinna put to him, but said little else, and after the meal he retired to his room. Behind his locked door, he spent long sessions, into the night, reworking new spells into the languages of the Ranu Ka Shehaala and Aelendyell, and modified the spells, simplified their casting, refined their power and made them his.

Seralinna kept quietly aside, watching, answering sudden questions he asked about language, or details in a text, patiently biding her time. She was in awe of A Ahmud Ki's appetite for learning, and she wanted to share what he was doing, but she knew that was impossible. What he was learning in a matter of days would take her most of her lifetime. She felt sorry for Lady Tarnyss. The High Council's President was becoming increasingly agitated by her protégé's rate of learning, and Seralinna knew that she was feeling the envy of seeing someone master knowledge in moments that had taken her years to learn. Tarnyss may have been planning for her own benefit by taking A Ahmud Ki under her wing, but Seralinna saw she was rapidly realising the enormity of the beast she'd let loose in her precious library, and guessed she was secretly regretting her decision with the passing days.

Lady Tarnyss intervened at the end of the fourteenth day. He was practising fire spells in the arena, while Tarnyss watched unobserved from above, but when he created a circular wall of flames about himself and made them march towards the wall of the arena, increasing their ferocity as they advanced, she could tolerate no more. That was an energy spell not even she had mastered. 'Enough!' she screamed from the Observation Chamber, and her agitation shattered his concentration.

He let the spell subside and peered into the haze of light forming the magical roof. 'You want something?' he nonchalantly asked.

'Yes. I do. I want you to come to the Inner Sanctum of the High Council. This evening. Ask an Attendant. One of them will lead you to its entrance. Oh, and bring your lady friend.' A Ahmud Ki responded by teleporting to her side, causing her to gasp, 'That too?'

'I've always had that skill. It's an Ithosen and an

Aelendyell spell, though neither group knows how to use it very well,' he politely explained. 'May I ask why we're being summoned tonight?'

Tarnyss' anger twitched in her cheeks, and he wondered what more he could do to aggravate her. She seemed to be mulling an idea in her head, so he switched his concentration to her thoughts, and was startled by the confusion he discovered there, and her outburst. 'How dare you! Don't fiddle with your mind spells on me!'

Her glare, he thought, would melt armour on a warhorse. 'I've always been fascinated by the fact that you're the only one I know in this land who's aware exactly of what I'm doing with that spell. The others sense something, but you know. I must find out how,' he mused.

Her glare intensified at his clinical observation, and her face reddened. 'Of little consequence! The Inner Sanctum. You will be there. Fail, and you will have tried my patience once too often. Understand?'

A Ahmud Ki nodded. 'Yes, Lady Tarnyss.' Tarnyss left him standing alone in the Observation Chamber.

A moment later, the door opened, and Seralinna entered with a quizzical expression. 'What was that all about?'

'You and I have a meeting tonight. With Tarnyss. In the Inner Sanctum.'

'Why?'

'I took the liberty of peering into her thoughts, but what I found was confusing,' he explained, 'but she's very much afraid of something in the Inner Sanctum.'

'She's jealous of you. And afraid too,' said Seralinna.

'No. Not entirely,' he replied, seriousness creeping into his voice. 'I'm part of it, but it's not specifically me that she's afraid of. I picked up images of the tapestries in the halls in her thoughts. Whatever is bothering her is very potent, and she believes I'm the key to her problem.' He knew Tarnyss was much like himself, a seeker of power, so he hoped she was inadvertently leading him to the very sources he was seeking to find since arriving in Targa. Tarnyss was afraid of raw magical power, a vast store of it, encased in the Inner

Sanctum.

'What are you thinking?' Seralinna asked softly.

A Ahmud Ki broke from his thoughts and took her arm. 'Nothing important. Come. We should eat and prepare to meet Tarnyss later this evening. I'm sure we're in for an entertaining night. But before then, I want you to show me a ship. I haven't set foot in your city yet. I might not get another chance.'

The streets followed twisting, narrow routes, beneath overhanging facades of wooden buildings threatening to fall together and crush pedestrians. In places, the streets were so narrow that only two walkers, or a solitary rider, could pass, and sunlight struggled to reach the ground. The streets crisscrossed in a mad pattern, with no common purpose, except as a procession to the docks. Stale odours of rotting food and human waste assaulted A Ahmud Ki's nose, and he contrasted the miserable conditions of the Targan streets to the clean straight thoroughfares of Yul Ithrandyr. The ramshackle disordered construction would be a terrible firetrap, and he was puzzled as to why the High Council had allowed the city to grow so wild and rank. Though very few people travelled the streets, he was aware Seralinna and he were being watched from shuttered windows. 'Shy lot,' he said indifferently, as they rounded a corner.

'Members of the Order aren't terribly popular. The common people avoid them,' explained Seralinna.

'Why?'

'Fear of magic. Contempt for anyone superior.'

'How come Council lets the city get so dirty?'

'They have no say. The City Aldermen are responsible for its upkeep.'

A Ahmud Ki stopped Seralinna by taking her by the arm. 'You mean Tarnyss isn't in charge here?'

Seralinna shook her head. 'No. Lady Tarnyss is President of the High Council. She is the leading figure in the Order of Power. She controls magic arts. The city is the province of the merchants. The City Aldermen control business ventures, here, and in ports in other lands. They control Targan money. Then there is the Lord Keeper. He controls the Targan Army.'

'But who makes the rules for everyone else? Who ultimately controls the Order and the Aldermen and the Army?'

Seralinna kept moving forward as she answered. 'There's no ultimate council or leader. They seldom have anything to do with each other. When they do, it's a business agreement. One agrees to work for, or finance, the other. Targa is a Federation.'

A Ahmud Ki pondered Seralinna's description of Targa as a nation of alliances. He had mistakenly believed the sorceresses were the rulers, as the Ithosen were in Yul Ithrandyr, but he was obviously wrong. Not everyone, in this land, respected magic. Such concept was outside his experience. Magic was the most powerful force of all, yet here were people who hated it. The smell of the ocean reached him. Years before, he smelled an ocean's saltiness, on his journey from Maheem's Tul to Yul Ithrandyr, but he hadn't forgotten it. His first vision of an endless expanse of blue water was permanently etched in his memory.

More people moved in the street. Merchants pushed barrows. Fishermen carried their catch and nets, and the stench of fish. Older men and women sat on cut down barrels, smoking pipes and mending nets or tools, turning to watch as they passed. Two full-bearded men, in baggy leggings and rough leather jerkins, leaning against a door, scrutinized A Ahmud Ki. Behind his back, after he passed, he heard one man spit and utter a low curse, and he tensed at the thought of an insult, but Seralinna caught him. 'Ignore them. Their kind always challenges strangers. This is their part of the city. The docks are just ahead.' Before the street spilled onto the docks, A Ahmud Ki glimpsed masts and rigging above the cluttered rooftops. Excited, he strode ahead of Seralinna onto the wooden boarding of the wharf.

The docks were busy. Labourers were hauling full cargo

nets off the decks of three ships berthed against the wharf. Sailors clambered up and down hawsers and rigging, ravelling canvass, and repairing or replacing worn and damaged equipment. Cartloads of timber, pulled by pairs of horses, lumbered along the wooden planking that was groaning and creaking under the loads. Out in the harbour, two ships rocked in the swell, anchored in waiting, their twin masts outlined against the sky. 'Amazing! I've never seen such craft before. What spell keeps them on the water?' A Ahmud Ki asked, as he moved to the edge of the wharf to stare at the ships.

'No spell,' Seralinna explained. 'Simple design.'

'Who designs these ships?'

'Shipwrights employed by merchants.'

A Ahmud Ki watched a young boy scamper to the topmost point of a mast on the closest ship. Gulls circled the boy as he clung to a rope and worked another free. 'Where do these ships travel?'

'I'm not sure. Most follow the coastline north and south to other ports. But sometimes they foray east, into the full ocean, and cross to foreign shores to trade, and gather raw wood. They're often gone for a couple of moon cycles on those journeys.'

'Have you ever been on a ship?'

'No.'

He looked out to sea. 'I'll have my own ship. After this appointment with Tarnyss tonight, I'll take you on a journey. We'll see other lands.' She looked at him, but his gaze remained fixed on the ships.

'We don' like your types nosin' roun' our docks.' The rough sea dog voice shattered A Ahmud Ki's reverie. When he turned slowly, four men faced them. All wore ill-made clothing, but one, with only two fingers remaining on his left hand, held a gaffing hook in his right. A second, a fat, shaggy bearded villain, carried a pike. The other two stood behind, flexing their fists. 'You got no right bein' 'ere,' puffed the fat villain, with a toothless grin. 'I thought you lot woulda knowed better.'

'People get hurt what shouldn' be down 'ere,' added a third, a rat-faced individual, head wrapped in a red scarf.

'We didn't mean any harm,' Seralinna calmly responded. 'My friend here only wanted to see a ship.'

A Ahmud Ki felt eyes scour him. 'e wants to see a ship do 'e?' growled the man with the gaff. 'That could be made right easy, that could, eh boys?'

His companions laughed wickedly. 'e could join th' crew!' shouted rat-face.

A Ahmud Ki saw several more sailors sauntering along the wharf towards their group, so he motioned to Seralinna, who looked up and saw them. Concern registered on her face, but he smiled. 'ere you. What do you find so funny, eh?' asked the fat man, fingering his pike menacingly. 'You won' be laughin' when you're aboard our ship in an 'owling gale fetchin' down the mizzen.'

'Seralinna,' A Ahmud Ki said quietly, 'I think it's time you headed back.'

'Not without you. I'm sorry this has happened. I should have known better,' she said.

'I'm not in any trouble. But you are, if you stay. Go now,' he calmly ordered.

She tried to argue with her eyes, but he fought her stare with a commanding gaze, leaving her no choice. She acquiesced. 'Alright. As you want it. But don't do anything foolish. There's more of them.' She indicated another crowd of sailors approaching along the wharf.

'Allow my lady to pass,' A Ahmud Ki said to the gathered sailors. 'She has nothing to do with this discussion.'

No response followed his request for a nervous moment. Then the man with the gaff grunted an order to the growing crowd, and a rough path cleared for Seralinna to leave. She walked cautiously through the men, aware of their curses and lusting stares, feeling as if she was betraying A Ahmud Ki, but a silent voice echoed in her head. Keep going. I will join you in the Hall of Study. Don't look back. You'll spoil the effect of your leaving. I'm in no danger from this rabble. She obeyed the voice and left the dockside, winding quickly, alone, back through the city streets.

'Your lady bit is gone, matey,' said the fat man scornfully. 'We keeps our promises, eh boys?' A chorus of voices backed his statement, as the press of sailors closed in.

'Ironim Ornyth!' said A Ahmud Ki. A gull flashed up out of the crowd's reach, chased by a flurry of oaths and shouts. It circled a mast of the nearest ship, and descended, settling on the boards several paces from the confused sailors. A Ahmud Ki resumed his shape. 'Sorry about that, gentlemen, but it was getting too crowded for me,' he quipped.

'Blasted tricks!' spat the fat man. 'You got no guts! All you can do is run away. A pox on your magic!'

'If it's a fight you're spoiling for, let's get on with it,' A Ahmud Ki offered, with a grin. The sailor's anger turned to glee. He closed in on the wizard, his gang of supporters moving with him. As he approached, A Ahmud Ki concentrated, and clapped his hands. A warrior in full shining mail armour, broad sword clasped in metal gloves, appeared in his place. 'Let's get on with it,' the warrior said, and swung his sword in a lethal arc.

Sailors leapt back from the sword sweep and scattered in fright. The fat man's face froze in shock as the sword blade cleaved his right hand from its arm, and he fainted. His companion with the gaff made a token lunge, had his weapon deflected by the sword, and collapsed with a broken nose from a mailed fist. The remaining sailors panicked and took to their heels, their retreat hailed by jeering onlookers who'd stopped work to watch the entertainment. A Ahmud Ki returned to normal shape and looked down at his victims, a smile spreading across his face. The fat man's hand was still firmly attached to his arm. The severing was illusion. The gaffer's nose though, smarted from the punch A Ahmud Ki had delivered within the illusion spell. The fat man was right, he thought with a grin, 'blasted tricks', but they were effective. He took a last look at the ships anchored in the harbour, breathed the ocean's aroma, returned to the form of a gull, and took to the air.

Twenty Six

Torches flickered the length of the steep stairwell that plunged deep into the earth beneath the Hall. Hand-hewn long ago through the limestone rock, the steps were clad with thick oak, wooden, like all buildings in Targa. The steward, who led the pair to this point, bowed and excused himself, explaining, 'I may go no further. The law forbids it, upon pain of death. Only members of High Council, and those they invite, venture beyond here. I will wait here for your return.'

A Ahmud Ki led the way down. He'd never ventured below ground, and the cool touch of stone and the air was a new experience, in part ruined by smoke lingering around the torches. Height above ground thrilled him, and learning Seralinna's shape-change spells that enabled him to fly high above the earth pleased him greatly, but the depth and angle of drop on the stairs caused him to move cautiously as he descended. They descended for what seemed a long time. At the bottom of the stairwell, they emerged in a broad space where ten people could comfortably stand. Ahead was a large double door, fashioned, A Ahmud Ki observed, very much like the doors in Jasmin's castle, clad with metal to strengthen it. It was the only visible entrance in the space, so A Ahmud Ki hefted aside the broad beam that locked it. 'Are we meant to do that?' Seralinna asked. 'It's locked to keep something in, it would seem.'

'Exactly,' echoed a voice from within, and Lady Tarnyss stepped through the closed door to join them. 'Replace the beam, young man. You must use a spell to enter this place. The door must never be unlocked or opened.' She moved back through the door. A Ahmud Ki picked up the beam and replaced it, and used a spell to follow Seralinna through the door.

Their eyes took a moment to adjust to the light as they

entered a vast cavern of dimensions that defied A Ahmud Ki's comprehension, and glowed with red light, like fireside coals. A mass of stalactites hung in long straws and ribbons overhead, and arched into the distance, rising beyond a light source hidden below, and the floor stretched away in red light, deeper into the earth's heart. Lady Tarnyss stood at the head of a spiralling path that was lit by a row of white orbs hanging on wooden poles. 'You are within the Sanctum of the Sorcerers,' Tarnyss announced. 'Only those the High Council permit come here. This place must remain undisturbed, according to the Laws of Abreotan. I warn you both not to touch a single item as we descend. There is a powerful but delicate balance of magic operating within this place, and if you interfere with it, even accidentally, the punishment is death. Follow, but do not speak until I say it is safe.'

She led them down the spiralling path into the enormous cavern's bowels. The white orbs intensified as they approached each one, illuminating the next portion of the path until they passed. The air grew warmer, until A Ahmud Ki broke into a sweat, akin to the kind he'd suffered in his first days in the Sands of Fire when he toiled to build his black tower. Warm water dripped from unseen stalactites, and, at one point, the path passed beside a precipice that dropped a great distance to what he saw as a river of fire. Slowly, the cavern changed into a chaotic mess of angled and razor-sharp projections, jutting in all directions, threatening to impale hapless individuals. The path became a tunnel plunging down a flight of steps, and the temperature dropped dramatically. They emerged in a new cavern, not at all like the first because everything was coated with ice, and it was biting cold beneath blue light. As they moved at a faster pace, A Ahmud Ki caught glimpses of creatures trapped in great chunks of ice, large creatures like the flying lizards, the dragons he'd seen woven in the tapestries. He paused, but Seralinna took his hand and pulled him forward, towards a huge iron door. They passed through it, without opening it, and entered a large hall. Marble columns ran in regimental rows through the hall, supporting a flat stone roof, but there was nothing ornamental or detailed, except that it was buried deep in the earth. Tarnyss led them to the end of the hall and a sweeping marble stairway. It led into a long corridor of light, which they followed to a door of gold, wrought with detailed images of the sun in its various seasons. They passed through it into a faintly lit area where the light emanated from two sources. Amber light from a large crystal in the centre of the space shone on a stone sarcophagus. Green light shimmered from a tall mirror to the left of the sarcophagus, between two columns. Steps led down to the sarcophagus.

Lady Tarnyss turned to them, and blue light shone brightly in her eyes. 'You are now within the Inner Sanctum of the Sorcerers. You stand at the Centre of Power.' A Ahmud Ki noticed the walls were crystalline because they reflected the amber glow. His nerves tingled with excitement because he felt a magical source of awesome magnitude, a presence that thrilled him as it drew him down the steps towards the sarcophagus. 'Where are you going?' Tarnyss asked.

'What lies in there?' he asked, pointing to the sarcophagus in the amber beam of light.

'The remains of an ancient Dragonlord,' she replied. 'You cannot enter, or even touch the beam. It is a glyph of imprisonment. One touch and you are vaporized.'

He heeded her warning. 'Who constructed the glyph?'

'The annals record that King Aian Abreotan's sword contained the power to cast many spells, including spells for holding. This is one such spell.'

Fascinated, A Ahmud Ki continued down the steps. Seralinna called him back, but he ignored her. He moved to the very edge of the glyph and glanced up at its source, the diamond-like amber crystal directly above the sarcophagus, and then down at the sarcophagus. On its surface was sculpted the figure of a tall man with a sharp-featured face, dressed in long robes. He immediately saw a strong Aelendyell resemblance in the features as if his own face was staring back at him. But a feature was missing – the eyes

228

were vacant, blank, as if the sculpting was unfinished. He read a precisely cut inscription in an ancient script at the base of the sarcophagus: 'Mareg Dru'artha Sutnavanistra'. A Ahmud Ki ran the ancient name through his mind, recalling all he could from the Aelendyell Book of Lore, but the name defied recognition. He stared at the words a moment longer, before returning up the steps to Tarnyss and Seralinna.

'Do you understand, now, why I brought you here?' Tarnyss asked as he reached them.

'Partly,' he replied. 'You believe the prophecies, don't you?'

'The resemblance is more than mere coincidence,' she answered with conviction. 'Your ability to learn magic with inhuman speed testifies to the fact.'

'That I'm a Dragonlord?' He shook his head and laughed, his voice echoing in the chamber. 'I don't even know what a dragon looks like. But I freely admit I'd gladly have the power these Dragonlords must have held if it takes a powerful glyph to hold down a dead body.'

'He is not dead.'

A Ahmud Ki stopped laughing and glanced down at the amber light. 'You said his remains -'

'His mortal remains lie there. But his spirit lives. The glyph keeps it locked eternally within the sarcophagus. And all his knowledge and power are trapped in there as well,' Tarnyss explained. The revelation heightened A Ahmud Ki's interest and senses, and he thought he glimpsed a faint, ghostly figure in the amber beam. Tarnyss touched his shoulder. 'If you are the prophesied wizard, meant to come to the land, your power lies here. Only a Dragonlord could do what you have done. This is rightly your inheritance – if you can penetrate the glyph. And if you do, remember, it was I who brought you to this place.'

So that's your plan, thought A Ahmud Ki. You want to buy a part of the prophecy in your favour.

'Another political game,' Seralinna said softly.

'And why not?' responded Lady Tarnyss. 'Politics is all about making the right decisions at the best possible moments. I told you I knew when I was wrong. I also meant that I knew when it might be necessary to alter my plans. Expediency, my dear sister Corinna would call it.'

'And if he isn't the wizard of the prophecy?' asked Seralinna. 'What do you do then?'

'Go back to my original plan.'

'But A Ahmud Ki is already stronger than you. He knows more speciality skills than anyone in Targa. You've even taught him your skills. Your old plan is finished, isn't it?'

Tarnyss looked at A Ahmud Ki, who'd ventured down the steps to study the glowing mirror. 'You forget, Seralinna. If he is the wizard of the prophecy, he must be able to penetrate the glyph. If he isn't, he'll perish, and nothing in Targa will have changed. I will still be President, and the Order will remain.'

Her admission shocked Seralinna, who realized the full implications of the visit to the Inner Sanctum. She called to A Ahmud Ki, 'You don't have to do this! It's a trick! A cheap political trick! You said yourself that you don't believe in prophecies. You only need go to the Council and fulfil your promise, answer the challenge and you'll be accepted. If you want, I'm sure the others will vote you onto the Council. How could they ignore you? They might even offer you the Presidency!' she added, glaring at Lady Tarnyss.

A Ahmud Ki turned towards her, laughing. 'No,' he said. 'Too simple. This is what I've been searching for, Seralinna. This is why I stepped through your portal. For power - raw power. And now it lies right before me. I can feel it. All these years I've learned the secrets of the Four Ki – the Elvenaar and Aelendyell Lore, the Ki of the Ithosen, and now your Targan magic – mastered them all, and they've led me here - to a power I never even imagined – a fifth Ki!' He stared straight at Tarnyss. 'I'm nothing to do with your prophecies – nothing at all. Prophecies are the province of limited minds. I resent being associated with your pathetic folklore.' He grinned at Seralinna. 'Their political games are fun, trivial as they are, but Presidency of the High Council isn't for me. When I've learned all that's kept in this place, I'll leave it all for Tarnyss and her High Council to puzzle over for the remainder of their lives. I'll be returning to another place where I have old scores to settle.' His voice softened. 'I'd like you to come with me, Seralinna.'

She'd seen the change in A Ahmud Ki, and the change frightened her. There was so much about him she still did not know, so much smouldering with dangerous fires. 'I - I don't know,' she said. 'If it's possible, I will.'

He laughed, as he strode up the steps. 'Go fetch your High Council, Tarnyss. Bring them to witness my learning in action. You brought me here. It's best if you have witnesses to offer you credit after the event. After all, Tarnyss, that is what you want.'

'With all respect, Lady Tarnyss, but this is madness!' old Lord Rattan complained, waving his staff. 'What if this upstart succeeds in releasing the Dragonlord?'

'Exactly!' chimed in Lady Gethrin. 'You've read the Scrolls. You know the Laws set down by King Abreotan. The Dragonlords must never be released from their entombment.'

'Havoc will be wreaked on us all!' warned Lady Nella.

'Be quiet, all of you!' Lady Tarnyss ordered. 'If he does succeed with his spells tonight, he will not be releasing the Dragonlord. He will merely take his powers. The Dragonlord cannot rise from his sleep. The dead are dead. You all know that.'

'But he's not dead,' Rattan insisted. 'His spirit lives in the light. You know that.'

Tarnyss scowled at him. 'Do we? How? Through the writings of a scribe dead these past thousand years!' She glanced around the assembled Council members. 'Who has seen the Dragonlord's spirit? Anyone? Of course not! For all their legendary powers, even they couldn't cheat death. Be still, and observe the proceedings. You could well learn a great deal from the young wizard.'

Gethrin leaned to her left. 'I say she had no right to bring him down here. She's playing yet another political game,' she whispered to Nella. She looked up, and Tarnyss fixed her with a menacing glare.

A Ahmud Ki watched the gallery of observers, from his position at the edge of the amber wall of light enveloping the sarcophagus, and smiled inwardly, wondering how many were wishing him to fail. He knew some feared the prophecy, while others feared the warnings from the Annals of Abreotan, and even a few feared the automatic gain in prestige Lady Tarnyss would earn, regardless of the outcome. What he most enjoyed was that the action pivoted on him. He was the key. He held them all firmly in his grip, even Tarnyss, just as surely as he now stood less than an arm's length from a being whose power surpassed anything he understood, save perhaps the magic of the Elvenaar High Priests and Priestesses who compiled the Lore Book. He was at the centre, as only he should be. He stretched his fingers and flexed them, and, in doing so, he caught sight of Seralinna, halfway down the steps where he'd asked her to be, holding an amber pyramid. He smiled, but he saw her nervous tension, and remembered how much he loved the young sorceress. If he hadn't leapt recklessly through the portal in the Sands of Fire, he would never have met her, or known the emotions she released in him. When this is over, he thought, she'll come with me, and all will be complete.

He moved parallel to the side of the sarcophagus, standing between it and the green glow of the mirror. The mirror was a portal, a powerful one, like he fashioned in his own tower. After he farmed the power of the Dragonlord, he intended to explore the portal to discover its construction and destinations. There was so much to learn. He focussed on the handsome visage etched into the sarcophagus' lid, the face with Aelendyell features, although more handsome than any Aelendyell he'd known, and he was flattered to think that he bore the same features. He shifted his concentration to the amber crystal suspended overhead, lifted his hands, and began a recitation of arcane words he'd stumbled upon in the Targan library – words from a past age.

'Djyurna! Djyurna artek merynoth. Asna!' 'Teraminus! Esta! Vordanna eirma meska Erinnor!' He hadn't translated them into Aelendyell, but it didn't matter. The spell would work if the words were correctly pronounced. 'Folminor! Folminor asna!' He felt a subtle changing in the energy of the amber light. Good. He'd broken a lock in the glyph. How many more are there? he wondered. He continued the litany, and slowly, inexorably, the light diminished, until it was a soft orange ray dancing on the sarcophagus figurine's forehead. A Ahmud Ki broke into a full sweat. He was drained from the effort of breaking down the glyph, but what wearied him more was knowing he was less than half done with the task of removing the contents from the sarcophagus without fully disrupting the glyph's control on whatever lay within; spirit or dust.

He glanced up at the faces peering down, and saw their features were lined with tiredness too. He'd lost sense of time. He relaxed his concentration.

The instant he relented, the last ray of amber light winked out. The sarcophagus lid exploded into a million fragments that scattered through the chamber, peppering stone and flesh. Screams, and cries of terror rose from the gallery, as Councillors fell, gashed by pieces of stone. The explosive force threw A Ahmud Ki backwards, against the base of the green portal mirror. And a smoky wraith rose from the sarcophagus.

A Ahmud Ki saw the chaotic panic among the Councillors. He turned to where Seralinna had been standing. She was swaying, about to fall. Blood pumped from a gaping wound in her side. Before he could react, a surge of bright green energy leaped from the wraith to the crystal in Seralinna's hands. The crystal exploded in a shower of blue-white sparks and Seralinna toppled sideways, down the steps. The wraith crackled with energy and metamorphosed into a being in gleaming ebony armour. Jagged edges jutted from the black metal, and hideous razor-sharp points curved from the shoulders. Flowing silver hair framed the same handsome visage that adorned the lid. The Dragonlord stared at A

Ahmud Ki, filling the wizard with indescribable fear because his pupil-less eyes burned red, like the red river of fire A Ahmud Ki glimpsed in the first cavern of the Sanctum. A Ahmud Ki knew he was staring at death, but the Dragonlord's attention was drawn to the gallery, where Tarnyss, screaming, was frantically weaving her hands, conjuring her most powerful spell, while members of the High Council scrambled for the door, pushing and shoving past the injured and dying. Tarnyss flung her hands outward to cast her spell. Fire leapt from her fingers, but it ran up her arms to engulf her, and she disappeared in a fierce eruption of flame, her writhing body dissolving to ash. The Dragonlord's deep, resonating laughter pealed in the chamber, causing the crystalline walls to vibrate and shatter, and the gallery walls cracked and collapsed inward, crushing the slower Councillors beneath crystal and rock. 'I am Mareg!' he roared, both arms lifted defiantly. 'Who dares to oppose the might of a Dragonlord?' He laughed again with the arrogance of supreme power. 'Let this accursed place be destroyed, and with it all the filth that dared to imprison me! I ruled once. I will rule again!' With a grand sweep of his arm, he initiated a chain reaction of spells in the structure of the rock. Deep rumbling began beneath A Ahmud Ki's feet as the chamber trembled violently. The remaining walls lurched forward and crumbled. The Dragonlord morphed into a bolt of white energy, which exploded through the collapsing ceiling and was gone. A Ahmud Ki lunged backwards, desperately plunging into the green shimmering portal.

"And there will come a great Darkness in the time beyond reckoning, and the Dragonlord will rise again..."

"Upon his face he will bear the mark of the moon as a sign to all that he it is who will smite the Dragonlord the death-dealing blow for all time."

"But first must he die and be born again..."

"He will walk as two upon the lands and some will not know him from the other."

"...and wield a two-edged sword, cutting friend and foe alike in his confusion to rid the Land of the Dragonlord..."

from Abreotan's Prophets, research papers gathered by Pak from the Great King's Library on behalf of Lord Advisor A Ahmud Ki

Twenty Seven

His back muscles screamed with pain and his shoulders ached. His arms had long ago surrendered to numbness, becoming part of the wooden pylon he held aloft. His legs were rock, but the knees were brittle and treacherous. Sweat trickled down salty paths and hung from his eyebrows. He tasted dust. He focussed on the voice again, heard its arrogance, hated it. 'Your backs are filled with fire. Your knees tremble. You cannot last much longer. None of you can. Feel your hips. Feel the weight grinding down on them, crushing them.' A groan – a wooden pylon thudded on the earth. Feet shuffled. Someone was dragged away. Sweat burned in the corner of his eyes. The voice hung close to his ear. 'Stings. Bites into your eyeballs. Irritates. Drives you crazy. Then you lose, you fall. You fail.' He tightened. Pain shot through his calves. 'Yes. Pain. Use your energy. Waste your strength.' Someone spat. The voice moved away. 'So. Still got some fight? Good. Very good.' Another pylon thudded on the ground. Andra gritted his teeth, eased his legs slightly, and fixed his eyes on the distant city.

The Great City, with its sprawling hovels and its business houses, clustered along the muddied banks of the Dragon River, halted before the towering cliffs of the Great King's Castle plateau that abruptly rose from the rolling Plains of Ky. When they first saw the Castle, it seemed to rest on a bed of mist, floating above the earth, and the vision filled Andra and his companions with awe. The stone walls sparkled with the early morning winter sun's cold light, while the great plateau lay hidden beneath the fog, but by the time they reached the encampment of the Great King's Armies the mist had evaporated into the ice blue sky. They hadn't gone closer. Devi Senok placed the Guardians of The Vale and the warriors of Tressel Deep in the charge of High Lord Mara, Supreme War-General of the Great King's Armies, and there they remained three full weeks. The recruits were given one day to orient themselves in the camp, while Senok and the Haardrishii horsemen rode on, towards the Great City.

The camp of the Great King's Armies was a bustling hive of activity. Andra and his companions were directed to a patch of ground between the clusters of hide tents, where a surly young warrior told them it was their responsibility to build their own shelters. They managed to draw from him that hides could be procured at wagons a merchant named Barnabus of Port brought each day to the centre of the camp. Not even Claarn's bulky presence intimidated the young man. He was wary, but his sour mouth was full of arrogance, and he left them a simple parting message. 'A soldier in the Great King's Armies must be resourceful.'

'That whelp will need lessons in good manners,' Claarn rumbled, 'and I should like to give those lessons.' He flexed his hands with menacing intent.

'It is likely we will meet many such as that one,' Stephen observed, as the subject of their discussion swaggered into the reaches of the camp.

Stephen, Alain and Andra spent most of the first day scouting the camp, learning its layout, and they were frequently surprised by their discoveries. The camp was deliberately regimented in the form of a gigantic wheel. At its centre was a large circular space that served as a meeting and market area. Roads led from the hub in gentle spiral arms, like curved spokes. The innermost circle contained huts, that were large and few in number, each differentiated from the others by multi-coloured pennants fluttering on poles placed before each hut. The largest, belonging to High Lord Mara, displayed one large banner: the half-lion, half-eagle crest of Great King Thana on a red field. Six soldiers in burnished plate armour stood at rigid attention before the building. Behind each hut, forming the second and broader circle, was a greater number of tents, and the occupants of these tents were the subjects and followers of various leaders in the inner circle. One group, immediately behind an inner hut wrought from green stained stone and hides, confirmed their thought, because they were mountain-people, Shaddites as Alain explained. 'Travellers to the Vale told my father about them. They dwell deep within mountains. in the south and west of the land. They live mainly by mining rich ores and jewels, and spend most of their lives below the earth. I don't know much else about them except that they are mighty warriors.' The three companions stared at a group of Shaddites gathered before a tent. They all had short, stocky builds - muscular, powerful. Each had a thick beard, intricately woven into braids and patterns, while their hair colour ranged from dusty auburn through to deep fiery reds.

Beyond the second circle, the third circle enclosed the camp, and contained the main body of the Great King's Armies. An enormous variety of people filled the circle. Although most were male, here and there, as with Claarn's companions, women were exercising or sharpening their weapons. The third circle was alive with warriors carrying out training drills, mock combat, building tents, while experienced soldiers barked abrupt orders at recruits drawn from across the Kingdom. 'It seems we will be kept very busy learning our new trade,' said Stephen, pointing to a group of trainees running in a circle, several paces beyond the edge of the camp. The runners cradled large granite rocks, while a formidable soldier, at the centre of the circle, goaded them with a large whip.

'That, my friends, is your trainer, Murdok.' The new voice, from behind, made all three turn to discover a young man, in simple leather breastplate and skirt, smiling at them. 'I apologize for startling you. I'm Tim Gaelus.' He warmly extended his hand in turn to each Guardian. 'I gather you've just arrived.'

'Not very long ago,' replied Stephen. 'We have yet to set up our tent.'

'So I see. Need any help?'

'No, I think not. Our companions will be here very soon.

But we appreciate your offer.'

'Tell us about Murdok,' Andra asked, as he watched the struggling circle of recruits. One had collapsed beside his rock burden, while the others stumbled on, ignoring him.

'There's not a lot to tell other than you can already see. He's a Trainer. He teaches recruits strength, endurance, perseverance, discipline. He does it through pain. He enjoys it. And he hates recruits. You'll learn soon enough.'

Andra listened with interest to Tim's words, but he was puzzled by a quizzical smile dancing about the young man's lips, as if he thought Murdok's treatment of his charges was a matter for amusement.

'And what do you do?' interjected Alain.

'Me?' Tim laughed. 'I serve in the King's Army.'

'Have you been a soldier for long?'

Another laugh. 'Too long. But not by choice, I might add. If I could, I'd slip back to the city tomorrow. I miss my old trade, and it misses me. This soldiering caper isn't for me. But that's not my choice right now.'

'And what was your old trade?' asked Stephen.

'Lads, so many questions?' he replied evasively. 'I came to find out about you. We'll be neighbours. That's my tent right there.' Tim indicated his compact, neat, hide construction. 'So, whom do I have the pleasure of meeting?' The Guardians briefly told Tim their tale and described The Vale with strong longing. Andra noted nothing more was mentioned of Tim's origin, but before he could broach the question Claarn and the others returned with hides and saplings for tent building. After a brief introduction to the warriors of Tressel Deep, Tim slipped away, and left them to the task at hand.

The Great City was sulking beneath grey skies. The castle brooded on the plateau, shadowy and sullen, and a solitary crow circled the northernmost tower that rose like an accusing black finger at the sky. Andra's back felt crushed. The pylon was part of him, his own weight, pushing down.

He felt the clouds grow leaden and sit on the supporting beam above his head. A tiny breeze ran cold fingers down his back and along his ribs. Time had stopped. 'Drop your burdens!' Obeying the biting voice, he willed his arms, against the taut resistance of his muscles, to drop the pylon. Through a veil of pain, he heard other pylons thump to the earth. 'To the crest and back! Run!' Don't question the voice. Run. Andra fought his body's rigidity, willing himself to move, forced one leg and then the other into motion. Pain. Sharp heat stung in his muscles. He was running. Awkwardly. Stiffly. His legs carried his upper body, but he couldn't synchronize his limbs. He was running in the boggy marshes of The Vale, battling to keep going, struggling to stay upright. The weight of the pylon was still crushing him. He would run. He must run.

The crest Murdok pointed to was eight hundred paces from the camp's edge, and the rise was gradual, except for a steeper section fifty paces from the top. Andra and the others had run the course countless times in the three weeks, under a mixture of conditions, to test their stamina. They ran in full chain mail armour, ran in pouring rain that left the topmost portion of the course a slippery morass, ran carrying another recruit on their backs, ran the course continually, until many dropped from exhaustion. Of the thirty recruits in their group, the three Guardians excelled at running because the Guardian Master had taught them well. Their ability to keep running, despite the conditions imposed by Murdok, irked rather than pleased the trainer. Andra saw him scowling more than once when he ordered them to stop at the end of a session. His scarred face, buried beneath its black bushy beard, was always angry, and he only smiled when a recruit faltered or collapsed, or when he offered a piece of sarcasm that pleased his wit. Otherwise, he moved his solid bulk among them like a violent thunderstorm threatening to burst, at any moment, without reason. This time, his devious mind created an exercise that tested even the legs of the Guardians, but Andra was determined not to break, not for Murdok.

Four hundred paces out, Andra was aware of someone gasping against the chill air. 'Wait. Andra. Wait. Let me catch up.' He slackened to a stagger, letting Alain draw alongside.

A glance told him Alain, despite his strength, was struggling. 'He's found a way to hurt us this time,' Andra panted.

'Uhuh,' was all Alain could muster.

A third voice came from behind; Stephen. 'Save your breath, there's a long way to go.' Andra fixed his eyes on the steeper slope ahead and ran mechanically.

The second morning after they arrived in camp, they were mustered with a host of warriors at the outer edge. Soldiers jostled and prodded them out of their tents before the sun even dared to peer over the ice-capped purple peaks of the mountains far to the east. The weariness of the long journey from The Vale, through the Valley of Rivers, and across the northern Plains of Ky, sat heavily on their eyelids, and even the irascible Claarn remained subdued as the soldiers herded them to an assembly. Casting his eyes about the milling crowd, Andra recognised Tim Gaelus helping to drive recruits to the assembly. Even in the pre-dawn darkness, his voice sparkled with teasing energy, a quality that fascinated Andra and attracted him to the man. But he didn't dwell on the thought. The freezing air forced him to focus back on himself, and he tried to stamp warmth and circulation into his feet. Clouds of steam issued from every mouth. Irritated mutterings and oaths rippled around the gathering.

Meek sunrays streaked the steel skies, and silhouetted the cold rain clouds, as a party of soldiers, bearing banners, moved from the inner circles, along a spiral road. 'Seems we are to meet someone important,' Claarn mumbled through his thick red beard, as he pulled his sheepskin over his shoulders. The party approached the head of the gathering and fanned out, revealing four armed soldiers in full plate and a fifth figure heavily robed against the cold air.

'On your knees scum!' bellowed a voice to Andra's left.

Soldiers moved quickly among the crowd, forcing slower ones into subservience.

Stephen kneeled beside him, whispering, 'It is The Way.' Andra kneeled as a soldier approached.

'You there! Down!' The soldier glared above Andra's head. Claarn was still standing with his companions. More soldiers closed in. The first soldier repeated his order with greater vehemence. 'I said down!'

'I kneel to no one, unless I choose.' Claarn's voice was as cold as the earth on which Andra knelt.

The soldier briskly strode across to stand directly before Claarn. He looked up into the red giant's burly face, seemingly undaunted by the size of the offender, and Andra recognised the arrogant young soldier who delivered them to their tent site. 'Kneel!'

'No.'

A second soldier moved behind Claarn, and at the word 'No' he went to bring the edge of his shield across the back of Claarn's knees, but the blow never fell. Marella's arm snapped out and smashed across the soldier's face, dropping him, stunned, to the ground. Claarn didn't acknowledge the motion. His eyes remained squarely fixed on the young man before him, but in the weak light Andra was certain he saw Claarn's white teeth grinning in the mass of flame-red beard. The soldier drew his keen-edged sword from its scabbard and pointed at the giant's chest. 'You'll pay dearly for your insolence. Now get on your knees.'

Claarn chuckled deep within his throat and glanced to his right. The glance distracted the soldier, and that was his mistake. The giant's huge hand shot out, gripped the soldier's wrist like a vice, and twisted the arm. Andra heard bone crack. The victim screamed and dropped his sword, collapsing to his knees at Claarn's feet, white-faced and trembling. The closest soldiers encircled Claarn's group, swords drawn, but the red giant bent forward, picked up the discarded weapon, and snapped the blade across his knee. He dropped the pieces beside the stricken soldier. The entire assembly stared at the defiant figure, standing a good head

243

above his circle of companions, and the surrounding soldiers of the Great King's Armies. People rose to get a clearer view of the individual who dared to disobey the King's men. Andra caught Alain and Stephen's attention, and appealed silently to them. Stephen was reluctant, but he nodded. If it was to be this way, then so be it. They stood.

'Get down!' boomed the voice that had given the order to kneel. Andra saw the solid figure belonging to the voice. The spreading light revealed a familiar individual, the man Tim Gaelus had pointed out – Murdok the Trainer. Though not as tall as Claarn, Murdok was at least as broad, and he carried as much threat in his body as he did in his voice. All who'd stood to gain a better view dropped to their knees out of fear and respect for Murdok's presence – but not the three Guardians or the warriors of Tressel Deep. 'If you are spoiling for a fight, I'm sure I can accommodate all of you at a pinch.' Murdok's voice was cool and measured. Andra recognised the strength and control of the Guardian Master and knew Murdok was no ordinary soldier for Claarn to carelessly brush aside, but the band of rebels remained standing. 'So be it.' Murdok motioned to the soldiers and stepped forward.

'Hold your places!'

Andra had forgotten the robed figure at the centre of the party, but the authority in his voice halted Murdok and the soldiers. The robed figure surveyed the assembly, and, satisfied he'd been obeyed, he walked between the kneeling warriors towards those who were standing. As he approached, Andra noticed the richness of his garb and his confident bearing.

Stephen tugged at Andra's sleeve, and said, 'Come. It is time to kneel again.' Andra went to ask for Stephen's reason, but Stephen simply spoke with his usual stoicism. 'It is The Way.' He knelt, and wondered how Stephen understood so much more than he did about when it was right to act, and when not.

The robed man stood before Claarn, dwarfed by the giant, and they seemed content to stare at each other, searching the face of the other for an inner meaning, until the robed one spoke. 'Do you know who I am?'

Claarn shook his great shaggy head. 'No. But I guess at it.'

'Would you serve me?'

'I have come to serve the Great King. I will not kneel before anyone who acts as though they are the Great King.' Claarn shot a sharp glance at Murdok.

'Be that as it is,' the robed speaker replied. 'I'm only a servant of the Great King, so I won't expect you to kneel before me. But I will give you and your companions an order that you will obey because you've come to serve the Great King, and because you are proud warriors. Go to the pavilion bearing the crest of the griffin at the centre of the camp and wait there.' The robed figure turned quietly and walked back through the crowd to the party at the head of the assembly. Claarn lifted his great paw and ran it through his shock of hair, puzzled, before he turned and, wordless, led his warriors from the assembly.

The slope magnified. Andra's legs wobbled, and threatened to collapse, as he forced his feet up the steep incline. Laboured breathing pursued him. Only another thirty paces. Thirty paces. Legs of wool. Chest of fire.

High Lord Mara stood before the assembly, facing into the rising sun, an effect that made him appear full of light and strength in the dawn's cold grey atmosphere. 'From this time, until the Great King Himself determines otherwise, I am your leader and your law. I hold, in my hands, your lives, your fates, your destinies. You have been chosen to serve His Royal Majesty as a soldier in the Great King's Armies. You will serve Him well, that I promise you, because here you will learn to be a soldier - disciplined, determined, strong. The Great Armies are one body, a mighty dragon, unified and powerful. Each arm, each link, each scale on the dragon's body is as strong as its neighbour. I order it to be so. You will

245

make it so. You will be trained until you hurt, and then you will be trained again. You will be asked to do what you believe cannot be done. You will find limits, and then you will go beyond them. You will be soldiers. You will be my soldiers. And you will make me proud.' Lord Mara paused. Andra hung on the silence, acutely aware that every kneeling figure at the assembly waited with him. Lord Mara passed his gaze over them all, before raising his arms defiantly, and shouting, 'Death to the Haagii!'

They responded as one. 'Death to the Haagii!' The bond was complete.

One push. One last lunge. The top. His shoulders and thighs burned with sharp fire. His heart pounded like a fist in his chest. Each gasp cut into his throat. Alain scrambled up the slope to join him and collapsed at his feet. Stephen followed, agony etched across his face. Andra put out a hand to help him up the final step. 'Come on, the worst is past.' Andra fought his body to breathe the words. 'Now it's all down.' He looked back at the camp, spread in its circles on the Plains of Ky. Six figures were strung out along the slope, struggling to run. So few had made it. The others were scattered on the ground between the runners and the camp, exhausted and beaten. Murdok's powerful frame stood at the edge of the camp, waiting, watching.

'Look,' gasped Alain. 'The others.'

'I've seen,' Andra replied. 'Murdok's broken them.' He helped Alain to his feet and glanced across at Stephen.

'Yes,' said Stephen hoarsely. 'I will make it. Let us run down together, as one, as the Guardian Master would expect of us.'

Andra mustered a smile. Alain nodded. Against their exhaustion, they started down.

Claarn, Talan, Marella and the others disappeared after the incident with High Lord Mara. When the Guardians were dismissed from the first assembly, they returned to their tent to find the belongings of the warriors of Tressel Deep gone. Stephen went to High Lord Mara's pavilion to inquire after Claarn, but the Lord's personal guard turned him away. 'I fear for their safety,' Alain said when Stephen returned, but Stephen shook his head.

'They will not come to harm. Of that I am sure. The High Lord has other plans for Claarn. In time, we will see those plans.'

The passing days carried wintry rains across the wide plains, and bitter winds tugged at the huddled tents in the camp. The Guardians searched for news of their friends, but heard nothing. Even the resourceful Tim Gaelus passed them, shaking his head when they pressed him for information. He echoed Stephen's words, and talked instead about their training under Murdok, laughing at their experiences and trials, and warning them of things to come with a twinkle in his keen eyes. 'You have the best and the worst, my friends,' he laughed. 'If you last, he'll make you into tough warriors for the Great King. But first you must last, eh?'

We will last, thought Andra, as the Guardians stumbled towards their goal and antagonist at the camp's edge. You did not tell us about this particular test, Tim Gaelus, but we will last. It is our Way.

Twenty Eight

'Where is your armour?' Murdok stared directly into his face, his dark brows knitted in anger, his dark blue eyes glittering dangerously.

'I found it clumsy to wear, Trainer Murdok,' Stephen explained.

'Where is your sword?' Murdok hissed between his teeth.

'I do not need a sword, Trainer Murdok. My weapon is my staff.'

Murdok thrust his face squarely into Stephen's face. 'A staff? A weapon?' He stepped back, glanced contemptuously at all three Guardians, and then moved among the other recruits, checking their armour and weaponry. Inspection completed, he strode back to stand before Stephen. 'The others come prepared to fight. They wear the armour of the army. They carry swords, shields, weapons of war. I don't play games with sticks here. Why have you dared to come so ill-prepared when I ordered you to come prepared to skirmish this morning?'

Stephen held Murdok's gaze calmly. 'We are prepared. In The Vale, a warrior wears no armour. The Guardian Master taught us the value of free movement. A staff is a light weapon, easily disguised, effective, and will only kill if necessary. It is The Way of Guardians, Trainer Murdok. You told us to come prepared to fight. You did not order us to wear the armour or weapons provided.'

Andra saw the heat rise in Murdok's face. Alain and he wanted to wear the gear delivered to their tent, but Stephen reminded them of their training in The Vale, so they dressed as Guardians. Now Stephen's wisdom was rapidly turning sour. 'You!' Murdok motioned to Stephen. 'Stand here,' he said, indicating a spot beside him. 'The rest of you form a circle, here. Wider.' The recruits shuffled into a ragged circle,

248

and Murdok stood at the centre with Stephen. 'When Spring returns, you'll be going to war. You'll be soldiers in the Great King's Armies. You will fight the Haagii. A soldier who wants to live needs five things. He needs fighting skill. He needs strength. He needs good weapons. He needs loyal companions. And he needs –' Murdok planted his elbow forcefully into Stephen's rib cage. The young Guardian crumpled to the ground. '– good protection!' Andra started forward to help his companion. 'You! Back into the ranks!' ordered Murdok. Andra looked at Stephen's face contorted with pain, but Stephen shook his head. Andra stepped back. Murdok glared at him. 'Armour reduces the places an opponent can hurt you, even with sword or spear. In close combat, any wound, even a slight one, will cost you. Armour reduces the chances of silly wounds that sap your concentration. And you will find in battle that the enemy will come at you from many sides, and never alone. Your armour improves your chances of surviving an attack, as you will now see.' Murdok gestured to two men in the circle. 'You. And you. Prepare yourselves. I want this one –' He pointed at Stephen who was struggling to his feet. '– forced to yield to you. He must kiss your feet.' Murdok stepped to the edge of the circle, as the two he'd chosen moved towards Stephen, swords drawn.

Andra tensed for action. Alain gripped his staff in readiness. Stephen's opponents circled with youthful confidence, seeing easy prey in the unarmoured staff-bearing Guardian. The shorter one, his long brown hair braided and crimped, began stalking Stephen. The watchers rallied to the challenge of the arena, and shouted encouragement to the two warriors, and urged their quarry to fight well. Warrior eyed warrior, eyed warrior. The short one lunged. Stephen bounced up, avoiding the point of the blade, and sidestepped. He flicked his staff into his hands as the attacker stumbled past, and brought it down across his opponent's haunches, sending him sprawling to the ground. Cheers and abuse rang from the audience as the humiliated warrior scrambled to his feet. He wiped his face, and rejoined his companion, both stalking Stephen around the ring. The shorter one charged again. Again, Stephen stepped aside, but this time he deftly turned the sword away with his staff and brought the free end sharply upwards, catching the warrior under the chin, jerking him to a halt. Simultaneously, the taller warrior made a hefty swing with his blade, but Stephen anticipated the attack and simply ducked under the sword. The short warrior keeled over, and lay on the earth, unconscious. Seeing his companion's fate, the taller warrior lost confidence, and stepped back. His hesitation galled Murdok, who ordered three more recruits into the ring.

Four to one. No Guardian would accept the odds. Andra pushed forward to stand beside Stephen. Alain joined them, and the three friends formed a triangle, facing outward. Their defiance provoked Murdok, and his voice bellowed above the clamour, 'All in! No killing blows! Fight until submission! Beat them down!' A roar of cheers rang out, and as one the circle of recruited warriors descended on the three Guardians.

The only consolation was that he gave out more bruising blows than he received, but his body ached as he lifted a moist cool rag to the swelling on the bridge of his nose. Fire raced through his sinews, and his head pounded as he sat up. A face hung before his eyes. 'Not a pretty sight, my friend. You look like you've been run over by half the King's mounted archers.' Andra heard a chuckle.

'Go away, Tim Gaelus. Let me die in,' he muttered. The effort set his head thumping, so he lifted the rag to his brow.

Tim gently took it from him. 'Oh no, I insist on staying. I'll freshen this.' Andra heard him dip the rag in a bucket of water outside the tent. When he turned towards the opening, the bright light forced him to close his eyes and turn away. 'Here,' Tim said, as he returned with the rag. 'This will ease the pain a little.' Andra gladly took it and pressed it to his forehead. The cold was soothing. 'Better, eh?' Andra grunted. 'Quite a fight you three put up.' Andra forced his eyes to squint open. 'Most entertaining,' Tim added.

'You saw it?'

'Most of it,' he replied. 'The best part anyway. You three had the others beaten, until Murdok grabbed more volunteers to enjoy the fun. Where did you learn to wield staves so proficiently?'

Confused by Tim's muddled outpouring, Andra mumbled, 'The Guardian Master taught us.'

'Then we need him here to teach the Great King's warriors a trick or two,' Tim declared, and laughed. 'Three against twenty, and I'd say the odds were even in the match. Impressive. I've never seen High Lord Mara laugh so much.'

Andra looked up. 'He saw it?'

'Indeed he did, my friend – at least the latter part of the melee. He and his entourage were riding the camp boundary and happened upon your sideshow. He was most amused by Murdok's frustration, and he applauded soundly when the last of your band was finally beaten down.' A tinge of anger touched Andra's eyes, but Tim saw it, and said, 'No, no, Andra, my friend. You mustn't take it so. Lord Mara was applauding you and your friends' valiant effort against the odds. He openly praised all three of you, in front of Murdok and the rest of your group of trainees. You are camp heroes.'

Andra let the words settle inside his head. Camp heroes. Murdok. Odds. Mara. Pain. 'If this is what a hero feels like, then no wonder there are so few.'

'Well said!' Tim responded, and clapped Andra enthusiastically on the shoulder. Andra winced, making Tim realize his mistake. 'By Teka, I am sorry my friend. I forget.'

Andra waved away the apology with his free hand. When he realized Alain and Stephen weren't there, he asked, 'Where are the others?'

'Ah. They've gone into the city.'

'The city?'

'Yes. You've earned a day's recreation, except you've spent yours in here.'

Confusion mobbed him again as he fought the pounding ache in his head. Tim wasn't making sense. 'Here? I don't understand.'

Tim smiled. 'You've been unconscious since they carried you in last night. Your head's not as thick as your friends. They left you here when they went into the city. After all, you wouldn't have had much fun in the city last night, in that state, would you?'

Andra began to understand why his head hurt so much. He'd lost a whole sun-cycle. 'I would like to have seen the Great City,' he muttered.

His disappointment surprised Tim. 'Are you saying you've never been into the city?' he asked. Andra nodded. 'By Teka, I don't believe it!' Tim paused, and grinned. 'That can't be allowed. A soldier in the Great King's Armies who hasn't even set foot in the Great King's city? We must rectify the problem. Tonight!'

Andra's confusion deepened. 'But you said I'd already missed the chance to go. I can't go to the city now. Murdok would have me whipped. That is the law, isn't it?'

Tim's laughter increased. He squatted beside Andra and leaned conspiratorially close to his face, speaking in a half-whisper. 'That's the law of the camp. All the more reason we should go. There's no fun where there's no risk, as Patti says. Besides, you've earned the right to go. High Lord Mara bestowed it upon you and your companions, so I'll be your guide.' He winked wickedly. 'You'll see many more sights of the city with Tim Gaelus than you would've seen with your friends anyway. We'll go. I'll make arrangements. You, my friend, will just have to relax here until sundown. I'll come for you then.' He grinned broadly, and rose to leave.

'Who's Patti?' Andra asked.

Tim stopped at the tent's entrance. 'You'll meet her tonight. I think she'll find you fascinating, for a man.' He bowed and slipped out.

The bright light from the entrance still hurt Andra's eyes. He slumped back among the animal hides of his bed, and lifted his right arm to cover his brow, and floated back to sleep on a dull sea of pains.

Voices. Andra listened at the edge of consciousness. 'Sh. He sleeps still.'

'Perhaps his injuries are too serious for healing.'

'No. He merely sleeps.'

'Leave him. Tomorrow he will be renewed. It is The Way.'

'I'll stay.'

'Come with us. We'll eat with Hendrik and his friends. Let him sleep undisturbed.'

'Sleep, my friend.'

Andra opened his eyes, and blinked in the soft semi-darkness, as footsteps shuffled away from the tent-flap. Camp noises carried to his ears. Soldiers sauntered by. Horses nickered. Unseen groups were gathering by their fires and preparing meals. He rubbed his eyes. The ache in his head had nearly ceased, but the bruising was still painful, and he gingerly moved to an upright position. The tent-flap flicked aside, and Tim Gaelus' slim figure was briefly silhouetted against the fading evening. 'Good. At least I don't have to wake you. How do you feel?'

'Sore.'

'Well, then, you have good reasons to go out to forget the sorry state of your body. Pity you probably won't enjoy everything the city can offer you.' Tim laughed quietly as he finished, but whatever he found amusing escaped Andra. 'Come on, my friend, time to dress. It's dark enough to leave, and most of those on recreational leave are back.' Andra accepted Tim's assistance. His aching limbs and chest painfully resisted, as he pulled on his jerkin and tried to lace a pair of leggings. Bruising along the base of his right shoulder burned whenever he raised his arm. 'Lucky I've only decided to take you sight-seeing tonight,' mused Tim, as he helped Andra pull on a pair of dusty boots. 'I'd hate to have to drag you along in the middle of a brawl or in a flight along a back alley. Your friends must have used you as a shield yesterday.' He chattered on, and Andra was content to listen, allowing his witty friend to fill the time. 'Let's go.' Tim tugged at Andra's sleeve, and they eased out of the tent.

The air was milder than it had been for many weeks, but Andra still felt the icy teeth of the bitter southerly wind invisibly lingering. Some soldiers wandered between the clumps of tents, but most were sitting close to their fires, eating, drinking, swapping tales, and sharing memories of their homes. Strains of song rose in isolated pockets. 'Wait,' said Tim, and he ducked back into the tent, reappearing after a moment. 'Your friends will now think you still sleep in your bed.'

He led Andra between the tents along the edge of the camp. They skirted the direct light of fires, and Tim made an effort to avoid overt attention, although twice he nodded to passing individuals who recognised him. They travelled several hundred paces before Tim turned towards a cluster of tents. There were no visible lights or fires. He halted, checked in all directions, and, when he was satisfied that no one was looking towards them, he bustled Andra into the tent nearest to the spiral arm of road.

Inside, Andra was blind, unable to see even his hands before his face, but the disorientation heightened his other senses. His ears told him Tim was moving in the darkness, trying to locate something, effortlessly avoiding invisible objects, as if he could see where he was looking. Tim whispered, 'They're here. Good,' and Andra sensed his friend approaching. A metallic object was pressed into his hand. 'Wear this around your neck my friend, under your jerkin. And put on this cloak.' Cloth was placed on his shoulder.

'What is it?' Andra asked, referring to the object in his hand.

'A talisman. A key. Where we go, you'll find it useful. But only when I tell you to use it.' Tim waited while Andra slipped the leather thong attached to the talisman over his head. 'We stay here for a little while. A wagon will pass shortly on its way back to the city. It belongs to an old friend, Karlin Wheeler. He's a furrier, and he'll have a light load of skins and furs aboard. He'll stop outside our tent, and that's when we climb aboard and secrete ourselves among the goods.

We'll travel to the city, warm and comfortable.'

Andra appreciated Tim Gaelus' planning to ensure roving soldiers on perimeter watch wouldn't stop them. The more he learned about this friend, the more secrets he seemed to have, but an immediate question nagged him. He turned in the darkness, towards where he guessed Tim to be crouching and asked, 'How can you see in here?'

There was uncomfortable silence as he awaited a reply. Tim touched his shoulder and said, 'Of course. I forgot you've never been beyond your tiny valley. I'm quarter-cast Aelendyell.'

Twenty Nine

The wagon bumped and rattled towards the Great City, and Andra was glad Tim had chosen a furrier's wagon because the thick furs cushioned against the jarring ruts and holes the wagon's wheels found. He tried to relax in the smothering warmth, but he continued to ponder Tim's cryptic explanation of being able to see in virtual darkness. What was a quartercast? No one Andra knew could see without light. Even the nocturnal animals he hunted, in the forest and hills around The Vale, needed a little light to find their food and their homes. Without light, they were dependent on other senses; smell, echoing sound. Yet, in complete darkness, Tim could see.

The wagon lurched to a stop. Andra thought it was too soon to have reached the city. He heard murmuring voices, and, although he couldn't hear them clearly, he assumed the City Watch wanted to see all was in order with the merchant, and he feared they might search the wagon. But the wagon jerked back into motion, indicating the disinterest the Watch held in apprehending offenders. When he felt they were safe, Andra whispered through the furs to Tim, 'We're lucky they chose not to be too nosy back there.'

'No luck involved,' Tim replied, casually. 'Karlin offered them a little payment to be less observant. That's the rules of the game.'

'You mean they knew we were in here? We bribed them?'

Tim laughed at Andra's naiveté. 'Of course; though, there's no way they could know exactly who we are. Not that they care. Call it what you like, Andra – drink money, blind payment, thank you money – the Great King's Armies pay a soldier one gold coin a month for his service, so he needs to get rich any way he can, and he needs to have good friends. After all, next week it might be them in this cart and us on

Watch. One looks after the other.'

Andra settled into the furs and wondered what he would do when it came to his turn on the Watch. Honesty was a matter of honour, an unquestionable value, The Way of The Vale, but here, in the heart of the Kingdom, that principle seemed readily discarded by everyone who saw it opportune to do so. He felt, and heard, changes beyond his cocoon of fur. The wagon shifted direction. Low voices passed, close. A burst of raucous song startled him, and the wagon stopped again. A hand thrust into his hideaway, followed by Tim ordering, 'Out of there, my friend. The free ride is over.' Andra threw aside his covering, and blinked. 'Karlin wants to go home and store his goods, and he doesn't want your useless carcass lying about, ruining the quality of his merchandise. Out you come.' Andra accepted Tim's arm and slid from the rear of the wagon. 'Welcome,' said Tim, with mock gentility, sweeping down in a grand bow before the young Guardian, 'to the Great City of His Royal Majesty, Great King Thana, Eternal Liege of the Kingdom.' He looked at Karlin Wheeler, seated on his wagon, and sternly commanded, 'That will be all, my good man. About your business now! I'm done with you.'

The merchant coughed, and bent towards Tim, to reply, 'Thank you, Your Grace. I am so humbled to have been of important service to one the likes of you.' Both men laughed. Karlin turned, and flicked his reins, prompting his horse into a slow walk.

Andra and Tim stood in a rough alley, with misshapen wooden buildings clustered either side. The buildings were dark, but for one from which yellow lamplight spilled through a window. The unfamiliar environment made Andra nervous as his senses struggled to take in the sights and sounds and odours. The alley smelt of rotting refuse – offal, decaying vegetable matter – and from the lighted window, voices rose and fell in excited pitch. 'Come,' said Tim quietly. 'This place allows us unseen entry into the city. We go this way.'

'What are they doing in there?' Andra whispered,

indicating the window.

'Alligator,' Tim replied. 'It's a betting game; dangerous and highly illegal. It's not our business to know about it. The City Watch are far too curious in this quarter. Let's go.' He led Andra out of the alley, and across the rear of a derelict block of huts, to a line of trees: willows, dipping into an inky river. 'Look along the edge,' said Tim. 'There'll be a boat hidden in the trees hereabouts. We'll cross over.' Searching in the dark was difficult for Andra, but Tim quickly found a poling skiff, loosely camouflaged under reeds. They boarded and poled thirty strokes through the dark waters to the opposite bank, where they scrambled ashore. Tim tied the skiff to an overhanging branch, unhitched his money purse, and tossed a coin into the skiff. 'I know,' he said, rejoining Andra. 'You wonder why I steal a boat to cross over and pay a copper coin. Call it a custom of the city. Boats are frequently used in this manner. The owners expect payment. It's our way of saying no hard feelings, no malice intended.'

'Are all cities like this?' Andra asked, his confusion revealed in his hoarse whisper.

Tim chuckled. 'Most likely, my friend; most likely.'

They slipped out of the tree cover and crept to the rear of a building. The windows were shuttered, and doors closed, but light glowed behind them. Tim put his hand on Andra's shoulder, and said, 'I have a moment's business to attend to within. Stay here and keep watch.' He knocked. A slide hatch opened in the face of the door, at head height. Andra couldn't see the features of the respondent within, because of the backlight. Inaudible questions and answers were exchanged, before the door opened, and Tim Gaelus entered. Andra waited, squinting apprehensively into the surrounding darkness, but he had no concept of where he was in the Great City. Black shapes of buildings, a treacle-slow and dark river, patches of lamplight, and black skies shadowing the chill air of night, revealed nothing. A brief splash of light spilled from the doorway, and Tim reappeared. He clapped his hand on Andra's shoulder, with cheerful abandon, and announced, 'All done and approved.

Let's go see the city sights.'

They walked between huts and houses, along short, winding lanes, until they emerged in a street wide enough for three wagons to travel abreast. Light filled several doors and windows, and groups wandered to and fro, or huddled in shadowy alcoves. Shouting and singing rose further along the street. Tim indicated that direction, and soon they stood before the entrance to a brightly lit tavern. 'The Inn of Dragons!' Tim announced. 'A fine place. The ale is excellent, the company interesting, if somewhat lively. Detton Tomas is the proprietor, a straight-speaking, no-nonsense man, who runs a thriving house, and brews ale like no other in the Kingdom.' Three men congregated under the lamp above the door, tankards in hand, ceased their conversation while Tim and Andra passed between, and Andra felt three pair of eyes scrutinize him as he stepped into the yellow tavern light.

The number of people crowded inside surprised him. The dozen or so tables were full, and a variety of characters leaned against the wooden bar and walls. Most were men, dressed in rustic clothing, although Andra caught glimpses of chain mail, partially concealed beneath better quality cloaks in the crowd. At a table, in the furthest corner, sat five men, whose unshaven faces, sharp eyes, and well-polished leather breastplates proclaimed them as seasoned mercenaries. Several youths skipped and dodged through the drinking melee, toting armfuls of mugs and tankards to waiting patrons, collecting payment and tips for their pains. Tim pushed through the mob, nodding to acquaintances who acknowledged him, and he found space at the bar. A pudgy-faced publican, with bright cheeks and piggy eyes, greeted him jovially. 'Tim, me lad! Soldierin' taught you 'ow t' walk through yon front door? Now tha's no such a bad thing is it? Ay, me lad, you'll grow an 'onest man yet, by my teeth.' Tim grinned and shook the publican by the ears. The man glanced at Andra. 'Oo's yon friend?'

Tim grabbed Andra's arm and pulled him forward. 'May I introduce Andra, my good lord publican, a fine young warrior from the Valley of Rivers, come to serve in the Great King's Armies.' Tim's exaggerated action and tone caused several men to stare at Andra, and he flushed at the unwelcome attention.

'Manners too, is it? I never thought t' see the day of it! You've embarrassed the boy! Well, young man, if you be a friend of Tim Gaelus, you be welcome in my house, 'n I'll be sorry for it. What'll it be, me lads?'

Detton brought the ales Tim ordered, and scuttled away to serve others.

Andra, unfamiliar with ale, found the bittersweet taste refreshing, but lacking the crispness of spring water. He followed Tim's example, and quaffed the tankard, only to discover that Detton as rapidly refilled it. After a second tankard, Andra felt his senses dulling, and the aches from his brawl easing. 'A great drop!' Tim remarked, smiling broadly. Andra smiled in response, and the tankards were refilled. For the third time, Andra noted, Detton didn't ask for money, and Tim offered none. 'Come on. Let's sit, and enjoy some good drinking,' Tim said, and he led the way between tables and customers. Andra was puzzled as to where Tim meant to sit, because there were no empty tables or stools in the tavern, but Tim moved unerringly towards a small table, pushed against the wall, with three chairs occupied by three men. Once there, he leaned forward and said something inaudible to one man. Astonishment filled the man's face. A second man, with a thin, straggly beard, and a scar across his forehead, began to protest, but his companions quietened him. They stood and vacated the table. Two nodded reverently towards Andra as they left, but the scar-faced individual gave him a bitter sneer. Tim beckoned for Andra to join him at the table.

'What did you say to them?' Andra asked, as he sat.

Tim chuckled. 'I said you were a Royal Assassin having a quiet night out, and you needed a place to sit.'

Andra had already heard references to the Assassins in the camp; murderers employed to conduct cold-blooded killings. 'They believed you?' he asked, incredulously. 'But I thought the Assassins were meant to be silent and unknown?'

'They are, usually, by trade,' Tim explained, 'but the Great King's Personal Assassins are very public people. They are known, and they go out of their way to be known. After all, they operate under the sanction of the Great King – they perform his duty. No one questions their coming or going, and no one, but the Great King, has authority over them. Their abilities are legendary, second only to the skills of the Guild's Hand, so no one dares interfere with them. Just pray, my friend, that one doesn't come to visit your house one day. They're not exactly friendly house guests.' Tim drank another measure.

'But why was the scar-faced man so grim?'

'His brother paid his dues to one of the Great King's Assassins a week ago.'

Andra looked over his shoulder, nervously searching for the three men, but they were lost in the crowd, perhaps even gone from the tavern.

By the sixth tankard of warm ale, Andra felt positively odd. Tim had been chattering about mundane events back at the camp, but Andra couldn't recall any details of his speech. The tavern became progressively rowdier, as more people forced their way in, to swell the crowd. Several tables attracted attention from audiences, and Andra guessed games were being played at them. The serving youths worked at furious pace, and frustrated voices frequently complained when orders arrived too slowly, or the boys failed to acknowledge drink requests. Heat poured into the room from the hearth of an open fire, and the mass of bodies and alcoholic fumes made the air so stifling that Andra was overwhelmed by an urgent need to escape outside to breathe cool air.

Ferocious voices sent shock waves rippling through the sea of revellers as a commotion erupted at the centre of the tavern. People turned to the source and Andra stood to see what was happening. The crowd was too numerous, so he clambered onto his chair, his head barely below the oak

261

rafters, and peered across the heads. Two men faced each other over an upturned table, eyes locked. One, in a leather jerkin and cord leggings, his dark hair tangled and knotty, held a sword's threatening point towards the second. The second man, completely bald, and wearing a thick woollen smock that hung to the floor, held both hands before his face, and he appeared to be mumbling. 'What's happening?' Tim asked with detached interest, from his seat. Andra quickly described the scene. 'My money's on the Apprentice,' Tim declared, and he quaffed another mouthful of ale.

'Who's the Apprentice?' asked Andra.

'The bald one,' Tim explained, without looking up from his tankard.

The crowd moved back, giving the men room. The combatants circled cautiously, the sword waving in the air, the pair of hands flickering in arcane ritual. Crowd shouts urged them to fight. Most of the encouragement supported the swordsman, but Andra heard urgency in the cries for him to attack quickly. The swordsman lunged. The Apprentice barely avoided serious injury, the blade ripping through his grey smock, and, as he stumbled backward, the swordsman swung at his head, the point of the sword slicing a gaping wound across the Apprentice's forehead. The crowd cheered approval. The Apprentice seized the opportunity to distance himself from his opponent, and his hands moved with greater speed, blurring into patterns. The swordsman stalked him, but as he raised his weapon to strike the Apprentice pointed a finger at the sword and it burst into bright blue flame. The onlookers gasped. The startled swordsman dropped the blazing sword, but anger quickly replaced his shock, and he whipped his dagger from its sheath. The briefest hesitation was what the Apprentice required. His fingers traced a pattern, and he opened one hand towards the dark-haired man. The crowd behind the swordsman jostled and shoved to avoid the Apprentice's line of attack. The swordsman's face lost all emotion, his eyes rolled up and he crumpled to the floor, his dagger clattering harmlessly across the floorboards. Everyone paused for a silent moment, to take in the tableau of the swordsman sprawled at the feet of the grey-robed Apprentice, before the hubbub returned as everyone returned to their private talks, arguments, drinking, and games.

Andra watched the bald head move through the crowd to the door and depart. Someone poured a mug of mead over the swordsman's face, and his friends hauled him to his feet, slapping him about the cheeks to rouse him. 'Sit down.' Andra looked down at Tim's laughing face. 'You look quite a fool standing up there on your chair. You're a Royal Assassin, remember?' Embarrassed, Andra awkwardly slid down into his chair, and Tim pushed a full tankard towards him. 'Here. One more measure of this lively liquid, and we must be off.'

'Did you see that?' Andra asked, awestruck.

Tim gulped a mouthful of ale before replying. 'It was a fight. And not a terribly good one,' he said nonchalantly.

'But the bald one,' Andra persisted, 'the Apprentice you called him – he did strange things. He had no weapons, but he won. And he didn't touch the other man. He had some kind of – power.'

'Power?' Tim shook his head. 'No. He just used a little magic.' Then he saw the puzzled expression on Andra's face and understood. 'You haven't seen magic before, have you?' Andra shook his head. 'Don't you have sorcerers, or sages, or witches in your lovely Vale, my friend?'

'No,' Andra told him. 'Nothing like this one who was here – perhaps one of the Council –' A fleeting memory of Master Geat flashed through his thoughts. 'No. No one had that sort of power in The Vale.'

'Well, relax. There are plenty of them around here. The King has a whole academy of apprentice sorcerers in his castle. You'll see many more like our friend. They look deadly, but they use tricks, and illusions, to make watchers believe what they see is real. But it isn't. That sword didn't burn, Andra. He just used his arts to make the swordsman believe it did.'

'But I saw it flame.'

'Perhaps you think you did,' said Tim, calmly. 'But that Apprentice is a small fish. Still, wise men don't mess with magicians unless they know how to deal with them.' He indicated the tankard before Andra. 'Drink up. This place is getting too rowdy, and we've got better entertainment elsewhere.'

Drinks finished, they pushed through the throng to leave the tavern. The night air was brittle chill, and light wispy rain drifted out of the darkness. The street traffic had increased, lanterns and torches swinging in rhythm with pedestrians and wagons, and the shadowy groups huddled in doorways had multiplied. At least four other taverns were open along the street's length. At the centre of the road, Andra spotted two Haardrishii sauntering towards them, almost invisible in their black armour, except for the metallic gleam reflecting light from nearby lamps and lanterns. He pointed them out to Tim. 'Ah, the City Watch, said Tim, with wicked malice. 'Now there's sport for the Thieves' Guild!' He sighed. 'If only we had the time –' His voice trailed away.

'Why?' asked Andra. 'What were you thinking?'

Tim chuckled, and replied, 'Nothing, my friend; nothing that can't wait tonight. I might show you another time.' He clapped Andra on the shoulder, and smiled into his face. 'Yes, indeed I might!' he laughed.

They followed the street, which became a road called The King's Way, as it curved through the city. After a period of walking, Tim turned to Andra and nudged him with his elbow. 'Wait here for me. I'll just nip in to see that we are welcome. Better still, wait in that alcove.' He indicated a dark doorway across the street. 'And don't go to sleep.' Tim slipped down a short alleyway, to an entrance, lit by two lanterns shaped like candles.

Andra moved to the alcove and slid into its protective darkness. From his vantage, he watched a pair of revellers stumble by, singing to the night about a soldier's lost fortunes and loves, in absolute disharmony, and, moments later, a lone horseman trotted by, heading towards the City's centre. He felt alcoholic numbness at the tips of his fingers and in his legs, and knew the icy air nibbling at his nose and cheeks was leaving no sensation because of the ale. He drifted, staring into the approaching torchlight, without understanding why it came towards him. Three figures stood somewhere beyond the light. A cold, brutal voice asked, 'Who is it to be tonight, Assassin? Your brother? Someone's mother perhaps?'

The questions were beyond Andra's comprehension. 'Who's there?' he asked.

A voice hissed. 'This!' Cold metal flashed.

His reflexes were dulled by ale, but Guardian instinct saved him. The sword point thudded into the door behind him, and he half fell, half dived into the street. Curses followed him, as he kicked to his feet, and shook his head to clear his thoughts. 'You can't take three of us, you pig-sticker! Not with no weapon!'

Andra tensed, but he spoke as calmly as he could. 'I'm not an assassin. I don't mean you harm.'

'Lies!' a bitter voice spat. 'We know who you are, with your fancy pigtail and black hair. Your friend told us at the tavern. Did us a favour really. I owe your Great King a favour from Lewin, my brother.'

The flickering torch revealed his antagonist's thin beard and scar, and Andra realized what was happening. A figure leaped, hoping to catch him unawares, but Andra caught the attacker under the chin with the heel of his hand, sending the man reeling backwards. The second assailant thrust his sword, forcing Andra to skip and twist to avoid the blade, and his evasion brought him around, until his back faced the first attacker. He grappled Andra from behind and squeezed. Pain shot through Andra's chest and shoulders, not from the squeezing, but the injuries he'd received the previous day. He lowered his centre of balance, reached for the hair of the man on his back, took hold, arched forward, and tossed his captor over his shoulders to land with a bone-crushing crunch at the feet of the man with the sword. Andra was aware of a half-choking gasp to his left, and, when he looked at the scar-faced man holding the torch, he saw terror etched across the man's features, eyes staring wide, pleading. For an instant, the man held his pose, before he toppled rigidly forward, torch spitting and guttering as it hit the ground. Between his shoulder blades was a dagger's black hilt, its blade buried deep. The sword-wielding attacker stared at his dead companion, dropped his sword, and took to his heels, shouting, 'Watch! Help! Murder! Murder!'

Tim called to Andra from across the street. 'Use your legs for better things than standing still. This way! Your screaming friend will raise the dead as well as The Watch. Come on!' Andra took a final look at the prostrate body, as Tim deftly withdrew his knife, wiped it on the dead man's jerkin, and returned it to its sheath beneath his cloak, before he hastily followed his companion across the road, and down the alleyway, to the door with the twin lanterns.

Thirty

The dirty room was cluttered with wooden crates, and enormous stoneware jars threw writhing shadows across the bare wooden walls. A lone torch struggled to light the room, kicking and sputtering in the dying juices of fat on which it fed. At first, Andra thought the room was unoccupied, until several piles of filthy rags moved, and thin hands, and gaunt faces with large, staring eyes appeared in each pile. 'Who are they?' he whispered.

'Them? Debris. Refuse. Leftovers of what were once a proud people – my people. They won't harm you, Andra. Give them a taste of rum, or mead, even ale, and they'll serve you all their days, when they're not drunk.'

Andra stared at the huddled individuals in the collection of storage and saw despair in a pair of deep almond-shaped eyes. 'Why are they like that?'

Tim ignored his question, taking his arm instead to lead him through the containers, winding towards a large pottery urn at the rear of the room. 'Have you still got the necklet I gave you to wear?' he asked.

'Yes,' replied Andra. 'Here on my neck.'

'Good. Pull it over the top so they recognise you're welcome here.'

'Who's 'they'?' Andra asked, becoming more and more curious about Tim's secrecy.

'Just do as I say, and hurry,' Tim demanded. 'The City Watch search everywhere, even here, in a disused warehouse, where derelicts hide.' While he spoke, he manipulated one handle of the urn, and pulled the urn away from the wall to reveal a dark passageway. He stepped in, and motioned Andra to follow. In utter darkness, unimpeded by the absence of light, Tim dragged Andra forward, descended a short flight of steps, and halted at the bottom. 'We wait,' said Tim.

'Who for?'

'You'll see.'

The cryptic response, and stifling darkness, stirred Andra's anger. 'No. Tell me!' he demanded. 'I'm tired of your secrets and games, Tim Gaelus. You nearly got me killed already. You've avoided answering my questions, and I -'

Brilliant light blinded them. Rough hands grabbed Andra, and held him firmly, and an invisible voice rasped beyond the light. 'Take it easy. They wear The Key. And I know this particular vagabond all too well.'

'How long do we have to wait here?'

'Depends,' mused Tim. 'If they don't see you as a threat to current activities, only a short while. On the other hand, if you pose a problem at this moment, you might be here for days.'

Shock filled Andra's face. 'Days? We can't be away from camp for days. Murdok will run me into the ground. And what will Stephen and Alain think if I suddenly disappear?'

'Well, you shouldn't go around killing people in the streets.'

'I didn't kill –' Andra began to bluster, but when he saw the broad grin on Tim's face, he eased his outburst. 'You know I didn't kill that man.'

'You didn't. But they need to make sure you weren't recognised or followed.'

Andra relaxed, and glanced about at the whitewashed room. A wooden door, solid and featureless, stood in the centre of one wall, and a single, smoky torch flickered beside it. 'Lovely place,' he remarked, in an attempt at sarcasm. 'Where are we?'

Tim's grin broadened, as he announced, 'You're in The Maze of The Guild.' Andra raised a questioning eyebrow. 'All right, my country friend, I'll tell you a few things, since it's obvious you know nothing of city life. The Guild is like a secret group, a large group, of people who share a common interest, who work together to mutually reach common goals and protect themselves from others who might threaten their success. There are lots of guilds in a city, but this one is interested in making a living conducting businesses that so-called respectable people think are wrong, or beneath their dignity. We earn our livings in a variety of ways, specialists you might call us, although we all started from the same basic beginnings. We're all called by the same title by the ignorant: thieves. Ever heard the word?'

'Only since I came to the Great King's Armies. Nobody in The Vale has reason to steal from another, or hurt them. The Way is trust and peace.'

'Well, in this world there is another 'way' as you put it,' said Tim. 'You get smart, or you die. Some people work for others, growing grain, or keeping animals. There are trappers, professional soldiers, merchants, artisans, scholars, minstrels. They all offer skills to others, only there are just so many skills to sell, and only so many people able to pay for those skills. No work, no pay. No pay, no eat. It's simple law; ruthless, but effective. If you have to steal to eat, you do it. Street children do it through necessity. But stealing takes great skill, and you become proud of your skill as you grow up. Thieving is a profession, Andra. The Guild has professional thieves of every kind - pickpockets, prostitutes, spies, assassins. It has rules and obligations, like any organization. It protects its own. And, once in it, if you break its rules, for any reason, you pay the penalty.'

'What's your skill?' Andra asked.

Tim's eyes narrowed, hardened, and Andra was struck by the similarity between Tim's eyes and those of the derelict he'd seen earlier, in the warehouse. 'I'm an assassin.'

There was no need to explain. Andra understood he'd been given information that went beyond the bond of friendship, knowledge sealed with the touch of death's icy fingertips, and he knew Tim would hold him to that bond, eternally. He broke the silence. 'You haven't explained the derelicts. Why are they like they are?'

Tim's smile faded, and the iron-fire of his eyes softened.

269

He dropped his voice as he spoke. 'It is too long a tale, for now, and one I know too little about. I can tell you've seen something of them in me. They're like distant cousins, some quartercast, as I am. Others have less Aelendyell blood in them. But they're dead. The Aelendyell are dead. Only these scraps remain. I began, like most of them, an orphan, loose in the streets before I can even remember, scavenging food, with dogs, outside the taverns, and stealing from the market, and the merchants' wagons – until Patti took me in. She's taken many of us in; strays, discards. But not all of them are so lucky. And there are many who run back into the streets, go back to drinking rather than face The Guild's discipline.'

Andra was fascinated by Tim's revelation. 'Who are the Aelendyell?'

'I don't really know. Patti said my grandfather was Aelendyell. He lived in the forests that grew to the east on the borders of Targa, but those forests are long gone. The Aelendyell were supposed to possess magic, but I have none, although it's why I can see in total darkness. My eyes sense heat, as well as light. Apparently the Aelendyell could do that. Strange, isn't it? But very useful in my profession. That's why I've been so successful. I can see when others are blind.' Tim moved towards the door, and he turned to stare at Andra with such intensity that Andra felt uncomfortable.

'What are you staring at?'

'The scar on your cheek - just curious.'

'Why? What's wrong with it?'

'How did you get it?'

Andra detected the note of concern in Tim's voice. He reached up and ran his fingertips over the crescent edge of the scar on his left cheek. 'I fell on a sharp root in the marshes.' Tim's eyes returned to the door, closing the matter, but Andra's curiosity was aroused. 'You're not telling me everything again.'

Tim cocked his right eyebrow. 'Well?' Andra demanded.

Tim shrugged his shoulders, and replied. 'All that talk of my Aelendyell heritage reminded me of an old legend. Patti used to tell it to us, as children.'

'So, what's the legend?'

'It's unimportant, Andra.'

'No. I'm interested now. What legend?'

Tim shook his head, but quietly began an explanation. 'There's a legend, a prophecy really. I've heard some of the older derelicts rave about it in their drunken binges. They say something like; when the Dark Lord returns, there'll come one bearing the mark of the moon, and he'll rise from the dead to defeat the Dark Lord. Your scar made me think of it. It's shaped like a crescent moon.'

Andra's eyes widened. 'Who's the Dark Lord?'

'Probably one of the old Dragonlords.'

'What's a Dragonlord?'

'They don't exist, Andra. Aian Abreotan slew them all in the Dragon Wars, a long time ago. It's ancient history.'

'But what about the prophecy?' Andra persisted.

Tim laughed. 'Prophecies are bigger lies than a woman's promise of love. They don't come true. Prophets are notorious for contradicting themselves, even over the same prophecy. I mean there's another common prophecy that claims the moon saviour will rise wielding a two-edged sword, killing friend and foe alike. And another says the one marked with the moon will appear as two. It's an old favourite as a motif, but nonsense, really, when you think about it.' Before Andra could respond, the door swung open, and a tousle-haired urchin, face darkened with grime, beckoned for them to follow. Andra saw Tim pause to regain his usual cheeriness, slipping it on like a favourite cloak, and ruffle the child's hair, as he reached the door, waiting for Andra to follow.

'You've been given th' all clear, Tim, you an' your friend 'ere,' said a stout ruffian, who lounged at a table, his boots on it, and a jug of warm mead in his left hand. 'Me an' th' lads 'ere are makin' th' most of a dull night. Why don't you join us?' he offered, indicating empty chairs. Andra and Tim sat. The room was warmed by a small hearth, glowing near the table, and a dozen boys and girls, all less than eleven years Andra guessed, by their size, were scattered about the room on rugs, chatting, or sleeping, or playing secret little games. Their clothing had the appearance of rags, but Andra noticed that it was cunningly constructed to appear worn and thin while remaining warm to protect the wearer. 'Street urchins. Beggin' children if you like,' explained their host. Andra was aware that the stout man was staring at him.

Of course, thought Andra, Tim already knows all this.

'We train this lot,' the man continued, 'So as they can earn their livin's by playin' on th' 'earts an' consciences of wealthy merchants, especially their wives. I mean, what woman could resist such a baleful pair of eyes?' He gestured towards a very young girl, who looked up at Andra with large dark eyes, and a pink pouting face smeared with dirt. Andra felt an immediate pang of pity for the poor child, but she burst into a giggling fit, and scampered away, to bounce back into a pack of her cohorts wrestling on the floor. 'Ha! See?' said the stout man. 'But that one needs a lot more trainin' at 'er actin' yet. She sees th' funny side of it all too quickly, an' laughs at th' point when 'er victims should be payin' 'er. What a vixen she will be!' He leaned forward, and offered his jug to Tim, who took a swig, before passing it to Andra. Andra tasted the sweet mead wine, but passed it back before drinking more than a dram. The ale of the Inn of Dragons still warmed his blood. 'So. I'm 'urrigan.' The heavy thief swung his boots down from the table and extended a large hairy hand towards Andra.

'And what's the news?' interrupted Tim.

Hurrigan leaned back again and smiled. 'Word 'as it that a man 'ose brother paid a debt to a Royal Assassin last week also paid a similar debt tonight.' Hurrigan winked at Andra, who shifted uncomfortably. 'Word also 'as it that a friend of 'is, that ran off to call th' City Watch, also met a similar fate. Obviously, this Assassin wanted to keep 'is identity secret.' Hurrigan grinned at Tim, who was chuckling quietly. Andra felt another conspiracy looming. Hurrigan settled back, before adding, 'Th' Guild is satisfied that th' incident 'as been quietly dealt with, and that no one 'cept th' Great King 'imself is implicated in th' deaths. You may as well continue your night's revelin'. Me, I'm for stayin' right 'ere, with me warm mead, in a nice warm room.'

Tim rose and tapped Andra on the shoulder. 'Hurrigan, we'd love to stay, but I've promised to be elsewhere tonight, and my young friend has an appointment. So we must be away.' Hurrigan nodded in understanding. 'But first,' added Tim, 'I'll need a blindfold for my friend. He's my guest, but you know the rules.'

'Aye,' laughed Hurrigan. 'I know th' rules indeed.'

Blindfolded, Andra was led along short passages, up and down steps, around sharp corners, and through doors. Twice, Tim stopped and pushed him against a wall to let others pass. Without sight, it was difficult to tell how far they travelled, or how many others passed them in The Maze. Eventually, Tim placed Andra's hand on a wooden rung, and they cautiously climbed a ladder, up through a trapdoor. His feet thumped on floorboards, and Tim removed the blindfold. A woman was staring hard at him, her eyes measuring, up and down, taking in every detail with consummate interest. Middle-aged, of ample build, several double chins wobbling beneath her florid face, surrounded by a halo of orange hair, what struck Andra was her height. At full stretch, she would be unlikely to stand taller than his belt, a feature that gave her an overall appearance of a bloated ball. If she were a full-sized person, she'd be enormous, he thought.

'You do pick up some unusual ones, don't you Timothy? This one wears a ponytail, I see. Different indeed. Still, he's right handsome enough, with those dark eyes and dark hair, and he looks strong. How old is he?' She spoke with a singsong cadence, harsh on an untrained ear, but not croaky.

'Well?' asked Tim, looking at Andra for a reply.

'I've seen eighteen sun-cycles,' he answered, and whispered to Tim, 'Who is this?'

'I'm Patti to you, lad. Plain old Patti,' she laughed. 'Aint that right, Tim?'

'There's nothing plain about you, Patti, except for what we can already see,' Tim quipped.

'You cheeky young whelp!' she chortled, in mock anger. 'For a copper coin, I'd lay one on you,' and she raised her hand as if to smack Tim's backside.

'Peace, you harridan! You've scolded and belted the living daylights out of me a thousand times before now. I won't risk another beating from you, even when you're old.'

'Quite right too,' she pouted. 'I'd still best you.' She stepped forward, and Tim bent to his knees to hug her warmly. 'Ah, but it's always good to see you, Tim, me lad. You was always a favourite, albeit a somewhat naughty one at times. But you've a good heart, you've a good heart.' She pushed him away, and took on a serious note. 'Well? What is it brought you to me tonight? Is it trouble again?' She hefted her hands onto her hips.

'No,' laughed Tim. 'Pleasure.'

Patti raised an eyebrow, and her face became cheerfully animated. 'Pleasure, is it? I might have guessed you'd come tomcatting. I take it he's one of your new friends from the Armies then? I might have known.' She looked straight at Andra. 'You'll do no good keeping company with this wild young man. He's more trouble than a pit full of wildcats. You'll do well to wash your hands of him.' She folded her arms across her ample bosom and addressed them. 'If it's pleasure you've come seeking, you'll get the best of it from my girls, without a word of bragging. Let me see your coin.' She held out a plump palm.

Andra looked to Tim, puzzled, but Tim motioned for him to relax, as he unhitched a money purse from his belt. He placed the purse in Patti's hand. 'You'll find plenty in there to feed yourself, and the girls, for a month, and a little housekeeping besides.'

Patti felt the weight of the purse and broke into a broad smile that ran crevasses in her face, and she hugged Tim a second time. 'Ah Tim, you're a wondrous lad.' She went to a door, directly behind her, slipped a key from her bodice, and unlocked a padlock. The door opened to reveal a corridor lit by green lamps, and decorated with obscure tapestries. 'Go through. Choose any door. None of the girls are busy at the moment, and I'm sure any one of them will be pleased to see you, Tim.'

Tim started for the door, but stopped when he realized Andra wasn't following. He took the young Guardian's arm, and led him past the chuckling Patti, and the door closed behind them. Tim stood before one of the six doors in the hall, and pointed to a second, directly opposite his. 'Go on. Go in. You know what to do. Enjoy. Patti's girls are the best in the city.' Before Andra could admit that he didn't know what to do, Tim entered his chosen chamber and closed the door.

The corridor was empty. Andra found the green light discouraging, and he shuffled his feet nervously. He'd never been with a woman, not like Tim was inviting him to do. In The Vale, young men weren't allowed to choose a woman before twenty years of age. It was the Law. It was The Way. He never thought of questioning it. The girls were all either older, and attached, or much younger, still children. He'd seen girls bathing in pools, near the village, and he'd been curious about their bodies, but nothing more came of it. His mother was a beautiful woman, with bright eyes and auburn hair, and he secretly hoped that, when it came to his turn to choose a woman in the village, she would have the same commanding beauty and intelligence as his mother. Then there was Marella. The warrior woman from Tressel Deep stirred different, stronger feelings within him. Her deep green eyes and full, athletic body entranced him, so much so he'd embarrassed himself with his own naivety when he spoke to her. He felt strength, sexuality, in her presence. He reached for the latch.

Five tall candles gleamed behind a paper screen in the far corner of the room, filling it with a faint red hue created by the ochre dye in the paper. A wood fire crackled in a small hearth to his left, and the warmth it generated pleasantly surprised Andra. The floor was covered with a mass of fur rugs, providing a thick bedding, and increasing the room's warmth and comfort. Tapestries on the walls, intricately woven in colourful threads, depicted naked men and women, frolicking in forested glens, or wrapped in a variety of sexual positions. The golden hearth light silhouetted a young woman's figure through her thin, silver-tinted smock. Her hair was long, longer than any Andra had seen, reaching to her waist in ringlets and curls, and it was dark, although the firelight caught flecks of gold. Her eyes were large dark pools, and her lips rich and full. She smiled and took his hands in hers. 'Welcome to my chamber, my lord,' she whispered, in a voice that made Andra shiver. 'I am Lisette.' She knelt before him and kissed his hands. She rose, and led him across the room to a tapestry, which hung full length from ceiling to floor, and gently pulled it aside. Beyond was a small alcove, lit by a single candle, and in it was a large tub of steaming water. She began to tenderly unlace his tunic. 'Come, my lord. You are cold and sore. I will bathe you, and make you feel whole again. I will soothe your body. Let me ease your aching with love,' she murmured.

Andra felt his body tingling, changing, responding, as she moved her soft hands over him. He glanced down at the gentle curve of her breasts, and felt an urgent need to touch, and be touched by, a woman.

Thirty One

Winter rains crisscrossed the Plains of Ky, turning roads into muddy quagmires, and fields into broad sheets of water. Endless oceans of slate-grey clouds rolled across the skies, defying the sun's feeble attempts to light the days, and casting inky blackness over the freezing nights, filling them with an evil presence. Winds whistled about the huts and tents, teasing loose scraps of hide, or ill-tied thongs, and maliciously ripped them away before the tent owners could repair the damage. Frost settled on everything, and water buckets were capped, every morning, with brittle ice mantles. Activity in the camp of the Great King's Armies all but ceased. Warriors huddled in their tents and huts over small hearths, telling tales, sipping boiling mugs of broth, and cursing the wild southern winds that lashed their flimsy shelters with rain drawn from the Lake of Tears and the Endless Sea.

Andra listened to the adventures of mercenaries who travelled deep into the Kingdom of Andros to the northeast, or foraged into the Federation of Targa to the east, where they constantly avoided the traps of sorceresses and wizards. He heard tales from men who ventured into the Endless Sea, and barely escaped alive from battles with weird sea monsters, and wild storms that turned the ocean into a seething maelstrom. Others described army service in fortified encampments on the western boundary of the Kingdom and told of encounters with barbarians who rode horses that ran like the wind. He learned fragments of older legends, of the greatest Warrior-King, Aian Abreotan, who defeated Mareg, the Dragonlord, and of the Elvenaar and Dwarven races, and their mystical existence in the Land before Mareg's reign of terror. He listened one night, awe-struck, as a warrior sang a haunting ballad about the death of the last dragon, describing, with accurate but poignant detail, the terrible beauty of the great winged creature. Long after the song, Andra pondered on the extinct race, creatures that must have been simultaneously magnificent and fearful to behold, and he felt sadness, because he would never see a golden dragon, gliding from mountain peak to mountain peak, against a sunset tapestry of pinks, blues, yellow-gold, and purple light.

Days were monotonous, in the main, although Murdok, and other trainers, used every available opportunity to order the warriors out of their tents and into the mud to drill them. The camp's organization – the positioning of roads, paths, camping patches – was precise, as Andra discovered. Each collection of tents and huts, bordered by designated paths, housed exactly twenty-five warriors, and was called a Group. Each Group elected a leader. Stephen was given that honour in their Group. Major walkways in the camp separated four Groups from every other four, and these were called Squads – one hundred soldiers under the command of a seasoned warrior who carried the rank of Trainer. Five squads formed a Spoke, under the command of a Devi, and each Spoke was separated from the others by a small road. Ten Spokes, five thousand warriors, formed a Wheel, led by a Captain, and there were four Wheels in the Great King's Armies, divided by four spiral roads that led from the centre of the camp. The Great King's Armies numbered twenty thousand warriors. The centre was the Hub, the base for the High Lord who commanded the Armies, and the High Lord's specialist retinue of two hundred soldiers, the Great King's Scribes, the Strategists who planned campaigns, Apothecaries, Priests, and minor attendant Lords who had the right to sit upon the War Council. Supplies, and other commodities, were stored at the Hub. It was the centre of the entire force, and the design carefully protected it.

Trainers were responsible for teaching recruits and warriors how to work together as Squads on the field of battle; how to form phalanxes, how to move into horseshoe entrapment, how to withdraw. Andra and his friends were glad to have the exercises, but they ensured just enough grumbling reached Murdok's ears so he didn't think they were too keen to be out in the wintry weather. Wet days were spent polishing armour and shields, sharpening weapons, altering harnesses, oiling leather equipment, and mending worn or torn clothing: menial tasks that taught them patience and discipline. For Andra, Alain and Stephen, the boredom and drudgery imitated the duty tasks they learned to abide as apprentice Guardians in The Vale, and they went about their days with cheerful resignation, an attitude that frequently irritated other members of their Group. Fights and arguments occasionally erupted between bored and frustrated warriors, but the Group Leaders, Trainers, and Devis quickly dealt with them.

Andra admired the ease with which Stephen adapted to his role as Group Leader, moving between the recruits and warriors as he subtly taught them fragments of The Way, altering their perceptions so they would function with greater harmony as a Group. 'The rain falls. It is The Way. Accept it, for, as it passes, the land, and all on it, is renewed.'

'Be patient. Flow with the events around you. Use their energy to carry you. Don't fight. Don't waste your own energy.'

'We are here together. It is The Way. We work together.'

The Guardian Master would be pleased with Stephen, thought Andra, as he watched his friend guide his Group.

Even before the winter rains eased, Murdok had his Squad training. He especially singled out Stephen's Group with demonic delight, and frequently set them to running across the slippery, muddy plain, scrambling up and down hills and embankments. He seemed determined to double the running he'd made them do before winter, and even when other Squads, and the rest of their Squad, were practising manoeuvres, their Group ran. Andra knew Murdok had a purpose, but the others in the Group constantly complained to Stephen, until he reluctantly agreed to act as their spokesperson and confronted Murdok, one afternoon, after they completed a particularly gruelling run. The Group watched, as Stephen approached Murdok and spoke to him. Andra saw Murdok place his hands, customarily, on his broad hips. Stephen was shaking his head. It appeared Murdok was laughing, because he tipped his head back and looked at the grey sky. Then he put his left hand on Stephen's shoulder, a gesture that sent a ripple of surprise through the Group. After that, Murdok moved back among the outer tents of camp, leaving Stephen to re-join the Group. 'Well?' asked the gaunt youth, Loric. 'What did old Mudrocks say? Are we his pet racing dogs or something?'

The others laughed. Stephen smiled, and waited for them to gather round. 'We were right. He is deliberately forcing us to run, more than any Group in our entire Wheel. Captain Fenwick ordered him to run us.'

'But why?' asked Alain.

'Haven't you noticed?' replied Stephen. 'We complete the running we are forced to do. We are better than most. We are chosen to be Runners.'

'What?' asked Nathaniel.

'Runners,' answered Stephen. 'We will carry messages between Squads, Spokes, and Wheels, whenever we are needed. We must be ready to run at any time, in any condition. It is what High Lord Mara requires. It is The Way.' Stephen let his news settle. Andra heard mixed reactions from those around him, some expressing pride in their specialist duty, others saying they felt cheated of their right to be warriors. 'There is one final thing,' added Stephen. 'The Great Armies march to war tomorrow. Great King Thana will come before us to review his Armies, and give his blessing, because he has ordered that it is time to strike north, at the Haagii, before summer is newly born.'

The buzz of voices rose around Andra, but he stayed silent, tasting a new sense of excitement; the thrill of knowing he was about to move from a place of stasis to somewhere different and unknown.

'Even the sun obeys the Great King,' said Alain, as he finished rolling his sleeping mat.

Andra looked about the camp. Everywhere, men and women were pulling down their quarters, and gathering their belongings, in preparation for the march. Trainers and Devis bustled back and forth, through the hive of activity, barking orders, urging their charges to hurry with their preparations. The pale sun sat on the rim of the Ureykyeu, making the snow tops gleam silver in the weak morning light, but, for a change, there was no rain and no bitter wind on the plains. The air was crisp, invigorating. Even the heavy, grey clouds were crested with tufts of woolly white. 'Perhaps,' said Andra, half in thought, 'Perhaps the Great King is going to become another of the legends of the land. The winter weather dares not mar his passing.'

'You should make ballads with words like that,' Alain scoffed.

'I might.'

'You?' said Alain incredulously. 'You've never touched a musical instrument in your life. And you sing like a wounded mountain bear,' he laughed. Andra playfully cuffed at his head.

'Enough! Finish your duties!' They looked up to see Murdok's stern face glaring at them.

Ranks of warriors formed, wavered, melted, reformed. Group Leaders spoke hurriedly with Trainers, and bustled back to their Groups, issuing orders. 'Five lines of five. Arm's length between lines. Horse's width between Groups. Stretch out, along the western radial. Once the Great King reaches the Hub, Groups to form into Squads within their Wheels. South Wheel to head the parade. North, East and West to follow. Each Wheel to be two Spokes deep, five wide.' Stephen repeated the instructions carefully until the Group understood. Then he added a final order. 'When the Great King has spoken, and calls upon the Four Armies to march, we remain in our places, until Murdok and Devi Korl and Captain Fenwick dismiss us.'

Andra shouldered his pack, adjusted the strapping on his breastplate, and wiped off a finger smudge, before bending to pick up his shield. He remembered how clumsy and inhibiting his Guardian friends and he found the soldiers' armour when they first arrived, and how they bested twenty others to prove the importance of simple mobility in combat, but Murdok insisted they mastered wearing of armour, and he trained them daily, until they could run freely in medium weight armour, but retain agility. Tim Gaelus' first comments about Murdok proved accurate. He was a harsh, but effective Trainer. Andra appreciated that after four months of drill. Now, he thought, as he walked with the others to the assembly point on the road leading to the Great City, now I am a soldier, a warrior in the Great King's Armies, and I will see more of this Kingdom than either my father, or his father.

The songs and stories of cold winter nights filled his head with delight and expectation. He'd set his foot upon the threshold of an amazing world beyond The Vale, and this morning his adventure would really begin when his companions and he marched forth to fight the Haagii, and drive them from the Kingdom, just as Aian Abreotan drove the dreaded Dragonlord from the lands centuries before. They were going to become heroes of future folklore. Andra revelled in the promise: conquerors of the northern lands, slayers of dragons –

'You! Dreamer! Watch your step!' The push of a hand and the rough voice broke his reverie. Andra turned to apologize, but the man who pushed him stood, mouth open, gaping. He was dressed like any foot soldier, but there was no mistaking the face marked with stubbly growth and wild eyes. The soldier turned, and melted into the throng, before Andra could speak or stop him. He was the second assailant who aided the scar-faced man in the streets of the Great City; the scar-faced man who died at Tim's hands. The startled stare warned Andra the man hadn't forgotten the incident.

'Andra?' Alain asked beside him. 'What is it?'

Andra collected his thoughts. 'That man,' he started to explain. 'He was the third one who attacked me in the Great City.'

'Are you sure?'

'I will never forget the face. I'm sure it was him.'

'Perhaps he's forgotten you,' said Alain.

'No,' he replied, shaking his head. 'He hasn't forgotten.' Andra stared into the ranks of soldiers forming along the road.

'Come on,' Alain urged. 'We'd better find our places.' He tugged at Andra's arm, but Andra continued to search the ranks.

A fanfare of distant trumpets drifted to their ears, heralding the imminent arrival of the Great King and his retinue. The warriors stood under the threatening glares of their Trainers, who were pacing between the ranks, but whispers and murmurs broke out, as excitement mounted with the approach of the man who was lord over all others in the Kingdom. Andra's Group was positioned three rows from the edge of the road, and he stifled his disappointment that he wasn't closer to view the passing Royal Party, but he knew he'd see more than those behind him, and for that he was thankful.

Across the heads to his right, he glimpsed the first banners streaming atop long lances, black banners, signifying the leading riders, the Haardrishii. The black armoured riders trotted into view, mounted on ebony warhorses: tall, silent, lethal in appearance. He watched the fifty-strong contingent pass, and recalled the battle in the Valley of Rivers when these warriors of the Great King ruthlessly and efficiently dispatched the Haagii. He remembered Claarn's appraisal of their virtue and smiled in memory of the rough giant of Tressel Deep. Andra envisioned the Haardrishii moving, like dark shadows of death, over the stagnant lands of the Haagii.

Behind the Haardrishii marched one hundred men in grey leather tunics and leggings, tall men, clean-shaven, and mostly blond-haired. Each carried a long bow, slung over one shoulder, and a full quiver of arrows, each arrow at least the length of a man's arm. Bright green banners, bearing the motif of a deer in full flight, fluttered above them. The trumpet fanfare grew louder. Andra saw bald heads bobbing along in the parade, and a troop of fifty Apprentices shambled by in thick woollen grey smocks. He leaned to the side, whispering to Alain, 'There. Those are the ones I told you about. They use magic.'

Alain took note of the passing group. 'They look ineffectual.'

Andra grinned. 'Just don't tell them that. I'd hate to face one.'

More groups passed: court sages, wagons bearing large logs strung from chains, and huge spoons pivoting on cross beams, a coloured group of performers and magicians, and a squad of trumpeters sounding the Royal fanfare, loudly and frequently, signalling the arrival of the inner circle of the Great King's retinue. Warriors, men and women in loincloths, with thick animal hides as cloaks against the chill air, appeared on horseback. The dappled grey and spirited horses frisked and nickered at the gazing soldiers. A large man with a mane of blazing red hair led the defiant riders. Andra elbowed Alain and pointed. 'I see! I see!' Alain responded.

Stephen, at the head of their Group, turned to catch the attention of his companions, and laughed, shaking his head. 'We should have known that great shaggy bear would find a way to the Great King. It is The Way.' Claarn rode on, unaware, but Andra caught Marella's dark eyes searching the ranks, and waved. She smiled brightly, shaking her long black hair, before spurring her horse forward. She would tell Claarn she'd seen the Guardians.

The next group, on foot, spread silence through the ranks. Each one was hooded and covered, head to foot, in a black robe, seamed with gold filigree. A silver dagger, tucked through a black leather belt, broke the absence of colour. Andra felt the chill of death stalking by. He recalled Tim's description of the Royal Assassins as very public individuals, people with recognisable faces, but these passing souls were faceless, cold, and assassins of fear. Behind them, alone, on a black steed like the Haardrishii horses, came a figure robed in silver, with long flowing locks of lead grey hair, and a dark, cropped beard. He sat aloof, erect, and held majesty in the angle of his head; a compelling aura of implicit power that set him apart from any man or woman Andra had ever seen. 'Who is he?' whispered Alain. Andra shook his head.

'That,' Murdok said gruffly from behind, 'is A Ahmud Ki, the Great King's Personal Advisor, and you would be wise to keep well clear of him.' Quiet warning delivered, the Trainer moved away, leaving Andra to stare in awe at the solitary rider. Five figures followed him, in ornate orange and red robes, swinging copper incense pots at the end of golden chains, as they chanted in an ancient language. Andra guessed they were the Priests of Teka, servants of the Goddess and patron of the Great City, but he knew little else.

Two powerfully built, bare-chested, warriors, riding snow white horses that were the equine counterparts of their riders, carrying oversized pennants, heralded the arrival of the Great King. The pennants displayed the royal insignia; gold rampant half-lion, half-eagle creatures gleaming from the sun's rays against red fields.

Behind them came a magnificent spectacle of beauty and opulence. Six white stallions, girded with jewel encrusted harnesses, ridden by six raven-haired maidens dressed in pale blue silken robes, edged with silver thread, drew an open gilt carriage, lined with exotic furs, and within the carriage sat a large man, clad in a peacock array of finery, displaying golden and silver chains, with rare, ornate jewels. A boy and girl stood in attendance above the figure, holding large grey feathers to shade his head. Great King Thana, Royal Highness of the Kingdom, Eternal Ruler of the Great City, Incarnate Son of the Goddess Teka, had arrived. Andra strained to see the Great King's features, but the man was snuggled deep within his bed of furs, blatantly ignoring the lines of soldiers his carriage passed on his journey to the centre of the camp. Two blond warriors trailed the carriage, and the tail of the royal procession followed them: Haardrishii riders. First and last, Andra observed, Haardrishii formed the Great King's shield.

Trainers barked orders along the ranks. Armour clinked,

weapons rattled as thousands jostled to form the Four Wheels. A babble of voices broke out, low enough not to interrupt the orders. 'Amazing!' declared Stephen.

'Did you see the precious gold worked into the carriage? My father would never have seen so much in his lifetime of crafting,' Alain said.

'I hadn't begun to imagine what the Great King looks like,' said Andra, 'but he's nothing like I expected.' He struggled with his thoughts, because something about the Great King's appearance wasn't right, but he couldn't express exactly what it was.

'The assassins sent a chill through my bones,' muttered Cornelius, another of the Group. 'They say the Great King smiles upon their work.'

'It's true,' replied Andra.

'You should know,' Alain teased. 'You've been one.' but his humour failed to amuse Andra, who remembered too vividly the unwanted trouble Tim Gaelus' joke brought to him in the Great City.

'Quiet!' warned Stephen. They all saw Murdok's dark eyes glaring at them and fell silent.

Andra peered across a sea of heads to a raised wooden platform, where High Lord Mara stood, with his attendants, the Devis and Captains, the Priests of Teka, the Great King's attendants, and the tall figure of A Ahmud Ki. The Great King sat on a large throne, carved in the shape of one of his heraldic beasts. Andra's Wheel was third from the front, so a full half of the Great King's Armies stood between him and the Great King. He couldn't see how he, or any behind him, would be able to hear the Great King's speech, and he was disappointed. He glanced at the banners flapping in a stiffening breeze, beneath the grey sky. The rising sun had climbed into the first layer of cloud, leaving the dull grey of winter in its wake. He shivered.

The Great King's Advisor moved to the foremost edge of the platform and raised his hands, arms outspread, until he appeared pinned against the background. His arms continued to stretch, until he appeared to enfold the entire assembly and touch the edges of the scurrying clouds with his fingertips. Then he shrank back into himself, until he was again a tall man in silver robes, standing at the head of the assembly.

But something had changed. Andra felt a presence, like static energy, causing the hairs on his arms to sit up. The banners hung limp. The breeze had died. He could hear his heart beating. He studied the assembly on the stage. With strength and precision, four warriors lifted the throne onto their shoulders, and carried the Great King to the front. They lowered their burden with ease and returned to their places. Great King Thana hefted himself out of his throne, and stood in his regal splendour before the Great Armies, gold and silver threads in his robes gleaming, and a ray of sunlight burst through the cloud, as if it had been awaiting its cue, shining directly on the Great King, giving him an ethereal quality. The Advisor moved behind, and to the right, of the Great King.

'O mighty warriors of Thana,' The Great King began. 'You form a host upon which we gaze with joy and bounteous pride. We are pleased, and enfold you unto our Royal heart, as children of the realm come to full age. Know that you are the arms and swords of our mighty crown, and we entrust, in you, our welfare and prosperity. Your duty is to rid us, once and for all time, of the nuisance of the hated northern tribes, those that are called the Haagii, and all who consort with them. Fill your hearts with courage and fire. March against our enemies, destroy them, and cause us to rejoice, and we will sing praises in your honour, even until the last of generations.'

The speech carried across the lines of soldiers, and reached everyone, as if the Great King was talking personally, and Andra was amazed at how powerfully and easily he projected his voice. As he listened, he focussed on the Great King and A Ahmud Ki, and saw the incongruities between the two. The Great King was framed in light. A Ahmud Ki stood in the grey half-light. The Great King was short, grotesquely rotund – a legacy of living too easily and too well – while A Ahmud Ki was tall, finely built, almost athletic. While the Great King had the trappings of a rich and powerful ruler, A Ahmud Ki emanated power; a stronger, more potent, darker power, beyond anything the Great King could hope to muster. Twice, Andra thought he saw the Great King glance back at his Advisor, the latter nodding slightly, although at this distance the movements were almost imperceptible, so he couldn't be sure. The words washed over him, and were gone, and a multitude of voices erupted, startling him with their spontaneity and violence.

'Death to the Haagii!' shouted the Great King.

'Death to the Haagii!' responded the soldiers of the Great Armies, and they repeated the chant, again and again. Andra joined in, mechanically, but he realized the Great King had long finished speaking, and was being held high on his throne by his four attendant warriors, sitting solid and supreme above them all, bathing in a pool of sunlight his Advisor controlled.

Thirty Two

They were chosen to run messages between sections of the Great King's Armies: five to each of the Four Wheels, and five to remain with High Lord Mara's Command Squad throughout the campaign. The Guardians were separated. Andra marched with the West Wheel. Alain stayed with the North Wheel. Stephen was appointed to High Lord Mara's Squad. For the first few days, Andra and Alain would be able to enjoy each other's company, as their Wheels headed west, through the Central Gate in the Andrakian Mountains, and onto the Plains of Axxon, but from there only the North Wheel would journey north. All three Guardians wanted to travel with the East Wheel, because its path lay northeast, through the Valley of Rivers, but that was denied to them. The South Wheel was commissioned to march southeast, to the borders of the Targa Federation, to act as a show of strength to Thana's neighbours while the Haagii were engaged on other borders. Stephen's course, with High Lord Mara, was directly north, into Forge Vale, to the fortress city of Anedya. The High Lord intended to conduct his operations from that city, using carrier pigeons to communicate between his base and his Armies, while the runners remained the means of communication, within each army, and between adjacent forces.

The North and West Wheels took two full days to reach Central Gate, but the pace was easy, and the weather cool. Andra was pleased to see the tall spires of the Andrakian Mountains smothered in a deep mantle of snow from close up, after months of living on the rolling, bleak Plains of Ky. Alain and he revelled in the crisp, fresh air of evenings, using precious time, after camps were set, to share campfires and talk about past experiences. Peasants, who waved, and ran after them with bundles of food as gifts, constantly broke the monotony of the march. The Haagii hadn't plundered so deep into the Kingdom, but people knew stories of those who were less fortunate beyond the mountains, and they were afraid the menace might penetrate the natural mountain barrier and ravage their land, so they gave eager blessings to the warrior hosts who marched by.

When they marched through the town of Ky, on the second morning, women and children sprinkled a path of spices and flower petals for their feet, so they might walk the path of the Gods in their quest. A small boy and his sister pushed a mongrel pup into Andra's hands as he tried to pass, and disappeared before he could return it. The animal was black, with a rolling red tongue that licked anything furiously, and Andra cursed his fortune, much to his companions' delight. In the evening, Andra and Alain inspected the pup, and found he was a robust, healthy creature, with no colour markings, but a piece was missing from his left ear, as if it had been bitten through. A slobbering tongue lashed them as they rolled the pup about. 'You'll never need to bathe ever again with this in your pack,' quipped Alain, dodging the tongue.

'He likes being clean, unlike you,' Andra retorted.

'What will you call this beast?'

'I haven't thought.'

'Perhaps Tongue,' suggested Alain. 'He'll always remind you of his name.'

Andra rolled the black pup over, scuffing him, until he growled and mouthed at Andra's hand.

'Perhaps Warrior,' said Alain. 'He has spirit.'

'Artega!' Andra said. 'I'll name him after the Guardian Master.' He picked up the pup by the loose scruff of his neck and held him before his face. 'You are Artega. That's what I name you.' The pup kicked, and a great rolling tongue licked Andra's cheek, and both young Guardians burst into laughter.

On the morning of the third day, the Armies prepared to climb the steep road into the pass of Central Gate. Passage through the mountains would take a full day, from dawn to dusk, and although the pass was the only major road from east to west in the Kingdom it remained a narrow and difficult way, especially for large vehicles and groups. The pass climbed several thousand spans, and wound through steep-sided, snow-filled valleys. The added danger of rock falls made the journey arduous, and in deep winter Central Gate was impassable, cutting trade between two halves of the Kingdom for part of each year. Royal engineers reworked much of the pass to accommodate the passage of a large force, but the Great King's Strategists urged retaining difficult sections to deter or delay invading armies, if any threatened the central regions of the Kingdom. At both ends of the pass, watchtowers and stone walls, built during the reign of one of Aian Abreotan's successors, protected and controlled traffic, and they were perpetually manned by garrisons who spent a full year at their stations, in the service of the Great King, before being transferred to another course of duty. The intricate, clever stonework in the watchtowers fascinated Andra. Legend attributed their fine construction to the ancestors of the Shaddites – the Dwarven. Each stone was deliberately and carefully hand-moulded into position, with no visible bonding to secure the rocks.

For Andra, Alain, and the other runners, the crossing was testing. Captains Fenwick and Westbourne were keen to maintain communication between all units of their Armies, as they laboured through the pass, so the runners were constantly on the move, reporting progress, and carrying instructions to the Devis. The siege machines presented the greatest challenge. Their size and weight made progress slow, and clumsy, and by the end of the first day they only reached the halfway point in the pass. Their crews were forced to spend a freezing night in snow, at the highest point of Central Gate, so Andra was thankful he was required to remain at the western end of the pass to carry first orders the following morning.

By midday of the fourth day, the Armies were camped outside Axxon, and late that afternoon the last siege weapons and wagons were safely out of the pass, in the low foothills near the camp. It was the last night the two Wheels would camp together. The runners prepared a common campfire and shared their meal. Campfires crackled, filling the night with red and golden hues, and the soldiers of the Great King relaxed, and told tales while they ate and drank. Andra held a second piece of salted meat out to the pup. 'Does that creature always have to eat?' asked Wallin, a scrawny, short man, who was bent over the fire cooking a leg of rabbit.

'He'll do better than you, bag-o-bones!' another scoffed, and the mocking comment brought a burst of laughter. Artega looked up at the laughing humans, and promptly rolled over, red tongue lolling out. 'Oho! A clown!' roared the mocker. 'We'll be entertained tonight.' He cut a piece of meat from his store, and tossed it to the pup, who showed appreciation by swallowing the offer.

Andra was peeved. He grabbed Artega by the scruff with a commanding grip, and sat the pup at his side. Another member of the group leaned into the light, and Andra recognised Samuel's lean face. 'Good,' said Samuel, with approval. 'You'll do well to teach him who's master. He might be the village idiot now, but one day, if he understands you are his master, one day he will repay you. Mark my words.'

'And so the prophet Samuel has spoken,' added the mocker, and he followed the jibe with a quick flick of his wrist, landing a second piece at the pup's feet. Andra's grip tightened, preventing Artega reaching for the morsel. 'Let the dog eat,' said Peter, the meat thrower.

Andra ignored him, and restrained the pup, while the others watched the struggle of wills. The pup tried to edge forward, but Andra pressed down, holding him firmly in place. At the point when highest tension passed through the dog, and receded, Andra quietly said, 'Now,' and released him to gobble down the offering. A sense of release also flowed silently through the watchers, and they relaxed, returning to their eating.

'There'll come a time when you'll be thankful of the discipline, you'll see,' said Samuel.

'That's just what Murdok the mongrel always said,' piped in tall Emmett, once a fisherman of the Lake of Tears, now runner, 'just after he finished running our legs off for the day.'

'I came to fight Haagii,' grumbled Turk, a swarthy peasant from the Plains of Ky. 'Murdok turns me into an athlete, like those the Great King laughs at in his Annual Games. So much for discipline. When do we fight Haagii? That's what I want to know.'

'I imagine you'll see them sooner than us,' said Andra. 'You march north tomorrow, towards the Haagii. We march west.'

'Plenty of marching for sure,' Turk responded. 'But we see no Haagii. What's all this talk of The Great Threat from the North?'

'We've barely started,' said Alain. 'The threat's real. We've already seen the Haagii in our mountains, plundering our land. Haven't we, Andra?' Andra nodded.

'What do they look like?' asked Emmett.

Andra stared into the fire, while he described the Haagii in the marshes, at the burial caves above the village, and in the Valley of Rivers. 'They sound even uglier than you, Turk,' said Peter dryly. Chuckles rippled around the circle.

'Their ugliness is on the inside.' Samuel's serious comment halted their mirth, and they stared at the stone face man, whose features were sculpted in fluid motion by the flickering flames. 'I had a brother. His name was Mark, and his wife, Lily. They had three children, beautiful children, happy children; two girls, and a baby boy. My brother was a trader, north of here. He traded ironware with peasant farmers and hunters. He was away, often, and he missed his wife and children when he was away. Last summer, he came to my house, and he said 'Samuel, I come to take my family with me. We're moving north to Haven, outside Dragon's Forest. That is where I will trade, close to my children, and my Lily.' Then he left. Ten days later, a traveller, a stranger, came to my house, and told me my brother was dead. And his wife. And the children. They were found in the foothills, near Riverfork. Robbed. Butchered. Cut up and left for crows to pick upon. Like bad meat. This the Haagii had done.'

The crackling fire lost its warmth, and Andra felt icy fingers inside his chest, and numbness, unable to respond to Samuel's tale. He felt inexplicably ashamed, and he could not look into the eyes of the men at the fire. Samuel quietly rose and walked into the heart of the camp. The desire to talk was dead. One by one, the runners bedded down, lost in private thoughts, unwilling to speak again that evening.

The two Wheels separated at the town of Hleo. Andra bade Alain farewell, with the reassurance they would meet again, soon, on errands between the two Wheels, or at the end of the campaign. Local folk informed the Captains that a sizeable group of Haagii and renegades were wintering in the Kobold Ranges, a full day's march northwest of the town. The North Wheel prepared to move in that direction, while the West Wheel was committed to the barbarian borders, beneath the Cliffs of Iron. Pairs of Spokes, totalling one thousand soldiers, marched defined routes to the west. One pair marched the road to Port Thana, the major trading centre in the western part of the Kingdom, and the remaining pairs headed across the plains, the northernmost pair passing south of the Kobold Ranges. A runner was appointed to each. Andra was attached to a central pair, under the dual command of Devis Farrow and Eli. Eli, a sour-faced, broad-shouldered warrior, with little patience for trivia, had a reputation for being quick to punish ignorance. Farrow was older, white-haired, and haggard. He, too, was firm with his soldiers, but he was humane with discipline, and Andra quickly learned that Farrow made a point of knowing each warrior by sight and name. He personally came to Andra's campfire to inform him he was the runner for their unit.

When the march west began, on the seventh morning, blue skies greeted the warriors, reviving their flagging spirits. Andra walked directly behind the mounted Devis and their attendants, and he observed the party throughout the day. Eli remained sharp-eyed and silent. Farrow warmed to the sun and clear sky, and contentedly talked to his companions, even taking time to rein in and speak to Andra, asking where he was born, and how long he'd served in the Great King's Armies. The man carried confidence like a treasured possession, making those around him feel acquainted and comfortable, and Andra felt immediate respect and liking for the older Devi. Others rode with the leading party. A Royal scribe in russet robes, and a flowing beard, sat uncomfortably astride an old bay mare, looking very much out of place between the warriors on stallions. There was also a figure who sat in complete silence on his horse, wearing a familiar, grey woollen smock. Andra was curious to see the Apprentice riding with them, part of the commanding party, being both aloof to, and ignored by, those near him, as if he simply did not exist. There were also five tall bowmen, in grey tunics and leggings, walking with the leading party.

By mid-morning, the bowmen struck up casual conversation with Andra, interested in his origins, and one, who called himself Derik O'Dale, was pleased to hear Andra mention The Vale. 'In the northern section of the Valley of Rivers?' he asked. 'I know it well. A Master Renfrey was head of Council when I last visited. Is he still?' Surprised, Andra replied he was. He couldn't recall ever seeing anyone like this bowman in the village. 'There was also a woman of the Council, one of striking beauty. Anedra was her name. I can never forget it. She had hair that shone with the scarlet hue of the setting sun.' Derik O'Dale spoke with a faraway gaze in his eyes that shocked Andra. Another man, not his father, was talking fondly of his mother – more than fondly.

'Anedra is my mother.'

Derik looked at Andra and smiled. 'Then well met indeed, my lad. You come from a marvellous home.' He extended his hand, and warmly shook Andra's hand like an old friend. Derik O'Dale introduced his companions: Marvin Bowmaker, Lester of the Lake, Ernest Fletcher, and Jeffry Merry. They explained their main trade was hunting, when times were peaceful, but they'd been trained since age eight to master all skills of the bowyer, the fletcher, and longbow marksman.

'We are happily married to our bows for life,' said Jeffry with a wry smile, 'although I've known Marvin here to sneak off to a wench's bed and be unfaithful to his wife.'

'You're not slow to break your marriage vow either, Jeffry,' Marvin retorted.

Derik spotted Artega's black muzzle poke from Andra's pack. 'A hound!' he cried. 'A veritable hunter's dog if ever I saw one! Where did you get this creature?' he asked, as he deftly lifted the slobbering pup from Andra's pack.

'Two children thrust him on me when we passed through Ky. I named him Artega.'

'After your Guardian Master,' added Derik. 'I know the man. I knew him before he left the Great King's service. Haardrishii warrior: one of the best. A good name for you, my little friend,' he said, with a shake of the pup. 'We'll teach you how to hunt.'

Andra was grateful for the company of the five Longbowmen. Their physical peculiarity attracted his attention. They were taller than he, taller than most men, and they all had flaxen hair, which fell to their shoulders, and green eyes. At a short distance, it would be difficult to differentiate them from one another. Their similarity puzzled him, like so many curious things about the people of the Kingdom, but especially so since he knew from the parade on the Plains of Ky that there were one hundred men who looked so much alike. There must be a reason, he thought, a purpose. The Guardian Master had taught him that all things existed, or happened, for a purpose. They were made to be. It was The Way.

As the sun sank into a looming bank of rain clouds racing in from the southwest, the twin Spokes settled on the side of a low hill in the centre of the plain, and soldiers swiftly toiled to raise shelters against the approaching weather. Darkness and the storm arrived at a furious pace, sweeping over the men and women who were struggling to push the last retaining pegs into place. The wind roared in with vengeance, howling through the wooden beams and struts of the battering rams, and under the supply wagons. The horses whinnied and strained against their halters, unsettled by the fierce gale lashing their coats. Later, when rain whipped across the crude encampment, and lightning and thunder rent the fabric of sky, the horses panicked, fighting fearfully to break free of their ropes, and only the grooms' desperation, at the storm's height, stopped the horses from bolting.

In the scurry for shelter, Andra accepted the Longbowmen's invitation to share their tent. They carried shared tenting equipment in their packs, and between them they erected a sizeable tent. Without their offer, Andra faced the prospect of weathering the storm in his simple, but inadequate, hide shelter that required him to dig a hollow in the ground for real protection from the elements. He felt sorry for the hundreds of soldiers relying on their military roll of hide. The Longbowmen's tent provided enough space for each man to lie down, but little else, and a fire was impossible. Body heat provided warmth. 'Cozy?' asked Jeffry.

Wind pressed against the tightly strung hides, and rain rattled on them. Rivulets trickled through gaps. 'Thank you,' Andra replied.

'Don't be so polite,' Lester interjected. 'It's cursed cold in here. And the roof leaks. If I had the money, I'd rent another room, one with a big, warm fire.'

'I'd be just as happy if, instead of you lot, I was trapped in here with five of those women warriors who went north with the other Wheel,' said Jeffry.

'Do you only ever think about women?' Derik asked.

'No,' answered Jeffry, with a grin. 'Girls sometimes cross my mind.' The others laughed.

'Let's eat, then sleep, while we can,' suggested Marvin. 'This storm will blow through by morning, and we'll be marching again.' Agreement followed his comment, and rations were organized with a great deal of awkward shuffling and wriggling, and frequent oaths and apologies for ill-placed elbows and knees. The Longbowmen shared a meal, and drifted into stories of hunting.

Andra lay on his back, listening to the murmur of voices, barely audible above the lashing storm, until his thoughts drifted to wondering if the same storm would reach Alain, or Stephen at Anedya, or Lisette, or Tim, wherever he disappeared to the week before they marched out of camp. Or even The Vale. He wondered if his father and mother were thinking of him at that moment. He missed them. He missed their voices and their presence. He missed the comfort of his bedding, the familiarity of his home. Four full moon cycles had passed since his leaving. He had only just reached the status of Guardian. His father gave him the gift. He twisted to face his pack. The sword was there, strapped to it, still wrapped inside the oilcloth. Andra carried it, as his father Malcolm instructed. He hadn't opened the cloth. Even when Murdok issued new weapons, he left the gift hidden inside his tent. He'd been warned to use it only when he felt it was time to do so, and that time had not yet come. Strapped to his back, the sword travelled like a silent friend, waiting to be called. A red tongue slashed across his face, breaking into his thoughts. 'Lay still, Artega,' he whispered, but the pup wriggled irritably, and bit his nose, seeking attention. A clap of thunder startled the animal, and the pup burrowed into his side, whimpering.

'He doesn't have his namesake's courage yet, but that will come,' observed Derik, and he laughed. 'Like the rest of us who grow less wise, as we grow older, he will lose the wisdom of fear.' Andra patted the pup's black fur, reassuring his companion, and lay back, and waited for sleep to soothe him.

Thirty Three

A rough hand shook him and he grabbed the wrist. 'Wake up Runner. You're called.' Andra looked into the face of one of Devi Farrow's attendants. 'Hurry. The Devis wait for you.' He struggled out of the low tent, dragging his armour and equipment after him. Rain spattered across his back. A stiff wind blew. Night sat on the land. He followed the attendant's dim, swinging lantern up the slope, with Artega scrambling behind him, until they reached the Devis' tent. Lit by lamps, it was sturdily constructed, roomy, and Andra thought of the soldiers along the slope, huddled in their rough digs where the wind, cold, and rain forced their way in, and wondered what they would give to clamber inside the Devi's tent. Artega nudged his leg, so he bent to pick up the wet pup. 'Runner,' announced the attendant.

The men gathered at the centre of the tent turned to him, and he read great concern in their faces, and anger in Devi Eli's eyes. In their midst, slumped on a pile of hides, cheeks bloodied, was Peter the mocker, staring beyond Andra with wide, glazed eyes. The sight stunned him. 'Haagii did this!' Devi Eli snarled, and he spat on the earth. 'Bastards of whoremongers!' he added, turning on his heel to face the rear of the tent.

Devi Farrow approached Andra, gently took his arm, and turned him towards the tent door. 'I understand your shock, Andra. Let it go through. There's little time for remorse. You must run it out. Your companion came from the company under Devis Rannoth and Wain. They were working the northernmost route, just below the Kobold Ranges, when the Haagii struck. Peter told us something about the Haagii coming out of the teeth of the storm, just as the company dug in to stave off the weather. The surprise attack did not go well for our people, so the Runner was sent. Haagii pursued him across the plains in the darkness and rain, and caught him. He killed four before the others were driven off. He barely made it here.'

Andra looked at Devi Farrow. 'He's dead, isn't he?'

'No. Not yet. The Apprentice will try his hand at mending him, if the surgeon cannot,' said Farrow. 'But you must run south and bring the other two companies to the edge of the Kobold Ranges, where we'll join the North Wheel. It appears the Haagii are based there and haven't pushed this far south yet. Tell the Devis and Captain Westbourne this, and bring them at once.' Devi Farrow noticed Artega lolling in Andra's arms. 'Yours?' Andra nodded. 'Leave him with me. I will look after him until you return,' Farrow offered.

'Thank you,' Andra replied. 'But I'll leave him with Derik O'Dale, Devi Farrow. He and his companions will take my gear for me.'

The Devi smiled, and clapped Andra on the back. 'As you wish. Speed of the wind on your task.'

There was little need to wish for the speed of the wind, Andra decided, because it blew strongly and sharply. What he wanted was direction. He ran across the dark, muddy plains, challenged by the conditions, but without moon or stars, and no sign of the impending dawn, he felt he was becoming hopelessly lost. The runner in him told him to keep running, but he listened to his Guardian training and chose to slow to a cautionary walk. Better to lose a little time by being patient than risk losing much more time by becoming lost. The wind dropped. Tiny patches of pale light spread across the eastern sky. Andra had direction. The land was dark, sodden, and forbidding, but he pushed his cold, aching legs into a jog, until he felt his body warming, his lungs working.

He found the first group not long after sun-up, after he retraced part of his night journey. They had travelled further west, but they were trapped by the storm on the open plains, so when he reached them the soldiers were wringing water from their tents, and repairing damage caused by the rough weather. Andra reported to the Devis, relayed his message, answered what questions he could, and schooled his fellow Runner, Wallin, to take the message on to Captain Westbourne's Company on the western road to Port.

Rested, he gathered his wits, and began the return run. Direction was easy in daylight. The Kobold Ranges sat low on the near horizon, like a dun predator crouching in wait for its prey, and Andra lengthened his stride towards the hills with fatalistic eagerness. The Haagii were wintering there, in force, and finally he would face them. They had interfered with The Vale, killed a companion there, plundered merchants and villages, killed Samuel's brother and his family, and probably killed Peter. He heard the words of High Lord Mara and Great King Thana echoing in the rhythm of his feet, and he chanted as he ran. 'Kill the Haagii. Kill the Haagii.' This was the path The Way had shown him. He was running it eagerly.

He had never seen a battlefield littered with corpses. Not just bodies, but chunks – arms, legs, heads – were scattered among broken weapons and equipment. Soldiers moved silently through the carnage, collecting undamaged weapons, searching for wounded, killing dying Haagii, piling the dead into heaps for burning. The stench of death – a sickening cocktail of blood, burnt flesh, urine and faeces – clung to everything, and clawed at Andra's stomach, until he was overcome with nauseating dizziness and a desperate need to scramble away to breathe fresh air.

'It gets you like that.'

Andra wiped his mouth free of vomit, embarrassed that someone saw him act so shamefully. Derik O'Dale was gazing across the low foothills leading into the Kobold Ranges. 'I've seen dead before -' Andra tried to explain.

'But not like this.' Derik finished Andra's sentence. 'The battlefield isn't a noble place.' He continued to stare outwards.

'Where's Artega?' Andra asked, after a moment of

silence.

'With Devi Farrow. He and the others are attending a meeting with Captain Westbourne, in the Captain's tent, over there.' Derik pointed to a red pavilion erected well beyond the battleground. 'They make plans to march against the Haagii entrenched in those god-forsaken hills. Come.' Derik led Andra down the side of the hillock that overlooked the field of dead towards their camp.

'When did they attack?'

'Not long after you left.'

'How many are dead?'

'Of Rannoth's Spoke? One hundred and thirty, according to the tally. Of the other Spoke? About ninety. Two hundred and twenty, and twice that many wounded. But six hundred Haagii will not sit at their campfires tonight. And they were lucky this battle surprised our people, or many more would have been slain and gone to serve their gods.' Derik's philosophical mood gave way to a jovial one, as they reached the tents, and he threw his arm over the young man's shoulders. 'Forget death. We will drink and sing, and share tales, and with luck, and a little persuasion, some of our female companions will favour us tonight. Jeffry's been hunting for women since we arrived, and he claims he's been successful. Tonight, we enjoy the fairer pleasures of life.'

The Haagii proved more elusive than the Great King's warriors anticipated. The hills were covered with thick clumps of blackberry bushes and stunted, twisted trees, and many slopes were steep and littered with shale, making them virtually inaccessible to all but the nimble-footed. A multitude of rocky outcrops and promontories, along the ridges, were pocked with caverns and holes capable of sheltering the Haagii, and the storm had washed fresh tracks from the hillsides and the narrow valleys. Soldiers sent to search the closest regions of the Kobold Ranges were forced to move along defiles in single file, unable to investigate the caves above them, and by the end of the first day most groups reported that they'd found no trace of their enemy. Old camping sites were found, but nothing fresh. Another group returned, before dusk, with the discouraging news that they'd explored a collection of small caves, at the summit of one hill, only to find they were interconnected and went deep underground. They hadn't risked venturing deeper into the maze.

Watches were drawn for the night. Andra walked to Devi Farrow's tent through a sea of campfires across the hillside, as five thousand warriors of the West Wheel prepared their evening meals. A lucky few had fresh meat from early morning hunting, like Derik and the Longbowmen, but most faced broth and dry gruel, the staple diet of the marching soldier, supplemented with stale fruit and vegetables collected near the town of Hleo. There was no shortage of good mead and rum, however, and song and storytelling grew as the night descended. Farrow welcomed Andra into the tent, and Artega bounded to the door to greet his master. 'I took him from Derik O'Dale so he couldn't forage among the dead. I hope you don't mind,' the Devi explained.

'Thank you, Devi Farrow,' was all Andra could offer in response to his superior's apologetic tone.

Farrow cleared his throat. 'I had a dog, for many years. He was a faithful friend. I love dogs. But Thana grew too old and died. Yes, I named him after the Great King. He was fat too,' and the grey-headed Devi chuckled quietly. 'But enough sentimentality. You'd better return to your post and rest. You and your friends will be kept busy tomorrow.' He bent to scratch Artega's ears. 'He'll be a good dog when he's grown.' He straightened to look Andra in the eye. 'Should it become necessary for you to leave the dog to do your errands, and Derik or his friends aren't able to look after him, then, like today, you'll bring him to me. I'll see he comes to no harm. Agreed?' Andra nodded, noting the serious expression in the Devi's eyes. The man's face softened, and he added, 'Besides, lad, that's an order.'

He watched Andra and Artega return to the Longbowmen's tent before he headed for the meeting quarters. He wished the pup was a little older. Hunting Haagii from cave to cave, across the southern part of the Kobold Ranges, was going to be time-consuming and costly, and a dog's ability to sniff out caves housing the enemy would be a valuable weapon against surprise attacks and blind holes. Now, he and the others were going to devise a plan of operation that could cost many lives.

Andra shared his meal with thirty companions. Derik O'Dale had gathered all the Longbowmen in the Wheel, the remaining three Runners, and a couple of new acquaintances, at the fire. Artega fed well on scraps as the warriors talked and ate. Conversation centred on the previous day's battle with the Haagii, as seven strangers at the fire were survivors of the encounter. One had bloodstained bandages wrapped on both arms, the result, he said, of parrying a sword after he lost his weapon. They detailed how the Haagii attacked in the blinding storm, and how they were driven from the hill onto the plain. They described the attacking hordes as a passionate wave of hate breaking against their shields, determined to kill or be killed in their initial frenzy, but once the Devis rallied the warriors, the tide turned, and the Haagii lost their enthusiasm against an organized defence. Andra listened to each warrior's account, content to sit back, patting Artega, observing the evening steadily pass, like the mead in their company.

The first warning came as a cry of 'Watch ho!' from the crest of an eastern ridge. Sharp yells and battle cries erupted, halting the storytellers mid-sentence, and they stared towards the eastern end of the camp. Behind them, groups continued to sing, unaware of what was unfolding. Andra thought he saw figures dashing about flickering campfires. Sparks flared from one. A tent flamed. Men ran towards them. 'By Teka, we're under attack!' yelled Marvin, scrambling to his feet. 'To your weapons!'

'Runners! Spread the word! To arms! To arms!' ordered Derik O'Dale fiercely.

Andra ducked into his tent to retrieve the oilskin bundle holding his great-grandfather's sword. When he emerged, dark figures were hurling themselves at the gathered warriors, screaming war cries as they rushed deeper into the camp. He hit one before he unwrapped the ancient weapon, swinging the heavy bundle across the back of a Haagii pressing Lester. More Haagii poured out of the darkness, and raced down the hill, setting fire to everything they passed. Andra ripped the oily cloth from the blade, and felt its weight balance perfectly in his hand, as he crouched to repel his next attacker. More tents erupted in flames. Haagii passed left and right, but one dark-faced warrior almost ran over him in the stampede. He stumbled to a halt, and swung wildly at the young Guardian, but Andra sidestepped and lunged, his gleaming blade neatly puncturing the Haagii's leather armour, burying deep into his chest. The creature's eyes bulged, surprised by the sword's sudden intrusion, and he fell backwards. Another loomed from the left, and a swinging weapon clipped the silver ring securing Andra's ponytail. Andra ducked, bringing his sword across the Haagii's hamstrings. The Haagii screamed and collapsed into the campfire embers.

Wild confusion followed. Andra fought Haagii after Haagii warrior, amid a discordant symphony of battle. Most of the enemy were determined to avoid him, and his companions, in their wild charge towards the camp centre, but he barred the way of as many as he could, forcing them, one at a time, to fight him. He let the trainings of Murdok and the Guardian Master flow through his athletic body, dodging, parrying, thrusting with the rhythm of the fight, and he drew greater strength and confidence with every blow of Cedwyn's sword. He was hit twice. One Haagii cut him across the back of his left hand. Another caught him a hefty blow from behind, but the blow came from the flat of a sword, and he rolled with the force, returning to his feet to cut down his attacker.

The enemy ceased coming. Stragglers appeared through the smoke and flames and were mercilessly cut down by the warriors around the Longbowmen's tent. Confusion and noise rose to a tumultuous pitch behind them, and Andra looked down at the centre of camp. Tents blazed more fiercely than campfires, and a dark Gordian knot of warriors writhed a short distance from the true centre. 'See?' yelled Derik, above the din. 'They failed to reach the centre!' The others gathered to watch, faces lit by fire, and stained with blood and smoke. 'We will go down and harass them from behind!'

So intent were the Haagii on pushing forward into the camp, they had packed into a deep wall, oblivious to the Great King's men attacking from behind. Many were killed without resistance, as Derik, Andra and the others moved along the rear of the crush, slashing and hewing. The living tide turned, and Haagii warriors broke into retreat, almost trampling Andra and his friends in their bid to escape. More Haagii died, charging blindly onto out-thrust weapons. As quickly as they flooded into the camp, they rushed into the night and hills, leaving a broad swathe of destruction, and their dead.

Andra surveyed the scene as the last Haagii scrambled away. The eastern section of the camp was ablaze, as was part of the northern, and the air was filled with smoke, the sounds of crackling fires, and the cries of wounded. Trainers and Devis hurried through the masses of soldiers, issuing instructions, directing them to extinguish fires and help the wounded. People came from the centre of the camp with buckets of sand, some with water. A squad of warriors set to executing wounded Haagii. Derik and several Longbowmen joined him. 'That certainly livened up the night's entertainment,' said Marvin laconically. 'Nearly as exciting as the women Jeffry brought last night.' They laughed, because the three women who joined them at Jeffry's bidding were pledged followers of Narigya, the Virgin Goddess of Chastity. They were pleasant company, but their religious affiliation proved too embarrassing for Jeffry, who retired early to escape his companions' smiles.

'I congratulate Andra on his fine swordsmanship,' Ernest remarked. 'Your training is obvious. Where did you get such a fine weapon?'

Andra glanced at the sword in his hand. The blade gleamed in the firelight, because, oddly, no blood stained its edge or face, even though Andra had slain many enemies. 'It was a parting gift from my father.'

'It parted a few Haagii,' quipped Derik dryly. He looked at Andra's feet. 'Where's the pup?'

Dread cut through Andra more deeply than any Haagii weapon. He sprinted ahead to their campsite to find their tents collapsed and bodies scattered about the sputtering fire. 'Artega!' he called. 'Artega!' The black pup did not come. 'Artega!' he repeated, as a sinking feeling filled the pit of his stomach. The Longbowmen searched through the chaotic jumble while Andra called the pup.

'Here!' Ernest yelled. The warriors saw him standing over a body, face down.

'Jeffry!' Marvin gasped. They gently turned him over, but he was dead, a bloodied slash across his forehead and a deep wound in his chest.

Derik stood and stared into the darkness of the hills. 'Damn them all!' he hissed.

Marvin covered Jeffry's face, and folded the dead man's arms across his chest, before he searched for Jeffry's longbow in the tents. When he returned to the group he carried a darker bundle. 'Think I found something,' he said and handed the bundle to Andra.

'Artega!' Andra gasped.

'He was hiding under the skins in the tent,' said Marvin. 'He's more sensible than he looks.' He returned to conducting the rites over Jeffry's body.

Pigeons fluttered out of the blue skies to perch on roosts outside the Captain's tent. Attendants took each pigeon, and unstrapped small leather cylinders from their legs. For four days, Captain Westbourne awaited replies from the other Wheels to determine his plan of action against the Haagii in the Kobold Ranges. The enemy attacked two more times, but were easily repelled by the vigilant Watch.

Jeffry's death dampened the Longbowmen's spirit, who were doubly angry for being kept on alert in the camp without action while wanting to exact revenge on the Haagii. Derik O'Dale spoke to Captain Westbourne to gain permission to attack the enemy, but his daily requests met with denial as the leaders of the Great King's Armies deliberated and waited for High Lord Mara's order. The Longbowmen's patience wore thin. When Andra returned to tell them the pigeons had arrived for the day, he found all, but, five had slipped out of camp. Tom Arrowshaft reluctantly told Andra where he thought the others were. 'But I wouldn't go nosing after them,' he added as a warning. 'There's too many Haagii waiting for a lone warrior in those foothills.'

'I'm trained to run and dodge. I'll do what I do best,' Andra replied.

Finding nineteen Longbowmen wasn't as easy as he expected. He searched quietly, carefully, putting his raw skill to practise, but they'd cleverly masked their movement along the ravines, and he would have bypassed them had not Derik neatly placed a shaft at his feet from the top of a ridge. The shot startled the young warrior, sending him instinctively tumbling for cover. Derik waved, signalled silence, and pointed to the easiest route to the top; a steep climb up a ragged rock face. The climb brought Andra to a position where he could see cave openings on the opposite face, openings invisible from the ravine floor. 'So, you're a curious Guardian?' Derik noted.

'I only wanted to see what you intended doing to fight Haagii buried in the ground,' Andra answered. 'I might learn something useful.'

'Where's your shadow?'

'Artega? With Tom and the others, eating as usual.'

'Now watch,' said Derik. He loaded his longbow, drew the full length of the arrow, and sighted along it, towards the cave openings. Their plan was simple, so simple Andra wondered why the Wheel leaders hadn't thought of it. Seven Longbowmen gathered brush, laid it at the entrances to the caves, and plugged every hole that might potentially be a vent or chimney for the cave system. Finished, they signalled to the archers by holding torches aloft, and lit the dry brush. As the fires crackled into life, they poured oil onto the flames and gouts of smoke rolled into the caves.

'How did you know the smoke would go in?' Andra asked.

'We tested, with candles. We looked for an inward lean of the flame. Two sets of caves weren't suitable. This set pulls air in.' Derik explained the tactic, while he maintained rigid concentration on the openings, and Andra marvelled at the Longbowman's discipline to remain perfectly primed under the strain of waiting. The smoke spread, and blanketed the face of the opposite hillside. A dark shape stumbled out of the smoke, followed by three more, coughing and hacking. Derik's bowstring sang. Arrows raced from different quarters. The four Haagii clutched at them, as they struck, toppled forward, and slid down the scree. More Haagii staggered out of the smoky holes to meet their fellows' fate, sliding or rolling crazily down the rocky slope into the ravine. The deliberate and efficient execution took a short time, the last Haagii crawling out of the diminishing smoke to die before he could take a breath of clear air. Derik waited patiently, for several moments, before giving a short, high-pitched whistle. The Longbowmen on the opposite ridge reappeared, stamped out the fires, and scrambled down the scree. 'I made that thirty-two. Agreed?' Derik asked, and winked.

'I didn't count,' Andra replied, still amazed by the ruthless efficiency of the blonde archers. They were his friends. When the camp was under attack they were like any other warrior with their swords, but now Andra had seen why they were set apart, and why the Great King had only so many of them. They were specialized killers.

Derik clapped Andra on the shoulder, and said, 'Jeffry will rest more easily now. We have avenged him a little. Tomorrow we'll add another batch of these animals to our tally.' With that, he led the group down the rock face.

Thirty Four

The Haagii were gone. For three days, squads of soldiers methodically moved through the hills, valleys, ravines, and defiles, scouting caves, constantly alert for ambushes, but none came. The hills were deserted, save for hundreds of wild goats, and a handful of straggly feral sheep, but everywhere they found evidence of their enemy's presence: hastily abandoned campfires, caves littered with crude furniture, tracks poorly covered, where companies and tiny bands of Haagii warriors headed north, out of the Kobold Ranges. They found dead Haagii, abandoned or killed by their fellows, left as mute testimony to the speed of their departure. The caves were systematically searched, but the Haagii left no clues as to the reason for their flight. Pigeon messengers brought confirmation of their movement. The North Wheel intercepted a large company of Haagii moving onto the plains west of Riverfork, but they missed the main contingent. Elsewhere, Haagii bands were reported moving out of the settled lands, out of the mountains and forests, trekking north, towards their homelands in Uz-Erhaag. Their withdrawal was good news to most people, but there were puzzles, disturbing pieces of information, connected with their movement. Winter was over. Spring was an excellent time to launch an offensive. The Haagii should have been preparing to attack, not retreat. Then there were the numbers. Daily reports estimated the combined forces of Haagii moving north exceeded twenty-five thousand warriors. Twenty-five thousand Haagii had infiltrated the Kingdom in the past year. The Haagii had never previously worked in groups larger than twenty or thirty, and yet an army marched out of the Kobold Ranges, quickly, efficiently, as if led by an experienced Captain.

Message running, between Devis, provided Andra with a perfect opportunity to gather information. He listened to

Captain Westbourne read pigeon messages that arrived from other Wheels and was privy to meetings between the Captain and his Devis. Runners heard and saw much more than most in the Great King's Armies, and Andra passed on as much as he could to Derik and his friends. 'It seems,' Ernest began, 'that we won't be needing a war, after all.'

'Why do you say that?' Marvin asked, as he stoked the campfire.

'I thought that would be obvious,' replied Ernest, with mock petulance, but he continued in a more serious tone. 'You know what I mean. The Haagii are going home. They're smarter than we think. They've seen what kind of army's been raised against them.'

Andra looked up at the two men. 'Captain Westbourne certainly doesn't think that,' he said, 'and Devi Farrow believes they're planning something much bigger than a few sorties in the hills.'

'Like what?' asked Ernest.

'They're not sure,' Andra replied quietly.

'I know one thing,' Derik interposed. 'This war is a long way from over. We've just seen the tip of it. We'll march north after the Haagii. That I am sure of.'

The order to march came from High Lord Mara within three days. The West Wheel was to join the North Wheel at Riverfork where High Lord Mara would arrive with the force he had based at Anedya. The news excited and disappointed Andra. The prospect of being reunited with Alain and Stephen filled him with joyful expectation, but he harboured a nagging fear that the campaign against the Haagii, a campaign most expected to take two or three months, was destined to drag on much longer than anyone imagined. He wanted to get back to The Vale, to his family and friends. If they had to fight the Haagii, he wished it could be soon. Then he could cover himself in glory as a warrior of the Great King, so that his return to The Vale would be full of celebration, and he would earn the respect due a Guardian who'd journeyed halfway across the Kingdom to vanquish a hated foe. When the march started in earnest, Andra was stationed with Captain Westbourne's party, along with the other runners. The parade ground order for the West Wheel was maintained, meaning Derik and the Longbowmen marched on the left flank, away from Andra's position. He was disappointed to be separated from his friends.

They reached the camp of the North Wheel after a full day's march, half a day west of Riverfork. Everywhere, the marching troops saw signs and tracks indicating the northward retreat of a large Haagii force. Discarded equipment and food highlighted the desperation of their flight, and Andra knew the slow Great Armies would never keep pace with their enemy, who were moving with swift intent towards their homelands.

Reunion with Alain was good. Alain related how the North Wheel circled through the northeast quadrant of the Kobold Range and routed several surprised Haagii companies. He proudly displayed a wound, the result of a Haagii spear that caught him in the wrist as he was running a message between Spokes during a melee in the hills. 'My sword hand is stiff,' he explained, trying to flex his fingers.

'Was there much pain?' Andra asked.

Alain grinned. 'If you were the Guardian Master or Murdok, I'd say there was none, but there was a great deal of pain, especially when I had to pull the spear out again. A soldier by the name of Kennett saved my life when I fell with the spear. The Haagii who threw it followed the throw, and was going to stick me with his sword. Kennett stuck him instead.' Alain looked up at Andra. 'And you?'

Andra scratched Artega's ears as he replied, 'There was one major skirmish. A lot of men died. It wasn't pleasant. Not a day later, the Haagii also attacked our camp at night, in force. There was a lot of fighting. I learnt the strength of this gift.' He patted the hilt of the sword strapped to his side. He added brief details of their march before he led Alain to the fire of Derik O'Dale and the Longbowmen.

The company of the Longbowmen had expanded to near

fifty, and their storytelling and song grew rowdy as they shared tales of each other's exploits in recent days. 'How do you know which one of these is your friend?' Alain shouted as they approached the sea of grey tunics and blond hair. 'They all look alike.'

'They do until you know them,' answered Andra. 'Close up they are as individual as you or me.' They found Derik merrily quaffing mead and singing heartily between quaffs. He clapped Andra on the shoulder, warmly greeted Alain as a brother, and ordered them to bring their fellow Runners to their drinking feast.

The West and North Wheels remained in camp for two days before the order to march was given. They headed directly north, to the western spur of the Abreotan Ranges, a line of sharp-peaked mountains that thrust angrily at the sky, threatening to rip open its belly with snow-frosted razor points. Along the southern edge of the Range huddled a dark, densely wooded forest, stretching east, until it ran up against the western wall of the Andrakian mountains. Giant beech, oak, and elm created a canopy of leaves thick enough to walk on, and the vision filled Andra with a longing for the forests of the Valley of Rivers. There was, however, little similarity in the two. While the forests of the Valley of Rivers were rugged because of the complex pathways of streams and rivers, they welcomed the presence and passage of people. This forest's gloom was foreboding, as if defying anyone to enter its depths.

The Captains called a halt at the edge of the forest and camp was set. The Runners were immediately ordered to the Command tent, from where they were deployed to carry a message to each Devi, and Trainer, that strict discipline was to be observed among the ranks while they awaited the arrival of the East Wheel and High Lord Mara. Andra knew the Longbowmen wouldn't appreciate the restrictions: no campfires, no song or merriment, no alcohol, strict rotation of Watch duty. The orders also meant the other Runners and he were required to bed down directly behind the Command tent, under the watch of Trainer Murdok. He knew Murdok wouldn't appreciate Artega's presence. Perhaps Derik would take the pup. He'd ask on the message run.

For six days, they waited at the edge of the dark forest. The first two days were tedious and uneventful. The Runners weren't required to move, and they would've idled time away by their tents if Murdok hadn't seized the opportunity to make them exercise. 'Runners run,' he said calmly. 'Fitness. If you sit around, like cheap whores, you'll get lazy, and when I need you to run you'll waddle. I make you do this for your sake, not mine.' And they ran – three times each day.

On the third day, Murdok allowed Andra and Alain to visit the Longbowmen. As Andra stuck his head inside the entry to the Longbowmen's tent, he was smothered with saliva from a gangly, black animal. The two rolled and wrestled among mats and fur and laughter. 'He misses you,' Derik said.

'What's he been doing?' Andra asked, as he rolled the pup over.

'Learning to be a hunter,' Derik replied.

Andra sat up. A couple of Longbowmen chuckled. 'Explain.'

'As I said,' Derik answered. 'He can't lie about all day. He'd drive us crazy with his puppy antics. So we've taken him into the forest to hunt game.'

'Into the forest?' Andra looked at Alain.

'Have you no ears? I did say forest, didn't I?' Derik asked in mock appeal to the other Longbowmen.

Marvin and Lester nodded, and Marvin added, 'I do believe you did say forest, brother.'

'There, see? Into the forest,' Derik concluded.

'But I thought the forest was off limits while we're camped here?'

'So it may be. But hunters must hunt, and what a perfect place to learn how to hunt if you're a pup as black as the inside of the forest. There's game aplenty for the taking. The Haagii haven't been in there. No sign of them.'

Andra grabbed Artega by the scruff to keep him off.

'And?'

Derik and his companions laughed. 'Hopeless, of course. But he'll learn.'

'He flushed out a clutch of quail yesterday,' said Marvin.

'It was hard to tell who was more frightened,' Lester chipped in.

Andra rolled the dog over. 'Do you know much about this forest?' he asked.

'This place? It's Dragon Forest. It was the home of a green dragon, a long time ago. Local legends say the dragon's spirit still guards the forest, but we know the last dragons perished in the Wars against Mareg when Aian Abreotan slew them. That makes the forest pretty much open invitation. We've only been in the fringes, where there's ample game for the taking, but Marvin is keen to look deeper, aren't you Marvin?'

Marvin gave Derik a sharp disapproving stare. 'There is no hospitality in a place so deep and dark,' he mumbled. 'But if you insist on going in, I go too.'

'Can we come with you?' Andra asked impulsively.

Derik's hesitation to answer disarmed Andra, and he wondered why the Longbowman needed to think about a simple request, until Derik nodded, and said, 'If it can be arranged for us to take a Runner, or two, we will name you.'

The fourth and fifth days passed without incident. The sun warmed the earth, and the long-standing winter dampness slowly dissipated, leaving a promise of fairer days. Murdok took them through their three daily cycles of exercise, but his manner was more relaxed as if the season was affecting the man.

The following morning, however, his fierce nature fully returned, and the Runners were turned out before sunrise. 'You are not here for leisure! Sleep half the day away, would you? Not while I'm your Trainer!' He pushed and prodded, as he passed individuals, and zealously shouted in their faces as they struggled into clothing and armour. 'You have work to do! And you will do it! Yes, you will! Runners run! And you'll get plenty of that today! That's what you're here for!

Running! Emmett! Boric! Merry! Wallin! To the Captains' tent! Move it!' The four named Runners gathered their weapons. 'Quickly!' Murdok barked. They scampered away, tall Emmett looking more like a strange apparition than a man in the semi-darkness. 'Turk! To Devi Farrow. You have much running ahead of you today. Prepare yourself. Remember your training. Run well!' Turk, a strong, muscled warrior, sprinted away. Murdok stood before Andra and Alain and his cold eyes fixed them. 'It seems you two have been directly asked for, by way of a favour.' Murdok's eyebrows rose to mock the last word. Andra caught Alain's eye with a wink. 'You are to go to the edge of the forest and await a company of Longbowmen. Go!' He moved past them to the others, as if Andra and Alain no longer existed in his world.

Faint morning light touched the snowy peaks as the pair reached the brooding forest. The absence of light at ground level intensified the forest's pitch interior, as if the forest was sucking the last remaining light of the world into its maw of eternal night. 'I think I understand why the Haagii didn't enter this forsaken place,' said Alain. 'Nothing moves in there. Nothing can be seen.'

'I think even Tim Gaelus' eyes would find seeing difficult in there,' responded Andra.

'Have you seen him since your excursion into the city?'

'No. I never saw him in the ranks on the day of leaving. He simply disappeared. I thought perhaps he'd been -' Andra stopped mid-sentence. Deep in the heart of the forest a keening wail broke the silence, an eerie sound that raised the hairs on the young warriors' necks. The cry echoed briefly and died.

'What was that?' whispered Alain. Andra shook his head, his pale fear mirrored in his companion's eyes. Rustling, slight, almost imperceptible, began in the outer leaves of the closest trees, and it seemed to spread rapidly through the canopy, moving away from the forest's margins to its heart. Traces of first sunlight tipped the highest boughs, and a shallow breath of air rolled out of the forest, brushing the cheeks of both young men. 'It breathes!' Alain whispered harshly.

They stared into the inky forest. A twig snapped behind them, and they span. 'Morning, my friends!' Derik O'Dale cheerily offered, before recognising their stance. 'A bit wary, are we?'

Andra relaxed and straightened up. Derik's companions were waiting with him. 'The forest set us on edge.'

'I understand,' Derik smiled. 'The inner parts are forbidding, but it's only a forest, as you will see.'

Their party comprised ten: eight Longbowmen and two Runners. An eleventh was produced inside the perimeter of the forest, red tongue slavering appreciation on anyone close enough to be appreciated. 'Carry him,' Derik advised, passing the pup to Andra, as they began to walk forward. 'His enthusiasm might be overwhelming for the animals we hunt.' Andra tucked Artega inside his jerkin, where the pup immediately set to chewing the talisman on the leather necklet Tim gave him. A quick tap of fingers on the pup's nose stopped his gnawing, and Artega suddenly preferred to peer out of the neck of Andra's leather tunic, ears pricked, nose impulsively twitching.

Less than thirty paces in, the verge ended, and true forest began. Rough undergrowth did not venture beyond the edge of permanent darkness. The forest floor became a thick mat of dead leaves, and decomposing matter piled deep between twisted roots, roots thicker than a man's body. The roots reared out of the organic carpet to feed huge tree trunks, broader and thicker than any Andra had ever seen. He estimated it would take fifteen men, at full stretch, to encircle the girth of a smaller trunk near him, and that trunk was a dwarf beside the colossi that disappeared into the surrounding darkness. 'Here.' Derik handed a lantern to Andra.

'I have a torch,' Andra replied.

'They won't be any use in here,' said Derik.

'Why not?'

'The forest puts them out,' said Marvin.

Andra looked quizzically at Marvin and at Derik. 'It's true,' Derik confirmed. He produced a torch and lit it. 'Watch.' The flame flickered into life, burned momentarily, danced, and died as a warm breath of wind snuffed it out.

'Well?' asked Andra.

'Well what?'

'Aren't you going to light it again?'

Derik sighed. 'If I did, it would only go out again. For whatever reason, one only the forest knows, there's enough breeze in here to put out torches. We discovered that two days ago. There's no point lighting the torch again.'

'I can't feel a breeze,' said Alain.

'That's what's strange,' explained Marvin. 'There is no breeze, until we light a torch. It's as if the forest - '

'Breathes!' said Andra and Alain in unison.

The Longbowmen stared at the Runners. Derik quickly broke the silence. 'Not quite. But it is strange. That's why we brought lanterns. You'll also need to wear these on the soles of your boots.' He produced two pair of rounded platforms, designed to strap onto footwear, made from pliable wood and leather strands. 'The floor of the forest drops away, ahead, even though it appears level, and the leafy mulch is deep and treacherous to walk on. These will help you stay on the surface.'

They made slow passage between the ancient trees, trudging cautiously across the spongy mat, clambering over and under larger roots. Their lanterns threw macabre shadows across the twisted wood as they passed. Above, in the darkness that refused to yield to lantern light, leaves whispered, and unseen creatures flitted back and forth. The damp air carried the stench of rotting vegetation, and no living creatures moved along the floor, or appeared in their bobbing circles of light. 'We don't belong here,' whispered Marvin. 'Even the Haagii had the good sense to steer clear of this place.'

Derik stopped and held his lantern so that its light etched his features and made his blond hair shine like strands of gold wire. 'I think you're right, Marvin. We'll leave soon enough. Just be patient a little longer. This forest fascinates my curiosity.' He turned and led the band deeper into the forest.

Time and dimension were empty. Andra felt he could wander, for days, weeks, in the gaping chasms between the gigantic trunks, along natural passageways. No one was willing to speak in the stifling atmosphere. The encroaching dark amplified their footfalls as they crushed dead plant layers with every step. They must have wandered for a long time, because Andra's legs ached from the softness beneath his feet, like walking on air or soft sand. And, then, unexpectedly, they entered a hall. In any other place, thought Andra, as he tried to discern trunks and roots at the extremities of his lantern light, this would be a substantial clearing, but even here the ceiling of leaves and boughs are solid and unrelenting.

'Far enough,' announced Derik. He turned on the spot, taking in the forest hall's majesty. 'Beautiful, isn't it?' No one replied. Agreement was tacit. The place came alive in the presence of the flickering lantern light. Shadows leaped and slithered between gigantic knots of wood. Huge grey moths appeared, and circled, inexorably closing in on the lanterns. Artega squirmed in his leather cocoon, forcing Andra to lift him out, and when Andra obliged Artega promptly relieved himself.

'Just as well you let him out,' Alain remarked and laughed, as he stepped across to join his friend. Artega was sniffing eagerly in the rotting carpet of leaves. 'He doesn't seem dismayed by this place.'

'He has no respect for beauty yet,' Derik added.

'Look!' The startled cry came from Lester of the Lake. He was pointing at Marvin who moved quite suddenly to the distant edge of the hall. A pale blue halo glowed ahead of him, on the trunk of an enormous old tree. In the blue haze, Andra saw a faint figure of an alluring maiden, her hair sweeping in a golden braid across her shoulder onto her full bosom. As he stared, Marvin reached the tree, embraced the beautiful vision in a passionate kiss, and melted into the tree, disappearing with the pale blue light.

'Marvin!' Derik shouted. The party ran towards the place where Marvin had been swallowed, and, as the last patch of light pooled on the trunk, Lester, first to arrive, plunged his right hand into the light. 'No!' Derik screamed. He grabbed Lester's arm to wrench it free, but his warning came too late. As the light dissolved, Lester's face contorted with agony, and he screamed wretchedly before passing out.

'There!' shouted another Longbowman.

A second patch of light formed on a tree trunk across the hall, a deep blue mirror, and a shape appeared in its midst. In a twinkling, Derik nocked an arrow and let the shaft fly. As it struck home, the light imploded. A brief, high-pitched scream pierced the air, and touched their hearts. 'Run!' Derik yelled. 'This place is cursed!' Swaying lanterns marked the retreat of the Longbowmen. 'Go with them,' Derik ordered, when he saw Andra and Alain hesitating.

'What about Lester?' Andra asked. 'And you?'

'Go!' snapped Derik. His tone warned the warriors not to disobey him. Alain grabbed Andra's arm, and they stumbled after the dwindling lights of the Longbowmen, as quickly as they could across the spongy forest floor.

Outside the hall, they waited. The trees seemed to crowd in, urging them to move on, but they were determined to wait for Derik. Time dragged. Out of the darkness, a lantern swung erratically towards them. Derik staggered forward, the limp weight of Lester slumped across his shoulders, his bow dragging in the mulch. He had freed Lester, but the Longbowman would never draw a shaft again, his right arm severed at the elbow. Cloth rudely bound the stump. 'We must hurry,' Derik panted. 'He's lost too much blood, and I fear for his life.'

The party regrouped to move along the dark pathways, but Andra span and stared into the forest depths at the dark hole leading to the forest hall. 'Artega!' he yelled. 'Artega!'

Derik stopped. 'You left him there?'

'I didn't mean to. I forgot. In the rush. Artega!'

'There's nothing you can do. He doesn't come.' Andra

320

stared into the darkness, but heard and saw nothing. 'Come,' said Derik, firmly but gently.

There came a sharp bark. 'Artega!' Andra cried excitedly, and the bark repeated, but the dog did not appear. 'He's still there. He's lost.' Andra grabbed Derik's arm. 'I've got to get him!'

'No!' Derik warned. 'It's too late. Come on.'

Artega barked again. Andra released his hold on Derik's arm and ran into the darkness. Alain went to follow, but a Longbowman grabbed him. 'Don't be a fool. There is evil magic in there. Your friend's already a dead man, like Marvin. Don't waste your life over a pup.' Alain shifted his weight, as the Guardian Master taught, and threw the Longbowman to the floor. He picked up the fallen lantern, and sprinted after his friend before the others could intervene.

Andra stumbled into the space between the trees. To his left, a circle of blue light radiated about a vixen-eyed nymph. She cradled a black pup in her arms. Without hesitation, Andra drew Cedwyn's sword, and lunged.

Alain ran into the hall in time to see Andra vanish within a blue haze that folded in upon itself, becoming the gnarled trunk of an ancient tree.

Thirty Five

'You erred in bringing him here. He bears Aelendyell protection.'

'I had no choice, sister. He was upon me before I could dissolve the light.'

'Why does a human wear an Aelendyell talisman?'

'It is a mystery, Niolanthe.'

'Things may have changed in the Outer World since we last caught a man.'

'Perhaps. But we must return this one. It's not right for him to be among us, even if he is a human.'

'Look. He bears the mark of the moon on his cheek.'

'Perhaps it is destiny he comes here, after all. But he cannot stay. He must be returned to the Outer World.'

'He stirs. Be patient, sisters.'

He was listening at the edge of consciousness, independent of his body, but sensations crowded in, dragging him swiftly into his physical self. His eyes opened. Amber light. He was staring at a carved wooden ceiling, interwoven with roots of trees, and packed with earth and stones. The stones radiated the amber light. As he rolled his head towards the voices, he had the distinct impression he was lying beneath the earth, in a natural chamber formed by disparate forces working in harmony. His eyes rested on eight sylvan figures clustered by his left side. The pale amber light masked the true shade of their hair, but their hair was light, with delicate braiding that fell to their waists. One leaned closer, to peer at his face, and her perfect beauty astonished him. Finely chiselled and high cheekbones underscored large almond eyes, and Andra thought of Tim Gaelus and the ragged derelicts hiding in the city warehouse. His thought vanished, as the nymph gently stroked his brow with her slender fingers, and he flinched. 'Do not be afraid, human,' she said, in a soft voice. 'You will come to no harm among us.'

Seeing her petite figure, and taut breasts pressing against her sheer attire, Andra looked away, embarrassed – until he remembered what happened. He scrambled to his feet, clutching frantically for his sword, to discover his scabbard was empty. The eight nymphs had not moved. 'Who are you?' he demanded.

The kneeling figure stood. 'We are the Alfyn Tree Keepers. I am Hyacinth.' She smiled and bowed her head towards him. 'You need not fear us,' she added, looking up. 'We know who you are.'

Now that he was standing, Andra realised the nymphs were no taller than children. Only the fullness of their figures revealed their maturity. 'Where is this place? And where's Artega?' he demanded, threatened by their casual reaction to his hostility.

'You are in Tree Home, our home,' Hyacinth replied, and she looked puzzled. 'Who is Artega?'

'The dog. My pup.'

Hyacinth turned to her companions. One stepped forward, cradling a sleeping black bundle. 'I could not resist him,' she stammered, handing the pup to Hyacinth.

'You had no right, Talatha. Animals do not belong here, and we cannot bring them in to serve our own selfish comforts.'

'I am sorry, sister,' Talatha mumbled, as she shamefully shuffled back to the group.

Satisfied Talatha had been remonstrated, Hyacinth held the pup in her arms. 'Here is your friend. He sleeps. He has come to no harm. Take him. He is yours,' she offered.

Andra studied Hyacinth's eyes for signs of deceit, but all he saw was beauty and sweetness, so he stepped forward, reached out warily, and accepted Artega's resting form. The pup snuggled comfortably against his chest, but did not stir. 'Where is Marvin?' Andra asked.

'There is another?' Hyacinth threw a querying glance at her sisters.

'I believe a sister on the eastern rim enticed a man to

follow her into Tree Home,' one nymph explained. 'That's why Talatha ventured to the Outer World, but I do not know who brought this human's companion within.'

'You must find out. Take Niolanthe to the eastern rim and learn what you can. Then return.' To Andra, as the two nymphs left, she said, 'Put down your burden and eat with us. We can talk of the Outer World and its happenings, and then we will return you there, rested and strong.'

'And Marvin?' asked Andra.

'If that is his will,' Hyacinth answered.

Andra followed his hosts through three small chambers, stooping to avoid hitting his head against the low tangled roof. The amber light emanating from the overhead stones illuminated each space. They stopped at a larger chamber where Hyacinth indicated he should sit. Plates of wild fruits and seeds were laid before him, along with a jug of nectar wine. Sweet fragrances tantalized his senses, and his distrust evaporated as the offerings increased in quantity and variety. Hyacinth directed all but three nymphs to other quarters, and joined Andra at the feasting table. 'Please. Eat and drink what you wish. If there is something you especially desire, ask. We may have it for you,' said Hyacinth, as she gestured gracefully across the fare. 'Except meats – they are forbidden within Tree Home.'

Andra nodded. He surveyed the food, and when his eyes found a bowl of familiar yellow fruit, he reached eagerly for it. 'Mada-fruit! I haven't seen any for months, and I've dearly wanted some in my rations. Where did you find it?'

'Here, in the forest, near the centre. How is it a human knows its value? I thought its bitter taste wasn't palatable to your people.'

'It grows in secluded valleys, near my home,' Andra explained. 'Its bitterness is a ruse for fools, the old people of The Vale say.'

Hyacinth asked a companion to pour wine, and as the nymph complied Hyacinth asked Andra to tell her who he was, and where his home lay. He saw no harm in her request, and he relaxed as he began to describe The Vale, homesickness running silently through his veins. 'But what brings you here, so far away?' she asked, when he finished.

'War,' he bluntly replied.

'For whom? Against whom?' Hyacinth's sincere interest sparkled in her eyes, but as Andra glanced down again at her near-naked body he blushed and looked away without responding. 'What is wrong?' she asked softly, fearing she'd offended him with too many questions.

Her question only heightened his embarrassment, and he stumbled on words when trying to explain. 'I'm sorry. It's just that I can't look -'

'I think I understand,' she responded. She leaned to one side and whispered to a companion. The three attendant nymphs left the chamber and returned dressed in russet robes, bearing a fourth that they handed to Hyacinth. She wrapped it demurely about her shoulders. 'There. I should have thought. Do you feel more comfortable now?' Andra nodded shyly. 'Good. Have you shared love with a woman?'

The questioned embarrassed him further. He blushed deeply and shyly replied, 'Once.'

Whispers raced between Hyacinth's three companions, but Hyacinth's face remained serious. 'I did not mean to pry. We will talk of less personal matters. What is this war you speak of?'

Andra explained how the Haagii had increased in numbers throughout the Kingdom, how they had embarked on looting, pillaging, and murdering, and he described Great King Thana's preparation and his Wheel's movement, up until his entrance into the forest. He observed Hyacinth throughout his tale, fascinated by the intensity with which she drew in every word he spoke, as if he was the centre of her world, and his words her breath of life.

When he finished, she was silent for a time, reflecting upon the information, before she asked, 'How did you come by an Aelendyell talisman?'

'A what?' Andra didn't understand, until he saw her staring at the necklet Tim gave him in the Great City. 'This?' he asked, fingering it carefully. She nodded. 'A friend, who said it would protect me at the right time, gave it to me.' Again, she nodded, and Andra wondered what secret she kept about the talisman, but he had other burning questions, desperate questions, and he wanted answers. 'I've told you who I am, but you've said nothing of yourself.'

'We are the Tree Keepers, as I said,' Hyacinth answered.

'But I don't understand you, or where I am,' he repeated, gesturing widely with his arms. 'Where am I really?'

Hyacinth indicated his goblet. 'Drink, and I will explain as best as I can to a human, though know well that what I am about to tell you is Sacred Lore, and it must not pass your lips, unless I bid. None of your people have heard the Lore and left Tree Home before. That is as it should be.' She sipped her wine, and rolled it on her tongue, while she gathered her thoughts, and she spoke in sombre tones. 'Long before your kind walked the earth, before your hated Haagii were spawned, or Kingdoms founded, the Land was rich and beautiful, beyond imagining. Our people, the Alfyn, were dwellers of the forests, and the Elvenaar were mere children of magic, laughing and dancing in the broad belts of forests that spanned half the world. It was the Time of Giants. The Giants laboured to shape mountains for their homes, dug rivers to irrigate their gardens, and planted magic in the earth from the Genesis Stone, after it fell from the sky. It was the Time of Shaping.

When the Giants took to their ships, and crossed the oceans to the east and west, then came the Time of Knowledge. The Elvenaar grew out of their childhood and learned the causes and sources of magic, and the purpose of harmony in all existence. Because the Elvenaar remained children of the forest at heart, they came to understand the nature and the needs of trees, and they formed an eternal bond with the Alfyn. The fellowship grew ever stronger, as the Elvenaar learned more about the magic inherent in trees, and it seemed peace would reign forever. And it did, for many generations, even after the first humans appeared in the Land. Even they seemed to understand the gift of the forests, the plentiful banquet they could provide, the protection and shelter within. And if it happened that one of them forgot his place in the balance of things, the Alfyn and the Elvenaar reminded him.

But humans were the harbingers of a rapidly approaching time, the Time of Change, when the Land began to decay, and be polluted and altered by increasing numbers of strangers. Humans multiplied. Soon they outnumbered the Elvenaar and Alfyn, and it was no longer possible to stop them burning and cutting down stretches of forest where they could run their beasts and grow their unnatural crops and build their cities. Still, change was slow, and it seemed much of the Land would remain untouched for a great many human generations.

Then the Black One came, sweeping across the Land on his great flying lizards, driving his rabid hordes before him, slaying and destroying everything that was good. So began the Dark Time, the Time of the Dragonlord. Your people were slaughtered or enslaved. The Alfyn and the Elvenaar were hunted mercilessly. The great forests were put to the torch, and the scorching breath of the Dragon Host turned the tree giants to ash. All hope was lost under the tyranny of the Black One, all beauty scarred forever. His minions devised pestilences to loose upon everyone in the Land, and a great many races perished. By the time the last of the Elvenaar and Alfyn were driven to make final stands against the Dragon hordes, in the fragments of remaining forest across the Land, all the surviving giant trees were ill. The Alfyn gathered here, at Tree Home, in the final fragment of Ethelreddor Forest, and prepared to perish by meeting the Dragon hordes in full battle. That battle never came. A mighty army of humans, and the remaining Elvenaar warriors, met the Black One, and the Black One was slain in combat by a human warrior.

There was great celebration, throughout the Land, at the news the Dragon Tyrant was dead. But in Tree Home there was only great sadness, for the last giant trees were dying, and no one could find the magic to alter or reverse the effect. In the last moments, when all hope to save the trees was lost, the Alfyn Ieldran made a covenant to forever seal

327

the bond between our people and the trees. We were honoured to be chosen from among the fairest daughters of our Alfyn family to serve the giant trees gathered at Tree Home: to serve them until their lives ended. The Ieldran prepared us, and inextricably bound our lives with the lives of the trees, so we could tend them. As long as our tree lives, we live. It is our source of magic and our life. We are the Tree Keepers.' Hyacinth ended her tale, but she stared into Andra's eyes, demanding his trust to keep the lore secret.

Unable to hold her gaze, he broke away, looking into the bowls of food. 'I understand, I think, but I promise I will never tell what I heard here.' He glanced up. Hyacinth was smiling. 'Can you never leave this place?' he quietly asked.

'Never. The magic of the Ieldran binds us here. Each of us cares for a tree. As long as our tree lives, we live, as I said.'

Andra shook his head. 'I –' but he left his statement unfinished. The power and presence of impossible magic, all around him, challenged his logic and senses. He took a deep draught of nectar wine, feeling its sweet, cool essence sooth his mouth and throat.

Another Tree Keeper entered, and glanced at Andra, before approaching Hyacinth to whisper in her ear. Hyacinth's eyes enlarged, as if shocked, but her serious expression returned. She whispered a reply to the messenger, who promptly left, before she turned to Andra. 'A tree is dying in Tree Home. One of your kind mortally wounded Tryolith with a foul arrow and killed a tree brother in doing so.' A tear formed in Hyacinth's eye and her three companions were visibly distressed.

Panic rose in the base of Andra's throat. He had to justify Derik O'Dale's action. 'We didn't know what was happening. You took Marvin, and Lester was trapped in the tree by your magic. He lost his arm. Derik only tried to protect us.'

'Be that as it may,' Hyacinth sternly replied, 'your kind has always resorted to violence when faced with something you don't understand. You destroy what you cannot alter because you have no magic in you, no love, no understanding of the Land. It has always been the same since your kind set ugly feet upon this place.' She paused, clearly angry, but she consciously altered her emotional state by force of will, an action that unnerved Andra, and a gracious smile returned to her lips. 'Please. I forget myself. I am not here to lecture you. It was not your doing. You must eat and drink, for soon you will be leaving. I remind myself that you wear the talisman, and bear the mark, and so you are an Aelendyell friend and must be treated as such in our home. Forgive my grief.' Hyacinth and her three companions stood. 'Remain here, until we return. I must attend to other matters, but I will also inquire after your friend while I am gone. Rest, if you wish. You look tired and troubled, and I would not have you be so in Tree Home.' She smiled again, and all four Tree Keepers left Andra alone in the chamber.

He listened, until he was certain they'd left the area. Derik's ill-timed arrow may have sealed his fate, though Hyacinth still said he was leaving. Why did they refer to his scar? He recalled Tim's interest and jumbled prophecies. Did the Tree Keepers know them? What about Marvin? What fate did he have in store? Andra reached for a second piece of mada-fruit and bit into the bittersweet rind. The taste reminded him that he could have been home, in The Vale, learning the arts of Guardians; but the eerie amber glow from the ceiling stones said he was in a place beyond The Vale, beyond the Kingdom – perhaps, he thought ruefully, perhaps even beyond help.

The entrance of a nymph broke his reverie. She wore only a sheer gown, and it clung to her, teasing his eyes, as she kneeled beside him. 'My sisters send me to give you a gift. Hyacinth knows you are the one who bears the mark of the moon, and this bracelet must serve its turn in the fulfilling of the prophecy. Give me your arm.' She held her hands forward, expectantly, and in her fingers she held a circlet of silver-amber metal, a spider web thin bracelet that sparkled, even in the soft amber light of the chamber. Andra allowed her to slide the gift onto his wrist. The bracelet fitted snuggly against his skin, and he was mystified by how it gently expanded to pass over his hand contracted to fit his wrist so perfectly. The gift tingled. 'Are you pleased?' she asked.

'Yes,' he replied. 'Yes, it's beautiful. Thank you.'

'Then it is good. Hyacinth ordered that you rest until her return.' The Tree Keeper maiden put her hands on his temples and bent his head towards her lap. He had so many questions racing through his mind, things he needed to ask, answers he sought, but he could not resist her; did not want to resist her. She ran her fingers through his hair, and across his brow, and crooned gentle words to match her touch. 'Be comforted, my weary warrior. Let sleep wash over your body, cleanse your senses, heal your mind. Let sleep caress your hair and kiss your eyes.' Andra relaxed, as her voice floated in ethereal patterns above and through him. Yes, he was tired, so tired, confusion drifting towards comforting darkness, soft night, warmth, to sleep.

It was dark, and he couldn't see beyond it. The darkness moved around him, became horses, men, herding him along. Haardrishii. Silently moving him. Someone prodded him from behind. He turned. Old Master Flintok waggled a crooked stick and pointed at a Haardrishii warrior. The warrior removed his helmet. The empty sockets of a dead sow's head glared with a sickening grin. Andra turned away, but a voice called, the Guardian Master's voice, ordering him to turn. He turned. The Guardian Master faced him, staff in hand. 'Fight!' he ordered. Andra shook his head.

'Fight!' shouted a chorus – Stephen, Erik, Mark, Renwith, his father Malcolm. Behind them, his mother, Anedra, shouted. 'Fight!' They crowded in, heckling, pushing him towards the foe. He clutched at his sword hilt, drew it from the scabbard. No blade. The sword had no blade. He looked into the face of the Guardian Master and saw Murdok grinning back. Behind Murdok, loomed a taller figure, a darker figure, faceless. Murdok lunged. The sword cut deep. No staff. Haagii warriors pressed in, heckling him, goading him to fight. 'Fight!' they sneered. 'Fight!' Something punched into his back. He looked down, saw the spear blade jutting from his stomach, saw the Haagii pointing. Murdok laughed bitterly, became Liam, angry and spiteful, holding a great golden broad sword above his head. A figure stepped between. Tim Gaelus. He laughed merrily and took Andra's hand. Andra tried to cry out, to warn Tim, but no sound came, except the silent fall of the golden sword, splitting his friend in twain. Now there were two Tims, then four, and as the sword flailed through them, there were more and more. A wave of Haagii warriors swarmed over them, but still they rose from the assault and multiplied. The dark figure beneath the cowl and cape wielded the sword, and it flamed and sparked as it struck one Tim after another. One by one, the images of Tim were cut down and disappeared as the flaming sword swept through. Trees, giant trees, crowded in from the edge of darkness, but they came too near the sword of flame and exploded in a ball of searing fire, until the whole world was full of burning trees. The dark face beckoned to Andra, called him to join him. Andra recoiled in fear, fighting the call, but it was strong, so strong, too strong, and he felt himself moving against the tide of bodies towards the golden sword of flame. He was holding it. He swung its massive blade through the crush of bodies before him, hearing screams and then nothing but utter silence. Only the vision of the sword remained, biting and cutting into the crowd, a crowd of almond-eyed nymphs cowering before him, before a wall of flame, and behind he could no longer see, only feel the presence of the Dark One, pressing down.

He woke with a start. Darkness pressed in, save for a tiny pool of light near his right hand. He sat up, and rubbed his eyes, and tried to determine where he was. The pool of light came from a shielded lantern resting on the leaf-strewn forest floor. Beside the lantern was a curled sleeping mass of black. Artega. Andra ran his hand over the pup's soft hide, but didn't wake him. A gleam on his wrist caught his eye. He turned it over to examine the source: a silver-amber bracelet. From where had it come? Where was he? He recalled seeing a blue haze on the trunks of the ancient trees. He leaped to his feet, deftly drawing his sword in the same motion, and circled, staring warily at the trees, but no blue light shimmered in the great hall, and it was silent, except for the beat of his heart and the soft murmurings of the sleeping pup.

He walked clumsily on the oval pads Derik fashioned, towards the base of the nearest tree, and touched the knotty bark, felt its rough texture against his palm, and tried to recall a deeper memory that eluded him, but there was nothing he could touch upon – except the mysterious bracelet that fitted his wrist perfectly, but offered no clues to its origin. He returned to where the pup lay asleep, gently picked him up, without disturbing his slumber, lifted the lantern, and shambled out of the dark hall, into the forest corridors.

"Failure is not a personal fault. It is strength, proof of effort. When one fails, one has merely taken another step forward on the long journey to enlightenment."

from The Third Ki, by Leiksha Ithrandyr Shehaal

Thirty Six

Dark. Absolute. Total. Smothering. He refocused his eyes, using Aelendyell vision to detect heat. Nothing. He was in a void. The only certainty was hard rock beneath his body. He lay motionless for a long time, straining to hear and see, but his senses were dead to everything beyond his heartbeat, and the ebb and flow of air he breathed. Tentatively, he stretched out his hands, his fingers, searching the rock on which he lay. It was smooth, worn, cool. His right hand ran into scattered fragments on the rock – sharp, uneven, invisible shards – and he recoiled, his heartbeat quickening. He waited. Silence and darkness waited with him. Again, he stretched out his hands, this time lifting them, palms cupped, and he whispered, 'Leoht.' A soft light sphere winked into existence, and the darkness shied away. He was at the centre of a vast chamber, a natural cavern, scooped into a hemisphere, deep inside the earth. The walls were smooth, the floor worn to a soft surface. Overhead, the ceiling was rough, as if formed by enormous boulders packed tightly into a gigantic hole. To his right he realised what his hand had discovered: the shattered crystal of a portal mirror, its green remnants glinting in the magical light.

A Ahmud Ki stood, but stumbled to his knees, disoriented and dizzy, and his light winked out. The Dragonlord's grinning arrogance filled his mind. He remembered the dying moments of the Inner Sanctum: Tarnyss shrieking in her death ball of energy; the High Councillors trampling each other in their frenzy to escape; Mareg's reverberating laughter rising above the din of destruction; and Seralinna, his Seralinna, falling. His senses were shocked by the impact of the stone floor against his cheek. He lay still, willed himself to be strong, and rose. He created a second sphere, brighter than its predecessor, and surveyed the cavern, searching for a way out.

A narrow, spiralling stone stairway led up into a tunnel, or corridor, and he cautiously mounted the steps. The stairway led to a dark antechamber, and two corridors headed in opposite directions beyond the antechamber. The one to his right, he figured, led over the cavern below, but it was blocked by a rock fall. The other corridor ended at a metal door. He approached the door, dimmed his light, and listened. It was silent. He placed his hand on the handle and tried to open the door, but it wouldn't budge. He recited a spell and passed through, to find the door was an arm's span thick, and heavily barred and bolted. There is too much similarity between this place and the Inner Sanctum, he thought. Perhaps I've only teleported to another part of the cavern beneath the city of Targa. His sense of danger heightened, aware the Dragonlord might not be far away.

He followed the corridor to the foot of another stairway, and ascended, only to find, part way up, the way was blocked by a collapsed ceiling. He sat and pondered the situation. Going back is pointless. The other corridor is filled. This one might be too. He thought of risking a spell, but if the collapse was too thick he could lose concentration and be trapped in the rubble. He resolved to dig.

The task was long and arduous. He cast a light spell on a rock to make it glow so he could concentrate entirely on excavating the rock from the stairwell, but he lost all sense of time as he dug. His fingertips began to bleed, and his hands were chafed raw by the rough surface, but he persisted, calling on his strict Ranu Ka Shehaala training to sustain him, until he collapsed, unable to push his exhausted body further.

He woke hungry, but with renewed spirit. I am A Ahmud Ki, he reminded himself. He tended his cuts and scrapes with Ithosen spells, and focussed his energy on the lessons of Targa, and shaping spells. A moment later, a soldier ant scrabbled up the face of the tunnel and tugged at small pebbles.

When the last pebble tumbled down the rock face, the soldier ant crawled into the adjoining dark space. A Ahmud

Ki cancelled his spell, stretched and shook himself, and created another sphere to see where his tunnelling had brought him. The room was square, with four doorways, one in each wall, but like the one from which he emerged they were filled with rock and rubble. He slumped against the wall, frustrated by the prospect of more pointless digging, and stared at a pile of twisted, rusted metal in the centre of the room. There was something familiar, and regular about the metalwork pattern. He stood and approached the heap, before recognising what it was – a ladder. He glanced up. A rectangular hole in the ceiling opened into a black shaft. That was the way out. He took another look at the wrecked ladder and the blocked passages. Someone went to a great deal of trouble to seal entrances to whatever lay in this place, he decided and wondered at the possibility of two Dragonlords buried beneath Targa, one so well hidden that even Tarnyss and her sorceresses had failed to discover his resting place. Perhaps he still had a chance to find a Dragonlord and tap into its power. The thought thrilled him. Once he ascertained out where he was, he could return, excavate the tunnels, reopen the chamber where the Dragonlord was buried, and complete what he started in the Inner Sanctum. Then he would be what Tarnyss knew he was destined to be - a Dragonlord! He concentrated and cast a levitation spell.

The shaft rose a greater distance than he anticipated, and his head struck a solid obstruction sealing the shaft at the top, which prevented him rising further. Like the door beyond the antechamber, the lid was substantial, and weighed down by a mass of boulders. Passing through unknown barriers was risky spell use, and his energy was drained by his last effort. He paused to rejuvenate, and when he was ready he wove his spell and passed through the obstruction.

He stood in darkness, on rock, listening to dripping water. The air was cooler, and no longer stale. His Aelendyell vision detected dots of heat emanating from clusters – small creatures, bats. He remembered what they looked like at night in the Aelendyell forests of his childling years, but he never ventured into a cave. The Aelendyell distrusted caves as the antithesis to their forest world. A Ahmud Ki grinned wryly at remembering another typically limited Aelendyell concept. He was underground, and saw nothing worrisome about it, except foolish Aelendyell superstition. It doesn't matter where you are with power, he thought, all things give way to power.

With a surge of passion, he flung his arms wide, spoke words of magic, and flooded the entire cavern with bright light. The confusion he precipitated amazed him. The bats, bewildered by the sudden light, fluttered into high pitched panic, and whirled around the cavern, weaving between stalactites towards patches of darkness, fear-blinded suicide runs averted only by their keen sonic ears. In squeaking groups, they cartwheeled towards a dark smudge in the far wall, which was an opening into darkness. And with them went four stumbling figures A Ahmud Ki hadn't noticed – four ill-dressed humans scrambling over the stalagmites and each other in desperate flight to escape the spirit that caused the cavern to explode into light brighter than day. At least there is a way out, he thought.

He dimmed his spell, allowing parts of the cavern to sink into darkness, and headed across the uneven floor, stepping around stalagmite formations, to the tunnel down which the startled humans fled. Bats hung in the recesses, watching A Ahmud Ki pass. The tunnel dipped and climbed and wound through limestone rock a short distance, but he saw torchlight ahead, and a wooden ladder rising out of the tunnel. He moved towards it.

The weighty impact threw the half-Aelendyell wizard against a wall. A sharp edge pressed against his windpipe, and strong arms bound his arms to his side. 'You're a dead man,' his captor whispered harshly. A Ahmud Ki fought his instinctive fear, using Ithosen mind spells to stay calm. If the blade at his throat moved, he could act. If not, he could wait. He felt pressure on his back, forcing him to stumble forward, his arms still pinned. Two figures emerged from dark alcoves and stepped into the torchlight, and A Ahmud Ki recognised their similarity to the men he'd frightened out of the cavern. They were unkempt, reminiscent of the sailors on the Targan docks, vaguely like the poorer citizens of Yul Ithrandyr. He never consorted with such people. They were limited in intelligence, worthy of nothing more than labour and drudgery. Their lives were brutal and short, used by their superiors, whenever necessary, for work and war. They represented no threat to A Ahmud Ki, but he acquiesced to his capture, content to let them lead him out of wherever he was. Humans, he secretly gloated, are so naive.

'Our problem with this intruder is that he found his way into the Deep Cave without being detected.'

'He couldn't have got past the Eyes and Ears. They've never failed.'

'The Eyes and Ears saw and heard no one.'

'He cannot be permitted to leave.'

'But if the King is expecting him -?'

'He won't arrive. He could've met a thousand fates on the roads from Targa, and no one could tell which it was.'

'He must pay the penalty then.'

A Ahmud Ki listened patiently to the discussion, and sensed bodies moving near him, despite his blindfolded eyes. He had little idea where he was, but he gleaned information from several minds, and knew more than the arguing voices were telling him. He wasn't in Targa. He was in, or below, the city of Thana. A King ruled the city. He remembered Jasmin talking to him about the western Kingdom. That was where the portal led him. One of his captors was called the Guild Master. His real name was Orrin – A Ahmud Ki learned that from mind searching – but no one spoke it. They spoke no names, except those belonging to people outside the room. His life was in the balance. A couple of lesser men were blunt about killing him. They wanted no threat to the security of their hideaway. The Guild Master was more calculating. He recognised A Ahmud Ki's potential as protection against the King's Law. The man was devious, shrewd, and clever, and A Ahmud Ki admired that. 'One more time,' a deep voice rasped, as a hand gripped his shoulder. A sharp blade pressed against his neck. 'Who are you? Where do you come from? Why are you here?'

A Ahmud Ki repeated his fabrication. 'I am Jonn of Targa,' he explained. 'I am an emissary from the Aldermen sent to speak with the King. I don't know how I came to be here. My master, Lord Carwold, cast a passage spell on me and I appeared in the cave. I couldn't help it. I don't know where I am. Where am I?' He modulated his voice carefully, simulating fear, a touch of confusion, and a suggestion of confidence, as if he was trying to bluff his interrogators with artificial courage.

'And where is your Lord now?'

'I don't know. Still in his Keep I guess.' His invisible interrogator released his shoulder.

'It's not enough,' another voice asserted. 'Since when has Targa showed interest in the Kingdom?'

'Emissaries have been sent before,' someone responded.

'It's too uncanny,' argued a third. 'He appears in the Deep Cave in a blaze of light. The chances of anyone accidentally appearing there, even by this so-called magic, are too remote. I say it's deliberate. And that makes him dangerous!'

'But how could anyone deliberately appear in the Deep Cave?'

'There's a traitor among us,' a voice scowled. Protests and curses exploded, and A Ahmud Ki felt the surge of animosity towards him.

'Enough!' snarled Orrin the Guild Master. 'I've come to a decision.' Silence followed his statement. 'But first, I'll speak to this one, alone. Go.' Mutterings and shuffling steps receded. A door closed behind A Ahmud Ki. 'Your neck is as good as cut, my friend,' Orrin said quietly. 'However you came to be in the Deep Cave, the fact is you know it exists, and for anyone outside the Guild to know that is death.' Orrin paused to let the gravity the situation pass to his captive.

A Ahmud Ki found a different message in the man's mind.

He wasn't going to kill him, but he was concerned other Guild members might defy his order. He needed a guarantee from his captive, something impressive, to gain the support of his men, but he hadn't tumbled to an idea. A Ahmud Ki would give him one. 'I will confess to you something more than I would tell your underlings,' A Ahmud Ki said. 'I have not lied about how I came to be here. I really don't know where I am. But I'm not an emissary of Targa. I have come to take my place as the right hand of your King. I have come to be his Advisor.' A Ahmud Ki refocused on the man's mind and watched confused comprehension take shape. Orrin had what he wanted – a powerful tool; a person close to the King he could manipulate. 'Your men are right,' A Ahmud Ki continued. 'If you kill me, your secrets will be safe, because no one will know where I went. But, if you let me live, I will be more than grateful for your mercy, and I swear I'll keep the secret to myself. I have nothing to gain from revealing it. Besides, I have no idea where I am, and if I'm kept blindfolded, until your men release me, I still won't know where I have been.' Orrin maintained silence, so A Ahmud Ki explored his thoughts. The Guild Master was almost convinced. Almost. There was still doubt, uncertainty. He recalled Lady Corinna's lesson. 'If you doubt my word, you needn't. I owe no loyalty to your King. I am Targan first. My position with him is purely political, for my own gain. Besides,' he added, 'in my land, when a man owes his life to another, it's called a blood bond, and it binds him to that loyalty above all others.' Impressive, A Ahmud Ki thought, as he finished fabricating his speech. He gave Orrin everything the man needed to feel confident about letting his captive live. He awaited the man's response.

Orrin removed A Ahmud Ki's blindfold, and A Ahmud Ki stared directly into the face of a man in his forties – a weathered face, with a broad nose, broken many times, and dark beady eyes set in deep sockets. It was an intelligent face, lined with weariness that mocked the strength in the man's voice. The eyes sharpened. 'Remember this, Jonn of Targa. You have looked upon the face of the Guild Master of

Thieves. This face holds your life. In every corner, in every dark night, in every smoky tavern, in every room of the King's palace there is a knife waiting to slit your throat. The Hand of the Guild is everywhere, and I will see and hear everything you do and say. Tonight, I give you your life as a favour because it is no longer your own. Cross me, or the Guild, fail to serve us when we call upon your service, and that favour is withdrawn.'

For a moment, A Ahmud Ki felt real fear creep through his nerves. Orrin held a very different kind of power – the power of a man controlling men. It was not magical, but raw, brute force: power over living and dying, the most primitive and basic power one man can hold over others. Orrin was a real danger. But A Ahmud Ki reined in his fear, letting only a mask of it remain in his eyes to convince Orrin his threat was effective.

Orrin replaced the blindfold. A Ahmud Ki heard him go to the door, open it, and whisper an instruction. The others came back into the room. Orrin waited for the noise of arrival to subside, before he announced, 'This one has the Oath of Death on him. Take him to the palace gates. Spread the word.' A Ahmud Ki heard arguing and muttering under breaths, most cursing the Guild Master for being a fool.

Hands grasped his arms, and he was forcibly conveyed from the room. He was half-carried, half-dragged through a maze of corridors and rooms, up and down steps, and through doors that slammed shut behind. Noises rose and fell. One large room was full of smoke and song and voices, and the pungent smell of wine. Another was equally as smoky, but the murmuring voices stopped as they passed, and resumed when they left. Children's laughter assaulted his ears in one corridor. Finally, he was hoisted roughly up, by rope, which cut under his armpits, and the sound of running water reached him. He smelt fresh horse manure and hay. The air was cold. His captors changed because he felt a difference in the strength of their hands. Someone steered him, and he felt cobblestone beneath his feet. They prodded and pushed and pulled him in different directions, for a short while, and carousing voices rose and fell in the distance. Then he was falling forward. Feet ran swiftly away.

He stayed still, listening to muffled sounds, until he was certain he was alone. Time to release myself, he decided. He began to cast a spell to serve his purpose, when he heard light, wary footsteps. He froze. They approached stealthily. He tensed, ready to react. Hands reached for his bound feet and arms, unknotting the ropes. His blindfold was slid off. Two dirty urchins, human children not yet ten years old, grinned at him. 'We's been told you might be looking for a guide to the palace,' said the taller one, in a girlish voice.

Thirty Seven

'Your Most Royal Highness, there is a stranger to see you.'

Great King Thana peered down from the majestic splendour of his golden throne at the stick insect figure of Lord Rheims. His Chancellor waited, head respectfully bowed, at the foot of the fifteen silver steps leading to the throne platform. Rheims is an insect, he considered, a pest annoying me with trifling requests. Thana looked disdainfully at his Chancellor's ill-fitting grey robes and golden chains that seemed to weigh the thin man down. 'Tell him to go away,' the Great King replied and pouted. 'We are being entertained.' Thana clapped his hands, and returned his bored gaze to the western stage, a flat area designed for dancing, feasting or fighting, depending on the Great King's mood. Two naked, athletic warriors emerged from behind purple drapes, muscled bodies glistening with oils.

'My Most Gracious King, the visitor is terribly insistent, and says he will not leave until he has seen Your Majesty.'

Thana shuffled his portly frame, in his throne, to present as much of his back to Rheims as possible, without tipping out. 'Rheims you are a boring little insect. Do not presume to bore Us any further.'

'Perhaps I could provide Your Highness with better entertainment.'

The intruding voice made Thana shift his weight to stare down at the base of the steps. Mouth agape, Lord Rheims was staring at a tall, motionless figure in silver and black robes. 'Who is this?' Thana grumbled.

Rheims stumbled for a reply. 'My most Royal Liege I-'

'I am A Ahmud Ki,' the stranger announced, and eased back the cowl of his cloak to reveal handsome Aelendyell features and long silver locks. As he did, guards moved forward from the edges of the Throne Room. A Ahmud Ki saw them at the periphery of his vision, and was pleased, because their presence would make his performance more impressive.

'Seize the nuisance!' Thana ordered. The guards lowered their flagged spear points and closed in.

A Ahmud Ki incanted a spell. 'If you want me gentlemen, I'm here.' The guards halted, and stared up at the throne, where A Ahmud Ki stood beside the Great King. Thana jumped with fright, and the Royal Personage tumbled ignominiously from his throne to land in a piled disorder of black, green, purple and scarlet robes at A Ahmud Ki's feet. The wizard extended his hand. 'My most humble pardon, Your Majesty,' said A Ahmud Ki with an apologetic smile, 'but I thought it would be less hazardous for my health if I was up here, rather than down there.'

Thana refused the proffered hand. He wheezed and heaved himself back onto his golden throne and tried to regain his composure. He considered ordering his guards to execute the man who was the source of his embarrassment, but he dismissed that thought when he stared into the half-Aelendyell's eyes, and measured the proximity of the wizard to his own person. 'Who do you think you are?' the Great King demanded.

'I am A Ahmud Ki, Your Highness,' A Ahmud Ki replied, with a slight bow of his head.

'Yes, but where do you come from?'

'My origins and purpose here are not for common ears, Most Royal Sir.' A Ahmud Ki cast a sideways glance at Rheims and the guards at the foot of the throne steps.

Thana looked down uneasily. 'We cannot dismiss the Royal Guard. How can We trust you alone?'

A Ahmud Ki leaned forward with a sly grin. 'Because,' he said softly, 'if I was going to kill Your Royal Self, you would already be dead.'

Thana recoiled, eyes bulging with fear. His Royal Guards were not far away, but obviously too far to stop this lunatic. What choice did he have? 'Very well, we will dismiss Our Guard – if We have your word that no harm will come to Us,' said Thana said, with as much authority as his terror of the intruder allowed.

A Ahmud Ki smiled benignly. 'You have my word.'

Thana raised himself from the throne and lifted his sceptre. 'We wish to hold audience with the stranger in private. You are dismissed, until We recall you.' The Royal Guard withdrew through a series of small doorways along the Throne Room wall, the warriors Thana requested for entertainment slipped thankfully behind the curtains, and only Lord Rheims remained. Thana glared down at him. 'Yes, insect?'

'Begging My Royal Lord's pardon, but is it wise to remain alone with this man, whom you do not even know?'

'Rheims!' bellowed the Great King. The thin Chancellor turned and scuttled out of the Throne Room, leaving Thana and A Ahmud Ki on the throne platform. Thana eyed the tall stranger cautiously, noting his confident bearing, feeling the fluid threat of his presence. 'We see you have Aelendyell blood in your lineage.'

A Ahmud Ki winced inwardly. 'You're very observant,' he acknowledged, hoping to dismiss the Great King's curiosity along that line.

'We are curious as to why that is so,' Thana persisted.

'It is a long and complicated story, not worthy of the Great King's ear. I am not Aelendyell, nor do I hold any love for the Aelendyell people,' A Ahmud Ki bluntly stated, but he noticed surprise in Thana's eyes. There were thoughts inside the man's head he might do well to peer into, but Mind spells were difficult to conjure and maintain in conversation. Words and thoughts became confused and coalesced into meaningless noise. 'I come from Targa,' A Ahmud Ki said. He had toyed with telling Thana he came from the Ranu Ka Shehaala, the Land of Barbarians as Seralinna called it, but he knew nothing of the political ties between this king and Shehaal. He did know the High Council of Targa held all neighbouring Kingdoms in contempt, so there was little risk Thana had any informed contact with Tarnyss, or her minions. Besides, Tarnyss was certainly dead, possibly along with all the High Council, after the Dragonlord's release. He could weave any story at all from the ruins of Targa.

'We know of this land. We thought only women were emissaries, and wielders of magic there.'

'As your eyes show you, not only the women hold power.'

'So We see. What is your purpose in so rudely coming into Our Kingdom?' Thana asked, endeavouring to restore his eminence. He was, after all, Thana, Great King of Thana, thirty-seventh descendant of King Aian Abreotan, Holder of the Dragon Sceptre, and Inheritor of All Lands. He was, after all, talking with a mere sorcerer, a wizard from a disjointed foreign state run by women. This stranger had to respect his status.

'I've come to serve as your advisor, Most Royal King. The High Council sends me to serve you.'

A Ahmud Ki's reply appealed to Thana's dignity. This is more like it, he mused smugly.

'If Your Highness will permit, I must now go into a trance. I bear a message from the High Council that was burned into my unconscious state, so that I would neither forget nor understand it entirely.' A Ahmud cleared all sign of emotion from his face, opened his eyes wide, and stared at Thana, a stare that so unnerved the Great King he almost shouted for his Royal Guard. A Ahmud Ki uttered from deep within his throat, 'Met Shehaal Kis! Ka Tarnyss akis n'tel jinn nyaru! Sek feran yaseem!' His form blurred, and sharpened into an image of Lady Tarnyss, glaring with disdain at Thana. Thana stepped back, alarmed.

'I am Lady Tarnyss, President of the High Council of Targa,' a strong woman's voice announced. 'I send not greetings to King Thana but a grave warning. A terrible power has been released into the world, a Dragonlord, capable of destroying everyone and everything in its path. It must be opposed and defeated. I send you this messenger, A Ahmud Ki, as the one user of magic who can protect you and your Kingdom from this menace. He will advise and aid you. I request that you provide him with all he needs, for the Dragonlord will seek vengeance on all who trapped him beneath the earth. By the time you receive this warning, I will have perished at the hands of the Dragonlord.' Lady Tarnyss' form blurred and became A Ahmud Ki again, staring blank-faced at the Great King.

A Ahmud Ki watched his deception work its fingers into Thana's mind. The Great King was sweating with fear, and A Ahmud Ki wondered how such a fat, simple fool could hold absolute power over a Kingdom. Corinna's lesson on politics rang truer the more he saw of the world. Shehaal was the only genuine ruler A Ahmud Ki had seen, because he held his position through intelligence, charisma, and genuine physical and magical strength. But even he was limited by his responsibilities as Leiksha of the Ranu Ka Shehaala. He could not afford to become too powerful, nor let anyone else rise near his level of power. Politics! Real power, the power he glimpsed in the Dragonlord, breaks free of political bonds. Real power is limitless.

Thana remained rooted to the spot, confused. Did I really see and hear what appeared? A Dragonlord released? Impossible. My ancestor slew them all. Hadn't the great flaming sword severed their heads from their black necks? He knew the history. Everyone knew the history. But this messenger said a Dragonlord was released. Lady Tarnyss of Targa was already dead. The monster was released, seeking revenge. And he, Great King Thana, was the forty-seventh descendant of Aian Abreotan who had slain the Dragonlords! 'Do you know anything about the message?'

'In part,' A Ahmud Ki answered.

'Is it true that the Dragonlord was released?' Thana hoped it was an elaborate lie, a political ruse. It had to be a lie.

'I saw it happen. I was there.'

Thana collapsed into his throne. The nightmare was real. He covered his face with his pudgy hands, jewel-bedecked rings sparkling on his fingers. He was King. He was Abreotan's descendant. The Dragonlord was his responsibility. He lifted his hands from his face and looked up at A Ahmud Ki. 'Is it true you possess the magical strength to defeat the Dragonlord?'

'Not quite yet, Your Majesty. But, given time, I will. All I require is your permission to create a sanctuary here, and the freedom to work as I wish. In return, I will advise Your Highness on the best plans to keep your Kingdom secure from the Dragonlord's threat.'

'And if I refuse your offer?'

A Ahmud Ki refrained from smiling at the Great King's naiveté, as he said, 'Then I will leave you to save yourself, and your people, as best as you can, when the Dragonlord comes.'

Thana winced. This emissary had trapped him. With lies? How can I tell? If the Dragonlord comes seeking Aian Abreotan's inheritors, bent on revenge, how can I fight such angry might? What will I lose by taking on this Targan advisor? What will I lose if I don't? A Kingdom? He'd heard prophecies of The Return, a time when the Dragonlords would again battle for supremacy over the Land. Is this The Return? Now? Why in my reign? Why couldn't it wait?

'Shall I stay, or leave, Your Majesty?'

Thana opened his eyes. The Targan emissary was waiting. Should he ask him to wait? Would he wait?

'Your Majesty?' A Ahmud Ki asked again.

The King sighed with reluctant resignation. 'Stay. I – We appoint you Royal Advisor. You are ordered to attend Our Royal Person at any time We request, and it is Our understanding that your magical powers are at Our disposal. Are We understood?'

A Ahmud Ki responded with a faint bow. 'At your Royal command, Your Highness,' he said, and smiled.

He came face to face with the Aelendyell in the long corridor from the Throne Room to the Great Meeting Hall. A Ahmud Ki pulled the cowl of his robe over his head, before leaving the Great King, which hid his features and shock of recognition when he saw familiar eyes and hair, and green robes approaching. He hadn't seen an Aelendyell since his escape from the hated forest into the wider world, years past, and he felt a twisted mixture of enmity and belonging stir. He turned his head, hoping to pass unnoticed, but his attendant tugged his sleeve.

'Advisor? Permit me to introduce Lord Laeowyth, the Aelendyell Representative on The King's Table. Lord Laeowyth, this is Great King Thana's new Advisor from Targa.'

A Ahmud Ki bowed his head, without looking directly at the Aelendyell. What magic does this one possess, he wondered? How many Aelendyell are in this palace, or in this city?

'Greetings Advisor,' the Aelendyell said politely. A Ahmud Ki reached out with a spell, touched the Aelendyell's mind, and found a consciousness waiting. Who are you to enter my thoughts so rudely?

I know what you are, who you are. And I hate you, A Ahmud Ki projected, before he broke contact and urged his attendant on, leaving the astonished Aelendyell dumbfounded, staring after the figure in black.

A Ahmud Ki was angry for acting impulsively. There was no point being rude to the Aelendyell Lord. Aelendyell curiosity would have caused their paths to cross eventually, but his capricious intrusion into the Representative's thoughts might have jeopardized his security because, if the Aelendyell Elders learned where he was, they would call upon their ancient laws to have him pay for murdering an Elder. Years of exile would not have erased his guilt from their memories. Aelendyell justice would pursue him throughout his lifetime. He had to choose a course of action, and it had to be swift.

'Lord Laeowyth has arrived,' Pak, his room attendant, announced.

'Show him in,' A Ahmud Ki instructed, while he moved to the centre of his room to admire his day's handiwork. The materials Pak gathered were the finest quality, better than the obsidian and ebony the Targan sorceresses used to build their portals, and he'd mastered the portal creation through Seralinna's help. It was perfect. He raised his hands, pointed at the black poles rising from the floor, and cried, 'Haeraeni!' Blue static flashed, and a Targan portal shimmered into life.

'Lord Advisor?' A Ahmud Ki turned to Pak and his guest.

Lord Laeowyth smiled, and he bowed politely. 'I came as soon as I was able, Lord Advisor.'

'Thank you, Pak,' A Ahmud Ki replied. 'I wish to speak with Lord Laeowyth, alone.' Pak bowed, and obediently withdrew. A Ahmud Ki advanced towards Laeowyth and lifted his cowl. 'Surprised?' A Ahmud Ki asked in Aelendyell, as he straightened his long silver locks.

'Somewhat,' replied Laeowyth. 'Who exactly are you?'

A Ahmud Ki grinned. 'Good question. Which answer would you prefer? Advisor to the Great King of Thana? Wizard of Targa? Ithosen of the Ranu Ka Shehaala? Perhaps Aelendyell bastard?' Laeowyth raised his eyebrows at the last comment. 'Yes, I am part Aelendyell, part of that proud race of people you represent.'

'That clearly offends you,' said Laeowyth calmly.

'It offends me,' A Ahmud Ki replied.

Laeowyth saw fires of hate burning in the Advisor's eyes, and he felt pity for a being so consumed. 'Be that as it may, I'm not here to be a target for your anger, whoever you are,' he said diplomatically. 'If that is all, I'd prefer to go about my business, with your permission.'

A Ahmud Ki acquiesced. 'No. No, that's not it at all,' he said. 'I'm sorry, but there's much in my past I want to change. I want to change it from today. I couldn't help passing my angry thought to you in the corridor, this morning. That's why I summoned you. I want to apologize. And not just to you. I haven't seen an Aelendyell for years. I've been isolated from my people for too long. I've let anger drive me too far from home. I want to start the journey back.' As he finished, he turned away, apparently to hide his grief.

The passionate confession touched Laeowyth's heart because he heard the cry of a lost Aelendyell spirit and instinctively wanted to help one of his kind. He placed both hands on A Ahmud Ki's taller shoulders in a gesture of understanding and love, and said, 'I am your brother. If you have lost your way, I will help you find it again.'

A Ahmud Ki heard the Aelendyell proverb and smiled. His victim's compassion for his apparent distress made the whole act more satisfying. He glanced at the blue portal. No Aelendyell could resist a fascinating form of magic. His guest would be no exception: a shame, really, because he had deliberately constructed a one-way portal, with no destination point. As he turned to Laeowyth, his face again solemn, he contemplated where the pathetic Aelendyell Representative to Great King Thana would be likely to wake the following day – if he woke at all.

Thirty Eight

Lord Laeowyth's disappearance caused consternation in the Palace for several days. The last person to see him, the Castle Gatekeeper, said the Lord left the Castle not long after he visited the new Royal Advisor. He had mumbled something about important business in the city that would keep him away for a time. No one had seen him since. The Gatekeeper never mentioned it to anyone, seeing no connection between the incidents, but later, that evening, he admitted the Royal Advisor to the Castle, although he couldn't remember allowing him to leave earlier that day.

A Ahmud Ki remained in his chamber, attended only by his servant Pak. He asked for writing implements and vellum, and spent a long time at his desk scribbling, recreating page after page of manuscripts and tomes he'd memorized and studied over the years. He ordered Pak to fetch particular crystals, and polished stones and gems, which the latter procured from the Great King's Treasury, after much argument with attendants there, under the false assurance the new Royal Advisor had the Great King's freedom of the Palace and he was to be unquestionably provided with everything he requested. Despite being immersed in his recording and experimentation, A Ahmud Ki noted his attendant's eager endeavour to serve and please, and he made time to commend the man. A reliable assistant is worth a thousand friends, he mused, and he needed a reliable servant in this new land.

A Ahmud Ki's arrival and news made Thana restless. His dreams became nightmares of Dragonlords plunging serrated lances through his heart. In every nightmare, he stood on a vast plain, alone, naked, staring at a dark wall of warriors marching towards him, chanting 'Death to Thana! Death to the Great King!' The army would melt into the fearsome form of a Dragonlord, charging on a black horse, twice the size of a Haardrishii warhorse, and the Dragonlord tore away his visor, revealing a skeletal maw, grinning with delight, as his lance pierced Thana's vulnerable, bare skin. When a week had passed, and he could no longer endure the nightmares or the mysterious absence of Lord Laeowyth, he ordered Rheims to assemble The King's Table.

Nine Lords were members of The King's Table. A Ahmud Ki and Great King Thana made the company eleven. They met in a spacious, but windowless, room adjoining the Palace Throne Room. Two doors opened into it. A double door led from the Throne Room, and the Lords entered The King's Table through this entrance. The Great King entered through the second door, a door of beaten gold that led to his Private Chambers. Two hearths were set in adjacent walls, so that, in winter, roaring fires would warm the gatherers. A large, rectangular table stood at the centre, hand carved from dark oak wood, and lined by fourteen high backed, oak wood chairs. At its head, closest to the King's door, was a gilt chair, padded with black material that had a dark green griffin motif woven into it. Ancient weapons and Royal armour, along with tapestries and paintings, mostly depicting the exploits of King Aian Abreotan in his war against the Dragonlord, decorated the walls.

Thana winced when he looked at the pictures. They'd dominated his childhood memories: a Warrior King, full of honour and courage, battling a fearsome foe, starting a new Kingdom. He revered his Royal ancestor, and many of his play fights involved Thana the Dragonslayer rescuing his people from the tyrannical grasp of a hundredfold Dragonlords. Now he cringed with the fear that his childhood fantasies were becoming adult possibility. He surveyed the gathering, and asked, 'Where is Lord Laeowyth?'

Lord Rheims bowed his head politely before answering the speaker. 'No one is certain, my Liege.'

'It's not like Lord Laeowyth to be late to the Great King's Table,' asserted a white-haired individual, in white robes, sitting at Thana's right hand.

'We are most disappointed indeed!' Thana pronounced,

indignantly. 'We have need of Lord Laeowyth's counsel on this issue. His people may know something Our people do not. Now We must proceed without that knowledge.'

'Perhaps,' the white-haired man suggested quietly, 'perhaps it would be wiser for us to wait until Lord Laeowyth returns, Your Majesty.' A Ahmud Ki spied a potential threat in the white-haired man's familiarity with Thana.

Thana coughed to demand attention. 'If it would please your Lordships to come to order,' said Rheims.

'I want to know who this new Advisor is,' a burly, full bearded man asked, from the end of the table.

'I am A Ahmud Ki,' A Ahmud Ki responded.

Thana coughed again, louder. 'Gentlemen, please. His Royal Highness orders you to attend to His wishes,' said Rheims with greater authority. When the Lords were silent, he introduced A Ahmud Ki, and each Lord, in turn, was introduced to him.

To A Ahmud Ki's left sat Lord Eustice, responsible for trade and monetary affairs of the Kingdom. Like Thana, he was fat, unused to rigour or work. He was also balding on top, and subdued, and A Ahmud Ki assessed him as a man who'd never take political risks. He would always be the Great King's man.

Next was Lord Nisus. Dressed in black, black, cropped hair, he was lean and athletic. Nisus led the Great King's Personal Bodyguard and the Royal Assassins. The nature of his responsibilities probably made him very loyal to Thana, A Ahmud Ki decided; too loyal, perhaps.

Beyond Nisus sat Lord Gerran. His was an alert, boyish face with twinkling blue eyes. Gerran was responsible for Royal and City entertainment, and Ahmud Ki saw little to concern him.

Then there was the burly soldier, Lord Dominic, who already challenged A Ahmud Ki's presence. A Ahmud Ki examined him closely, and realized the man, despite his apparent physical strength, was quite old. Not that it made him less dangerous. He was responsible for training an elite force of King's warriors called Haardrishii and A Ahmud Ki knew it was essential he learn more about this elite force.

High Lord Haephus was introduced next. He wore fine orange and red robes and was High Priest of the city's religious sect of the city: the Priests of Teka. A Ahmud Ki recognised the style of the Ithosen in Haephus' clean-shaven face, and wondered how much magic a Priest of Teka could summon. The Ithosen of the Ranu Ka Shehaala held significant political power in that land, but they were kept in check by Shehaal's charismatic leadership. What political influence did the Great King's priests have?

When Lord Kerry, who handled the Kingdom's foreign affairs as well as internal disputes between different races of people, was introduced, A Ahmud Ki thought he detected the faintest mark of Aelendyell heritage around the man's eyes, though it was obvious the heritage was ancient. Kerry could know more about Targa than A Ahmud Ki would like a person at the table to know. He would watch Kerry closely. The success of his ruse might rest on this Lord's knowledge.

Two Lords remained. High Lord Mara was the Great King's military general in control of the securities of the Kingdom's borders, and in time of war he called together and controlled the Great King's Armies. Mara was a key to A Ahmud Ki's plan. The last, the man with the halo of white hair and white robes sitting at Thana's right, was introduced as Lord Waeron Ardath, the Royal Drycraefter. Rheims added no further explanation of Ardath's role, a point A Ahmud Ki noted carefully, because he sensed power in the man's presence, the quiet confidence of a practitioner of magic. Was Ardath the Great King's secret strength?

As Rheims finished his introductions, Thana stood at the head of the table. He wasn't tall. Apart from his excessive weight, he failed to cast an imposing figure. A Ahmud Ki had difficulty accepting the supreme importance of a man so facile.

'Hear and know why We have summoned The King's Table, and why We have appointed a new Advisor,' Thana began. 'A Dragonlord is loose again in the world. This We have been told by our new Advisor. If his word is true, and the sorceresses of Targa have so meddled with the Ancient Dark Ones, then We must prepare our Kingdom accordingly. Each of you will bear a task. Lord Mara will summon the Great Armies from the people of Thana. We order a full representation from every village and town. Lord Dominic will instruct the Haardrishii to enforce Our Law in this summoning of the Great Armies. Lord Kerry will instruct Our emissaries to Andros, Targa, and the Barbarian peoples of the West, to gather what he can from these lands regards their understanding of the threat and their preparation for it. He will also negotiate with the Shaddite King on Our behalf. Lord Laeowyth, when he returns, will speak with the Aelendyell Councils and gain their aid in Our cause. Lord Eustice will redirect the profits of mercantile business for Our general preparation for war. High Lord Haephus must seek divinations from Holy Teka to guide Us in Our choices.'

The Great King paused. Lord Rheims spoke. 'My Liege awaits your questions.'

High Lord Mara shifted in his seat. 'Are we certain there will be war?'

Everyone focussed on A Ahmud Ki. He looked to Thana for approval. The Great King nodded, his chin wobbling. 'I saw the Dragonlord released,' A Ahmud Ki explained. 'A creature of such immense power would want nothing less than everything. There can only be war.' Lord Mara nodded approvingly. High Lord of the Great King's Armies for twelve years, in that time there were no wars of significance, only minor border scuffles, and a handful of peasant insurrections in the southwest. He was bored. A war would prove his right to be High Lord.

'Your Highness, begging your pardon, but the merchants and traders in Port won't take kindly to losing their profits to the Royal Treasury,' Eustice argued politely.

Thana banged his chubby fist on the table, and A Ahmud Ki was mildly surprised by the Great King's outburst of temper. 'They'll take even less kindly to losing their greedy heads if they choose to question Our authority! Remind them Our Kingdom comes first!'

357

'Please accept my apologies, My Liege. I'd only meant to pass on an observation,' said Lord Eustice, looking downcast.

'Are there further questions?' Rheims asked.

'Yes.' They all turned to Lord Dominic. The Lord of the Haardrishii was glaring fearlessly at Thana. 'Why is it my soldiers are treated as henchmen to beat unruly peasant boys into obeying the King's Law?'

'That is Our wish,' Thana replied.

'Then I do not like your wish,' the Lord bluntly responded.

Several gasps rose around the table. 'Lord Dominic!' Rheims chided.

'Don't patronize me, Rheims, you sycophant,' said Dominic. The coldness of iron crept into his voice. 'You treat the Haardrishii as though they are any soldier of the King's Armies, but you all choose to forget they are warriors with pride and discipline, each one worthy a thousand of Mara's petty soldiers, or Nisus' Assassins for that matter.' A Ahmud Ki saw Nisus stiffen in his chair at Dominic's slight. 'Haardrishii will not play policemen on the whim of a King's belief in an unknown stranger.'

'Lord Dominic!' Rheims yelled. 'You are at The King's Table!'

'I know damn well where I am!' said Dominic, pushing away from the table, and standing. 'I will not be responsible for deciding that Haardrishii will serve as whipping boys. Lord Mara has soldiers who can do menial jobs. Let them chastise uncooperative peasants. If this wish of the Great King remains after I've left, Dominic is no longer Lord of the Haardrishii. I will join the Council of the Elders.' He marched from the room, leaving the double doors open in his wake. A servant appeared briefly, and pulled the doors shut.

A Ahmud Ki was fascinated by the scene. He felt the antagonism in Lord Dominic's demeanour when they were introduced, but he hadn't suspected it to be anger directed at the Great King, if not at everyone else at The King's Table. He wanted to edge his way into a strong position with the Great King, and find ways to fragment the power of those around Thana to increase his own, but he hadn't expected to discover bitter rifts and rivalries already prying the Lords apart, so publicly, so soon.

'Always his precious Haardrishii,' grunted Nisus.

'Go after him, Mara, and bring the hot-headed old fool back,' said Rheims.

Mara shook his head. 'Not I. I'm tired of his arrogance. Let the Haardrishii do a soldier's work. If they have the iron discipline that he says they have, they'll do it more efficiently than soldiers anyway.'

'But they respect only Dominic,' chipped in Gerran. 'Bring him back.'

'No.' A Ahmud Ki seized an opportunity. 'No. Let him go. He's more dangerous to you all than you realize.'

'How?' asked the Great King.

'Against the Dragonlord you'll need unity, one strength. That's where the sorceresses of Targa failed. They were divided powers, each too concerned with their own greed to see the dangers they were tampering with. If you bring Dominic back, who's to say he won't use the loyalty of his Haardrishii against you for his own gain? What guarantees do you have that he won't walk out again, in the middle of a crisis? He will divide you against yourselves. Find another to replace him. Find one who is loyal, who won't question the orders of the Great King, who will do as he is told.' A Ahmud Ki had played his first card, and he waited, gauging the effect of his speech on his listeners.

'True enough,' Nisus agreed. 'Dominic is forever defending or promoting his beloved Haardrishii. I believe they hold stronger allegiance to him than to you, Your Royal Highness.'

Thana looked up at the tapestries. Abreotan was whirling his flaming sword as a dragon swept in towards him, its great ugly jaws spouting fire. The ancient King was tall, muscular, powerful, twice the man of any warrior near him. Thana was never that, except in his boyhood fantasies. He could never face a dragon. Not alone. Why was Dominic so unreliable?

A Ahmud Ki needed no mind spell to read the man's thoughts. Nisus' comment was working its poison unwittingly well. Or is Nisus merely furthering his own plans, A Ahmud Ki wondered?

'Well, I have a task,' said High Lord Mara. 'Does Your Highness require us further?'

Thana looked at his general. He was a man to be trusted. Mara would drive away his enemy. 'No. We have decided on Our plan of action. It will remain. If Lord Dominic will not obey Us, then We shall appoint another to his task. The King's Table is dismissed.'

Lord Dominic resigned. In his place the Great King appointed an unusual successor – a mercenary who served time in the Royal Assassins, according to the rumourmongers, although no one publicly suggested it to Lord Surdrok's face. It was generally believed he was promoted at Lord Nisus' behest, but gradually opinion divided, because the new Royal Advisor also favoured Dominic's successor. No one, but Thana, knew the truth when he proclaimed Surdrok Lord of the Haardrishii, three weeks after the eventful meeting of The King's Table. What was certain was that Dominic had fallen from the Great King's favour. Speculation beyond that was scandalous and dangerous.

Within weeks, reports arrived at the Palace that foreign mercenaries were infringing on the Kingdom's northern borders. Lord Kerry's emissaries to Uz Erhaag sent two letters warning that a change in attitude towards the Kingdom of Thana was rapidly occurring in that land. They recorded that Uz Erhaag's capital, Azikhaag, was filling with greater numbers of mercenaries, and fringe tribal warriors. A third letter arrived, hastily scribbled. In it, the emissaries said Azikhaag's Tribal Assembly was being forcibly disbanded. In a surprise coup, a new leader declared himself King of Uz Erhaag, and Overlord of All Lands and, miraculously, he succeeded in uniting the normally warring tribal elements and was using them against the Assembly. The emissaries said they were heading northwest from the city, with thousands of refugees, to escape the bloody factional fighting. After the third letter, the emissaries ceased correspondence.

Haagii mercenaries began plundering the northeast outlands of the Kingdom. It wasn't uncommon for Haagii mercenaries to make brief incursions over the northeast border, but by early winter, reports were widespread that Haagii warriors were moving in organized bands through the western plains, into the fertile Valley of Rivers, attacking travellers and shepherds, burning hamlets, and raiding larger villages.

Whatever else A Ahmud Ki's opponents thought of him, they conceded that his warnings of an attack on the Kingdom were plausible, though none took his tale seriously, of the destruction of the Targan High Council. Only Thana believed a resurrected Dragonlord threatened them, and his cold fear drove his passion against the invading Haagii. The Kingdom was placed under martial law, the Great King's order to assemble His Great Armies was dutifully instituted, and every warrior of age was summoned to the Plains of Ky. There, High Lord Mara, finally being fulfilled in his role, organized his professional soldiers to train raw conscripts in the strategies and discipline of army life. Not all were willing to comply with Thana's order. The Haardrishii, under Lord Surdrok, patrolled the Kingdom with silent, ruthless efficiency, to ensure every warrior obeyed the Great King's command; unquestionably. Slowly, steadily, the Kingdom of Thana shook off its peaceful lethargy and mobilized.

Less overt, but significant, changes were underway within the Palace. The new Advisor opened a school for mystics, under Great King Thana's sanction. The Royal Advisor invited young men to study magic under his tutelage. They swore an oath of austerity and obedience, shaved their heads, donned grey woollen gowns, and were given the name Apprentices. They were seldom seen outside the Palace.

Waeron Ardath questioned Rheims on Thana's wisdom, in giving the new Advisor unreserved freedom, but let the matter drop when Rheims responded he was obligated to pass Ardath's query onto the Great King. Instead, he withdrew quietly from the political stage to observe, and learn. He distrusted the Royal Advisor, because he knew the stranger with the Aelendyell features was lying behind his apparent truths.

One other change was notable. In the Castle's northern grounds, between the Palace Gardens and the outer wall, almost overnight, a black tower appeared. Great King Thana and his Lords came to marvel at the structure that seemed to have sprouted magically from the rocky plateau on which the Castle stood. The tower wall was rounded, smooth, glistening in the sunlight, without a visible joint line marring its perfection. No door. No windows. Like a black finger, it pointed at the heart of the turning sky, and the onlookers gazed with a mixture of wonder, envy, and dread.

"The world does not wait for us, nor does it owe us anything. It moves forward, and we can only choose to be carried with the current or drown fighting against it. It is better to let the current carry us, and hope that we are not pulled down."

excerpt from The King's Diaries in the reign of Great King Thana.

Thirty Nine

'How long?' Andra asked.

The old man shuffled his worn boot stubs and tugged at his straggly tuft of beard. 'Nigh on four days, come eventime. Isn't that so, Mart?'

His young scrawny companion nodded vigorously. 'Aye. Four days it were. An' there were much ado, an' a great many soldiers, an' banners, an' important ones there were,' the lad prattled in his excitement. 'Wi' their swords an' shields, an' armour an' horses, an' wagons full o' things too.'

'Aye, an' you would ha' gone, if you were of age, eh lad,' chuckled the old man.

'Aye, an' I would ha' too, to be soldierin' in such finery.'

'Aye lad, an' I'm sure you would,' added the elder. 'Be you a soldier, young man?' he asked, screwing up his rheumy eyes to slits, to take a sharper look at Andra.

'Yes,' Andra answered, but he was lost in confusing memories of a dark forest and amber light, and was only half-considering the old man's questions.

'Then you best hurry on, or you'll be missin' the fightin', lad. With so grand an army, there's sure to be a mucky battle or two. Aye, an' if I were a younger man, I wouldn't be here mindin' sheep, I wouldn't. 'Tis a long time since these arms held the pike for the King, but they'd be willin' I'm sure, if it were possible. But I'm an old man, an' I must tend sheep with a half-grown fool, eh Mart?' The gawky lad grinned, revealing a mouth with less than half the teeth remaining. 'You'd best get a goodly supply o' water, afore you follow yon army. Dragon Breath Plains is a cursed dry course to walk, an' there be no wat'rin' places twixt here an' there, where you be goin'. Mart, fetch yon empty water bag.' The old man pointed at a pack slung across his sagging mule, and the youth loped to the unfortunate beast. 'An' there's a spring hidden in them rocks, at th' base of yon hill, as near's

365

I remember. Fill the bag well, son, for I've little doubt you'll need every drop of it, I'm sure. An' luck be with you.' The lad handed a worn waterskin to Andra. Artega's tongue lolled out as the young shepherd scratched his ears. 'An' we must take our leave, my fine young friend, for yon sheep are a wand'rin' lot, an' it would please them greatly if the lad here, an' I, were tardy about our work, an', please our Masters, we're not.' The old man wagged his grey head, as if thinking of more to say, shrugged his shoulders, and turned to follow the lad and mule, ambling after the spreading herd of sheep. Andra picked up his pup, and watched their stick shadows dwindle across the landscape, before he headed north.

The route of the Great Armies cut a beacon through the spring grasses along the western spur of the Abreotan Ranges, so Andra followed the track to the edge of the Dragon Breath Plains. He searched among the rocks at the foot of the last hill, as the old shepherd advised, and found a tiny spring dribbling out of the earth. He filled the aged waterskin to capacity. He let Artega drink his fill, before he climbed to the top of the hill to look north, across the expanse of Dragon Breath Plains, and he beheld a wasteland unlike any he imagined.

The plains were flat and grey to the far northern horizon, and only at the edge of sight could he see variation: a dark smudge rising from the grey. To the west, a stark, jagged mountain range jutted out of the waste, forbidding its progress. To the east, again at the reach of his vision, he glimpsed a bright glitter of reflected light, as if from water. Perhaps it was a mirage, an illusion. From where he stood, the razor peaks of the Abreotan Ranges marched eastward, forming the southern border. The Dragon Breath Plains were desolate, except for twisted, bleached skeletons of long dead trees dotted tragically across the landscape, their bones mute warning to anyone foolhardy enough to venture there. What terrible forces met to form a place of such vast devastation and despair that all life should eternally shun it, Andra wondered? Into the desolation, the Great Armies had marched, his friends had marched: to face what? What could they hope to find alive out there? Perhaps his friends thought he was dead. He was lost in the forest for four days according to the shepherd's report. If so, he had no need to plunge headlong into this deadly grey world. He could walk away, find a village to call home, live there, and forget the war. But his friends were out there. He would reach them, if he could. It is The Way, he reminded himself. A Guardian has few choices. He took a final look at the alien landscape from the hilltop, and headed down onto the plains, followed by a dark shape bounding at his heels.

The Great Armies had entered Dragon Breath Plains on a broad front, leaving a churned highway of grey dust in their wake. Wagons had cut deep ruts into the flaky surface, and Andra guessed the grey dust would have formed one continuous, voluminous cloud as the Armies advanced. He scooped a handful of dust to examine, and discovered that it was powder-fine, deep, and lacking a trace of arable soil: a truly dead land. He couldn't afford to dawdle, so he picked up Artega by his scruff, thrust the pup into his pack, strapped his sword scabbard across his back, under the pack, to make running easier, and set off at a steady pace.

The Plains were not as flat as they appeared from the summit. Low dunes of grey dust rose erratically, and the path of the Great Armies constantly faltered and changed direction, meandering between longer and larger dunes. Most low dunes ran north to south, suggesting the bitterest prevailing winds swept in from the east because their eastern faces were concaved and windswept. Throughout the afternoon, Andra ran, tiring more rapidly than he wanted to tire, but the soft, broken surface worked against his calf muscles and wore him down. The afternoon sun leapt from cloud to cloud, and he was thankful the overcast sky protected him from the heat. A full summer sun would be merciless. When last light faded behind the western mountains, he sank into the dust, exhausted.

Continuing at night was impossible without light, and the moon was in its last phase, moving like a pale sliver of cat's eye through a cloud sea. The Plains melted into black sky.

Andra lit the lantern he kept from the forest and laid out small shares of rations for Artega and himself. The pup bounded about, pleased to be rid of the cramped confines of the pack. They shared water, and Andra relished washing the dust from his mouth and throat. He wondered if Alain, or someone, had kept his small tent and personal belongings when they broke camp. I could do with them now, he thought, instead of having to sleep in the cursed dust, but he was tired, and sleep would be a pleasure.

The dry scratching of Artega's tongue woke him. The morning sun was perched on the flat eastern horizon staring through a grey haze. Andra patted the pup's muzzle and poured him a handful of water that Artega lapped up enthusiastically. The drops that fell on the grey earth disappeared without trace. Would heavy rain do the same, he wondered? Or would the plains turn into a slithering, impassable quagmire of mud, as inhospitable as the dust in full summer? Andra drank, hitched his gear, and set out on the day's run.

The clouds deserted him, leaving the burning eye of the sun to beat down on him throughout the morning, and he was forced to stop several times to walk and take water. He passed a flattened area of dust he guessed served as the Great Armies' campsite at the end of the first day's march. Not long after that, he came upon a decomposing Haagii warrior, face down, hand clutching a torn water bag. He moved through a grove of bone white tree trunks, cracked and baked by heat, dust, and lack of water, feeling the eerie silence of a lifeless forest in a dead land. Later that afternoon, he hurried out of the way of a swirling dust vortex twisting its erratic path across the low dunes.

By the second evening, he clearly saw the source of the dark smudge on the northern horizon. A mountain wall reared out of the earth, and it ran, unbroken, from west to east. He stopped to rest, having pushed his body to the limit of its endurance, in difficult conditions, and he slipped into a deep sleep, oblivious to the dark world.

The third morning, he woke, aching from the bitter cold of the night, and the previous day's running, to a bright and hot day. After they ate and refreshed, Andra estimated the mountains to the north were at least a full day's running distance, assuming he could maintain a steady pace. Artega was restless and hungry, and tired of being cooped up in Andra's pack, so he decided to let the animal run as far, and as often, as he could manage. The two companions ran on, the pup gambolling, and stopping frequently to scratch and explore, the young warrior determined to make distance, despite the heat. There was no escaping the sun. No friendly patch of shade offered respite. They stumbled across carcasses of horses that had collapsed through exhaustion and been left to die. They found empty water bags, discarded as useless baggage on a forced march, and more bodies of Haagii warriors, dead at least a week. Artega skirted death, his tail between his legs, each time a corpse lay in their path, and Andra slowed his pace, picking up the pup as he grew tired. He drank more frequently from the waterskin, but took smaller amounts, since it was more than half empty. The mountains loomed blacker and larger, and they perched atop a mighty scarp, a cliff that formed an unbroken wall across the northern perimeter of Dragon Breath Plains. Dust whirlwinds spiralled on their mad journeys from nowhere to nowhere, but they passed safe distances from him, and he was glad. By nightfall, he could see fires burning atop the cliff, though they were far away, and of little comfort to him. He slumped into the dust, supported only by the knowledge that, if the fires were campfires of the Great Armies, as he hoped, he would reach them within half a day's running. Then he could rest properly.

He woke, frightened, and wet with perspiration, though he didn't know why. The last moonlight had been eaten by the shadow of the earth, but high in the sky he thought he heard

369

a keening, a shrill cry that sent a shiver down his spine, and made him clutch the hilt of his sword. It was a sound like one he heard before, deep in the forest beneath the Abreotan Mountains, and he listened intently. He soothed Artega's head, as the pup whimpered and buried his nose under Andra's arm, but there was no repeat of the cry, and the desert silence bore down on him. When he drifted to sleep, it was a fitful and cold sleep, full of dreams.

The fourth morning, he shared a piece of dried fruit with Artega, but the pup refused the offering. He took a measured sip from the almost empty waterskin and stared at the dry grey dust. The sun was ready to torment the desert world. He picked up the pup and began the cruel run.

Within a short time, he could see the base of the cliff wall, and after another burst he made out a long line of tents and huts near the base. He picked up pace, knowing he was reaching one part of the Great Armies. As he arrived at the camp, hot, tired, he stumbled to his knees at the feet of the soldiers who came to meet him, and gasped out his name, told a brief portion of his story, and waited, expecting to be offered a drink. No one moved. He fumbled for his waterskin, and eagerly drained the last mouthful. As he lowered the empty skin, aware of staring eyes, he asked, 'What's wrong?'

A soldier, a bald spear bearer, replied with another question. 'Was that the last of your water?'

'Yes. Yes, it was. I barely had enough.' They stared. Puzzled by their demeanour, he started to ask again what bothered them, but he was interrupted by a minor commotion behind the soldiers. A hulking figure, with a huge mane of fiery hair, strode into view.

'What have we here? One who comes back from the dead? This world is full of mysteries.'

Recognising the giant with the booming voice, Andra cried, 'Claarn!'

'Last time I looked, I was,' Claarn replied. He bent and easily lifted Andra into his arms. A yelp came from Andra's pack. 'What magic is this?' asked Claarn, in mock alarm. 'A pack that barks?'

'It's Artega,' Andra answered. 'Put me down. I'm a warrior, not a boy!'

'Warrior you may be, but you are exhausted. Besides, I need the exercise. You'll be carried, like it or not. Better than being dragged, which is your other choice,' the red giant warned, and laughed. Claarn wound through the maze of tents, huts and wagons, until he reached the Command huts. He put Andra down where a group of warriors, men and women, excitedly greeted him. Alain and Stephen pushed through the crowd.

'By The Vale! I had given you up as one who'd passed beyond the Twin Guardians of the Dead!' Stephen exclaimed.

'You're alive!' shouted Alain, joyfully. 'But how? What happened?'

Before Andra could answer, Claarn interrupted. 'In time, in time. You've a warrior's tale to tell, and we will listen to it. But tonight, at the fire. For now, you must rest and regain strength. The rest have duties to perform. His own will tend to him.' Claarn shepherded the warriors aside, except Alain and Stephen. As Andra watched the others depart, he glimpsed Marella smiling at him.

Stephen and Alain unpacked Andra's meagre pack, brought him a hide to rest on, and food, and a small bowl of water for Artega and he to share. Alain squatted beside him, but Stephen stood. 'I feared I was not to see you again,' Stephen said quietly. 'But this time it was not The Way, and I am glad. I cannot stay. Alain is excused to remain, but I must return to my post at High Lord Mara's command. At sunfall, I will return.' He smiled, and he vanished between the tents.

Alain fed Artega, the pup greedily gulping morsels of dried meat as his tail wagged appreciation. 'I see he hasn't learnt new manners crossing the desert,' laughed Alain, as he scuffed the pup's ears affectionately. 'It's good to see you. I didn't think I would. How did you return from the tree? We searched and searched, Derik and I, but we found no trace of you.'

Andra swallowed a mouthful of water, before replying, 'I know less than you. I remember running at the blue light, and then I woke at the base of the tree, with Artega asleep there, and a lantern. And this.' He held up his wrist for Alain's inspection.

The Guardian studied the bracelet. 'It fits perfectly. Does it come off?'

'No,' said Andra. 'It's as if it's part of my arm. I can't even move it. It seems to be fading into my skin.' He tried unsuccessfully to twist the bracelet.

'It passes understanding,' said Alain.

'And there's more,' Andra continued. 'When I came out of the forest, I learned from an old shepherd that you'd marched four days beforehand. I lost four days, and yet I wasn't thirsty or hungry.'

'Did you say we marched four days before you came out of the forest?'

'That's what the shepherd said.'

'Then you lost seven days.' Andra registered amazement as Alain explained. 'We didn't break camp for three days after you disappeared. We waited for High Lord Mara's Wheel to arrive from Anedya, and they were a day late. We spent much of that time searching for you.' Andra stared into his bowl and took a deep swallow. 'Drink,' urged Alain gently, 'but not too quickly. There's no water on this desert, and we've nearly used the little supplies we have left after crossing the grey wastelands. There are soldiers who have no water of their own to drink.'

Andra suddenly understood why the soldiers at the edge of camp had stared so oddly at him. 'Why don't you get more? There must be pools or springs at the top of the cliffs, or in the rocks at the base?'

'There might be, but we can't reach them. The Haagii stand between the water and us.'

'But I saw fires -' Realization struck Andra mid-question. 'The Haagii have you trapped on the edge of this forsaken plain?'

Alain nodded. 'They were waiting. An army sits at the bottom of the cliff to block our way up, and they're supplied with food and water by an army at the top who lowers supplies to them.'

'Aren't there other ways to the top?'

'None known. None that can be found within a day's march, east or west of this point. The cliffs of The Rim Shield are high. The road that winds up is ancient, carved from rock forged in great fires at the root of the Fire Mountains. Yesterday, we Runners were sent to find a way around the Haagii. There is none. Now the High Lord sits in council, with the Captains and Devis, deciding how to fight a battle the Haagii have made inevitable with their trap.' Alain took a breath and frowned. 'If we don't fight, we'll perish from thirst.'

Forty

Andra's first full view of The Rim Shield volcanic scarp filled him with awe. Sheer granite cliffs dominated the immediate landscape, smothered with basaltic encrustations that dropped in enormous columns to the grey volcanic dust of Dragon Breath Plains, and immense mountain peaks soared to dizzying heights above the cliff wall. He guessed The Rim Shield rose five hundred spans out of the desert and understood why it was an ancient barrier to warring parties from either north or south. He traced a persistent zigzag line, cut into the rock of the cliff face from top to bottom, representing the only visible access: a narrow road clinging to the wall. At the base, a short distance from where he was, a dark stain spread twice the width of the encampment frontage of the Great Armies. Ragged pennants hung listlessly atop tall poles. Hunched figures scuttled across the front of the mass of the Haagii army. Alain was right. Battle was inevitable. Their position was untenable. Retreat or withdrawal meant they would perish of thirst in the dust of Dragon Breath Plains. Advancing meant fighting an army twice their number and being exposed at the base of the cliff to attack from above. The steep, narrow, winding road up the cliff face suited skirmishing or fighting withdrawal, but not an attack by an army. Even with his limited experience, Andra saw there was little in their favour. The impending battle would be bloody and costly for every piece of land they gained.

'Not very promising, is it?' Andra turned to Derik O'Dale's tall, grey form and blond head. They embraced in a backslapping hug. 'Alain came to tell me you returned. Good news indeed!' Derik grinned, briefly but he became more serious. 'Did you see, or learn, anything of Marvin Bowmaker?'

'No,' Andra replied. 'Nothing.'

Both men stared respectfully across the space at the Haagii lines for a moment. Another voice broke into their thoughts. 'There's to be a meeting, my friends. High Lord Mara wishes you to attend him, Derik.' Ernest Fletcher clapped Andra on the shoulder. 'Well met, young Guardian! We need your fortune here, Andra of The Vale, but you may regret finding us,' he added wryly.

'I don't regret finding old friends,' Andra answered with a grin. 'Besides, you need all the help you can get against the Haagii. I want this war over.'

Activity increased in the Haagii lines. Throughout late afternoon, reinforcements wound down the cliff road to swell their ranks, and companies formed and moved to precise positions directly opposite the Great Armies. Derik's meeting with High Lord Mara was brief. When Andra next saw the Longbowman, he and his fellows were climbing raised wooden platforms, constructed from beams and planks. Small catapults were wheeled closer to the front ranks, and Devis organized their Spokes into battle readiness. Murdok emerged from the milling crowds and ordered the Runners to their feet. 'There'll be no running tonight. Prepare your armour. You will not be in the front ranks to repel the Haagii, but if they break through you must fight like soldiers of the Great King's Armies. High Lord Mara has decided we will defend our position this night, and tomorrow, early, we will move against the enemy. Don't waste water, or food. Now, to your task. Assemble here as soon as you've readied yourself.'

'Andra!' yelled Alain. 'Most of your armour is here.' He pushed a pile of leather and metal towards Andra.

A rattle of metal against metal was followed by a full-blooded curse from Emmett. 'Blast this bloody metal cage! I'll never get the hang of it! No wonder fish jump eagerly into my nets at home. It's because they have to live their lives bound in scale skins!'

The Runners laughed at Emmett's tall, lanky frame struggling into an ill-fitting breastplate. 'If the fish are as poorly made as you, fisherman, it's little wonder they don't become soldiers too!' Merry quipped.

Andra slipped his chest plate on and tightened the buckles, and Alain and he assisted each other with more difficult strapping. Andra's last act was to tether an unwilling Artega to his pack inside his tent. 'Better you stay here,' he crooned softly to the pup. 'Haagii may have more of a taste for you than you for them.'

Throughout the camp, men and women moved with deliberate haste, as the sun dipped towards the western peaks and shadows lengthened. When the light of day dissolved, leaving a blood red stain streaked across the western horizon, an eerie silence fell in the space between the two armies. From where they stood, the Runners could not see the Haagii lines assembled at the base of The Rim Shield because of the rows of warriors ahead of them, but dots of light, fires and torches, hundreds of them, sprang into life along the cliff verge, like fireflies swarming at dusk. Up there, Haagii warriors are probably watching the impending cataclysm, Andra thought, with the same fascination and fear I'm feeling. He touched his sword hilt, the sword his great-grandfather had wrought with a blade that refused to be stained with Haagii blood, and wondered why that was so. He recalled his father handing him the gift, and Anedra weeping silently.

'They come!' called a voice from a nearby wooden tower. Agonizing seconds passed. Abrupt shouts and deep-throated war cries reached Andra. He heard them answered by the bass thrumming of longbows high on the platforms, and screams rose amid the approaching battle yells. The noise morphed into the clatter of weapons against weapons joining battle among hundreds of voices.

'What's happening?' Alain called to a watcher on the closest tower.

'Hold your position!' Murdok growled.

The cacophony reached frenzy and Andra fought his overwhelming desire to rush through the waiting ranks and join the warriors clashing with Haagii on the front line. His companions' faces were searching the sea of sound for clues to the battle's progress, and they were nervously fingering their weapons in anticipation of a Haagii attack. The riot of arms evaporated. Loud cheering broke from the front line, carried rapidly back through the ranks. 'They run! The Haagii turned away!' yelled the watcher from his perch.

Andra felt relief and heard it echoed by those around him. He put his hand on Alain's shoulder. 'I've fought in one brief skirmish, but I'd rather fight a hundred such battles than be made to stand here like this and not know what is happening.'

Alain nodded, and smiled, but a sharp voice cut in from behind. 'One good battle, Andra of The Vale, and you'll wish otherwise.' Murdok handed him a torch. 'This is but the very beginning. You won't have long enough to wait -'

A shout from the watchtowers cut him short. 'They come again!'

Four times, the Haagii charged out of the darkness at the ranks of the Great King's warriors, and four times spears and swords, shield walls and arrows repelled them. The Haagii suffered staggering losses, but they cut successively deeper into the ranks of High Lord Mara's army, because night served them better than it did the Kingdom warriors. Fires crackled the entire length of the Great Armies' defensive lines in a desperate attempt to light the battlefield and reduce the odds in favour of the Haagii. The Runners waited. They heard the battle, saw wounded and the dead carried back through the ranks, but no one called for them. When it was certain the fourth attack was the Haagii's last for the night, the Runners sank to the grey dust, exhausted from the tension of waiting, and several, including Andra, drifted into restless sleep.

Someone vigorously shook him awake. Stephen. He picked up Artega, and stumbled out of the tent, into a world of yelling and fire. 'Watch the sky!' Stephen shouted. 'Warn us if the flaming missiles come this way!' Andra gazed into the night and saw two comets trace fiery paths through the darkness from the cliff top to the camp. They plummeted to earth near the western edge. Tents and huts and wagons were burning, and men and women scurried through the wild dancing light, frantically tossing dust over the fires. There was no water. The Haagii were smarter at planning a battle than the Great King's Generals had assumed, Andra grimly considered. Another flaming ball smashed into a nearby wagon.

For a long time, invisible catapults on The Rim Shield hurled fiery meteors into the heart of the Great Armies' camp. Twice, Andra warned those working nearest, as burning stones rained down. Many missiles landed ineffectually in grey dust, but enough struck flammable targets to keep the Great King's soldiers occupied with smothering flames threatening to engulf valuable equipment, and the missiles felled soldiers caught unawares by their fall.

As suddenly as it started, the bombardment ended, and people ran to quell the lingering flames. Andra remained at his post, waiting, watching The Rim Shield for further activity. Fires burned brightly along its edge, clear and strong enough to suggest the watchers did not intend to sleep. Stephen approached, saying, 'You have watched well, Andra. Thank you. Rest now.'

'Something's not right,' Andra said, without taking his eyes from the cliff top fires. 'They're not finished.'

'What makes you say that?' asked Stephen. 'What is it you can see?'

'The fires.'

'They burn every night. Haagii are night creatures.'

'Yes. But if they are night creatures, why do they need light all the time?'

'For warmth. It would be colder on The Rim Shield than here.'

'Perhaps,' Andra mumbled. 'But these Haagii are more organized than I ever thought they'd be. Haven't you noticed? They've planned everything with unusual care, better than High Lord Mara or his Devis anticipated. Or else why would we be caught here? Something's being planned up there right now, and not by the Haagii.' Andra heard a sound in the air. An instant later, he heard a thud and a scream. Shouts rose at the centre of the camp, and torches whirled in chaotic motion. Another cry of surprise came from the left, and figures dashed out of the darkness towards them.

'Rocks!' one man yelled. 'Rocks fall out of the sky!'

Something heavy thudded into the earth, directly behind them, and Andra span to see a boulder, an armspan wide, half buried in swirling dust. He grabbed Stephen's arm. 'Quick! Get the others out of the tents and out of the camp!' The Guardians woke the sleepers and ushered them towards the eastern perimeter. Confusion spread as massive rocks tumbled silently out of the darkness to crush whatever they struck. Warriors rushed in blind terror, while Devis and Trainers tried to contain the panic. The Runners escaped into the desert's dusty darkness, and precious time passed as people called to each other to draw their fugitive group together.

'No light!' someone shouted. 'Don't light anything.'

Andra stared at the campsite and heard cries and occasional screams, and figures appeared and disappeared, silhouetted against the campfires. He clutched the black squirming mass in his arms. 'Easy, Artega. You're a warrior. Be brave.'

'Here!' Murdok called. Andra trudged through the dust that tugged at his feet, until he could vaguely identify people. 'Who's that?' Murdok called.

'Andra.'

'Good. That's everyone, except Stephen,' said Murdok. Moments later, Stephen stumbled into the group. 'How does it go?' Murdok asked.

'Badly. But they are all leaving the camp. Rocks are still falling. It is not safe there,' Stephen informed them.

Andra heard Alain call his name, so he searched for his friend in the dark circle of Runners. 'Here. I'm here,' Alain half-whispered. The friends embraced.

Sleep was impossible in the shin-deep dust, and Andra was too cautious, too fearful of the Haagii crouched beneath the cliffs, to sleep. So, he stood with his companions on the Dragon Breath Plains, waiting silently for the first morning rays to paint pastel hues across the sky and eradicate the cold blanket of night.

When the dawn came, the warriors were forlornly strewn across a broad front, clustered in pockets, staring bleary-eyed at The Rim Shield. If the Haagii army attacked now, Andra knew they stood little chance, so fragmented and so broken in morale. Yet no attack came. Slowly, reluctantly, the clusters returned to the shattered campsite, where fire and stone had left their mark, regrouped, and searched the debris for salvageable gear, and the bodies of those slain by the silent rain of rocks. Several small catapults were damaged, three irreparably, and food stocks in one section of the camp were destroyed. Andra's tent was crushed beneath a sizeable boulder. He bent to rub Artega's ears, thankful he remembered to take the pup with him when Stephen first woke him.

By mid-morning, the Great Armies had reassembled, facing The Rim Shield, but the warriors were tired, and thirsty. Haagii corpses were scattered across the gap between the opposing armies, piled deeper before the front ranks where hand-to-hand fighting had taken place. The Kingdom's dead were carried to the rear, and one Spoke spent the morning burying bodies in the infertile desert. The Haagii waited. The invisible catapults beyond the edge of the cliff top were silent. Only the sun moved in its slow, tedious, hot path towards the zenith, and it glared with indifference on the two forces.

High Lord Mara rode to the front of the ranks, flanked by Captains Westbourne and Fennik. Riding in their wake were Claarn, Marella, and the warriors of Tressel Deep, and a group of grey robed Apprentices appeared, their bald pates shining in the sunlight. Orders rippled through the ranks to close, so Andra and the Runners shuffled forward to hear what the High Lord had to say. Mara wore full plate armour, gleaming beneath a yellow cloak, but his head was bare, and Andra saw a ragged piece of cloth wrapped across the High Lord's forehead, haphazardly proclaiming him a victim of the previous night's clash. The Apprentices gathered in a circle before him and synchronised an intricate pattern of finger movements that reminded Andra of the first time that he saw the Great King's Advisor. Magic: he knew what it was, now, though he was puzzled how he knew. He absent-mindedly fingered his bracelet as he watched the pattern completed and the Apprentices withdraw. Just as the Great King's voice had been amplified on the day they marched from the Great City, so now was High Lord Mara's. Even distant ranks to the sides and rear could clearly hear their leader, as though he stood beside them in normal conversation. Mara's tone was solemn, his voice firm, but Andra detected uncertainty in the voice, a fragment of the man's vulnerability.

'Warriors of the Kingdom,' Mara began, 'I greet you as brothers and sisters in arms. Before us stands the enemy, our enemy, and he has strength, an arrogance that goads us. You do not need to tell me we are caught in a trap, or that there is no going back. There is only going forward. Our water is gone. Our food is low. We stand on barren ground, exposed to fire from the cliffs. An army waits at the bottom. An army waits at the top. We can no more stay here than go back over the desert. Our enemy knows that. He intends to make us wait. Tonight, like last night, he will attack again. He wants to weaken us, break us, destroy us. But we will not give him that satisfaction. We can only go forward. There is no waiting, no going back, only going forward. We must go forward. And we will! Summon strength to your arms, and courage to your hearts! Make your weapon edges keen and hungry, like your bellies. Think upon your hate for this foe, this enemy that is your enemy. Think upon those he has already cruelly slain, whom you now must avenge. Think upon the greatness of the Kingdom for which you march, and to which you will return, wrapped in heroes' glory. Here you will become part of legend! After this day, your name will be sung through the generations, and your name will become one with Aian Abreotan, and Larsen Ironhand, around the fires, and in the long halls of warriors everywhere! Today you crush the enemy on the very doorstep of his homelands!' Mara drew his long sword from its scabbard, and every warrior followed suit, lifting his or her blade high to sparkle in the sun. Andra hefted his sword, its ancient runes carved by sunlight and shadow, and felt its weight pulling down, against his will. 'Death to the Haagii!' shouted the High Lord.

'Death to the Haagii!' chorused the warriors of the Great King's Armies, but Andra heard a hollow uncertainty in their response, echoing the masked sentiment in Mara's voice. It was, Andra realized, as if everyone knew they were doomed to fail.

Forty One

A Ahmud Ki stared at the opaque sphere resting on the pedestal at the centre of his Communication Room. His Apprentices were maintaining vigil over Thana's Great Armies, reporting their progress to him three times a day, and he received their first-hand knowledge through the crystal, before deciding what was relevant for the Great King to know. Power, he reminded himself, lies in the hands of those who controlled knowledge. The precious communication crystal he stole from Tarnyss was proving its value in the eight months since he became Royal Advisor to Great King Thana. High Lord Mara's forces fanned out through the Kingdom, when winter ended, and in a matter of weeks they were forcing the Haagii northward, back to their homelands. Reluctant as he was, to let Thana and his Lords know how easily the Great Armies were driving back the enemy, A Ahmud Ki kept them informed. Because his information was corroborated by messages couriered by pigeons, from the Wheels, and from High Lord Mara to the Great King, his standing with Thana grew. At least that is pleasing, he decided.

But something was wrong. He warned Thana that a Dragonlord was loose in the lands, and the Lords of The King's Table believed the Haagii were rallying under the Dragonlord in the northern lands of Uz Erhaag, yet the Haagii were retreating, as if afraid of the Great King's Armies. There was no strength, or defiance in their withdrawal, nothing to suggest their incursions into the Kingdom of Thana, even in large numbers, were more than organized raids on a larger scale; nothing suggested they were working under the direction of Mareg Dru'artha Sutnavanistra.

A Ahmud Ki descended to his Visiting Room. As his feet settled on the floor, he focussed on a prostrate figure, face down, awaiting him. 'Rise, Pak.'

'Thank you, Master,' Pak answered, and stood.

'Any news?' A Ahmud Ki asked, as he walked towards the stairs to the bottom level of the tower.

'Master, Lord Ardath requests an interview.'

'When?'

'As soon as possible, Master Ki.'

A Ahmud Ki paused to consider Pak's information. 'I have news for our Great King,' he said. 'Find Lord Ardath and bring him to the tower tonight. I'll speak with him then.'

A Ahmud Ki passed through the tower wall, into late afternoon light. He no longer needed a crystal to come and go from his new tower, because he'd made it an integral part of his fibre, sensitive to his touch and movement. He had perfected the Ithosen skill, transferring the magical energy of a crystal key required to enter a tower into an aura of personal presence he shared with the tower's magical creation. He could come and go as if there was no wall barring his passage. Pak emerged and scooped up the special amber crystal key A Ahmud Ki created for him, and trotted after his master.

They walked through the Royal Gardens. Thana's gardeners maintained a resplendent area of rich green plants, bright flowers, and an artificial babbling brook for the Great King's private retreat. Stone terraces, laced with hanging ferns, encircled the Gardens, and Thana had three caves built in the rock terraces for secluded excursions with suitable young ladies of his court. A Ahmud Ki always found the caves amusing. In eight months, he had never observed Thana in the gardens. Maidens did not offer themselves to the Great King because he was fat, unattractive, and too shy to force his royal pleasure on an unwilling victim. His circumscribed desires reinforced A Ahmud Ki's perception the man was an inept, weak ruler. The Dragonlord would crush Thana with one meagre blow, if ever they should meet.

Inside the Palace, as Pak scurried off to find Lord Ardath, A Ahmud Ki smiled. Pak was useful. He was intelligent. He understood power in a basic, but clear way. He knew his adopted master was more than a mere Advisor, and knew it was better to serve power than be its victim. A Ahmud Ki wondered if Pak had hopes of gaining power. Perhaps. He was faithful, reliable, and consistent. One day, he would have to die for the same reasons. Sad, thought A Ahmud Ki briefly. Sad.

Thana was waiting on his throne when A Ahmud Ki entered. 'Well?' the Great King asked.

A Ahmud Ki didn't bow. He never bowed. Bowing was an act of subservience, and he served no one. What he hated was the fat king's condescending attitude whenever he was in Thana's presence. Thana believed he was the most powerful man in the Kingdom – after all, he was the Great King – but A Ahmud Ki knew otherwise. He surveyed the attending Lords, noting who watched and listened as he gave Thana the latest news. 'Your Majesty, the Great Armies, under High Lord Mara, pursued the Haagii across Dragon Breath Plains, and are currently camped before The Rim Shield. They will attack the Haagii army tomorrow.' Most of it was true, although he left out his Apprentices' concern that the Haagii held a strategic advantage, meaning Thana's Great Armies were at stalemate for the first time in the campaign. He couldn't settle his concern that something was amiss at The Rim Shield, but he masked his emotion from Thana.

'Good news! Good news indeed. Then tomorrow night We will celebrate victory!' said Thana with enthusiasm. 'Lord Rheims! Order Our Royal Musicians to prepare, and see that the Royal Kitchens know it is Our intent to feast and enjoy. Go organize entertainment for Our Royal City, Lord Gerran.'

Gerran's supercilious grin signalled his departure to obey his Liege, but Lord Rheims' protest halted him. 'With respect, Your Majesty, aren't you being premature in your preparation? The battle is not yet fought.'

Thana looked peeved and glared at A Ahmud Ki. 'Will there be a battle tomorrow?'

'That is what I've been informed, Your Highness,' A Ahmud Ki answered in a detached tone.

Thana shifted his weight in the throne to stare back at

Lord Rheims. 'Did you hear that? The Royal Advisor says there will be a battle. Therefore, High Lord Mara will be victorious over the Haagii. That is an end to it. Obey Our wishes.' Lord Rheims bowed grandly and withdrew ahead of Gerran. A Ahmud Ki turned to follow.

A Drycraefter practised magic. A Ahmud Ki learned that information from Lord Rheims, five weeks after arriving in Thana. Lord Waeron Ardath was the Great King's Royal magician. The knowledge aroused A Ahmud Ki's curiosity, and caution. He waited, observing Ardath's actions whenever possible, but the magic user never once publicly displayed his skills, and kept very much to himself, except when the Great King required his attendance at Royal gatherings. A Ahmud Ki, therefore, had no sense of the power the man possessed, and he needed to know, in case Ardath blocked his path towards power in the Kingdom. Even Ardath's loyalty to Thana was ambivalent. He reminded A Ahmud Ki of himself, except Ardath was content to merely observe the actions of others at The King's Table, only sometimes drawing attention with his controlled warnings; never blindly following Thana's lead, yet unwilling to lead either. Except at sittings of The King's Table, the two had avoided meeting during the eight months since A Ahmud Ki's arrival. A Ahmud Ki wanted to meet Ardath, but the latter declined his invitations, reinforcing A Ahmud Ki's suspicion that Ardath was a dangerous man in the Palace. Now Ardath was seeking to meet him, so he was curious as to why there was a change of heart.

A Ahmud Ki waited in the Visiting Room. The furnishing was austere, Ithosen in taste and decor. While he preferred more lavish furnishing, he also wanted to retain the atmosphere of an Ithosen tower, so the Visiting Room was fitted with a low marble table, stools, and plain white walls. A light sphere floated a hand span below the ceiling. Footsteps rose from the stairwell, and Pak appeared, and behind him came Lord Waeron Ardath, in his customary white robes, his white halo of hair giving him a charismatic presence, an image of tranquility. A Ahmud Ki motioned Pak to withdraw, before greeting his guest with the Ranu phrase, 'Irand shadu arat shehaal,' intending to impress his visitor. 'Welcome,' he added.

Waeron Ardath politely bowed his head, and replied, 'Irand shadu arat shehaal.' The language of the Ranu Ka Shehaala ran naturally from his lips.

'You speak the tongue remarkably well,' A Ahmud Ki said, surprised by Ardath's fluency. 'Are you an Ithosen?' he asked.

'No,' Ardath answered. 'I learned the language when the Great King's father sent me to the barbarian land, as his ambassador – before border skirmishes ended diplomacy between the two Kingdoms. That was thirty-two years ago.'

A Ahmud Ki's curiosity heightened. 'How long were you in Yul Ithrandyr?'

'I saw the Holy City once, from a distance, on horseback. Leiksha Shehaal was never told I was an ambassador. The Ithosen never took me to him. I spent three years in Tul Yareek, living a lie. You see, we are the barbarians to their culture, as they are to ours. Senseless, really.'

A Ahmud Ki noticed Ardath wasn't asking how he also came to speak the Ranu tongue. The man had no curiosity. 'I don't mean to be an abrupt host, Lord Ardath, but what prompted your visit to my tower?'

Ardath sat on a stool and looked up at A Ahmud Ki from light blue eyes beneath white eyebrows. 'We use magic, you and I. We're driven by the same passion: curiosity. I've always wanted to see the inside of an Ithosen's tower since I was a young ambassador. Now that one's planted at the doorstep to the Great King's Palace, I've come to look.'

There are games being played, thought A Ahmud Ki. More than mere curiosity drives me. What drives you, Ardath? 'Then I'll show you,' he politely offered. He would test Ardath's abilities. He would learn what a Drycraefter could do. But he would not take the man to the tower's highest levels. Never reveal too much to an enemy, he remembered. 'Follow me.' He concentrated, whispered arcane words, and rose to, and through, the ceiling, where he waited, but when Ardath did not appear he descended, to find the Drycraefter sitting meditatively. 'Why didn't you follow?'

Ardath shook his head. 'I have no such ability. It would be pointless to try.'

More games, thought A Ahmud Ki. Or was the Drycraefter a limited magician? 'That's unfortunate. The upper levels are only accessible by levitation and passing spells,' he explained bemusedly.

'Then I will never see the inside of an Ithosen tower,' Ardath replied, and sighed. 'I guess curiosity can't overcome every obstacle.'

Better a direct question, A Ahmud Ki thought. Cut through the games. 'I've been told you're a Drycraefter, Lord Ardath. What powers do you possess?'

'I have a little magic. It's not a discipline like yours,' said Ardath, 'but it has its place.'

Another game. A riddle. A Ahmud Ki toyed with using a mind spell. He'd get the real answer. He focussed on Ardath's thoughts, clearing his own mind, but something was wrong. As he reached out mentally, he saw a vision of white static rolling towards him. It touched his mind, sparked and crackled, and hurt. He shut down his spell and stared at Ardath.

The old magician's expression was stern. 'Mind spells as well,' said Ardath, calmly. 'You are talented. I apologize for the wall. I never mastered mind spells, but my Mentor taught me how to stop them. The reaction is automatic nowadays.'

A Ahmud Ki was learning nothing about Ardath except greater mystery. The less he knew, the more powerful his opponent was, and Ardath had to be an opponent. 'Why did you really come here, after all these months?' he asked.

Ardath stood. 'To confirm what I feared was true. I speak Ranu, remember? Your name: seeker of power. I know why you're here, why the Dragonlord obsesses you. I even know why the Dragonlord was released. It was no accident by the Sorceresses of Targa. You released him.'

A Ahmud Ki stared directly into Ardath's eyes, but he saw no malice or threat. What he saw made him angry. Ardath pitied him. 'A nice theory,' he replied flatly.

Ardath shrugged. 'As you wish.' He walked to the head of the stairs.

A Ahmud Ki's anger smouldered. Ardath was the danger he suspected from the outset. There would have to be a confrontation. It was inevitable. 'You said you had advice, and a warning?' A Ahmud Ki coldly reminded him. 'Before you leave.'

'Yes,' said Ardath. 'The advice is simple. Underestimation is fatal. If the prophets of our great grandfathers are accurate in their foretelling, we are embarking on bloodier and darker times that either you or I have imagined in our nightmares. Don't underestimate anyone, Lord Advisor. In the right circumstances, even an ant can fell a man.'

'And the warning?'

Ardath smiled for the first time since entering the Visitor's Room, and vanished.

The amber crystal ball glowed in the low light. A Ahmud Ki stared into its depths, concentrating, searching for contact with a mind, an Apprentice. The crystal core began to oscillate, shivered and cleared. A face formed. Where have you been? A Ahmud Ki projected, fuming. Ardath's frustrating visit had incensed him, and he would not tolerate tardiness from his Apprentices.

Much is happening, Master Ki. The Haagii bombarded the camp from the height of the cliffs. There's confusion. We moved out of the main camp to avoid the missiles.

Will the attack continue in the morning?

Yes, Master Ki. High Lord Mara has no other choice. If he doesn't attack, we'll perish from thirst in this desert of dust. There is also a possibility that – The Apprentice's thought waves disintegrated.

A Ahmud Ki intensified his concentration, trying to push through the substance of the ball, reaching towards The Rim Shield with his most powerful spell amplified through the crystal. A possibility of what? He focussed his energy. The opacity dissolved and the crystal ball sparkled within, like polished glass, a degree of clarity unlike any A Ahmud Ki had experienced. The new energy purified the crystal. What had his Apprentices discovered? A face appeared and A Ahmud Ki recoiled in horror. The eyes glowed burning red, burning into him: pools of fire. He couldn't turn away – those eyes. They compelled him, drew him. He could only stare into the face of Mareg Dru'artha Sutnavanistra, stupefied, as a hideous grin spread across the Dragonlord's handsome features.

I sense familiarity. This mind intruded on my domain before. The Dragonlord's thought speech cut into A Ahmud Ki's mind, and he winced, but he fought his terror, determined to be strong. Who are you? A Ahmud Ki hesitated. He was reasserting his strength. Who are you? the Dragonlord demanded, with the ferocity of a whip across A Ahmud Ki's mind.

A Ahmud Ki. I am A Ahmud Ki.

You presume too much. I will teach you respect, you pathetic creature.

A Ahmud Ki was racing, retreating from the depths of the ball, escaping incomprehensible danger he knew was chasing him through the crystal's chambers, intent on mutilating him, annihilating him. The ball filled with blood red light, closing in, engulfing the paths his thoughts abandoned. His consciousness plunged blindly through the choking scarlet mist, and lunged desperately out of the ball, narrowly escaping a massive concussion as the crystal imploded.

He gingerly opened his eyes. Soft, amber mist dissipated through the Communication Room. A Ahmud Ki listened warily, before easing his aching body into a kneeling position. Shards of shattered crystal were scattered across the floor. He leaned forward, lifted a crystal chunk, and examined it. The crystal was opaque, the amber tint dissolved. Somehow, the Dragonlord had drained its magic, destroying it. The power of the Fifth Ki was awesome, beyond all measure of the other four. A Ahmud Ki stared at the shard – if he could find a way to embrace the Fifth Ki.

Forty Two

The order came. The North Wheel would lead the attack. The Devis ordered their Spokes into position on a front, five Spokes wide, two deep: almost five thousand warriors. The Longbowmen went with the North Wheel to provide covering fire, and the King's Special Guard – the warriors of Tressel Deep – marched with them. Runners assigned to the North Wheel would carry reports of the battle to the forces remaining in the rear. The three Guardians were separated again: Alain with the North Wheel, Stephen to the Command tents, Andra with the West Wheel. They parted, wishing each other fortune. Andra passed Artega to Stephen. 'He'll be safer at the tents with you.'

Stephen took the bundle of fur and red tongue. 'I will see he comes to no harm. He will be waiting for you at the battle's end.' Andra affectionately scuffed the pup's head before retiring reluctantly to his station to watch the initial stages of the battle.

The North Wheel advanced in regimental order, spears and swords ready. As the distance closed, Derik's Longbowmen loosed an arrow storm that fell among the Haagii at the base of The Rim Shield with devastating effect. Companies of Haagii reinforcements moved rapidly down the cliff road. The two armies clashed, and the North Wheel's ordered ranks disintegrated. Smoke swelled, mixing with muffled cries and yells, as the first reinforcements reached the base and charged headlong into the broil. The North Wheel warriors were outnumbered, three to one, but slowly, inexorably, they made headway towards the upward road through the seething sea of Haagii. Andra felt relief and excitement mounting around him, in the ranks of those watching, as their fellows gained ground. The Longbowmen shifted position, waiting for the second company of Haagii reinforcements to round the last switchback of road, and as they ran into range the Longbowmen released a wall of arrows, cutting through the enemy like a sharp scythe. A second volley cut another swathe through their ranks, and the survivors hesitated. When a third spray brought down more Haagii, the remainder turned and ran blindly into the third company arriving at the corner. In the ensuing chaos, Derik's men released two more swarms of arrows. The demoralised Haagii scattered in wild retreat up the roadway, leaving the dead and dying in their wake.

Two warriors from the North Wheel ran full tilt across the gap towards High Lord Mara's tent and disappeared inside. A short time after, Captain Westbourne emerged from the tent. He took a prominent position at the head of the West Wheel, and yelled, 'We march in slowly!' The warriors moved forward, obediently holding rank, but Andra felt and understood everyone's eagerness to join the battle, because he was curbing his own compulsion to charge in, flailing Cedwyn's great sword with reckless abandon. He knew his Guardian training did not permit him to follow impulse, but he felt it regardless, as the West Wheel marched to the base of The Rim Shield.

The North Wheel advanced up the climb, and Andra spotted twelve riders, one with a fiery mane, leading the charge. Good, he thought, with a wry smile, Claarn will be enjoying this. Corpses were piled thick where the Haagii front lines had been, and the battlefield stank of blood. The West Wheel moved through, killing wounded Haagii, but when they reached the road they were forced to reorganize their ranks to continue upward. The front ranks began the ascent, stepping over the dead. Further ahead, the Haagii were in full flight, the warriors of the North Wheel in close pursuit, and Andra glimpsed Claarn on horseback, hacking down straggling Haagii, but the road was steep, and afforded few views. Now and then, someone would call a warning, as a Haagii body tumbled from a higher ledge, victim of the pursuing vanguard. Andra watched a corpse bounce, and spin crazily to the dust below, and hoped Alain was faring well. He turned his head, to look back, and saw the

Apprentices walking through the plundered Haagii camp, leading High Lord Mara and his bodyguard. How easy for a leader, he thought, but rebuked himself for his cynicism when he remembered the wound Mara bore on his forehead. He looked up at the rugged, twisted cliff face, wondering why the enemy weren't dropping oil or rocks on the attackers and, again, he felt instinctively that something was amiss. His pulse quickened. He turned and followed the others up the road.

The upward path was strewn with corpses, and Andra wondered how many Haagii had to die before the Kingdom could claim victory. The dark rock was awash with thick streams and pools of blood, and twice he slipped. Near the crest, however, the leading ranks slowed, and shuffled forward, as though their advance was being hindered by those further ahead. The sounds of battle diminished rapidly, and ceased, and an unexpected hush descended over The Rim Shield. 'What's happening?' Andra asked a soldier in the rank ahead.

'Don't know. Wish these bastards would move forward so we can get some action,' he growled.

'I think we've already missed it,' grumbled another.

'Bet the gutless mongrel Haagii raised a white flag,' added a third, behind Andra.

'But no one's cheering,' said the first soldier.

The pack steadily pressed over the crest, and Andra pushed forward to stand with the others at the top of The Rim Shield. He saw the reason for the veil of silence. Instead of sweeping along the edge of the cliff, as Andra expected, the soldiers of both Wheels were massed together, rooted to the spot like confused, caged animals. Above the walls of the Fire Mountains, dark, unnatural clouds were rolling down, sprawling like a thick, choking blanket into a deep valley, directly ahead of where Great King Thana's warriors stood on The Rim Shield. Someone nearby groaned, and a soldier jabbed his left elbow and pointed, crying, 'O holy Teka! We're doomed!' Andra saw the vision and acid melted the pit of his stomach. He lowered his sword.

A vast, dark mass covered the valley between the mountains, like a shadow of the surging body of black clouds, but the mass was a sea of running figures, an immense army of Haagii warriors, filling the breadth of the valley, and the shallower slopes. They came on, silently at first, but the drumming of their feet against the earth reached the ears of the staring warriors, drowning their heartbeats long before the first wave broke upon them. And, in the air between the twin floods of darkness rushing towards them, came something else, creatures Andra couldn't comprehend, except as black winged shapes breathing gouts of fire.

Panic flashed through the milling soldiers, and Andra was embroiled in a violent struggle as warriors scrambled back to the road in frantic bids to escape. For desperate moments, he fought to keep his feet, before the dark wave crashed into them, and swept over them with a roar and high-pitched scream. Balls of flame exploded among the terror-stricken warriors. Some perished, obliterated to ash by searing heat. Others danced, screaming in the crush of bodies, setting friends alight with their fiery touch. The cloud tide swept over The Rim Shield, blotting out the sunlight, plunging the cliff into preternatural darkness and heightening the chaotic terror among the Kingdom's warriors. The push to the road became so frantic that those at the edge were pushed over the cliffs, and the air was filled with the pitiful howls of their struggles and dying. The winged creatures banked over Dragon Breath Plains and swept in again, flames from their ragged jaws scorching and searing everything in their paths.

Andra couldn't move against the tide of bodies, so he desperately worked across the current, towards the western edge. Poor light made it impossible to see more than a few spans. He knew he could never hope to find Stephen or Alain in the turmoil, but he was determined he would be a warrior fighting the Haagii to the death, if that was meant to be his Way, his path. He spied a party of soldiers engaging the enemy a few paces ahead, so he gripped Cedwyn's sword and grimly plunged into the fray. A Haagii warrior intercepted him, but Andra mercilessly cut him down, and waded into the pressing sea of enemy warriors. He thrust, and stabbed, and hacked relentlessly, slaying Haagii after Haagii, their bodies forming a temporary wall, but their fellows clambered defiantly over the corpses, possessed with a consuming desire to reach Andra and the Great King's warriors. The party of defenders rapidly diminished as, one after another, overwhelming numbers beat down the Kingdom warriors. Andra's sword arm throbbed with exhaustion, and his strokes became more desperate as the Haagii hemmed him in. He would stand as long as he could.

A fierce shout came from his right, and the ring of encircling Haagii broke open, forced apart by a wild-eyed, giant with red hair, and two raven-haired women swinging battle-axes. The Haagii pressed forward, hindering their own fighting strokes in their bid to force Andra and Claarn and their companions to yield, a strategy that made their slaughter easy. Andra lost count of the number he slew, yet still Cedwyn's blade was bloodless, gleaming in the oppressive darkness, and though his sword arm ached unbearably, his sword grew lighter with every blow, as if it was aiding him of its own volition.

Their tiny party lost ground, forced back, towards the cliff edge, by sheer weight of numbers. We must go right!' Claarn roared above the din. 'The way down is to the right!'

Andra summoned his inner strength and moved beside Marella, but a quick glance revealed a woman he barely recognised. Cut, splattered with her victims' blood, her teeth bared with hate, she was like a rabid she-wolf. Do I wear the same grim mask, he wondered? A sharp pain in his leg broke his thought like shattered crystal, and he parried a second spear thrust, before hewing down its wielder. They reached the lip of the road that plunged over The Rim Shield, where a much larger body of warriors were making a stand. Andra spied three tall blond figures, working their bows in unison behind the embattled defence, and went to them. 'Where's Derik O'Dale?!' he shouted.

They shook their heads, but one said quickly, as he nocked another shaft, 'We were separated in the confusion.

I saw him with a group at the centre of the battle earlier, but not since.' He released his arrow, dropped his bow and drew his sword. 'Perhaps I'll see him soon enough!' he yelled, and pushed through to the front line.

They held the Haagii army at bay, as the dead piled up, and the dark ocean across the valley floor rolled and swayed, as those at the rear tried to move forward against the wall of those caught at the front. Black clouds swirled and twisted. Flashes of dull lightning and claps of thunder rent the sky. Through the maelstrom, the flying creatures swooped across the battlefield, lashing patches with sheets of yellow flame, before climbing sharply into the blanket of cloud. Andra scrambled to a vantage point in the milling crowd, to see what was happening, but darkness hid the surging masses, until a continuous sheet of lightning lit the centre of the battlefield with eerie blue-white light. Andra saw the Kingdom's warriors clearly, against the tapestry of struggle, their swords and shields shining as they rose and fell among the dark hordes. He glimpsed the banners of Captains Westbourne and Fennik, and saw Derik O'Dale, other Longbowmen, and Alain trapped at the centre of the vortex. A second flash revealed three more pockets of warriors vainly resisting the Haagii, but they were collapsing under the enemy's ferocious onslaught.

Long moments passed before another burst of light exposed the stage. Andra saw a huge, winged form, with long snaky neck and tail, and a rider on its back, outlined against the clouds, hovering above the centre of conflict, its huge talons bared, its ugly mouth opening. Beneath it, bowstring taut, shaft trained at the creature's underbelly, stood Derik O'Dale, caught with lightning silvered hair, like the warriors of ancient legend described at the campfires. The vision remained static, a picture, but the bowstring thrummed, and the arrow sped upward, as a crackling stream of fire rushed from the jaws of the suspended creature to explode over the desperate band – and darkness collapsed upon the centre.

The Haagii's momentum changed, as the whole force

coordinated its attack against the line of resistance at the top of The Rim Shield. 'Back! Down the cliffs! We can't hold this place!' shouted a Devi. An instant later, a Haagii spear impaled him. Haagii burst through the front ranks, and Andra beat a hasty withdrawal, down the first paces of the cliff road, to avoid being trapped. Others were less fortunate. A sharp cry echoed above, and the vibration of huge wing beats frightened him. He flattened against the rock. An intense heat wave passed over with a thunderous roar, and the air trembled with screams. Bodies writhed and twisted in angry tongues of flame, before plunging from the cliff, or being cut down by Haagii, whose flat, fierce faces were carved into death masks by their victims' flames.

He ran blindly: ran as he had never run before. The mad scramble down The Rim Shield road left him cut and bruised from numerous falls as his body outstripped his feet on the steep decline. He leaped and tripped over corpses of Haagii and Kingdom warriors, and he was pursued by the cries of those who fell behind whistling like wind in his ears.

As he turned a bend, he came upon a group of Haagii encircling two bald Apprentices. At their feet lay the prostrate body of the Great King's High Lord, a spear in his back, and the bodies of others of his retinue piled where the Haagii had ambushed them. The Haagii were playing cat-and-mouse with the surviving Apprentices, jeering, thrusting their weapons, daring them to fight. An Apprentice raised his hands and rapidly weaved an arcane pattern, until a ball of flame erupted in the cup of his palms. The Haagii mocked his actions, laughed and cajoled him. Infuriated, the Apprentice lunged, pressing his flaming hands on the face of the nearest Haagii, who recoiled, screaming with pain. But his victory was brief. He jerked upright as a Haagii disembowelled him.

Andra glanced back up the road. A black tide of Haagii warriors was pouring over The Rim Shield lip. He had no choice, but to fight through the Haagii blocking his escape. Resolved, he swung Cedwyn's sword above his head and charged. Two Haagii fell before their fellows noticed Andra's intrusion. A third dodged, caught his foot on the edge of the roadway cliff, stumbled, and fell. The others joined battle. Action and time blurred. He anticipated cuts and thrusts directed from all quarters, and deftly parried them, rolling and ducking his head and body, avoiding blows with ease. He moved into a staccato rhythm, dancing a death ritual that defied the Haagii's attempts to stop the young Guardian moving through them. His sword blade shone in the dull light, as it flashed from victim to victim, slicing with uncanny accuracy through their leather armour like it was made of cloth. He stood in a temporary space beside the Apprentice, facing the remaining Haagii on the road below. 'Who are you?' the Apprentice asked.

Andra turned to answer, and saw astonishment etched on the Apprentice's face. He was staring at Andra's weapon. 'Andra of The Vale. Have you any of magic left?' The Apprentice shook his head. Andra picked up a sword. 'Then you better use this.'

The Apprentice gaped in disbelief. 'I have no idea how to use one of these things.'

'Then you better learn. Look.' He gestured up the road, where the Haagii moved steadily towards them, a black wall of warriors descending like judgement. Andra thrust the sword hilt into the Apprentice's hand and turned to face the Haagii blocking their way down. Beyond, he glimpsed a second wall of Kingdom soldiers on the road, and at their head was a familiar figure: Claarn. Perhaps there was still a chance. He summoned his courage and tightened his grip on the hilt of his sword, testing its weight. 'This time,' said Andra, and he plunged into the Haagii.

Andra's sword wrought havoc. A dozen Haagii stood their ground, but several bolted up the road to join the approaching army. One by one, the Haagii fell as the sword of Cedwyn swept in deadly arcs. Two, seeing a weaker foe, made for the Apprentice, who awkwardly heaved his sword up in desperate defence, but the leading Haagii's first blow sent the sword spinning from his hands. The Apprentice shut his eyes and raised his hands in a futile attempt to ward the next killing blow, but it never fell. When he opened his eyes, one Haagii was staring past him with glazed bewilderment on his rugged features, before he toppled sideways to lie with his dead companion. Andra was yelling. 'Come on! Let's get down the road!' The Apprentice stumbled after the young Guardian who saved his life. If they should, by a miracle, survive this massacre, he would tell Master Ki what he'd seen. No normal warrior could've slain the Haagii like this one had, and no normal sword cut as deep, without a trace of blood or damage tarnishing its surface. It was powerful magic, magic that the Great King's Lord Advisor would pay dearly to have.

A phalanx of warriors filled the road. Claarn saw Andra and bellowed above the clamour of thunder, 'Come on, young Guardian! Join us! We make our last stand here!' Andra met Claarn's embrace and went to join the ranks, but a large arm held him. 'By all that is in the power of the gods, I have seen fine warriors since leaving Tressel Deep, but what I witnessed up there by you, my friend, is worth many a song at a warrior's hearth fire. If The Vale has more like you, ten such Haagii armies could not take it.' Their eyes locked, and Andra saw his own fear mirrored in Claarn's face. If he was destined to die in battle, what better company to die in? He braced his sword arm, as Claarn released his wrist and turned to face the advancing Haagii.

Dark clouds boiled and seethed overhead. Through them soared the black winged lizards, barely visible in the darkness. The press of warriors, with whom Andra stood, barely numbered a hundred – the sole survivors of the slaughter on The Rim Shield. The Haagii on the cliffs were innumerable, and their strength poured down the road, driven by an insatiable passion for blood.

'Look.' Andra followed the pointing finger of a woman. The front ranks of the Haagii were halting, barely thirty paces away.

'What are they doing?' someone asked.

'Baiting us,' a veteran snarled, and spat. 'They mean to savour the last kill.'

A subtle ripple spread through the Haagii ranks and four

figures emerged. They strode arrogantly across the space between the opposed warriors and halted five paces from the front ranks of the Great King's warriors. Two were Haagii, impressively built, wearing chain mail under their leather jerkins, and carrying black helmets bedecked with long curved teeth. But Andra's attention was fixed on the leading pair. They weren't Haagii. They looked like Haardrishii: tall, athletic, wearing shining black armour. One carried a blood red pennant fixed to the tip of a lance. Andra studied the detail worked into their armour. Intricate runes and patterns adorned every visible surface, and at the joints were spikes and sharp edges; embellishments Andra did not associate with the more austere armour the Haardrishii wore.

The taller man removed his helmet, and long fine blond locks fell to his shoulders. His clear-featured face was surprisingly fresh, and undeniably handsome, but there was a hard touch to his dark eyes, and a grim line in his thin lips. 'E'dammaragg,' he said, lifting his hand to his forehead before touching his chin. 'In my tongue is formal greeting to ones worth of respect.' He cocked his head to one side, before continuing. 'Is one still lead you?'

Andra heard confusion buzz through the tight knot of Kingdom warriors and was acutely aware of the silence that descended on the Haagii. Claarn faced the stranger, his fiery mane bedraggled and matted with blood. 'I am Claarn. I will speak for us.'

The blond stranger looked up at the giant, and Andra saw the man's eyes narrow, measuring Claarn's worth. 'I will be brief with you.' He glossed over the warriors behind Claarn, assessing them with the same cool calculating intensity. 'My Master give you tiny glimpse of His power. He spare your miserable lives so you carry to Great King word of what you see here. You carry warning too. Tell Great King his time end. Ancient Ones' prophecies fulfilled. Mareg Dru'artha Sutnavanistra returns to claim what is His. He One Lord of All Lands. Always that be so. Take this to Great King.' As the last syllable left his lips, the blond warrior turned curtly on his heels, and led his three companions back into the Haagii ranks, leaving the Great King's warriors staring after them. Claarn remained rooted to the road as the Haagii began to withdraw, a black river slowly retreating, maintaining their eerie silence, leaving the littered carnage of battle in their wake on the bloodied road.

'Why are we standing here?' someone asked quietly, breaking the stunned silence.

'Waiting.'

'There's nothing to wait for,' muttered a warrior behind Andra. 'That was it. The battle's over.'

'The bastards!' a stocky man growled.

'Praise Teka for mercy,' whispered another soldier, bleeding profusely from a gash across his right cheek. 'Let's go before they change their minds.'

'Where?' asked someone else. 'Into the desert? Have you got water?'

Puzzled warriors turned their weary, battle-scarred faces away, pushed past Andra, and began descending the narrow road.

Andra remained with Claarn. The red-haired giant was staring after the Haagii hordes pouring back over the lip of The Rim Shield. Marella joined Andra, her haggard face watching Claarn. 'He wanted to fight them,' she said in a hoarse, tired voice. 'Now they turn away. They mock us, and him, Andra, and he can do nothing. They've cheated him of a warrior's death and honour.' The giant man was trembling. 'Help me bring him away,' she said, through her exhaustion. Together, they approached the warrior of Tressel Deep who stood alone on the road. 'It's time for us to go,' said Marella softly. She rested her arm on Claarn's. 'There's nothing more we can do here.'

Passion trapped within the warrior exploded. He wrenched his sword from its torn scabbard and flung it up the road with a demonic yell. The blood-spattered blade cartwheeled and shattered as it struck a boulder. 'Claarn will be revenged on you!' he roared at the cliffs. 'By all the gods and goddesses there be, I will be revenged!' For a moment, he seemed more terrible and powerful than any mortal

Andra had seen, and the Guardian stepped aside, but Claarn's anger subsided as quickly as it ignited, leaving him looking smaller and weaker in stature in the dull light beneath the dark swirling clouds. Marella took Claarn's heavy arm and led the weary warrior, from his torment, towards the base of The Rim Shield.

When they reached the base, they saw other survivors picking through corpses, and the charred remnants of the Haagii camp, searching in vain for water vessels. They salvaged little from their own abandoned campsite. Gradually, groups of spiritless warriors drifted into the endless grey desert, blindly heading for homes beyond the southern horizon.

Claarn, Marella and Andra were last to leave. Andra searched for Artega, but he found no sign of the pup. The fire-breathing lizards had ravaged the campsite, destroying every living creature. If Artega survived their inferno, it was likely he would have followed Andra up The Rim Shield road. To what? To death, like Alain, and Derik, and thousands of warriors in the name of the Great King? And he'd run away, in the end, like a coward. Even the dog had more courage. He had covered the title of Guardian with shame.

'Come,' Claarn's big paw rested on Andra's shoulder. 'There'll be time enough to measure our sorrow while we cross this grey, motherless dust. After that, we can prepare ourselves to avenge what is lost here. One thing is certain. This One Lord they speak of will come searching for us soon enough.' Claarn hoisted Andra to his feet, and placed his other arm on Marella's back, and forced a tired smile, as he added, 'And we, my friends, we will be ready for him.'

As the companions turned from The Rim Shield's brooding face and walked into the grey wilderness of Dragon Breath Plains, a dark ocean of clouds rolled back from the sombre Fire Mountains, and winged ebony shapes raced silently northward towards the heart of Uz Erhaag. From beneath a charred wagon, a small black nose tentatively sniffed the air.

ABOUT THE AUTHOR

Australian writer, Tony Shillitoe, entered the fantasy field in 1992-3 when Pan Macmillan Australia published his popular and successful Andrakis trilogy. He followed the trilogy with a stand-alone coming-of-age fantasy novel, *The Last Wizard*, which was short-listed for the inaugural Aurealis Awards Best Fantasy Novel in 1995.

From 2002-2008, Tony published two more fantasy series – the Ashuak Chronicles trilogy and the Dreaming in Amber quatrology – with HarperCollins Voyager Australia, and *Blood*, from the Ashuak Chronicles, was shortlisted for the Aurealis Awards Best Fantasy Novel in 2002.

Tony branched into Adolescent/Young Adult novels in 1999, with the publication of *Joy Ride* by Wakefield Press. Tony's second teenage novel, *Caught in the Headlights*, a HarperCollins Angus and Robertson imprint, was listed as a notable read for Older Readers in the 2003 Children's Book Council Awards, and subsequently appeared on Premier's Reading Lists around the nation.

Tony has written and published short stories, scripts, poetry, professional writing course books and ghost-edited a variety of projects. More information about his work and life can be found at his web site The Phoenix Rises: http://www.tonyshillitoe.com.au

BOOKS BY THE SAME AUTHOR

FANTASY NOVELS
The Andrakis Trilogy
The Waking Dragon
Maker of Kings
Dragonlord War

The Ashuak Chronicles
Blood
Passion
Freedom

Dreaming in Amber
The Amber Legacy
A Solitary Journey
Prisoner of Fate
The Demon Horsemen

The Last Wizard

STORY ANTHOLOGIES
Tales of the Dragon
The Red Heart

TEENAGE NOVELS
Joy Ride
Caught in the Headlights
In My Father's Shadow
The Need